Harbour of Secrets

Kate Lance

SEA
BOOKS
PRESS
seabooks.net

Print ISBN: 978-0-6489851-5-0
Ebook ISBN: 978-0-6489851-6-7

Published by Seabooks Press
seabooks.net

 A catalogue record for this
work is available from the
National Library of Australia

BY THE SAME AUTHOR

Fiction

Embers at Midnight
Testing the Limits
Silver Highways
Atomic Sea (As CM Lance)
The Turning Tide (As CM Lance)

Non-Fiction

Alan Villiers: Voyager of the Winds
Redbill: From Pearls to Peace

To Margaret Mary Lance
8 October 1928 – 26 May 2021

Table of Contents

PART I. GHOST NOTES

1. Tina: Me Too

Look, I love a party—and it's not as if this one's going to be a big deal, just a get-together for my brother and his wife—but I feel oddly on edge. Perhaps it's the people coming tonight?

Probably not. Just the usual crowd, a few of the girls from my old signals section plus assorted husbands, and a handful of Nikos's workmates, dull as ditchwater and always talking about seaplanes and flying boats and flarepaths and pontoons. Yawn.

I may have been an airwoman myself, but most of us mustered in the WAAAF as clerks, cooks, drivers or mechanics: we certainly didn't *fly* anything—and planes themselves bore me to tears.

All the same I loved my work in signals. But when peace came I simply wanted out of that regimented world, to return to freedom. I thought marriage to Nikos and a new start would mean ... what? Now, three years later, not *this*.

Perhaps I'm just annoyed at Nikos. With his usual efficiency we got to Sydney Central on time to meet the Newcastle train, but it's late. Naturally. The wind is rushing cold and gritty along the vast concourse and, despite a cardigan over my dress, I'm freezing.

There's a whoosh of steam as a train stops at the railheads and smoke drifts across the skylight in the great barrel roof above. Unfortunately it's not the Newcastle train. People are streaming through the exit now, passing us where we're waiting beneath the clock at the timetable board. Is it them, perhaps?

It's late 1948 for heaven's sake, yet quite a few blokes ambling past are still wearing items of khaki uniform. Some are arm-in-arm with women whose dated hairstyles and hard scarlet mouths suggest their best days are behind them as well.

Are mine?

I sigh, and a young woman in a suit gives me a friendly glance as she passes, her bag slung stylishly over her shoulder.

I gaze at her with envy. She looks like someone on her way to a job, a *real* job. Something that tests her and engages her and makes her glad to be alive. Like the job I used to have.

A pair of thugs swagger by in double-breasted jackets and pegged trousers. They look me up and down, then notice Nikos and take an interest in the timetable board instead. Imperturbable Nikos glances at them. Tall and strong, his brows as dark as his neat beard, if I were a thug I wouldn't ogle his wife either.

Perhaps it's the reminder that spivs like that are everywhere now? The newspapers seem to be full of the doings of racketeers who received a fine weapons training in the war. I suppose Sydney's always been notorious for its gangsters, prostitutes and drug dealers, especially around Kings Cross, but in these drab post-war days, crime seem more *blatant*.

Like all those illegal gambling rings patronised by social butterflies rich enough to risk a thousand pounds—three times a workingman's annual pay!—on a single flutter.

Keeping a sly eye on the libel laws, the papers hint that the baccarat rings flourish because they're patronised by the highest ranks of government. Given our squalid politicians and the corruption I saw during the war, it's not hard to believe.

But I don't think that's what's weighing on me, either.

Nikos checks his watch for what must be the twentieth time and, thankfully, the Newcastle train finally chuffs to a halt a few platforms down. Carriage doors open and another crowd of people emerge chatting, and Nikos says calmly, 'There they are.'

He says everything calmly. Our women friends who fancy him imagine that means he's manly and dependable: they have no idea how dull such calmness can be. And irritating.

But soon my older brother Harry and his wife Eliza are approaching us, laughing, and suddenly I forget my bad mood. I reach up to hug Harry, nearly as tall as Nikos, and kiss Eliza, small and bright-eyed as a sparrow.

I admire her little red hat and she compliments my dress, then we walk out to the car park, to Nikos's beloved Chevrolet, all long plump curves and soft leather.

Harry and Eliza are staying the weekend with us. They plan to catch up with an old mate of theirs who's arriving this evening from Perth—Billie Quinn, one of those determined lady aviators who flew with a women's transport unit in the war. She sounds daunting, although Eliza says she's witty and elegant.

We set off along George Street and I turn to her in the back seat and say, 'Everything's just about ready for your friend tonight. Can't remember—did I meet her in 1936, when Mum and I visited you in Southampton—a tall woman with short red hair?'

'With a fairly *brisk* way of expressing herself,' Harry says dryly.

'And she sent you a telegram out of the blue, asking to meet?'

'We used to write all the time, she was my closest friend,' says Eliza, a little wistfully. 'Then the letters trailed off to nothing, and suddenly this mysterious telegram arrived.'

At the wheel, Nikos says, 'The name's familiar. Didn't she set a flying record in the late twenties?'

'Yes, that's Billie,' says Eliza. 'After the war she came back to Perth and opened a training school for pilots. The papers made a great to-do about the homecoming of the 'glamorous girl aviator,' which annoyed her terribly.'

'And in the war she flew with the—what was it? Air Transport something?' says Nikos, as we drive through shabby Glebe.

'Air Transport Auxiliary,' says Harry. 'Surprised you know of it.'

'I'd see articles in Picture Post,' says Nikos. 'Women in Spitfires were always newsworthy.'

'The ATA had male pilots as well, but they weren't quite as photogenic,' says Eliza wryly. 'Still, they all did the job of flying new planes to the fit-out airfields.'

'Did they *really* do that without weapons or radios?' Nikos shakes his head as he turns the car. 'Hard to believe.'

'It's true,' says Eliza. 'Another friend of ours in London, Yvonne, was an ATA pilot too. You can ask Billie about it when you meet.'

Nikos laughs. 'Ask about planes? Now if she'd sailed on ships like you two, or even the odd boat, we'd have something to *talk* about.'

With another twinge of irritation I watch the sooty houses passing by on Victoria Road. Beyond even the Chevrolet, my husband's deepest passion is his yacht, *Wind Rose*. Of course I used to go sailing with him, but the novelty soon wore off.

We turn into Darling Street, then drive down a cul-de-sac to our modern two-storied house. It's incongruous among the old semi-detached terraces, but Nikos's parents live nearby and this house was their wedding present to us. It's too large as well—we only needed space for Nikos's grumpy son Stavros—but at least the extra bedrooms make it useful for guests.

Eliza and Harry look tired after the long trip, so I serve them sandwiches and tea, then send them off to rest for the afternoon while we prepare for the party tonight.

Nikos makes himself busy in the kitchen (my husband's saving grace is his love of cooking), while I tidy the living room's low-slung sofas and occasional tables, and vacuum the rug. Then I go upstairs, have a bath, and put on my new gold taffeta gown.

After a few people have arrived, Harry and Eliza come downstairs. Eliza is in a darling blue dress that shows her shoulders, and thankfully Harry is looking brighter than before. My poor brother spent much of the war in a prison camp in Singapore and, even now, I'm not sure he's completely recovered.

Nor Eliza, for that matter. She had a dreadful time escaping from Singapore, and then worked in some stressful hush-hush job in London that left a streak of silver in her dark hair.

At least when Harry came home from Changi she finally became pregnant with the child they'd wanted for years, my adorable nephew Leo. Grandmother Jessie (my mum) is minding him at home in Newcastle this weekend. I think it must be his parent's first time alone since they had him, poor sods.

'Meet our friends,' says Nikos, waving them into the room.

'Everyone, this is Dr Harry Bell, Tina's big brother, and his wife, Eliza. They're from Newcastle—but of course if they had any sense at all they'd live near us in Sydney.'

'But we love it there, Nikos,' says Eliza, laughing. 'Perfect for Leo. So where's your young Stavros tonight?'

'With my parents.' Nikos shrugs. 'Doesn't want to bother with boring grown-ups. Now what are you drinking? We've got potent cocktails, champagne or red wine from my cousin's vineyard.'

I offer around a tray with drinks. 'Ooh, *cocktails*,' says a woman, wife of one of Nikos's workmates, all red lipstick and come-hither looks at my husband. Silly cow. If nothing else, he's a faithful man.

Harry takes a glass of wine and Mrs Lipstick turns her gaze on him. 'And you're Tina's brother, Harry? Goodness. Tina must be a bit older than she'd like us to believe.'

'Not at all, there's—what, Tina?' he says. 'Sixteen years between us? She was just a shy little thing when I left to study in London.'

'I think I grew up fairly quickly once the war came,' I say.

Harry smiles. 'When you dashed off to study wireless telegraphy?'

'Best thing I ever did. I'll always be grateful you and Eliza got me into that training course.'

He nudges me gently. 'Ah, you only wanted to escape Newcastle and spread your wings.'

I laugh. 'That's true. And I certainly did.'

Mrs Lipstick interrupts with a smirk. 'Oh, *do* tell us more about tonight's visitor, Harry. An old friend of yours, I hear.'

'Well, yes,' he says. 'We first met Billie in the early thirties when we were living in England. She and Eliza's brother Pete came over to do some advanced aviation courses.'

'Have more wine, Harry,' says Nikos, re-filling his glass.

'Goodness, an *aviatrix*?' says Mrs Lipstick. 'How *dramatic*. And this—Billie is married to Eliza's brother?'

Harry takes another mouthful of wine. 'Oh no, they went their different ways. Billie came home and Pete stayed on his Hampshire farm.' He chuckles. '*He* ended up marrying—and divorcing—my flighty first wife, and certainly came to regret it.'

I'm a little surprised. Harry is rarely so personal, but the drink must have gone to his head.

'Such drama, mate,' says Nikos. 'We're pretty dull in comparison.'

You can say that again, I think.

I take the last glass of champagne and hand the tray to Mrs Lipstick, saying, 'Mind bringing us some appetisers from the kitchen, dear?' She flounces away.

'This wine is bloody good, Nikos,' says Harry, 'but you're going to have to stop topping me up.'

'What nonsense, Harry, it's a party.'

The doorbell rings, and Nikos says, 'Ah—our visitor at last,' and goes out to the hall.

Eliza comes over and takes Harry's hand. 'I'm so excited, love. I've missed her terribly.'

I hear Nikos's deep welcoming voice outside the door, then he ushers a woman into the room.

Harry stares and murmurs, 'Eliza—?'

Eliza whispers in shock, 'What on earth's *happened*?'

I try not to stare myself, and say brightly, 'Welcome to Sydney, Billie!' I'm good at being bright.

'Reckon the taxi brought me here via Brisbane,' she says. 'Um, can I put my bag—?'

Eliza cries, 'Oh, *Billie!*' and hugs her as the now fairly well-oiled guests cluster happily around.

'Let me—' Billie says. 'I just want to—'

'*Right*,' I say in the voice that kept the girls in Hut 12 in line. 'Give the poor thing a bit of space.'

Billie glances at me gratefully, then says to Eliza, 'In a few minutes, Lizzie—'

'I'll show Billie her room, then you can all catch up.' I take her bag and usher her upstairs. 'The bathroom's along there, first left. Fresh towels too. Can I get you anything? A drink?'

'No, let me tidy up, then I'll join you.'

I leave her. She's going to need more than a tidy up. Her face is grey with—what? Fatigue, dust, illness? Her greasy hair is pulled back with a rubber band. She's in a stained shirt and jeans, which hardly disguise the fact she's so thin she's practically a skeleton.

Where's the elegant redhead I've heard so much about?

I resume my hostess duties. Time passes. A few guests leave, then a few more, until only me, Nikos, Eliza and Harry are left. Finally Billie comes downstairs. She's washed her face and changed her clothes, though they'd still suit a mechanic.

I hand her a glass of champagne, which she quickly downs, then give her another and say, 'Let's have something to eat.'

I play my wifely role and produce something tasty Nikos made earlier. Fortunately the conversation ambles along, and we hear about Billie's delayed flight and Harry and Eliza's train trip and young Leo's well-being. Tomorrow we can find out what's going on, but for now let's be diplomatic.

After the food, Nikos switches on the gramophone. Eliza and Harry dance quietly together and I feel envy at the way they seem so lost in each other. The music is the sort Nikos likes, the dance tunes of wartime.

I prefer jazz myself—the sparse, drifting lines of saxophone I'd listen to late at night, when my mind yearned for emptiness but was still echoing with the ghostly dit-dahs of Japanese signals.

Life and death signals.

The record ends and Harry and Eliza sit down. Nikos loves to dance but knows perfectly well I don't, so he asks Eliza.

She says, laughing, 'Try Billie, she's so much better than me—you always says dancing and flying go together, don't you, Bill?'

Billie doesn't respond but simply sips her drink.

Nikos changes the record and turns. 'Then I must insist, Billie. Let's see what you're made of.' He takes her free hand and pulls her from the lounge towards him.

She stares and throws her drink in his face.

*

Next morning I'm awake early—old wartime habit—and go downstairs to the lounge-room. I gather glasses and plates and start washing up in the kitchen. Still, it wasn't a bad party. People seemed to enjoy themselves, apart from the bizarre Billie.

Her face blank with shock she simply stood staring at Nikos, champagne dripping on his shirt, his face as astonished as hers. She put down her glass (a very nice crystal—I feared she'd throw it as well), then murmured 'Good-night,' and went upstairs.

The door slams. Stavros must be home.

He slouches into the kitchen, glances at me with dislike and opens the refrigerator. He pulls out some titbit from last night and I say automatically, 'Have you had breakfast yet, Stavros?'

He mutters, 'Call me *Steve*,' and leaves.

The fridge is still ajar so I grit my teeth and close it, and go back to the washing-up. Stavros is fourteen and not my son.

Nikos's first wife died some months after she had him, so he never knew her, and I don't understand why he dislikes me so much.

Nikos and I met during the war and married as soon as it was over. He was in the Naval Reserve then, skipper of a small ship—when the war began the Navy requisitioned almost everything that floated, from luggers to ferries.

Nikos used to joke they sent anyone who knew port from starboard off to sail them, but as he'd grown up playing on boats, then crewed as a teenager on a relative's fishing vessel, he was probably more than good enough for the job.

He was on sick leave in Brisbane then—a broken arm from a fall during a storm, not a war wound—and I was out with one of my Hut 12 girls who vaguely knew him.

We stopped to chat, then went for a few drinks and a meal, but I wasn't in the mood to flirt. I'd been badly hurt a few months before by a pilot who'd taken my heart and virginity both, then disappeared on me.

A few days later Nikos and I met again by chance, walking in the Botanic Gardens. He had maturity and gentleness and intense dark eyes, and by the end of the afternoon I was more than in the mood. He kissed me politely on the cheek as we were parting, a kiss that turned suddenly passionate, anguished, heart-thudding.

He had a room not far away, a blessedly private room, and that night I shed another kind of virginity, an innocence about myself and what I was capable of desiring.

After a few wonderful weeks Nikos had to go hundreds of miles north, back to Townsville where his fleet was berthed, but soon afterwards my radio section was relocated to Townsville as well.

We got to see each other more than most wartime couples, although it was never enough. We were always hungry, always desperate for each other.

But now? The joy has ebbed from our life. We love each other—I think we do—but Nikos is almost never around, and when he is he drives me to the point of fury.

I've just put the kettle on when I hear footsteps. Billie comes into the kitchen, then hesitates at the sight of me.

I say, 'Cup of tea?' and of course she says yes, simple politeness.

I make the tea and we go to sit in the sunroom. She's washed her hair, thank heavens. It's a nice auburn, richer than my own strawberry blonde, and she's got those dark lashes and brows some redheads have that don't need makeup. Lucky girl.

'Wouldn't have a rubber band?' Billie says. 'Mine broke.'

'No,' I say. 'And you shouldn't use rubber bands, it's bad for the hair and looks dreadful. I thought you were famous for your stylishness. What happened?'

She shrugs. 'Too much effort. Easier to pull it back when I was working on engines.'

'Well you're hardly working on engines now.'

We sip our tea. Billie says, 'Did it stain the rug?'

'The expensive French champagne, you mean? No, the rug's made of that new nylon fibre. Could cope with an atom bomb.'

'Oh. Good.'

After a silence I say, 'What was too much effort?'

'Ah, just—I don't know, things.'

'No, that's not it.'

Billie looks at me, surprised. 'Pretty sure of yourself, aren't you?'

'Got to be if you're short and everyone calls you love. Or blondie. Or *you stupid bitch.*'

'Army?'

'Women's Auxiliary Australian Air Force,' I say. 'Signals.'

'Oh, intelligence stuff like Eliza.'

'Since we're sworn to eternal secrecy we'll never know. But yes.'

'Accounts for the bossiness,' Billie says. 'Or air of command, take your pick.'

'Bossiness—I was a sergeant. You?'

'Nah, civilian. Air Transport Auxiliary.'

'Civilian? Still no excuse.'

She smiles. 'Sorry again. Bit of a dampener on the party.'

'We were winding up anyway. But why?'

After a time Billie says, 'Men. Cocksure, arrogant men, certain you'll do whatever they want, certain you'll get up and dance with them, do anything for them, then they leave you out there on the floor, abandoned in the spotlight—' She stops.

'He's not like that, Nikos,' I say. 'He doesn't mean to hurt anyone.'

'Men never do. Until they do.'

Eliza enters, yawning. 'Anything left in the pot? Yes, please.'

I pour her a cup and she sits down beside us in the sunroom. It looks out onto a garden with a shady pergola, and this morning it's full of light and colour.

Eliza says, 'Bill, come on, what's happened?'

Billie glances at me then shrugs and says, 'Suppose it's not really a secret. Ah, Lizzie. You know my mother died a few months ago—'

'Of course, you poor thing. Are you still feeling raw?'

'A bit. But then the doctor realised Dad had dementia. My aunts and I had noticed he was getting strange, but with Mum so sick, we didn't … anyway, he had to go into a home, an expensive home.'

'But your family's well-off, isn't it?' says Eliza. 'They can afford it.'

'Once upon a time. But we didn't realise how mad Dad had got. He'd thrown away all the family money—gambling, donations, bad investments. A lifetime of frugality blown in months.'

'Did it affect your flying school?'

'Could say that,' Billie says. 'Dad had a financial interest in it, so the creditors took my planes and my savings—couldn't even pay the mechanic or the hangar rent.' She laughs bitterly. 'Another man calling me out to the dance floor then leaving me helpless in the spotlight. My own bloody father.'

'And there's no way to recover?' says Eliza.

'Nah, it's done. And *this* time, Lizzie, I can't pick myself up and try again. You know how I have before, but whatever mainspring's kept me ticking all these years is broken, bloody broken.'

Billie's face is stony. She's not crying but it might have been better if she were. 'Oh, Billie, love.' Eliza puts her arms around her, and I take the teacups out to the kitchen.

When I return I say, 'So what will you do?'

Billie takes a deep breath. 'Dad's happy in the home now and all I've got is in that bag I brought last night. I can't stand Perth a moment longer, so I'm going to get a job, any job, here in Sydney.'

'*Any* job?' says Eliza. 'Not flying?'

'No, not flying. But I've done other things—jeez, Lizzie, remember the cardboard box company?'

Eliza smiles. 'Didn't you say bombing it was the only time the Luftwaffe did us a favour?'

'Look, I can cope with that sort of boring office stuff,' says Billie. 'But I can't take risks any more. And I can't trust some smug, fancy-footwork bastard to stand by me. Never again.'

I say, 'Okay, wait a minute,' then go and get a towel, a comb and some sharp scissors.

'Put this round your shoulders,' I say. 'I used to cut the girls' hair in Hut 12, and if you're trying for a job you've got to look at least semi-human.'

*

Funny what a haircut can do. Eliza gets all misty-eyed and Billie, who looks much better after my ministrations, says, 'Thanks, Teen. Feel a lot less godawful now.'

Later, Harry comes into the kitchen. 'Good move, Sis. The rest of us were so aghast we were useless, but what you did was perfect.'

I put a plate on a shelf and say, 'Glad to help, Harry.'

'You know, the other day I was thinking how we've spent so much of our lives apart, and I've never really got to know the grown-up married woman you've become.'

'Oh, not so grown-up. Maybe not so married either.'

'Ah. I wondered. Wartime relationships can be difficult.'

I sit down. 'I just can't cope. Nikos is never here and Stavros hates me. I want to scream every time I serve a meal, make a bed, sweep the floor. Of course it has to be done, but is it *me* who has to do it? Can't I do something interesting like I used to? When Billie said she was getting a job, I nearly cheered, *me too!*'

'But what would Nikos think about that? I assume he's got fairly traditional attitudes about women staying at home.'

'Oddly, no. His father would be horrified, but his mother's Australian and she's always been the bookkeeper for their business. She brought Nikos up with one or two modern ideas.'

'So it's not him holding you back?'

'No it's me. I have no idea what to do. Look, my WAAAF work wasn't very high level but still it mattered. I had responsibility, I did my job well and Harry, I *loved* it. But what could compare to that? It's peacetime now.'

Harry says, 'Not necessarily. The Russian atomic program is racing ahead to catch up to the Americans, and God knows what'll happen if they do. Wars never pass, Tina, there are just lulls. And look at all those colonies demanding their independence.'

'But the Yanks gave the Philippines their freedom and the Brits are letting India go too. Surely the rest will follow.'

'Doubt it,' he says. 'The French are tangled up in some spat in Vietnam, the Dutch have a death grip on the East Indies, and the Madagascans had a bloody uprising last year. The old colonies are simmering with rage: promised their freedom for helping in the war, then kicked in the guts as soon as we won.'

I shrug. 'But they're just little places, far away.'

He says ruefully, 'Little places have triggered some pretty big wars over the years.'

'Not *nowadays*.'

Harry smiles. 'All right, let's forget world affairs. Basically you want to do something like your wartime service.'

I think for a moment then shake my head. 'Actually, no. I don't ever want my job to be a matter of life and death again. What I'd really like is to work somewhere that brings people *happiness*. A restaurant, a theatre, a club perhaps.'

'Perhaps lack of experience might be a drawback?' he teases.

'Hey, I've got office skills and worked in a shop before the war,' I say, exaggerating only a little. 'I'll start where I have to, Harry, but I can organise *anything*. I just need the chance to prove it.'

2. Billie: Dancing and Flying

Holy hell, I look good. I gaze to the left, to the right. Tina's a miracle worker. She didn't cut the hair as boyishly short as it usually is, but left it shoulder length, with a fullness around the temples—don't know how, but jeez it's flattering.

And jeez, how I needed that small comfort.

I hadn't actually expected to turn up in Sydney looking like something the cat dragged in, but my flight was delayed for hours and some idiot spilled coffee over me.

That wasn't all. I'd spent the previous days moving everything from the hangar to a shed—my mechanic was going to sell what he could to recover his wages. So of course I was filthy and didn't have a moment to clean up before the flight.

I look in the mirror again. Stark collar-bones, wrists like twigs. I haven't felt like eating and anyway, I spent my last penny on the flight. I'm stupidly skinny, but Tina says she's going to feed me up.

She's a funny one. No-nonsense, bristling with good sense, but because she's small and buxom and bright, men treat her like an adorable fool.

But she's clever, as clever as Eliza. At least being tall and thin and cranky has helped me avoid a lot of unwanted attention. I sit down on the bed and laugh a little.

And poor old Nikos! He's been tiptoeing around me as if I'm an unexploded bomb. I tried to explain I was a bit touchy about losing my business, but didn't tell him all of it of course. Haven't told anyone, not even Eliza.

One almost-last straw was a bloke in Perth who'd follow me round with big mournful eyes. He drove me mad and I treated him like shit, but really, it was the poor bastard's sorrow I couldn't bear: that familiar, hopeless yearning. It hurt. I'd felt that way too often myself and couldn't stand it.

And Nikos? Everyone treats him like the man in charge, the confident big boss. But all I could see in that split second, as he grabbed my hand laughing and pulled me towards him, was the pain in his eyes. The vulnerability.

I couldn't bear it and wanted him to stop, to go away, to never show me those dark sad eyes again. So I threw my drink at him and it worked perfectly. He's hardly spoken to me since.

After the weekend Lizzie and Harry returned to Newcastle. I'm so happy to see Harry home safe from the war and Lizzie the mother she always wanted to be, and now we'll only be a hundred miles apart. Not much more than than the distance from London to Southampton, and we used to go back and forth often enough then; between Toby's house and Pete's farm.

Pete's farm.

And there it is. The news I've been keeping secret, the last straw in the heap of last straws that's finally crushed me.

A fortnight ago a letter arrived from Pete's daughter, Vivian. She's only eleven but she's a good correspondent and, ten thousand miles apart, we're closer now than ever before. One of my most painful realisations (among many) has been recognising how little I offered Vivy when she was a small child.

Then, before the war, I was simply a friend of the family, the old affair with Pete a matter of history. I was with Wilf, a lovely man, and Pete was married to wild Charlotte. She gave him Vivy and ran away; then Wilf died and the war took over all our lives.

As a friend I still saw Pete and Vivy, but a child was so far beyond my experience all I could do was offer her the occasional toy aeroplane and take her for walks. A bit like playing with a puppy, I think with shame.

But finally Pete and I found each other again, and it seemed we'd broken through into sunlight: until the war ended and I wanted to come home. My mother was ill, I had no chance of a flying job in Britain, and I'd simply spent too long in that chilly country.

But Pete loved his farm too much to even consider coming back to his birthplace. So that was that. Yet funny little Vivy, who forgave her restless mother Charlie for flitting in and out of her life, forgave me too for leaving her.

Her letters are a great comfort. They remind me of the glittering stars above Hamble airfield, the old living room with its welcoming fire, autumn days in the hills around the farm, and the long sweet nights with Pete.

As everything got harder and harder here, I sometimes thought perhaps, perhaps? Could I swallow my pride and go back to Pete? Despite our separations, the love between us has always been deep and constant. Then, a fortnight ago, I got Vivy's letter.

Did I misunderstand? I sit and open my satchel (a handbag substitute that appals Tina), take out the letter and read it again.

Dear Billie,

It's the middle of summer now and the holidays are such fun! I've been riding Taffy up in the hills, and out to the old field—remember the one with the poppies where we used to lie under the oak trees?

Guess what? <u>Charlie</u> came to visit us! She's looking very chic (that's a French word) and is getting married soon to a French General. She says I can visit them at his château in Brittany. I'm not sure what a château is but I love the little hat on top of the word. So I'll be getting a stepfather—I do hope he's nice.

My music lessons are going well. I'm learning jazz singing from my new teacher, Miss Price, and I love it. She's Australian like you, and it's so nice hearing her voice. Her name is Janet.

Daddy was worried about me learning modern singing, because my old teacher said I could have a classical career if I put in the work (and I <u>do</u>, Billie), so he went to see Miss Price and now they've become good friends.

She visits for dinner a lot and he takes her to the theatre. I don't suppose you'll mind about that because you and Daddy told me the two of you were parting forever. Daddy says everyone moves on and you've probably got another boyfriend by now. Have you, Billie?

I hope some new students have joined your flying school. Only very silly people would be scared of learning flying from a woman! Daddy says you're the best pilot he ever met.

Remember when you took me up in his Moth before you left? I loved that day. A few weeks ago he took Miss Price flying too but I don't think she liked it very much. He's going to sell the Moth soon, he says.

Anyway, that's all for now. School starts again in a week (ugh) but it's so pretty here when the autumn leaves are red and gold, I don't really mind.

Love, Vivy (and Taffy)

I was hoping it wouldn't hurt so much but it still kicks. I didn't misunderstand. There's no way back with Pete.

After the letter I stopped trying to salvage my life. I found foggy-eyed Dad a bed in a nursing home, my aunts said they'd close up our old house, and I emptied out the hangar and got on a plane to Sydney. And here I am.

Perhaps I can find a new life in Sydney and forget, finally, the life with poppies and oak trees and autumn leaves, the life with Pete and Vivy I was so stupidly, stupidly convinced I had to leave behind. Perhaps.

A month has passed since I turned up on Nikos and Tina's doorstep. They've been welcoming and the house is large, but sometimes there's more tension between them than was obvious at first. The son, call-me-*Steve*, is a bad-tempered presence as well.

At least I'm feeling calmer now. Every day Tina and I check the newspapers for work, but nothing so far. She's tried for jobs in a cafe and a pub and was laughed at. I applied to be a secretary and didn't even get an interview.

I drop the paper beside my chair in the sunroom, and the house cat, a grey thing called Shadow, leaps unasked into my lap. I've never had a pet so it's taken a while to get used to this.

She has the habit of lying coyly on her back, then tries to draw blood if you rub her tummy. I'm more cautious now, but she settles herself and lets me stroke her neck.

'Of course Pete's moved on,' I say to the cat and she purrs.

I told him he should, and said I would myself. Surely we'd simply returned to each other during wartime out of nostalgia for the past? But I've just turned forty-two and I've got to be realistic about two things: I can't go back to Pete, and I can't keep flying for very much longer. And although it's hard to admit, I'm not even sure I want to any more.

'I've given it up before,' I say. The cat looks unimpressed.

After Wilf died of his wounds from the Spanish Civil War I didn't fly a plane for three years. Not until the war demanded I do something useful, and the only possibility for a woman pilot was the Air Transport Auxiliary.

And now I don't even care about teaching any more, not the way I did in the early thirties. That was when I first met fresh-faced Pete, who strolled into my training school and declared (like every other young fool in the country) he wanted to be a pilot.

But even then I wondered if he lacked something essential. Perhaps it was the connection Lizzie mentioned, the link I've always felt between dancing and flying, and Pete hated to dance.

In his heart he's always been tied to the earth, the farm his deepest passion. At the end he said bitterly I'd never understood how he felt about the land, how it grounded him.

'Oh, I understood, Pete,' I say, and the cat yawns. 'It was you who didn't see it for so long.'

He learnt to dance at the end too, to impress me when he hoped we'd stay together. And I was impressed, but not enough to freeze forever in that old, smug, hypocritical country. Australia's hypocritical too, but it's warm and young and doesn't have a lot to be smug about.

I sigh. The cat turns around and settles itself again.

But now, what will I do with my life? I don't have Lizzie's focused intellect, nor her yearning for a child (had my tubes tied years ago).

I don't have Tina's bluntness—well, yes, I do—but I don't have her desire to organise and push through obstacles. She must have made a great sergeant.

'Really, cat, all I *can* do is dance and fly.'

'Surely not,' says Nikos, coming in the door with two small plates of the nutty, delicious pastry his mother bakes and sends over. 'Baklava?'

'Oh. All right. Thanks.'

Now I've been here a month we're a little more comfortable around each other, but we still haven't spoken much. Nikos sits down and says, 'You've got a great throwing arm, Billie, so cricket's always a possibility.'

'Jeez, are you *ever* going to let me forget that night?'

He smiles. 'No, and nor is anyone else.'

'I can play hockey. Any future in that?'

'Not in Sydney. Now if you could sail a boat you might be useful.'

'Sail?' I laugh. 'Talk to Lizzie, she's the ship-mad one.'

'She and Harry only love their old windjammers. No, I need an extra hand for my yacht, a friend can't make it this weekend.'

'Well, don't look at me. The closest I've ever been to the sea is a flying boat, and the whole idea was to get off the water, not play around on top.'

He's surprised. 'I know you're a pilot of course, but flying boats? Where was that?'

'Hamble airfield, near Southampton. We taught snotty-nosed recruits for the RAF Reserve in the thirties.'

Nikos looks at me oddly, and I think, Typical. Yeah, mate, flying boats. And they were a doddle compared to the four-engined heavy bombers we had to ferry across the country with nothing but an old road-map on our knees.

'What sort?' says Nikos, leaning forward.

I shrug. 'Cutty Sark amphibians. Avro seaplanes. During the war I took a repaired Sunderland back to Pembroke Dock.' I look at him a little mockingly. 'ATA women weren't supposed to pilot flying boats but there was no one else around with the experience.'

He nods. 'I suppose you know there were Empires based here in Sydney before the war, out at Rose Bay? Civilian version of Sunderlands, massive beasts.'

'Of course. But it's mostly Catalinas now isn't it?' I lick flakes of baklava off my fingers.

'Yes, though a few outfits have war-surplus Sunderlands and the newer Solents, too.' Nikos is quiet for a moment then says, 'Billie, can you read flight plans and meteorology reports?'

I laugh. 'I'd have been dead long ago if I couldn't. Why?'

'What about using teletype machines?'

'Yeah, had one in an old office job. *Why?*'

'Well, I actually work at the flying boat base at Rose Bay.'

'Oh. You've never mentioned that before.'

'We've hardly spoken.'

'Tina's never said anything either.'

He smiles briefly. 'She's not much interested in what I do. But yes, that's where I work. Look, there's no chance at all of a pilot's job there—'

'—for a woman—'

'For a woman, but the Aeradio section needs a teletype operator. The word's come down from on high we must only use teletype for position and weather reports, but no one's got the experience.'

'Good pay?'

'Not great, but not awful. But look, I really do mean there's no possibility of flying. So if you're thinking it might be a way back into aviation, it's not.'

'I never said I wanted a way back—just a job,' I say. 'Where's this Rose Bay, anyway?'

'Oh, about six miles east of here, through the city and Kings Cross. It's out towards the Heads, the entrance to Sydney Harbour.'

'And what do *you* do there?' I say. 'I thought you worked with boats, not planes.'

'I manage the small vessels section. Our control launches go out day and night to clear debris and mark the takeoff and alighting areas. Bloody hard shifts and so is the teletype job. Still interested?'

Nikos gazes at me, and his eyes aren't dark and vulnerable after all. That's a relief—perhaps I was simply overwrought that first night and quite misread him.

And he's offering me a job, so who cares how sad the sod's eyes are anyway?

Tina is amazed when I tell her. 'But I thought you wanted to get out of flying, Billie,' she says, putting a saucepan away in the cupboard. 'It's just typing, isn't it? Sounds pretty dull.'

'Pays better than a secretary, and I've done that before.'

'I'm sorry, I never even thought of the flying boat base for you. It's always seemed such a dull, bureaucratic place. I know they've got good equipment—we'd have killed for transmitters like that in the war—but I want *people* in my life, not bloody headphones!'

'Have you seen anything in the paper today?' I say.

She nods. 'One possibility. A restaurant that needs a bookkeeper.'

'Can you do that?'

'No.' She smiles. 'But Nikos's mum Ruby said she'd teach me the basics, then I'll try to bluff my way through.'

The phone on the hall table rings. Tina goes out and answers it and chats for a few moments, then calls me. 'It's Eliza,' she says, handing me the receiver. 'News about some old friends of yours.'

'Billie, guess what!' Eliza says. 'Klara, Yvonne and little Claire are coming to Australia!'

'Really? When? For how long?'

Eliza laughs. 'In two months, January. But it's not a visit—they've decided to *emigrate*.'

'But Klara always said she couldn't live anywhere but the romantic old cities of Europe.'

'That was before the war,' says Eliza. 'Now she knows what happened to Jews like her in those romantic old cities. Her letters have been horribly bleak lately and Yvonne says she's been depressed and is having nightmares. Now it's all too much and they want a new start.'

'Brave of them to pull up sticks and emigrate, though,' I say. 'Still, so many people have done that since the war, why not? It'll be fantastic to see Yvie again too.'

'And Claire—she's four now, and must have changed so much. Oh, Bill, isn't it *marvellous*?'

'So this Klara is a poetess?' says Tina.

'Yeah, Klara Virtanen. She was well-known in the thirties. Small, very fair woman from Finland, long hair to her waist, and she'd dress in all sorts of bizarre things.' I smile at the memory. 'When the war came she chopped all her hair off, so Toby called her a pragmatic little Nordic pixie.'

'And Toby was her husband, the author Toby Fenn?'

'But they only married to protect their daughter, Claire. Toby had no interest in women and Klara was living with Yvonne.'

'Then how on earth did they have a child in the first place?'

'Ah, Teen, you probably don't want the gory details, but it involved a glass jar and a syringe.'

'Good God. That's certainly pragmatic.'

'She and Toby were still very close. He was a dear man, killed in the war. He owned the house in London where Lizzie and our other friends lived. Yvonne and I would catch the train from Southampton to take them extra farm rations.'

'Is Yvonne one of those muscular, no-lipstick ladies? We had a few girls like that in Hut 12.'

I laugh. 'Yvie? No, she's tallish and dreamy, her hair always falling down. You mightn't notice her in a crowd but she's got a lovely smile. She was a good friend to me at Hamble, a great pilot too.'

'Well, they're very welcome to stay here when they arrive in January,' says Tina.

'You're a hospitable lady, Teen.'

'I am, aren't I?' Tina laughs briefly. 'Nice to have people around, really. That's all.'

3. Yvonne: Calm Blue Harbour

'I can see *Billie*! Look, near that blonde woman,' I say, leaning on the bulwark as the liner nudges slowly against the dock and the wharf labourers secure the lines.

'Beside that bearded man? Oh, Yvonne, yes!' says Klara. 'She is waving, she sees us. What a crowd is down there.'

'I suppose most people have friends or family here. It'd be hard to emigrate if you didn't. We're so lucky Billie's here, and Harry and Eliza just a hundred miles away.'

'We shall find our new home in Sydney, my love, I am certain of it.' Klara bends down. 'Look Claire—see the woman with red hair who is waving to us? She is our old friend Billie, who knew you when you were a baby.'

'I don't remember her, but that was a very long time ago.'

Klara and I smile at each other over four-year-old Claire's head.

'Well,' says Klara. 'Let us go now to see this new land.'

After we've collected our baggage and satisfied the burly Customs man we're not smugglers, we go out to the visitor area, and there's Billie at last. We laugh and kiss, and she introduces her friends.

The blonde woman is Tina, Harry's sister. Petite and pretty, she has his grey eyes and no-nonsense air. Her husband Nikos, the tall bearded man, takes charge of our baggage trolley.

'Now, you don't need to find a hotel,' says Billie. 'Tina and Nikos would love you to stay with them—and me—until you get settled.'

'All of us? Are you certain?' says Klara.

'Of course,' says Tina. 'And Nikos has a cousin in real estate so he'll help you find a place to live.'

Claire is gazing around wide-eyed and Nikos lifts her onto the baggage trolley. 'You'll have a much better view from there, young Claire,' he says. She thinks for a moment, then settles herself and smiles regally at those of us unfortunate enough to have to walk.

Billie says, 'Lizzie and Harry are staying with us overnight—they've come down from Newcastle especially to see you.'

'Wonderful!' I say, and Billie grins her dear familiar smile. With Claire on Klara's lap, we all fit into the car, and Nikos drives us to Rozelle. The sun is shining in a deep blue sky, the air is warm and fresh, and I sigh with relief.

Everything will be all right now.

Billie and I first met in 1942, when I joined Ferry Pool 15, the ATA women's unit at Hamble. I was twenty-four, shy, and loved classical music. I loved a woman too, but she'd left me by then. Billie was my first friend at Hamble and we'd swap books and listen to records in the mess when things were quiet.

Women flyers were accused often enough of being 'man-haters' and 'lezzos,' so those of us who weren't actually much interested in men had to play it straight. But Billie didn't care who you liked in bed as long as you flew well. It turned out she knew the poetess Klara Virtanen, my idol for years, and introduced us. It was the start of my life, my real life.

Billie and I did the same hard job and knew each other's fears as only another pilot could. Once her fuel almost ran out, and when she landed I wrapped her in a blanket and rubbed her frozen hands until the blood returned. Another time, after a near-crash, I was shaking uncontrollably and she held me till I was calm enough to take my delivery chit to the airfield office.

To the world we were absent-minded Yvonne and sardonic Billie, but we understood each other like sisters. On the long train trips from Southampton to London, taking precious eggs, vegetables and bacon from Pete's farm to Toby's house, we used to talk about our hopes for the future.

Hers were to leave 'this bloody *refrigerator* of a country,' return to Australia and teach flying once more. When she and Pete became lovers again they were so happy I thought she might stay in England, but in the end she still left.

My hopes were always to go into publishing—my father ran an old-fashioned printery and taught me the trade. It turned out that Klara used her own small letterpress to hand-print her poetry books, and when it broke down it was Billie who sent me to help her mend it.

When Klara and I first met I swear light radiated from her face, that elfin face with its dawn-blue eyes and short silvery hair. People call her angelic, but they have no idea of the lusty woman who drew me laughing into her bed, both of us covered in ink and dust, stars glimmering through the window and, in my sweet, foolish mind's eye, drifting around us as we made love.

Klara always called London her spiritual home, and it was in London she worked tirelessly for the *Kindertransport* refugees, the children sent away by their parents to save them from the Nazis. But a rocket killed Toby and almost killed her, and after that she seemed to lose some essential strength of heart.

When the war ended we went to Finland to visit her parents (alive because Finland protected its small Jewish population) and Klara discovered that her family tree had almost ceased to exist.

Cousins and aunts and grandfathers and babies living quietly all over Europe had been slaughtered without mercy by a bureaucracy beyond comprehension—although not beyond the comprehension of the sadists, the *infinitely* damned sadists, who did it.

Back in London the papers endlessly reported what had happened to the Jews, and every day, although it seemed impossible, every day was worse than the day before. One evening I came home to find my love sitting in the dark.

'The Americans found a warehouse, Yvonne, full of children's shoes,' said Klara evenly. 'Jewish children's shoes, taken from their soft baby feet to become the shoes of German children who, being alive, naturally had greater need of them. Such impeccable logic.'

'Oh, my darling, have you been thinking about that for hours? Where's Claire?'

'Claire?' she said.

'Our *daughter*. Where is she?'

Klara shook her head, puzzled.

I raced into the bedroom and there was the child, lying still in her cot. I felt rigid with horror, then Claire murmured. Trembling, I went back to Klara, who now simply sat, unresponsive. She lay without moving in bed all night. Every time I checked, her eyes were still open. Next day the doctor gave her laudanum drops, and she slept at last.

She stayed in bed for two weeks. She'd eat a little food from a spoon and relieve herself as obediently as a child when I took her to the bathroom, but for two weeks she didn't say a word.

Then she spoke again, as elusively as she always had, the voice of her poetry. She was sorry she had *gone away*, she said, but now she was back. And she was indeed back, the loving mother of Claire and companion of my heart: in the day at least.

At night she would wake up trembling, crying out, sobbing. Of course she could no longer write her beloved poetry. For two years I looked after Klara, our child, our flat and the other tenants in the house, and every moment was razor-edged with anxiety.

Then one day Klara said, 'I think we must leave, darling Yvonne. London has become a place of death, and we need to see different light and hear different sounds and live beneath different skies.'

We considered moving to the country, to Finland, to America: but Australia, home of our dearest friends, seemed right. We packed our things and sold the house and got on a ship.

It's marvellous to see Eliza and Harry, but next day they return to Newcastle, insisting we visit them as soon as we can. We spend the following weeks with Billie, Tina and Nikos, although we don't see much of Nikos's rather surly son, Stavros.

Nikos introduces us to Kostas, his cousin in real estate. We already like this part of Sydney very much, so Kostas helps us find a house to buy in Balmain, close to Rozelle.

Balmain rambles across a broad harbour peninsula, with shipyards, warehouses and factories clustered along the water's edge. It's a proudly working-class area and we're greeted with kindness in the small shops of Darling Street, especially when Claire is with us.

Our new home is near a park on the water. It's a run-down Victorian terrace, with two storeys and a basement flat. We can afford to buy it because we're not badly-off—I have a small inheritance, while Klara gets the royalties from Toby's books and also did well on the sale of their London property.

The rear of the house faces north, which in the southern hemisphere is the warm side, and from upstairs it has a striking view to the water over the next street's buildings. Klara and I love the place. We have it repainted and tidy the garden, and buy furniture from local second-hand shops.

Klara makes one bedroom her study and tries to write poetry, but even in this new land she cannot. She slowly becomes more silent and I wonder if she's slipping away from the world again. And if so, dear God, what will I do?

Still, we go to the park and sit under the great trees, and take Claire to splash in the nearby swimming pool. It's protected with wire netting, a shop-keeper tells us, because there are sharks in that calm blue harbour. (Are there sharks circling Klara too?)

Claire goes to kindergarten three afternoons a week. We see our old friend Billie and new friends Tina and Nikos. We walk around the steep twisting streets of Balmain, and discover this country does indeed have different light and sounds and skies: and all are brash and enchanting.

But Klara still sometimes wakes up sobbing and I am still afraid.

Toby's house in London's Fitzrovia was also Victorian—a red-brick interloper among the elegant Georgians, Toby would say. We called it simply 'Whitfield Street' as if it were the only thing in the neighbourhood, despite the pubs and nearby police station.

Toby's house had a cellar, four floors and an attic. Klara had a study in the attic but after D-Day, when the Germans started raining V-1 rockets onto London, she started working downstairs.

So it was cruelly bad luck that she and Toby were up in the attic one morning. Klara was packing books, Toby telling her the new ending he'd dreamt up for his novel, when a V-1 exploded in Whitfield Street. It wiped out the police station and half a pub, but amazingly left Toby's house almost untouched. Almost.

The V-1's engine sounded like a motorcycle, until the moment it stopped and the rocket spiraled down. Toby heard the clatter and the silence, and flung Klara beneath a desk to save her: but could not save himself. She held his body, promising him she would not forget; and went on to complete his novel just as he'd wanted.

All his life Toby had loved a man named Stefan, and Klara loved me, but she yearned for a child. Farmers had long used artificial fertilisation with their stock, and clinics in Switzerland had started discreetly providing the same service for humans, but with a lot less fuss we only needed kind Toby, a jar and a syringe.

Klara conceived almost immediately, as if her body had been waiting for such a miracle. She and Toby married to protect the baby and she became Klara Fenn, no longer Klara Virtanen.

She says she's glad to carry Toby's name and it doesn't matter to her readers: she won't be publishing any new poetry for a long time. (*If ever* remains unspoken.)

Toby died four months before Claire was born and how I wish he'd had a chance to see her. She has his blue eyes and high cheekbones, but more than that she has his calm air of remoteness from the world.

Sometimes he'd say, laughing, he'd always expected to observe the human condition from a distance, at least until Klara's blessed glass jar came into his life: but I think his shell was shattered long before that, when Stefan left him.

Poor Toby. I didn't know him very well, but still I miss him.

*

Our house is one of a pair with a common wall, and the inhabitants of the mirror residence are Valma and Reg. We meet them one day as they're going out, and they stop to admire Claire.

Valma has a permanent wave and Reg has slicked-back hair and a walking-stick. Reg says, 'And what brings you lovely ladies all the way from England to Balmain?'

'Klara was married to my cousin Toby in London,' I say. (He wasn't really my cousin but a family connection makes our shared life more plausible.) 'He died in the Blitz and Klara wanted a new start. I came too to help with Claire.'

Reg nods sagely but Valma's smoothly pencilled eyebrows lift slightly. I expect she thinks Klara is an unmarried mother—the war has provided rather a lot of useful cover stories.

Claire points to the walking-stick. 'Why have you got that?'

'Lost my leg at El Alamein, chicken,' says Reg, which confuses me for a moment till I remember it was a battle in Egypt. 'See, it's a wooden one now.'

He taps his ankle with the stick and it clacks.

Claire is impressed. 'Does it hurt?' she says.

'Not any more.' His forehead tightens fleetingly and I expect it once hurt a great deal.

'But how do you do your work?'

'Sitting down, princess, sitting down.' Reg chuckles. 'Used to be on the presses but my boss found me a desk job.'

Klara hasn't been paying much attention, but she looks up and says, 'Presses?'

'Williams Printery. In the lane behind the shops.'

'Oh yes,' I say. 'Thought I smelt ink there the other day.'

'Small publisher. Magazines, catalogues, textbooks,' Reg says. 'Not going very well though, the equipment's too old.'

'You have old presses?' says Klara. '*Hand* presses?'

'Oh no, they'd be too slow. Electric ones, but the boss won't do the maintenance so they break down a lot.'

'I had a hand letterpress once,' says Klara, 'but we left it in England. I miss it.'

Reg looks at small, slight Klara in surprise. 'You had one? Whatever for?'

Valma shifts impatiently.

'For printing books, of course,' says Klara.

'Well, I never,' says Reg. 'Now I think of it, we used to have an old hand press at the back of the shed. Maybe the boss'd sell it to you cheap.'

'If we don't get a hurry on, Reg, we'll miss the tram,' says Valma.

'Must go. Tell me tomorrow if you want to have a squiz.' Reg tips his hat and they leave.

We go to the park and sit under a tree, watching Claire as she plays on a swing.

Klara says, 'I would like to have a squiz, Yvonne, if that means to have a look.'

'I expect so. But if you did get another press, love, what would you do with it?' I say gently.

'Yvonne, I have written nothing worthwhile lately. I know I must be patient, but I have been thinking about all the poets of today, not just myself. The war was a cacophony, a clamour that drowned out every human voice.'

She looks up, her eyes tired but smiling. 'It occurs to me I could edit a book of some of the poetry that went unheard over those years. I cannot create fierce words of my own, but still I would like to be surrounded by them.'

With relief I realise Klara's silence has been one of contemplation, not despair. 'My dear,' she says, 'will you help me?'

The following Saturday Reg takes us to the printery. It's closed but the owner is there anyway, a harried elderly man flicking through a pile of papers on his desk.

'The *hand* press? Are you serious, Mr Frisket?' he says. 'It's ancient. Well, you can show the ladies, I've no time to do it.'

Reg takes us to a large shed. Two long machines and three smaller ones lie beneath dustcovers. At the rear is a square form beneath a blackened canvas, which Reg removes. Klara steps forward and gazes at the old press.

She slowly runs her fingers over a beam and says, 'The platen is rotted, the frisket is gone and the screw is stripped. The stand has termites and the metalwork is corroded beyond repair.'

'Perhaps not beyond repair,' says Reg uncertainly. 'But a big job, no mistake. A big job.'

Klara sighs. 'We could try to mend it, but I do not love this press. I loved my own, but that was a long time ago. Now I realise I no longer have the patience or the strength for such labour.'

'That old skinflint never has anything properly maintained,' says Reg. 'Mind you, he probably discarded this one some time around the Boer War.'

Klara smiles a little and looks at me. 'I think I shall still do the book, Yvonne, but I will use modern machinery. It is the poetry that matters, not how it is printed.'

'Well, we've got a few good presses, don't get me wrong.' Reg looks around. 'With a bit of care this could be a good printery, but the old sod wants out. If he doesn't get a buyer soon I reckon he'll just shut down.'

We walk to the exit and Mr Skinflint scowls from his desk.

At the door we thank Reg, then Klara says, 'Is your name really Mr Frisket?'

He grins. 'Had to be a printer with that, didn't I? No. Matter of discretion, really, sometimes you got to get yourself a new name. Thought it fitted.'

4. Harry: The Double Tenth

What a treat to see Klara again! Last time I saw her—my God, ten years ago—she was as flighty as a finch. As a mother now she's more settled, although she still has that elfin air. I haven't met Yvonne before, of course: she's tall and wispy and a little other-worldly, but she seems pleasant and Eliza is very fond of her.

After dinner we sit in Tina's lounge room, and Claire goes to gaze at the book-case. I haven't met her before either: she was born in London while I was in Changi. She's a striking child with a cloud of silvery-blonde hair and her father Toby's deep blue eyes.

'How did you enjoy the ship, Claire?' Eliza says.

'I don't like travelling,' she says with composure. 'I like our house because my books are there now. They had to go in a crate on the ship and I couldn't read them.'

'Claire is not fond of disruption,' Klara says. 'Yvonne says she has the look of an angel and the soul of a librarian.'

Claire nods firmly. 'I like libraries. Yvonne used to take me to one in London and now we're going to join one here.'

She yawns and rubs her eyes. It's clear they're tired. We don't have much time to chat that night, but they're invited to stay with us in Newcastle after the dust has settled.

On the train home next morning I feel refreshed: surprising given that Eliza and I were enjoyably awake together in bed until the early hours. She turns to me and sighs with pleasure.

'Oh, wasn't it *lovely* to see Klara again? And did you like Yvonne?'

'Very pleasant woman,' I say. 'Do you regret living in Newcastle, so far from your old friends? Would you prefer to be in Sydney?'

'No, I like Newcastle and besides, it'd break your mother's heart if we took Leo away.'

The train arrives at Hornsby, the big station on the outskirts of Sydney, and I notice a man walking beside our carriage as we slow down. I think, shocked, surely that's not ...? Christ, it is.

Eliza says, 'What? You look so surprised.'

'Ah, someone I used to know.'

She glances back but the man doesn't come into our carriage.

'What's wrong, Harry? Was he a friend?'

I take a breath. 'No, not a friend.'

'From Changi?' She sighs and takes my hand. 'Oh, love.'

We've talked about my imprisonment, of course. There was no avoiding it when I first came home, but I didn't go into the details and she knows I'm determined to put it all behind me.

'A horrible man, but I never thought at the time—well, you wouldn't have been so naïve, but I was. I simply couldn't imagine one of ours could betray ...'

'A spy?' she says.

'That sounds so melodramatic, all trenchcoats and invisible ink. No, more a seeking of favours, of privileges granted. I'd see him with the high-ranking Japanese, and wonder. Of course our senior men had to talk to them, but there was something in his bearing, even his eyes, suggested ... he *approved* of them.'

'You can't conceive of that?' says Eliza.

'Good God, no.'

She pauses. 'Darling, more people approved of the Fascists than you could imagine. And they didn't give up their fantasies when the war started—and sometimes not even when it ended.'

'But how could anyone want to *help* those bastards?' I say.

'Perhaps they had grudges against their own,' she says. 'Perhaps they were so afraid they'd have done anything to save their bacon. Perhaps they simply hoped to be on the winning side.'

I sigh. 'I've always hated that tribalism, our side and theirs. Despite Changi, despite everything, I still hope our common humanity will bring us all together one day.'

She says gently, 'Oh, Harry. Many conservatives are still in power and they'd say your hopes are treacherous and Communist.'

I nod wryly. 'Remember when we met on the barque? I made it clear then I was a Socialist, my mentor that notorious Red, Professor Fischer.'

'I admired you for it, and Otto became one of my dearest friends.' She elbows me. 'But you didn't have to go and marry his bloody daughter.'

I laugh. 'That was a certainly a mistake, but be fair—I got out of it as soon as Charlotte ran off with Pete. I can't blame her on Socialism, or Socialism on her.'

'Charlotte's certainly more a force of nature than a philosophy. A cyclone perhaps.'

I gaze at Eliza. 'Did you mind, love, really? All that time we had to wait until I was free?'

'I minded that she made you so sad, but no, that's the odd thing about Charlotte. She behaved appallingly but she always had such a brave, vulnerable side. Even when I was furious with her, I couldn't hate her.'

'So when does her third lot of nuptials take place?'

Eliza opens her handbag and pulls out a letter.

'Um, in a couple of months, at the famous château. She sent us a snapshot—look. So well-groomed and Parisian now, hardly the blonde seductress we once knew.'

'Well, she's got a French general to live up to. Did we get an invitation to the wedding?'

'We did, as it happens,' Eliza says as she puts the letter away. 'I'll have to write and *ever*-so-regretfully decline.' We laugh and chat about getting home, and soon I completely forget who's sitting in the next carriage.

After a time Eliza yawns. 'I still haven't caught up on sleep. Leo was awake half the night before we left.'

'It'll be better once he's older. Or so total strangers feel obliged to tell us all the time.'

'Don't they just. But motherhood's so *complicated*. Sometimes it seems as if I've gone to the moon and back and have no idea where I am. Or even who I am.'

That worries me. When we first met on the sailing ship *Inverley*—Lord, nineteen years ago—she was such a wise, brave young woman.

After we married in 1938 we wanted a child, but time passed and our hopes slowly faded. Four years later, when Singapore fell, our hopes became a little more basic: would either of us survive? Brutal days.

Yet even the worst of days must end, and by a miracle Eliza became pregnant as soon as we were reunited. I wasn't much more than a walking skeleton myself, but nothing mattered then except to lose myself in the sweet slim body of my wife.

I say, 'Put your head on my shoulder and have a snooze.' She kisses me and in moments is fast asleep.

As a lad I'd often take this train between Sydney and Newcastle, and always loved the trip. Soon we're approaching the new steel bridge across the Hawkesbury River. The old bridge's remaining sandstone piers are like miniature castle towers set in the swirling green eddies.

Rows of timber posts out on the river bear racks of shellfish that grow plump and delicious in these pristine waters. Most of the Hawkesbury oyster farms are family businesses, Nikos tells me, many run by Greeks.

His uncle owns one and wants Nikos to take it over, but my cosmopolitan brother-in-law just ruefully shakes his head. He's Australian-born and hasn't the slightest interest in that kind of hardscrabble life.

Nikos is a few years younger than me, although still a lot older than my baby sister Tina. She's not a baby now, of course, just turned thirty. But I must say I was surprised a few months ago when she said she was unhappy, even yearning for the past.

Most people were delighted to put their war years behind them. I bloody was. I shift a little in my seat to ease my back—it never quite recovered from a vicious beating in 1943 and still gives me trouble.

Across the river, I see glimpses of old shacks, the homes of the local fishermen and oyster farmers, set along the waterline of the steep, stony hills; then they disappear as we pass into a tunnel.

Through a few more short tunnels, then we reach Woy Woy. After a brief stop we steam across the causeway, and soon other station platforms are flashing past as the line runs beside sunny Brisbane Water.

When we reach Gosford, half-way home, Eliza stirs but doesn't wake up. I'd hoped meeting her old friends again would help her feel more like herself. They were in London together through much of the war, although the last time I saw them was in 1939.

That was when Eliza and I sailed away on what we so innocently called our Singapore adventure. (Turned out to be too much bloody adventure for anyone's liking. But it's over. I refuse to let myself be defined by that time. It's *over*.)

I unclench my fists and take a breath.

The whistle toots and we're off again. The green scrub and grey-trunked trees flickering past the window are hypnotically soothing. We stop at Ourimbah and Tuggerah, and then to the west emerge the indigo mountains of the Watagans, the range that ends in symmetric blue Mount Sugarloaf, a sight so reminiscent of home it always tightens my throat.

More bush, a stop at Fassifern to pick up people from the Toronto line, then a string of little stations, their names as familiar as my own—Booragul, Teralba, Cockle Creek, Cardiff, Kotara, Adamstown—and finally, Newcastle.

Yawning, I get our case down from the luggage rack and we leave the train. I know I should be cautious now. When I get too tired I jump at noises and fear the guards will … (Stop it. The guards won't. The guards are *gone*. Retribution for speaking or moving or just existing will not descend upon me, not ever again).

As we're queuing to hand the inspector our tickets I turn and he's there. I feel nauseous. His eyes are as colourless as I remember, although they're baggier, his jowls heavier.

He stares at me. 'Bell.'

After a moment I say, 'Godfrey.'

The queue isn't moving, a woman ahead is arguing about her ticket. He glances at Eliza. She says calmly, 'How do you do, Mr— Godfrey, is it?'

'Doctor.'

'My wife, Eliza,' I say. I'd rather introduce her to a crocodile.

He clears his throat. 'Visiting?'

'No, we live in Newcastle East,' says Eliza. 'You?'

His face is pale, but that's his usual dead-fish complexion.

'Just here till tomorrow.'

I say, deliberately, 'An old comrade of ours lives in Newcastle too. Maybe you'd like have a drink and catch up.'

'Oh?' He swallows and Eliza glances at me.

'Caswell. You'd remember *Caswell*, of course.'

The queue shuffles forward and I hand the inspector our tickets. We pass through the gate and I turn as Godfrey comes out.

'Will I give him your regards?' I say. He looks at me with hatred, pushes past and hurries away.

I left the car parked at the station so we drive to Mum's house, a few streets from ours. After Leo's ecstatic greeting he falls asleep on the sofa, and we sit down to a nice hot dinner.

When she was a young teacher Mum was as pretty as Tina, with the same red-gold hair. Now hers is white and neatly coiled but she's kept her sharp mind and good looks, and is always amused to hear of my ex-wife Charlotte's adventures.

'French *general*, is it?' she says in her soft Scottish accent. 'Oh my. He'll have his work cut out for him. He's used to telling people what to do and I doubt the lassie'll pay him any heed. Whatever happened to that lad Stefan she was going to marry?'

'He promptly moved on,' Eliza says. 'He'd already flitted from Toby to Charlotte, then he married some poor girl with a title and a bun in the oven. Last I heard he was living it up on the Riviera with a famous playwright.'

Jessie solemnly shakes her head. 'Changeable young things. Nothing like that in my time.'

I smile. 'Mum, you're hardly some ancient dowager and I'm sure people aren't very different today.'

She laughs. 'Och, I was just teasing. My best friend at school was never quite sure if she was Arthur or Martha. So you're not going to Charlotte's nuptials, then?'

'Too far, too costly, Jessie,' says Eliza. 'And can you imagine Leo on an aeroplane for a week?'

'The bairn's always welcome here, but I take your meaning.'

We finally get Leo home to his cot, and as we're getting ready for bed, Eliza says, 'Why did the name Caswell make that nasty little man flee?' She turns. '*Ned*? That man had something to do with what happened to poor Ned?'

'I was always pretty certain of it. Did he seem guilty to you?'

'Yes. Completely, Harry. Tell me.'

'Not tonight, love. Let me dig out something to show you first.'

Before the Japanese invaded Singapore I was head of a malaria unit at the General Hospital. My duty was to stay with my patients, but I insisted that Eliza leave. I could hope she was safe, but she had no such comfort, especially after the massacre at the Alexandra Military Hospital.

Most of our staff survived capture, although some of the patients weren't so lucky. We were marched to Changi peninsula, the site of a prison and three army barracks. Allied soldiers were sent to the barracks while we civilians were interned in the prison.

It was built to hold eight hundred, but three thousand men and five hundred women were crammed inside, rigidly segregated. As the days, then weeks, then months crept by, our hopes of repatriation faded.

It took half a year for the Red Cross to pry even a list of our names from the reluctant Japanese: Eliza says she'll never forget as long as she lives the day she heard I was still alive.

Life at Changi was dull and repetitive, although we held games and concerts and gave lessons to keep our minds active. Rations were slashed to killingly low levels, so we dug gardens and ate anything that grew, including weeds, but there was never enough.

People died from illnesses that we helpless, humiliated doctors could do little about: malaria, dengue, typhus, cholera, and the cruel vitamin deficiency beri-beri, with its water-swollen limbs and fist-deep tropical ulcers.

I was sick myself, but in truth I was lucky too, so lucky. Civilians didn't get sent to work on the railway in Burma, and although we endured bizarre, unpredictable cruelties, I was never beaten so badly my bones were broken.

A spirit of resistance bound us all, marred only by some of our own who were once in power and now were not. Men like Godfrey, who did not despise our captors, but preferred instead to curry their favour.

In the kitchen next day, while Leo is asleep and we have an hour or two of peace, I open a dusty cardboard box on the table and take out three old sketchbooks.

'I've never shown you these before—' I say.

'Why not, love?' says Eliza at the sink. She wipes her hands on a tea-towel and sits down.

'Just wanted to put it all behind me. But they might help you understand. Of course you know what the papers said about Changi, but that wasn't the whole picture. Well,' I laugh a little, 'nor are these, but—'

'Oh Harry, were you still *drawing* all that time? You never said.'

'I wasn't the only artist in the camp, either. It was hard to get pencils, but one of the blokes was a genius at making pigments out of odd things, so I ended up doing more painting than drawing.'

Eliza gently opens one of the three scruffy booklets. 'You were always so good with people's faces and bodies—I remember those sketches you did on the ship years ago.'

'That was mainly trying to capture you, the rest was just for camouflage.'

Eliza laughs, and slowly turns the pages. 'Oh, there's Ned! But he looks so young.' She looks up at me. 'And unscarred.'

I nod. 'He was.'

Edward Caswell—Ned—was a young surgeon, a bone specialist, who arrived at Singapore General a few months before the Japanese declared war and, when we were taken prisoner, marched beside me on those agonising twenty miles to Changi.

Eliza turns another page. 'Where are the men in the lorry going? They look pleased.'

'Soldiers from Changi Barracks being taken to work on the railway in Burma. The Japanese told them they were going to new, healthy camps, and the boys were joking about freedom and fresh food and wild women.'

Eliza turns some more pages and looks up at me. 'Oh, *Harry.*'

'Yes, that's a few of the poor bastards who came back. If I hadn't seen those broken bodies myself I couldn't have imagined the kind of abuse they went through.'

She turns a page. 'Godfrey with some of the guards?'

'They didn't mind us painting, as long as we did a portrait of them now and then. The one on the left wasn't too bad, but the man in the middle was pretty awful. And on the right, he's one of the officers Godfrey was so fond of.'

'He's certainly cosied up to him, isn't he?' She turns another page. 'Ah. Ned and the boys playing football. My goodness—look at Godfrey's malevolent face, watching them.'

'He always was a spiteful little bureaucrat. He disliked most of the doctors, but he absolutely loathed poor old Ned. It mightn't have been important, but see the date at the bottom?'

'28th September, 1943. Why?'

'That was the day we heard that six enemy ships had just been blown up in Singapore harbour.'

'Oh yes, the famous commando raid, Jaywick. But how did you hear about it?'

'Some of our men built radios to get the BBC news, hiding them in shoes, brooms, buried in the gardens. Unfortunately the secret police decided it was us who'd guided the saboteurs with our hidden receivers. Of course it wasn't, although every man would happily have done so.'

Eliza sighs. 'So that was the start of the—what was it? Double Tenth? The tenth of October, when the secret police started dragging civilians away to force them to confess?'

'Yes. They took nearly sixty people—even a bishop, a woman doctor and a military doctor's wife. The poor bastards endured months of gaol and starvation and bestial torture.'

Eliza is pale. 'And they took Ned.'

'What none of us could figure out was how they chose who to question. But when they arrested Ned I saw Godfrey's face, and painted this.' I turn a page.

She gasps. 'Harry, he's *pleased.*'

'I went over and said, What the hell are you smirking about, Godfrey? He just sneered and said, Shut your mouth, Bell, or you'll be next. Then he strutted away.'

'*You'll be next?*'

'But too many people had noticed, and after that Godfrey was shunned. They called him the *White Jap.*' I sigh. 'It was five months before Ned and the others came back. Well, some did—a lot died. After the war, the torturers were prosecuted and a few were hanged. Not enough of them, though.'

'And Godfrey?'

'Slithered through the cracks. The military, the government, they were all too busy hiding the evidence of their own stuff-ups. Who cared if someone ratted on his mates? Of course a few did it to survive, but I doubt many did it out of sheer spite.'

'But why on earth did he hate *Ned?* Such a dear man.'

'Remember Jean, that nurse in my ward who was killed just before Singapore fell? I think he fancied her, but she preferred Ned. I have to assume Godfrey's wounded pride made him want revenge, but that's the sane rationale.'

I gaze at Eliza. 'We both know by now there are plenty of people around who don't need any sort of rationale to do terrible things.'

She nods. 'After this war I don't understand very much about human psychology, Harry. I'm simply glad we have each other and Leo, and can live out our lives here in peace.'

5. Tina: The Starlight Lounge

My second-best suit, I think. My best is an expensive Paris copy and I don't want to look too prosperous. Anyway, the second-best has a hint of turquoise that makes the most of my eyes. A white blouse, grey hat. I check in the mirror.

Yes. Now I look like a smart young woman who's perfectly capable of being a bookkeeper. Nikos's mother Ruby has taken me through the basics of the art and I've always had a good eye for discrepancies—with a bit of luck I can apply that to numbers as well as people.

I check my watch, the gold one Nikos gave me when we married —plenty of time before the tram. The watch catches the light, dainty and elegant: Nikos has good taste, in things at least.

Women? The first wife was apparently a paragon of the virtues. She was tall, like the girl he was seeing before me. That ended pretty smartly when we fell in love. He said it wasn't serious, yet I wanted him so much I wouldn't have cared if it had been.

But like a lot of wartime couples, perhaps if we'd had more time together we might have discovered how incompatible we really are. I love clothes and parties and people who gossip—the only thing I don't like is dancing. I'm not well-coordinated and usually feel a fool, especially beside my husband who's so annoyingly good at it.

Nikos is cheerful and welcoming too, so people simply assume he's as sociable as me. But it's just a habit of hospitality, his Greek side coming out. More usually in private he's quiet, and his methodical habits drive me crazy. He reads boring things too— textbooks and science fiction and magazines with pictures of engines on the covers.

I check my handbag. Purse, compact, lipstick, a fresh handkerchief. I sit down on the bed for a moment and sigh. It's not really Nikos's magazines are the problem.

It's more that I think he doesn't love me any more, though he tries. I know he's fond of me and wants our family to succeed, especially in the eyes of his parents (who are perfectly nice, I'd just rather they didn't run my life).

He needs me to be a mother to his grumpy, motherless son, and he's happy for me to have a job, as long as I'm home in time for dinner. Neither of us likes this large, soulless house his father bought as a wedding present, but Nikos could never admit it.

And yes, he does a lot of the cooking and sometimes even helps with the housework, but the whole dead weight of it still seems to be completely mine.

And oh, how I *wish* he'd make love to me the way he used to, as if he'd die if I wasn't in his arms. That was the edge the war gave all of us. Of course you fling yourself into such intensity when it might be your last few moments on earth.

But when it's not? When your soulmate becomes an everyday obligation, what then?

And now of course it's not Nikos I'm talking about. Seeing happy couples like Eliza and my brother Harry, even strange little Klara and quiet Yvonne, has shown me something is wrong, deeply wrong in our marriage.

So perhaps it isn't Nikos who's fallen out of love.

He's twelve years older than me, another generation. I know it was his maturity and the sense of security I felt that attracted me in the first place. My father died when I was only nine, and perhaps that's why I fell for an older man—who knows?

But lately I've been waking up in the early hours, my throat tight. Is this is all I have to look forward to for the rest of my life? I don't *want* dull obligation in a gloomy house, I'm young and I want passion and dizziness and lighthearted happiness.

And more than that I'm *bored*, bored out of my mind. I want a real job to do. Come on, Tina. Go and catch that tram into town and find it.

*

I get out at the Town Hall, cross George Street and walk a block or so in the direction of Hyde Park. The Starlight Lounge is on the right, a little dated with the sort of curved chrome strips on the window that were all the rage when I was a girl.

Inside it's larger than it seems from the street, with tables and leather-lined booths around the walls, a dance-floor in the middle and a small bandstand at the rear. It's not lunchtime yet and there are only a few customers. At the counter a sulky-faced blonde with a lot of makeup is arranging teacups on a tray.

'I'm here about the bookkeeping job,' I say steadily. The woman glances at my clothes and says, 'Yeah? Come out to the office.'

I follow her to the rear of the restaurant and into a corridor next to the kitchen, with a staircase at the far end. She taps on a door to one side and says, 'Jimmy? Lady about the job.'

The door opens and a man says, 'Thanks, Pearl. Come in, doll.'

There's someone else there, a big thuggish type who stares at my legs. The man says, 'All right, Davy. You go sort it out now.'

'Okay, Mr Kelso.' The big man looks me over again and leaves.

'Now, Miss—?'

'Mrs Loukas. Tina Loukas.'

'Good to meet you. Have a seat. I'm Jimmy Kelso.'

He doesn't have to say, I'm the boss, that's quite apparent. He's slim and medium height, brown hair that'd be curly if it weren't smoothed with lotion. He's not immediately good looking, not like Nikos, but he has a certain quick charm.

He sits down, scribbles something on a piece of paper and says, 'Now, we've had a wee disaster. Our man Mr Truscott has had to leave unexpectedly and I need someone immediately. Trouble is, most fellas have to give a few weeks notice. So first off, can you start straight away?'

'Yes, that wouldn't be a problem,' I say, my heart pattering.

'Haven't seen many ladies in this line of work. What's your experience?'

'I do the books for Loukas Foods, well, my mother-in-law and I do the books.' Calm down.

'Oh, indeed? *That* Loukas.' He scratches out 'Lucas' on the paper and writes 'Loukas.'

He looks at me with oddly light grey eyes beneath dark brows. 'Now why would a smart thing like you not be staying in a comfy job with the family firm? What brings you to my fine establishment?'

His accent is Irish, crisp, like that of a Belfast girl in Hut 12. She'd say, 'Now the southerners, they'll charm you out of your knickers, but the northerners'll just order you to take them off. I like it either way.'

I can't think for a moment for a vision of knickers being sultrily removed, then say, 'Well, that's why. It's the family firm—too close to home. I want to prove myself.'

He smiles with one corner of his mouth. 'Me, I'm all for independence too.'

He takes a ledger from a pile on the desk and opens it. 'All right, Mrs Loukas, take a look at that and tell me what you think.'

I take the ledger, praying my hands aren't shaking, and gaze at the numbers and swallow.

'What a poor host I am.' Jimmy Kelso goes out and calls, 'Pearl—glass of water here, thanks.'

I run my eyes frantically up and down the handwritten columns. What am I looking for? Think, think, Tina. Something that doesn't add up, something not right. There's an error in addition in the credits column, but surely that's too obvious.

Wait on, *there*, shouldn't that be an eight, not a zero? And repeated in the debits column too, so it doesn't show up in the total. Odd. I turn the page. Same thing. Again, a few pages later. Doesn't make sense, unless—

Jimmy Kelso returns with a glass of water and I take a sip.

He sits down, lazes back in his chair and says, 'And how're you going, Mrs Loukas?'

I turn the ledger towards him and point to the obvious error, 'There's that.'

'Good girl.'

'And that. Doesn't show up in the reconciliation because it appears twice.' I sit back in my own chair as casually as Jimmy Kelso. 'Someone's been cooking the books.'

A pause.

His eyes hard, Jimmy says, 'Well I'll be buggered. No wonder our man was so keen to leg it.' He looks me over, my hat and blouse, the handbag on my lap, and smiles.

'Well, Mrs Loukas. Let me show you to your office. You'll need these.' He lifts the pile of ledgers. 'I'd like to know how much in total the bastard's skimmed. By the end of the day.'

'Today?'

'Something better to do?'

After a lot of scribbled notes and adding and subtracting, I manage to reach a total of the amount the previous bookkeeper stole—around six hundred pounds, taken over a long period so it wasn't obvious.

When I tell Jimmy Kelso he says, 'Well, well. So that's where last year's pin money got to. Clever sod, I'm too trusting by half.'

'Can't you report him to the police?'

His eyes bright with mischief, he says, 'Ah, Mrs Loukas, not sure I want the police in my hair. No, I'm a great believer in what the Orientals call—karma, is it? *Karma*. Fate will sort that foolish boyo out. Now it's getting late, so you'd better go home to Mr Loukas. We'll see you tomorrow.'

The tram lurches around a corner and halts with a squeal of brakes, but all I can think is, I did it, I *did* it. Already I wonder about some of the legal niceties Jimmy Kelso's fine establishment seems happy to disregard, but who cares?

I've got a *job*. From my stop it's just a short walk home, but now I know what 'floating on air' means.

Unfortunately the feeling ends as soon as I enter the house. It's seven and I can hear Nikos in the kitchen. I sigh, put down my bag, and go in.

'Ah, there you are,' he says, closing the oven door. 'Just heating up something Mum sent over.' He hesitates. 'Did you miss out again? I'm sorry—'

'No, I *got* it! I'm the new bookkeeper at the Starlight Lounge!' I'm suddenly happy again. 'The previous bookkeeper was skimming the take. I saw it when no one else had even *realised!*'

I hug him and he feels strong and warm and safe, and all my irritation is forgotten.

He laughs. 'Wonderful! Tell me about it.'

As in the old days we eat in the kitchen, not in the cold, formal dining room. Stavros slouches in and sits with us as well, and even smiles now and again. Poor kid. He's spotty and gawky, but when he bothers to smile he has all his father's charm and his own touch of sweetness.

Later that night Nikos and I make love. It's not the blind passion of our early times but it's warm and pleasurable. Everything's okay after all. I shouldn't have worried so much.

That weekend I take Billie into town for some shopping. She needs some new clothes and I'm buying her a few things as an early Christmas present. We find a nice pair of grey tailored slacks, with wide hems we can let down to fit her long legs. She also chooses two plain white cotton blouses which are a little severe for my taste, but she just grins when I say so.

'Got to be ungirlish when you're working with men, Teen, they're so easily confused.'

'But what about a day dress? And an evening gown—you *must* have an evening gown.'

'Yeah, a cotton dress would be good, it's been hot lately,' says Billie. 'But I've got an evening gown Eliza gave me years ago, silk jersey. That'll do for now.'

'What colour?'

'Jade green.'

'Yes, that'd look good with your hair. But what about shoes, stockings, underwear?'

'Don't wear a bra, just a camisole. Not much need for it.'

I sigh. 'Heavens, wish I could say the same.'

'But the rest'd come in handy. What about you, Teen? I saw you eyeing up that aqua lace thing.'

'It's gorgeous, isn't it?' I say. 'I buy too many clothes, though.'

'You're a working woman now, you can afford it.'

I laugh. 'True. I'll see if they have it in my size.'

I get to know the others at the Starlight Lounge. Pearl, the restaurant manager, used to be a dancer. Her bobbed blonde hair suits her sullen, feline style. She rarely smiles so I thought at first she disliked me, but now I know it's just her.

Big Davy is the thuggish man I saw on the first day, round-faced with too much hair lotion. He does the heavy jobs and harbours a not-so-secret passion for Pearl, who treats him like dirt.

Jimmy Kelso, the boss, has a rough tongue (though not nearly as rough as some of my Hut 12 girls), but he's easy to be around, and we're all on a first name basis by now—the formality only lasted as long as the job interview.

I start to feel at home at the Starlight Lounge, and one thing I especially like is the music. On most evenings there's a dance band, and at the afternoon high teas the pianist, a European refugee called László, plays the sort of jazz I love.

I often sit humming to myself in my office, and Jimmy jokes about how he'd make me his musical director if I weren't such a good bookkeeper.

One day I sort out a problem we've had with a gin supplier, using charm and a rigorous accounting of exactly who owes who the ten pounds in dispute.

Later, Jimmy says, 'Well done, wee Tina. That'd be the first time those buggers've paid a bill on time. In fact, you've already saved me so much money, why don't you and the hubby come out for an evening here on the house?'

'Thank you! Oh—but we've a house-guest staying—'

'Ah, bring him along too, everyone's welcome.'

'It's a woman, Billie Quinn.'

'All to the better,' says Jimmy, grinning. 'We'll see you Saturday? That's when the new band is starting and you know I've got a tin ear. I'd appreciate your thoughts on their competence.'

On Saturday I wear the aqua lace gown. It's cut wide on the shoulders with a fine belt that emphasises my narrow waist.

My heels are high, my hair falls in gold-bronze waves, and I know I look damned good: and in the jade green jersey, with her auburn colouring, Billie looks almost as good.

She borrows an evening bag of mine, we get in the car and off we go. Pearl, in a long black dress, greets us formally at the door, and when we've checked our coats she shows us to a booth.

I'm excited—I haven't been out for ages, and the lights at night make the everyday restaurant seem so glamorous.

Jimmy is working the room in a well-cut evening suit. He comes over to our booth and I introduce everyone. He orders a bottle of champagne on the house, and Nikos asks him to sit down with us.

'Well now, it's a pleasure to meet you all,' Jimmy says, raising his glass. 'And here's to Tina. A real asset, she's saved my business single-handed.'

'Tina'd be an asset to anyone, Mr Kelso,' Billie says. 'She has so much experience at this kind of work, after all.' I kick her gently under the table.

'Please, just Jimmy between friends.'

He grins at her but I notice there's no real spark between them. I'd wondered if there might be, because Jimmy is single—'between women,' Pearl says—but he's only of medium height and in her heels she's taller, and that seems to worry some men.

The lights dim a little and the small band comes onto the stage. They launch into a recent swing tune and people get up to dance.

I listen for a time. 'Jimmy, they sound pretty good to me. Nikos, what do you think? You know this sort of music better than me.'

'Yes, they're not bad—tight and melodic, but loose when they need to be.'

His head is moving to the beat, and I say, 'Go on, you're dying to dance. Maybe Billie'd give you a second chance.'

Nikos looks at her. 'We'll just push the champagne out of arm's reach shall we?'

'You're damned lucky I'm in the mood this time,' says Billie.

They get up and join the people on the dance-floor, and as I expected, they move well together, smoothly and skilfully.

Jimmy watches them and takes a drink. 'You don't like dancing yourself, then?'

I shrug. 'I get intimidated out on the floor with Nikos. He's an excellent dancer and I've got two left feet. And I'm small and he's tall, so I always feel a bit foolish.'

'Ah, it so happens I've two left feet as well, but I'm not as lofty. Let's give it a whirl.'

The band launches into another catchy number, so we get up and join the crowd. After a few moments I realise Jimmy is right, he's a better height for me. He doesn't have Nikos's flair, but I don't mind that, he dances simply and easily.

His hand in mine feels warm, his touch on my waist is firm, and he has a pleasingly masculine scent of leather and tobacco.

'There we are, you see?' says Jimmy as we move into a slower number. 'Somehow two lots of left feet work perfectly in the end.'

'It's good,' I say. 'Almost relaxing.'

'Almost? You're breaking my heart, wee Tina. You're a natural and I'd no idea—and here's me hired you half for your skills.'

'Only *half* for my skills?' I say, laughing. 'What's the other half?'

'Looks, of course,' he says. 'But without your skills, your looks wouldn't be much help.'

'And without the looks?'

'Ah, you'd be in trouble then, too. But I'm a lucky man. You've got both.'

6. Billie: Rose Bay

I'm in the kitchen when Call-me-*Steve* comes in and gives me a dirty look on his way to the refrigerator. Enough, I think.

'Sit down, kid.'

'What?' He doesn't even look around.

I slam the fridge door. 'I said sit *down*. Kid.'

He looks at me as if I'm mad and backs away, but a chair is just behind him so he's forced to obey. I sit and take a deep breath.

'Jeez, I'm fed up with you. What's your problem?'

He looks away. 'Don't have a problem.'

'Yeah? Haven't said a civil word to anyone since I've been here. Look, is it me? You don't like house guests?'

'Don't care.'

'Only thing you care about is your name, is that it?'

He goes red, which highlights his acne. 'Want to be called Steve, that's all. Stavros is stupid.'

'Who says?'

'Everyone says. Sick of it, sick of—' He clamps his mouth shut.

'The other kids making fun?'

He swallows and stares at the floor.

I nod. 'Yeah. Must be a pain in the arse.'

He still doesn't say anything, but his eyebrows move in surprise.

'Ought to try being called Wilhelmina.'

He snickers. 'Wilhel-*meena*? No wonder you call yourself Billie.'

'I rest my case—there are worse names around than yours.'

'So if it's all right for *you*, why can't I call myself what I want?'

'When you're older you can.'

'I don't care about when I'm *older*. I want it different now, but Dad won't listen. Some stupid deal about how it's his father's name and it'd be disrespectful to change it. Who cares? Nothing to do with me.' He scowls. 'And, yeah, I don't like having a house guest too.'

'Join the club, I don't like being a house guest. I'll move out as soon as I can.'

Stavros sits back and crosses his arms and stares at me. 'And I don't like you, and I'm sick of all this—*bull*—about you being a lady flyer too. No such thing.'

'Never heard of Amelia Earhart?'

'That was the olden days and she was a freak.' He looks me up and down. 'Yeah. All skinny and tall and cropped hair. Probably a man in disguise.'

I nod. 'If so, life'd be a lot more convenient for me and Amelia both, but you have to work with what you've got, mate.'

'Yeah? You and Dad, you're always going on about planes and all that stupid stuff—prove it, *prove* you're a lady flyer.'

I shrug. 'Given the lack of actual Spitfires around Rozelle I probably can't.'

He sneers. 'Spitfires? Ho, ho, pull the other one. Douglas Bader now, are we?'

'Not everyone flying Spits was fighting, kid. We used to ferry new ones to airfields for their fit-out, so blokes like Bader could actually do their jobs.'

He stands up. 'You're crazy.'

That stings. Pete used to call me *crazy lady*, but in fun. Or awe.

'Sit down, you fucking idiot,' I say. 'Don't move a muscle.'

He lowers himself, mouth agape, as I run upstairs and riffle in my bag. When I get back to the kitchen he's still sitting, astonished. I throw the notebook on the table.

'Check that out, sonny Jim.'

The spine has two large rings for easy opening, and the cover is navy with yellow writing: Air Transport Auxiliary, Ferry Pilots Notes, For Official Use Only. (The lack of apostrophe in Pilots used to annoy the hell out of Yvie.)

Stavros casually open it and says, 'Huh, Moths? Old-fashioned canvas things. Big deal.'

'Keep looking.' The covers of the notebook are worn and I vividly remember the feel of it in the knee pocket of my flying suit.

'Oxfords?' He shrugs. 'Twin engines, not bad. Ansons? Ancient.'
He snickers. 'Mosquitoes?' He stops snickering. After a few more
pages he stops. 'Oh.' He swallows. 'Spitfires. With *superchargers*?
What's that date at the top?'

'When I first flew one.' I sigh. 'Friday, 5th September, 1941.'

He glances at me then flips more pages. 'Hurricanes? Really? And
Lancasters ... you flew *Lancasters*?'

'Yup.'

'But they're so *big*.'

'I always say they carried us, we didn't have to carry them.'

'Four *Merlins*. Wow.'

'We had co-pilots and flight engineers, didn't fly them all by
ourselves.'

'You did with the Spits, though.'

I nod.

'What was that like?'

I smile. 'Like dancing the most thrilling, dangerous, magnificent
tango in the world.'

'Dancing? Huh. That's *stupid*.'

He turns the pages, reverentially murmuring the names of planes
I might only have been in once or twice. That was the beauty of the
notebook—it had everything we needed to fly a kite we'd never
seen before, and nothing we didn't. Take-off, landing, flaps, fuel,
boost, trim, glide, stall, peculiarities.

Sometimes we'd be frantically studying a new bird moments
before we had to climb into it and take off. The RAF boys couldn't
believe their eyes.

Stavros closes the notebook and is silent, then says, 'But you're
not going to fly when you go to Dad's work at Rose Bay, are you?'

'Nah. Just transmitting flight plans, weather reports.'

'Won't you miss it?'

I shake my head and get up and put the kettle on. 'Do you like
planes, then?'

'At school you can't be one of the gang if you don't. But I don't
want to be a stupid pilot.'

'What do you want to be?'

He hesitates. 'I like music. Want to play piano.'

'But there's no piano here.'

'I play it at school. The music teacher lets me stay after lessons and practise. I tell Tina I'm at my grandmother's house, and tell her I'm here.'

'Why can't they know?'

'My grandfather'd blow a gasket. He just likes *bouzouki* music, says only wastrels and thieves play other stuff. Can't believe *anyone* says wastrels nowadays.'

'You play classical music?'

'Yeah, but I really like jazz the best.'

'Tina likes jazz,' I say. 'Why don't you chat to her about it?'

He looks puzzled. 'Does she?'

'Don't you even talk to that poor woman as she's making your meals and cleaning up after you?'

He goes scarlet, and shakes his head. 'All the other boys laugh at her.'

'Why?'

'They say things. She's young and pretty and—you know—big, um, here.' He gestures at his chest and goes even redder.

'*That's* why you treat Tina so badly? Jeez, mate. She's your mother, the only one you've got.'

'She's only been my mother for three years. If my *real* mother was here she'd be old like Dad, and the boys wouldn't laugh at her.'

'Yeah but she's not,' I say. 'You'll be out of school soon and what those nasty little swine have to say will mean nothing. Appreciate your family while you've got it, believe me.'

He's silent, looking down for a time. 'Tina likes jazz? Didn't know.'

'Likes piano too. Could be an ally if you've got a battle ahead with your grandfather. Anyway, how come he gets the final say on everything?'

'How it is in Greek families.'

'Yeah, but your Dad's only half Greek, so you're pretty diluted.'

'But you haven't met my grandfather.' He looks at me. 'And even if you *are* a lady flyer, I still think you're stupid.'

'So does everyone have to do what your father says?' I say, as Nikos and I are doing some cooking before Tina comes home from work. Well, Nikos is cooking, I'm washing up.

'My father?'

'According to Stavros, he's a modern-day tyrant.'

Nikos laughs. 'The grandfather, Papous, has the most sway in a Greek family. Just tradition.'

'He's the reason poor old Stavros can't be Steve?'

'He's named after him, and it'd upset him if Stavros changed it. I was named after my grandfather in the same way. Tradition.'

'Bet you got called Nick in the navy.'

'Got called a hell of a lot worse than that,' he says dryly. 'But yes, usually Nick, though I never told my grandfather.'

'Then why not?'

'Suppose we could. Need to be formal around Papous, though.'

'I reckon young Steve could deal with that.'

'If it makes him happy, why not?' He hesitates. 'Do you think perhaps I didn't—take him seriously enough, Billie?'

'Ah, it's the sort of thing no one takes seriously, except the poor bugger who's complaining.'

Nikos sighs. 'I raised him by myself for eight years before the war, then was away for another three, so I couldn't have done it without my parents' help. Guess I've bowed to their greater experience more than I should have.' He scatters cheese on the dish he's preparing, then places it in the oven.

'I'd hoped when Tina and I married it would all work out, but— anyway.' He looks at me and quickly smiles. 'Thanks. Helps to have an outsider's view.'

He brings two glasses and a bottle of very nice red wine to the table. He sits and pours, hands me a glass and says, 'Yamas.'

'Cheers.'

'Where are you thinking about moving to?' he says after we've had a few sips.

'Somewhere around Kings Cross. It's cheap and on the tram line to Rose Bay.'

'Convenient, but can be a pretty rough area.'

'Anyway, it's all theoretical till I get a job,' I say. 'So next week's the beginning of my future—hopefully.'

'Yamas, again. It'll be quiet without you, now Tina doesn't get home till late.'

'But she's so happy,' I say. 'Are you complaining?'

'Not in the slightest. I like it when she's happy.'

'You've got doubts about her employer, though, haven't you?'

He takes a mouthful of wine. 'I've heard rumours. Jimmy Kelso keeps himself pretty clean and the Starlight Lounge seems above board, but some shadowy people still hang around. Sydney can have some ugly secrets beneath the surface.'

On Monday I wake up early to get ready for the interview. I put on the navy skirt from my old uniform—it'll be hot with stockings, but I'll wear a cotton blouse. I'm looking pale so a dash of lipstick helps. I dab some powder on my nose, brush my hair, and I'm ready.

'What's his name again?' I say to Nikos in the car.

'Mr Willoughby. In civil aviation since the early thirties, now he's the station manager. Bit of a fuddy-duddy, but not too bad.'

We drive from Rozelle through the city and Kings Cross, then Double Bay, Point Piper and finally Rose Bay, where we turn into a road running along beside a sports field, then park at the end.

Along the waterfront is a two-storied white building: the passenger terminal, the control room upstairs. Beside the terminal are clusters of office buildings and workshops—expanded during the war, says Nikos.

A vast hangar sits on a concrete apron, with a slipway and rails running into the water. In front of the terminal is a pier with several small boats tied up to it—Nikos's control launches.

'Bigger than I expected,' I say.

Nikos nods. 'It's a real airport. The runways might be out on the water, but we've still got to have space for customs, quarantine, kitchens, airlines, electronics, repairs—everything.'

Inside he introduces me to the manager's secretary, Mary, then leaves. She shows me to an office, saying, 'Miss Quinn for the job, Mr Willoughby.'

A man looks up and blinks, slightly surprised. My heart sinks. He's one of those tubby, thin-moustached blokes, the sort who prefer women to stick to baking cakes and churning out babies.

'Do sit down, Miss Quinn. Well, Mr Loukas said you might be suitable for an opening here. As you'd appreciate, air travel is greatly expanding. Like most airports this is run by the Department of Civil Aviation, and we provide services for many companies, including the government's own Trans Australian Airways.'

'What other companies?' I say, to show I'm paying attention.

'Well, Australian National Airlines, new Trans Oceanic Airways, servicing the Pacific islands, Tasman Empire Airways from New Zealand, and Qantas of course, flying to Europe and Asia.'

'So you must be very busy sometimes,' I say helpfully.

'Indeed. Now, the position is in the Aeradio section, relaying messages to and from air traffic controllers, weather reports and speed or route variations. It involves teletype machinery and some air-to-ground radio. Mr Loukas assures me you're familiar with the technology. Now, do you have your qualifications with you?'

I take a folder out of my shoulder-bag.

'There's my private A and commercial B licences.' I place them on the desk. 'Navigator, Ground Engineer and Wireless Telegraphy qualifications, and my instructor's licence with endorsements for a number of aircraft.'

I plonk down the final item. 'And my ATA pilots' notebook, covering a rather greater range of kites.'

'Ah, no, I'm sorry, Miss Quinn, not precisely what I meant. Your qualifications as a teletype operator. You do appreciate this is not a flying job?'

'Yeah, but *this* is so you know I know what I'm talking about. And I don't have teletype qualifications. Just test me out and see.'

He picks up the Navigation certificate and adjusts his glasses. 'Air Service Training at Hamble? Quite a reputation. Mr Loukas mentioned you're familiar with some seaplanes.'

'Yes, but that's not why I'm here. I want a ground job.'

'Unusual for a pilot.'

'Feel like a change. And we both know I've got Buckley's chance of getting flying work with all our lads home from the war.'

'Indeed.' He takes his glasses off and rubs his eyes. 'Are you perhaps the Billie Quinn who set the flight speed record between Adelaide and Perth in—what was it—1928? Foolish question. Of course you are.'

'It was no big deal. The record was broken a few weeks later.'

'As I recall, that was in somewhat less harrowing conditions.' He gazes at me silently for a few moments. 'I can only assume with this background you'd have a certain level of self-discipline and a serious approach to your work.'

'A fair assumption.'

'And you're hardly a flighty young thing looking for a husband.'

'Another fair assumption.'

'You do appreciate that some of our senior staff are ex-pilots, and may find it difficult to accept a woman with a similar sort of background?'

'No one seemed to object when we were bringing them Spitfires.'

'Indeed not.' He writes something down. 'It has also been suggested that a female voice on air-to-ground radio might not provide the—ah—*reassurance* to pilots of a male voice.'

'Plenty of women on the other end of the radio in the war.'

He smiles a little. 'Certainly were. In fact I've made it quite clear to my staff we must move with the times. You'd need to be tested of course.' He looks up at me. 'That is, if you still want the job?'

'Guess so.'

'Then Mary will take you to the Aeradio section for testing and, all being well, will introduce you to your colleagues. Good luck.'

'Oh, is that it? Right, then. Thanks.' I gather my qualifications and notebook and place them in my shoulder-bag, then stand up. 'See you round.'

'By the way, Miss Quinn, I should apologise for my surprise when you walked in.'

'Hardly noticed. I seem to surprise everyone.'

He smiles slightly. 'As it happens, you have a look of my daughter —similar adventurous spirit, I expect. Insisted on being a nurse. Singapore and all that.'

'A friend of mine, Harry Bell, was a doctor at the General Hospital there.'

'Dr Bell? Yes, she mentioned him in letters, and a Dr Caswell too. She nursed in the malaria section.'

'Nice coincidence. I'll tell Harry. What's her name?'

He hesitates, his face tight, then says, 'Her name was Jean.'

I nod gently, but don't say anything more. I've seen that look before.

Mr Willoughby clears his throat and offers me his hand.

'Welcome to Rose Bay, Miss Quinn.'

7. Yvonne: Poetry

Klara works long hours at her new project, the compilation of wartime poems. She sends out letters by the dozen to poets famous and not-so-famous, but receives few replies.

'I suppose they do not think a book by an obscure Finnish poetess will have many sales,' she says. 'And they are probably correct. But I have had an idea, Yvonne—let us visit Newcastle and see Eliza and Harry. They are unaware of it, but they know a fine poet I would like to include. However he is most reclusive and I am told he wishes only to forget.'

'Perhaps you should let him then.'

'A poet must never be allowed to forget,' she says sternly.

On the train north I'm entranced by the wild scenery, the rugged wide river, the distant blue mountains, and the small towns scattered by the water's edge and set deep in the bushland.

We arrive at Newcastle station shortly before noon. Waiting on the platform is the familiar trim figure of Eliza, while Harry, in his gold-rimmed glasses, is holding a small fair boy of about three.

'Oh, darling Klara, Yvonne, Claire!' says Eliza. 'This is Leo!'

'Who's *that*?' says Leo, pointing at four-year-old Claire, who's gazing coolly back at him.

'It's Claire, Leo,' says Eliza. 'Perhaps you can be friends.'

'Can't,' says Leo. 'Her eyes are *sharp*.'

'Your eyes are *slippery*,' says Claire, and turns away.

'Sorry,' I say. 'She's usually friendlier. Perhaps the trip was tiring.'

'And Leo just needs a nap,' says Harry, as the boy says loudly, 'Do not,' and falls asleep on his father's neck. 'Now, out this gate. Here's the car, but the house isn't far anyway.'

We drive a few blocks, then Harry parks beside a terrace house. Eliza turns from the front seat. 'Klara, I've organised it, just a quiet dinner party. You'll explain the skulduggery later, won't you?'

'All will become clear,' says Klara. 'But you live so close to the water? How fortunate you are.'

The ocean is at the end of the street and I smell salt on the air. It's not a wealthy part of town—the houses are old, a tram depot nearby—but it seems quiet and pleasant.

We eat lunch, then Harry goes to work and Eliza takes us for a walk. It's a sunny autumn day, and we stroll past an army base to a viewpoint above a long beach.

Before us is a sandy breakwater running out to distant Nobbys Head, topped with a lighthouse. To our left a railway yard sprawls down to the docks, while smoky steelworks line the far harbour.

'This is a rough industrial town, rather like the original Newcastle on Tyne,' Eliza says. 'It was settled early on as a penal colony and they've been mining coal here ever since.'

I turn and gaze at the town straggling over a hill, a cathedral near the summit, the low blue mountains to the west.

'Still, it is strangely beautiful,' says Klara.

Eliza laughs. 'But only the visitors ever seem to notice.'

After the children go to bed that evening, we're sipping drinks with Harry in the lounge room when the doorbell rings. He answers it and ushers in a pleasant-looking man wearing glasses, with a ragged scar down one side of his face and neck.

'This is Ned Caswell, a bone surgeon at my hospital. Ned, these are our friends Klara and Yvonne, visiting us from Sydney.'

'Aha,' says Klara. 'Ned? Or perhaps we meet Edward *Quest?*'

Ned's scar goes white as he blushes and suddenly sits down.

'Have a drink,' says Harry, handing him a glass. 'Edward Quest? Klara, what's this about?'

'Surely you know the name, Harry?'

'Vaguely—wasn't there a well-received book of poetry after the war? Rain, orchids, jungle, very striking images I recall.'

'Indeed,' says Klara. 'Yet Edward Quest has not published since *Tropic Dusk*, although I have it on good authority he has written more—and better too.'

'Good authority?' says Ned. 'Not that drunkard of a publisher?'

Klara smiles. 'I cannot reveal my sources. *Well?*'

Eliza comes in. 'Well what, Klara? Ned, are you all right? Look, I'm ready to serve the roast, come and chat over dinner.'

'Just didn't want to revisit it, that's all,' says Ned, putting down his fork. 'The published poems were written in the early days at the camp, when I still had hope. Those that came after were full of rage. I just want to forget that period, like everyone else.'

'But poems of rage should not be forgotten, and I wish to make certain they are not,' says Klara.

'She's right,' says Eliza, leaning forward. 'You, Harry, everyone who suffered—how you felt should never be lost.'

'I'm astonished, Ned,' says Harry. 'You were always scribbling things down in the camp, but I didn't realise you'd actually published. I wish you'd told me—we could have celebrated.'

'But *you* were always painting, Harry, and damned good work too,' says Ned. 'So I did think you'd exhibit afterwards. Why not?'

'Ah, the same thing. Putting it all behind me.'

'Did you keep your sketchbooks?' says Ned. 'Hope they're safe.'

'He did,' says Eliza. She goes to a bookcase and brings them back.

Harry says, 'I don't think, Eliza—at a dinner party—'

I turn the pages carefully. Klara stands at my shoulder and says, 'Harry, these are beautiful.'

'Hardly what I'd call beautiful,' he scoffs.

'But they are,' I say, gazing at a picture of palms in stained-glass greens against a charcoal sky.

'Oh my goodness!' says Klara. '*Ragged emerald sawtooth elegies*— Ned, now I see. I did not understand before. How wonderful.' She looks up. 'Harry, you should exhibit these pictures.'

'Wait on,' I say, excited. 'We could *print* them with Ned's poems— they'd illuminate each other!'

Ned reaches out and turns a few more pages. He stops at a picture of a young man held by Japanese guards and an older man who's smirking at the sight.

'Jesus, mate, didn't know you'd caught that—' He swallows, and with horror I realise the young man is Ned, an unscarred Ned.

Klara turns the pages to the final image in the book, a dashed-off sketch of guards in a cluster.

'Are they attacking someone?' she says, puzzled.

Harry slaps shut the sketchbook. 'I have absolutely no intention of exhibiting *anything*.'

He takes the books out of the room and when he returns he says, 'Sorry. Don't mean to be dramatic. Just embarrassing little daubs I did because I couldn't bloody do anything *else*.'

Eliza refills our glasses and says quietly, 'Sometimes I wonder. We won the war, but how do we even begin to reconcile it? All those stolen years. Youth and hope gone forever.'

I hesitate. 'We lost so much, but some of us gained as well. We got to work, fly, travel, do jobs we'd have been blocked from before. But yes, how do we reconcile such an era?'

'We leave it in the *past*,' says Harry firmly.

'No,' says Klara. 'We must tell of it.' She is suddenly stricken-faced. 'Or perhaps it may happen again.'

'Then *you* tell of it, Klara,' says Harry with surprising curtness.

'I cannot,' she murmurs, gazing at her glass. 'I am unable.'

I find her hand under the table and hold it. 'But that's why we mustn't let anything be forgotten. At least Ned's work exists here and now, and it should be seen.'

Ned nods slowly. 'I suppose at heart all writers want their words witnessed—I can't pretend I'm any different.'

Klara is still gazing down, and Ned say gently, 'All right, take my poems of rage, Klara, do with them what you will. Just let me have my pseudonym or I'll never live it down at the hospital.'

After a moment Harry shakes his head. 'No. I'm sorry, I can't help. Those pictures are private.'

Klara says, 'It is all right, Harry. The poems alone are enough.' She gazes at Ned. 'You should know there will be few royalties.'

He shrugs. 'What's new?'

'But how will you *do* all this, Klara?' says Eliza.

'Yvonne has worked that out,' says Klara.

I dab my mouth with my napkin. 'Well, I've always wanted to publish books, and a small printery in Balmain near us is closing down. I've decided to buy it. The bread-and-butter work like texts, magazines, catalogues, will help finance the book.'

'And we can also reprint some of Toby's early works,' says Klara. 'I still get requests for them.'

'What a wonderful project!' says Eliza. 'Here's to your success.'

Harry says ruefully, 'Sorry, everyone, for being a bear with a sore head. Best of luck with it all,' and Ned slaps him affectionately on the shoulder.

Later, over coffee in the lounge, the atmosphere is lighter. Ned says, 'Eliza, didn't you mention you were taking a holiday?'

'Next month—a sentimental journey.'

'An expedition to Port Victoria,' says Harry. 'We'll fly to Adelaide, then hire a car.'

'Port Victoria?' I ask. 'Isn't that where those giant sailing ships you love come in?'

Eliza nods. 'Only two are loading up this season, probably for the last time ever. Heavens, there were twelve four-masters working when we sailed on *Inverley*.'

'That was twenty years ago, love. Unbelievable,' says Harry.

'Sailing ships?' says Ned. 'What—like clippers, Spanish galleons? In this day and age?'

Eliza smiles. 'No, these are steel windjammers that take the grain harvest to Europe. Used to be ideal for the job in the old days, but steamers have taken over now. Sad, but inevitable.'

'You owned one, didn't you, Eliza?' I say.

'Not really. I had a small financial share in *Inverley*, which I sold after the war. But she'll never sail again. These ships are German-built vessels with a few more years of life in them.'

'Good Lord,' says Ned. 'Do you mean you've actually been around the famous Cape Horn?'

'Yes, we saw Cape Horn,' says Eliza. 'Harry and I first met on the ship.' They glance at each other and smile.

'And you've been together ever since?' says Ned.

'Oh, no. We were just friends,' says Eliza. 'Took us years to figure it out. We're both *terribly* slow on the uptake.'

Harry laughs and goes to the cocktail trolley. 'Brandies?'

'Heavens, after all that lovely wine?' I say. 'But I suppose we only have to totter upstairs.'

Harry starts pouring drinks and says, 'Eliza, don't forget to give them Izabel's news.' He turns to Ned. 'That's her aunt, Izabel Malory—Klara and Yvonne know her well from London.'

'Oh, yes,' says Eliza happily. 'The latest letter from Hong Kong! Izabel says the civil war is almost over and corrupt Generalissimo Chiang is losing to the Reds. Soon she'll be able to start searching.'

'Searching for what?' says Ned.

'Her lover, Laurence Kuan.'

'Ah, so the lover is fighting with this Generalissimo?' says Ned.

'No, Laurence is a Red,' says Harry, handing around brandies.

'Sorry, are we talking about the same Izabel Malory? The famous *actress*?' says Ned, puzzled. 'What's she doing in Hong Kong fighting with the Communists?'

'Yes, the same. She went back to Hong Kong after the war, but I doubt she took up arms for the Reds—although who knows?' Eliza flings her head back, laughing. 'Oh, dear, after all that wine summing up Izabel's life in a few sentences is quite beyond me.'

Let me try,' says Klara. 'Izabel was very unhappy in London, her husband Felix—'

Eliza and I laugh and groan simultaneously, 'Not bloody *Felix*.'

Harry says, 'No, wait on, you lot. Felix wasn't that bad, he just became a bastard over time.'

'You're far too kind, love. He was always a bastard,' says Eliza. 'But he he filled out an evening suit so handsomely nobody noticed.'

Harry says, 'True. Ned—this Felix sod destroyed Izabel's career, and it was completely his fault she and Nancy were in Singapore during the invasion. He should have got them out earlier.'

'Ah, and *Nancy* would be—?' says Ned tentatively.

'Laurence's daughter,' I say. 'Izabel adopted her. *Honestly*, Ned, you have to keep up.'

We're all laughing now, and Ned shakes his head. 'Amazing, Harry, I had no idea your family was so exotic. Revolutionaries *and* the great Izabel Malory?'

Harry laughs. 'I'm no revolutionary, mate, just a common-or-garden Socialist.'

After a pause, Eliza says, 'It wasn't really Felix's fault Izabel stayed in Singapore. None of us could bear to admit it would fall, not even the Socialists.'

There's a silence, then she says, 'Izabel saved Nancy and me, but she paid dearly for it. Rather sad, really. Not funny at all.'

The lamp beside the bed casts a soft glow. I get in, arrange my pillow and put my arm around Klara.

'That got a bit heated with Harry earlier,' I say. 'Are you all right?'

Klara says quietly, 'I have a sense he wishes to hide something.'

'A secret? From Eliza?'

'I do not know. Perhaps it is from himself.' She snuggles against my shoulder. 'Ned seems a very pleasant man, although perhaps rather lonely.'

I kiss the top of her head. 'Yes. Poor man. He should be like us and have someone to love.'

She looks at me. 'No one else in the world could be like us, Yvonne. We are beyond poetry.' She kisses me and her breath seems the very essence of spice and desire.

'Beyond poetry, dear heart?' I murmur. 'That's heresy isn't it?'

I feel the curl of her smile against mine.

8. Harry: Port Vic

For most of my life I've dedicated myself to studying malaria, but in Changi I had to witness the disease at its most virulent, bitterly standing by as people suffered and died. After that, I knew I could never go back to pure research.

So I joined the staff of Newcastle Hospital, where Chris McCaffrey, a crafty and farsighted Medical Superintendent, was assembling a range of modern teaching facilities.

With the local unions and industry he set up an outpatient clinic, where for just sixpence a week whole families could receive treatment from hospital doctors. (The bureaucrats had the nerve to call it creeping Socialism!)

My job was to train junior doctors in techniques of cell staining and microscopy, but lately I've been spending more and more time in the outpatient clinic. I've been surprised to discover how much I enjoy such a broad range of problems.

Now the clinic is where I do most of my hours. It's been an odd change of direction perhaps—from specialist to generalist—but for me it's felt like a necessary one.

A few days after the dinner party, Ned sits down beside me in the doctor's lounge saying, 'Wonder what this new Chief Administrator will be like?'

'Don't know. It seems to have taken them ages to find someone.'

'Anyway, thanks again for the other night, Harry. Still not sure I'm doing the right thing, but I posted those poems off to Klara. Do you really believe they can publish a book?'

'I think so. As you probably noticed, quiet Klara is an unstoppable force. And while I don't know Yvonne very well, Eliza assures me she's equally single-minded.'

'I made a carbon copy for you as well.' He adjusts his glasses and smiles shyly and holds out a small ream of papers. 'You seemed to quite like what that Edward Quest fellow published.'

'Thanks, Ned, that's thoughtful of you.'

I take the papers, but wonder if I actually want to read anyone's poems of rage. It's hard enough keeping my own emotions under adequate control.

'Might be a relief to have them published, after all,' he says. 'It's reassuring when you run across readers who understand—like a friendly conversation. Do you find that with your paintings?'

'Hadn't thought about it that way.' I smile at the younger man. 'But it's an academic issue anyway as I certainly don't intend—'

The Medical Superintendent enters the room with an entourage. 'Good morning, ladies and gentlemen,' he says. (Yes, we do have several dedicated female doctors.) 'I've called you together today to meet our new Chief Administrator, and I'm sure you'll make him feel most welcome.'

A figure steps forward.

'Please let me introduce Dr Aylwen Godfrey.'

I feel as if I've been thumped in the chest. Ned gasps and starts to tremble beside me.

'It's all right,' I murmur and grasp Ned's arm, as the Superintendent blathers about Godfrey's marvellous qualifications.

He shakes his head. 'No. No, it's *not.*'

Mercifully, after a time, the Superintendent takes his entourage and leaves.

'Sit tight, I'll get you some tea.' I pour Ned a strong brew with sugar to help with the shock.

He swallows a mouthful, staring and whispers, 'Dear God, Harry, what will we do?'

'I actually met the bastard very briefly a few months ago,' I say. 'Didn't want to mention it. He said he was here for a visit and I never expected to see him again—'

'A visit to interview for this bloody *job* I expect. Shit, oh shit. Can we report him?'

'For what, being a bastard? We've no proof. Only the Japanese stood trial for the Double Tenth. None of our people were mentioned, let alone implicated.'

'No one dared hint at collaboration,' says Ned bitterly. 'That can of worms was too big to open.'

'Don't forget, we all wanted to leave those memories behind us, to get *home*. I planned never to think about the camp again, let alone bloody Godfrey.'

'But he's just kept going. Flourishing too,' says Ned.

'Look, maybe he won't be the blue-eyed boy the Super wants—'

'Don't kid yourself, Harry. All those qualifications? He always was an efficient swine. He'll be everything the place needs and more.'

'No, Ned, hold on. Something's not right. It's only been three years since we came home, and that degree the Super mentioned is a four-year course. And Godfrey certainly didn't have it when we were in Singapore.'

'Are you certain?'

I nod. 'I was on the committee that hired him at the General Hospital, so yes, I am. If he'd had a qualification like that he'd have shouted it from the rooftops.'

'That's interesting,' says Ned, gazing at me.

'Look, I'll have a word with the Super, try to find out a little more, see if—'

'See if the treacherous bastard's a bare-faced liar as well?'

I put my hand on his shoulder. 'Don't worry. He can't hurt you now.'

Ned is silent, then says, 'People like that … they don't stop. They can't. The greater the wrong the harder they try to justify it. They double down, they don't slink away.'

'Chris! A word?' I sprint down the hall after the Medical Superintendent.

'Harry? Of course, come in.'

He sits down at his desk and rubs his hands happily. 'At last, eh?

Thought we'd never find anyone. We liked a few of the others, but they withdrew for one reason or another and Dr Godfrey was still interested. Lucky for us! Now, how can I help you?'

'Actually, it's to do with Dr Godfrey. I know him—rather well in fact.'

'Odd—he didn't offer you as a reference.'

'Not odd.' I hesitate. 'Chris, this is highly confidential. I worked with him at Singapore General Hospital before the war, and was with him in Changi Prison.'

'Ah. Go on.'

'He's an extremely efficient medical administrator, I'd never say he wasn't, but he also has a side that—' I rub my brow. 'Look, it's impossible to sugar-coat, I'm sorry. The man was a traitor. He collaborated with the Japanese.'

'Good God! What happened?'

'He dobbed Ned Caswell in when the secret police were searching for hidden radios. Ned had nothing to do with them and, as you know, suffered five months of torture as a result.'

'Of course, that was appalling. Was Dr Godfrey tried?'

I shake my head. 'At the end everything was chaos. The Japanese torturers were convicted and hanged, but in that atmosphere, who'd accuse one of our own? We all know how officialdom was only interested in rushing to sanitise the record.'

The Super nods. 'The war was a litany of official cock-ups, but that doesn't mean Dr Godfrey was a traitor, Harry. Do you have any *proof*?'

'Things I saw and heard—his high regard for our captors, his joy when people he disliked were taken away. That's what I *saw*, Ned and I both, and so did our fellow prisoners.'

'Dr Caswell is our finest orthopaedic surgeon, but I think we're all aware his tragic experiences have left its mark, Harry, and not only physically. I'm sorry. Without proof I can go no further. Perhaps we should give the man the benefit of the doubt. They were dreadful circumstances after all—'

'What about his impressive higher degree then?' I say. 'Oxford?'

'What about it?'

'He didn't have it when we hired him at Singapore General, he certainly didn't study for it in Changi, and he hasn't had time since. Surely that sounds as suspicious to you as it does to me?'

'Ah.' The Super shuffles some files on his desk and lines them up neatly. 'I'll tell you what he told our committee, in some embarrassment, I might add. He'd done the greater part before going to Singapore, then dropped it because of a breakdown over a failed love affair. But he did complete it after the war.' He gazes kindly at me. 'Harry, we've got a Xerox copy of the degree.'

I feel deflated, sick, foolish. 'Very well, nothing more I can say. Except—please keep this in mind, Chris. The man I knew in Changi won't have changed, and I don't believe he bodes well for this hospital or for any of us.'

The Super stands and shakes my hand. 'I won't forget, Harry, but sometimes bygones really do have to be bygones.'

'You're a pirate.'

'I'm not a pirate and sit down, Leo,' says Eliza. 'Your shoes are hurting my knees—you're getting to be a big boy now.'

'I'll be three soon won't I, Mummy?'

'Yes, you will, love.'

'I won't stand on your lap then.'

'I can hardly wait. Look, we're almost to Central, then we'll be going out to the airport.'

'Daddy's a pirate.'

'Pretty sure I'm not, little man,' I say. 'But look, sit down, you can't jump up and down on your mother, and certainly not in your new shoes. Pirate boys don't do that.'

Leo sits down and thinks for a moment. 'If I'm a pirate boy then you must be a pirate daddy.'

'Dear God, if I hear one more word—' murmurs Eliza. 'I could kill Ned for giving him that book.'

I laugh as the train slows, and stand to get our bags from the luggage rack. 'He certainly didn't quite grasp the difference between a four-master and a skull-and-crossbones galleon.'

'Suppose not. Come on, darling, let's go and see Aunty Tina and Uncle Nikos. They'll be surprised to see how much you've grown.'

Tina and Nikos are waiting near the indicator board, just as when we met them eight months ago, but my sister's clothes and makeup are now stylish and sophisticated in the extreme.

Eliza says, 'Oh, Tina, don't you look gorgeous!'

'Demands of the job,' she says, pleased. 'And how's our little Leo? Give me a cuddle, darling!'

Leo obliges, and I shake hands with Nikos, who says, 'I think you've got time for a cup of tea before we have to be out at Mascot.'

'Dear God, yes,' says Eliza. 'I'm already exhausted and we've barely begun.'

'Are you sure, Nikos?' I say.

'Plenty of time, you'll be fine. Once you're in the air the flight to Parafield will take about five hours, then you can go to your hotel and have a good rest.'

'Don't like rest,' says Leo, and yawns. I swing him up to my shoulder, where he promptly falls asleep. I mutter, 'Would have been bloody useful if you'd done that on the train, mate.'

'Oh dear,' says Eliza. 'If he sleeps now he'll be wide awake by the time we land. Still, not having to talk about pirates for a while will be wonderful.'

We go to the restaurant at the end of the concourse, give our order to a waitress and sit down at a table. Leo is half on a chair and half on my lap.

'Are pirates the latest obsession?' says Tina.

'Obsession's the word for it,' says Eliza. 'Our friend Ned got him a book on pirate ships, thinking they're they same as modern steel windjammers! Leo knows Harry and I sailed on a four-master, so now he's convinced we're pirates and just refusing to admit it.'

Nikos laughs. 'I'd believe it of you, Eliza—I can just imagine you and Billie swearing and swinging your cutlasses to repel boarders.'

'Ah,' says Eliza, delighted. 'How *is* she? Going well at the base?'

'On duty today, but sends her love. Yes, enjoying herself—a few old fogies were miffed at working with a woman who'd flown bigger planes than they ever did, but even they're over it by now.'

'I'm so glad,' says Eliza. 'And your boss, Mr Willoughby? She wasn't sure about him at first.'

'No, they get on,' says Nikos. 'She told you about his daughter?'

'Jean Willoughby?' I say. 'Yes, that was particularly tragic.'

'What happened?' says Tina.

'A couple of days before Singapore fell a bomb hit one of the wards,' says Eliza. 'It was awful. Ned—our doctor friend who so unwisely gave Leo the pirate book—cared for her rather a lot.'

The waitress brings us tea on a tray and after we've poured, Tina says, 'That's Ned the doctor-poet? We had Klara and Yvonne over for dinner and they were telling us about their book of poetry and the mysterious Edward Quest.'

'Yes, Ned Caswell,' I say. 'He uses a pseudonym to keep his medical and writing lives separate.'

'Klara's still surprised you wouldn't let her publish your paintings, Harry,' says Tina.

'Surprised?' I say. 'I made it *perfectly* clear my amateur daubs are not for publication.'

There's a silence.

'Ah,' says Nikos gently. 'Apparently Klara didn't get a good response from many other poets, so she's going focus entirely on Ned's poems. She says in any case it's outstanding work.'

'Marvellous!' says Eliza. 'That might cheer him up.'

'Why does he need cheering up?' says Tina.

'Oh, some dreadful man he and Harry knew in the camp has taken a job at the hospital, and it's weighing on Ned's nerves.'

'Is that a problem for you too, Harry?' says Nikos.

'So far he's stayed out of our way.' I'm still feeling a little irritated at people harping on about my paintings.

'Good to hear,' says Nikos. 'Now, we should get moving. You pirates have to fight your way onto an aeroplane.'

'Yo-ho-ho,' says Eliza.

*

In Adelaide next morning I'm feeling brighter, yesterday's annoyance forgotten. Leo stayed asleep all night too, a bonus. Eliza rinsed his nappies and they were dry by morning, so we seems to have that side of travelling with a small child under control.

I collect the car I booked from a garage and we set off for Port Victoria, one hundred miles to the west, on the shore of vast Spencer Gulf. As we leave the city behind, the countryside around us is flat and brown in the warm autumn air.

Eliza looks at me and smiles. I squeeze her hand. 'All right, love?'

She nods. 'Everything's seemed quite unreal till now, but suddenly I'm excited. It's been so long since I've seen a four-master —do you remember the last time?'

'Just before the war, 1939—we took the train from London to Cardiff to visit *Inverley.*'

'And poor old *Olivebank* was there beside her,' says Eliza.

'Was poor old oleever-bunk a pirate ship?' comes a voice from the back seat.

'She was a barque, my darling, like those we'll see today,' says Eliza. 'A beautiful thing. She was sunk by a mine in the North Sea, and people we knew were killed.'

'But a mine is a hole in the ground.'

'This sort of mine was a bomb, Leo. It blew up the ship.'

'Why?'

Eliza laughs sadly. 'I don't know.'

'Did pirates do it?'

After a moment Eliza says, 'No, Leo. Bad men did it.'

I can tell from her voice she's close to tears. I squeeze her hand again and she gives me a shaky smile. Fortunately Leo shuts up, and we manage to get another twenty miles before he starts again.

'I know, I know! You *are* a pirate, Mummy! You've got scarves in your cupboard and pirates always wear scarves!'

Eliza half-sobs and covers her face. Then she looks up and says, 'Yes. Yes, I *am* a pirate, and so is Daddy.' She turns around to him.

'But it's a secret, so you have to stop talking about it.'

'A secret?' Leo says uncertainly.

'Pirate boys have to keep secrets or they can't be pirate boys,' I say. 'Everyone knows that.'

'Oh. But—'

'A *secret*, Leo,' I say.

'All right,' he says in a small voice. His breathing slows.

I whisper, 'Is he?'

'Thank God, yes,' says Eliza. 'He'll certainly have something to tell his psychiatrist when he grows up, won't he?'

'Better than both of us going bonkers on the road to Port Vic.'

She smiles then says, 'There's something else, Harry.' She hesitates. 'I'm sorry I've been so on edge. I was feeling … well, I was afraid I was pregnant again. Luckily I discovered this morning I wasn't.'

'Even so, I wouldn't mind,' I say. 'Leo's hard work but he's still the best thing that ever happened to us. I'm sure we'd survive.'

'I'm not,' she says quietly.

'Eliza?'

'I'm forty-one, Harry, and I'd simply assumed it wouldn't happen again. But faced with the prospect?' She shakes her head. 'You know how hard I've struggled with this—*gloom*—I've had since Leo was born. I really don't think I'd have the strength to do it again.'

'I'm sorry, love, I had no idea you felt that way.'

'Nor did I.'

'Then we should start taking precautions, like the old days,' I say.

'Caps and douches and French letters? What a prospect.'

'We could just be careful. Work out the fertile times of your cycle.'

She nods. 'Bit rough on you, though.'

'I'd rather be frustrated than have you miserable,' I say. 'And remember all those years in the war I had to survive without you? Just being together now is enough.'

'Is it?' she says, smiling.

'Well, I actually want to sob like Leo when he loses his teddy bear, but I'm sure I'll cope.'

She laughs. 'I'll make it up to you at other times, I promise.'

'Only if you want to, you know that.'

'I want. Always.'

She touches my hand and, with pirate boy asleep in the back, the miles pass in easy silence. We finally reach Port Vic (as the sailors call it), a tiny country town with a single main street.

I pull over and turn off the engine. We're parked on a rise, and the road ahead runs down to a beach and a jetty that stretches into the water beyond. Small ketches are moored around the jetty and, perhaps a mile offshore, are the ships we've come to see.

To farewell.

Passat and *Pamir* ride at anchor, their ranks of masts straight and tall, their long hulls graceful. They're riding low in the water, each weighed down with fifty or sixty thousand bags of grain, carried out by the ketches and stowed by hand in those great deep holds.

'I didn't actually believe—after all these years. They're almost unearthly,' says Eliza. 'And what a funny little place this is! Port Lincoln was practically the big city in comparison. Remember the day we sailed on *Inverley*? You were awfully chilly towards me.'

'I thought, who's this young flibbertigibbet coming along on our sensible, manly voyage? She'll probably fall overboard and then we'll all be in strife.'

'I was twenty-one.' She smiles slowly. 'I liked your voice.'

'I liked your courage. Then I liked everything about you.'

I take her hand and kiss it, and she rests her head on my shoulder and together we watch the sea and the ships.

We know the captain of *Passat* from the old days, so we spend the time happily visiting vessels and talking to sailors. Wide-eyed Leo is made much of by kindly young men, although he's puzzled no one will show him where they store the cutlasses.

Pamir leaves at the end of May, but we decide to stay on at Port Vic for a few more days until *Passat* is ready to follow her sister over the horizon.

On 2nd June 1949, we assemble at the shore with one or two reporters and a small crowd of people who've been greeting, or loading, or crewing the giant barques for more than twenty years, and watch in awe as *Passat*'s thirty-two massive sails are unfurled, one by one, flashing bright in the morning air.

'An acre of canvas all told and twenty miles of running rigging,' Eliza murmurs. 'And today is probably the last time anyone in this country will ever witness the sight.'

I take photographs with a box camera, and we ask a passer-by to take one of Eliza and Leo and me, *Passat* in the distance behind us.

'They're not *really* pirate ships,' says a small, firm voice. 'They're four-masted barques. The captain told me that.'

'You believe him and not your own parents?' I say.

'Daddy, he's the *captain*.'

'Can't argue with that.'

Passat begins to move. 'Goodbye, barque, *goodbye*,' Leo calls out.

'Goodbye, youth and hope,' says Eliza wryly.

Away from the harbour, *Passat* catches the wind and her sails blossom full and round. The massive ship heels and surges through the foam flying white from her bow, and people around me sigh.

I remember a moment like that twenty years ago on *Inverley*'s deck. I remember the sense of power when she took to her element as brave as an albatross; and the singing of the lines and the rushing of the water on her hull and—beyond everything—the vast and glorious silence.

Goodbye, youth and hope.

We stay one more night at our lodgings in Port Vic. I wake just before dawn. Leaving Eliza and Leo sleeping I go to the tiny kitchen to make a cup of tea, then sit by the window and watch the first light on the water.

I've got Ned's poems out, his poems of rage. I think he's hurt I haven't said anything since he gave them to me, so I brought them along hoping I'd feel serene enough on holiday to read them.

With a sigh I turn to the first page.

The poem is about one of the quiet days, when we didn't have to stand in the sun for hours to be harangued or randomly beaten. When we had a talk on Shakespeare's plays, or gardened, or repaired the plumbing with bits of old tin, or added bitter weeds to the soup of our single meal to try to ward off beri-beri, or thought about our loved ones. The last stanza:

> *The round golden clouds in the evening*
> *The haze soft as bruises beyond*
> *An ending of sorts but how could we know*
> *How lucky, how lost, how forlorn?*

Exactly. Life as a prisoner was tedious, yet almost peaceful compared to the Double Tenth that followed. You caught the feeling well, Ned. One of my paintings, showing rain on the horizon, has a similar mood. Of course that's irrelevant.

I turn the page to 'Games of Betrayal.'

> *Boyish amusement*
> *Rushing and kicking*
> *Carelessly playing:*
> *Who knew the match*
> *Was chess with Iago?*
>
> *Free from God's kindness*
> *White Jap's betrayal*
> *Broke all the rules as*
> *Pawns are discarded*
> *In endgame's despair*

A hint of Godfrey's name in *Free from God's kindness*. Clever. And the sod himself as jealous, malignant Iago, watching lighthearted men playing together? Certainly captures the dreadful day Ned was taken away. Next page, 'The Abattoir.'

We sit, we sit, we sit
We ache in raw uncushioned hips
Hands on knees like Buddhas
Staring straight ahead
To deviate brings beatings
Until the bamboos shred

We wait, we wait, we wait
In fear of final looming fate
Flank by flank like bullocks
Bound for abattoirs
In dung and squalor weeping
From wounds on top of scars

We stink, we hurt, we bleed
We live in unrequited need
Innocence defenceless
For torture cannot cease
While no admission qualifies
To bring exquisite peace

From everything I've heard, that's exactly what it was like for the prisoners in the dungeons of the Double Tenth. Of course innocent people have nothing to confess, so how can they end their ordeal?

I'd sit beside Ned's bed when we weren't certain if he'd recover. Once I sketched his bare shoulder and arm flowing down to his half-open hand, a line as pure as a Classical statue. But I wasn't a father then, and now, more than anything, the memory recalls Leo's dear small body. I blink and turn to 'The Scar.'

I forgot, I said
Of course I did.
They say it's over but
If it's not

What use for them to know
That Torquemada has fruit
on his platter
To taunt and show who's boss?
(Of course he is)
What use for them to know
That torch-bright batteries
Sear incandescent pain?
That gentle balm of water
Brings drowning more than once?
They say it's over but
If it's not
What use for them to know
That platters (shattered)
Scar?

I'm stunned. *Scar?* I'd always wondered what caused the wound on Ned's face. He told us he couldn't remember, but of course the jagged edge of a broken plate would do it. Then my scalp crawls.

Ned told us he *couldn't remember.*

He was delirious after he came back so it was easy to believe, easy to accept. But he'd forgotten nothing. He went on to rework these dreadful memories into poems, bearing witness to the horrors I'd tried so hard to forget.

Oh God. I'm a doctor—the suffering I've seen, the bad news I've had to break—I thought I could bear almost anything. But this? Memories rush through me, all the things I'd hoped were forgotten, all the pain, the guilt, the horror. I feel sick with shame.

'Are you all right?' Eliza comes in, her nightdress pale, and puts her hand on my shoulder.

I take a shuddering breath. 'Not really. No.'

She gazes at the papers. 'Ned's poems? They're that powerful?'

I collect myself. 'I knew some of it, of course. But I hadn't felt for myself how much he suffered. He's a brave lad.'

It's not the entire truth, but it's plausible at least.

Eliza sits down and says gently, 'It sounds as if you feel his words deserve to be seen. Perhaps you should reconsider and let your paintings be seen with them. What did Yvonne say? They could *illuminate* Ned's work.'

I rub my eyes. 'But, you don't understand—I'm not as brave as him. I couldn't bear to face all those dreadful memories again.'

(That's honest, if nothing else.)

'Putting those memories into words seems to have helped Ned cope a little better than you, Harry.'

'Eliza, it's as if, all the time—shadows haunt the edges of my senses, carrying the fear—no—the *knowledge* that for no reason, in some ordinary moment, a beating will begin and pain will descend again, *inescapable* pain.'

She takes my hand.

I gaze away in despair. 'When it happened we'd laugh it off, tough it out, she'll be right, mate. But usually we'd weep ... *I'd* weep—in the night.'

After a time Eliza says, 'You never told me that before, love.'

'My God, how *could* I? Sudden noises, loud voices, quick gestures —they bring it all back and my heart almost stops in terror. And Christ, I had it easy! Look at poor Ned.'

'Expressing it helped him, Harry. Showing the world your art might help you too.'

'But ... I'm ashamed.'

'Of what?' she says, incredulous.

I should have done more, but sometimes it was too *much* ...' That's as close as I can come, and my throat convulses in denial.

Eliza gazes at me silently. I try to recover.

'I'm such a coward you see.' (That's true enough.) 'I couldn't take on such a burden. To choose to step out of the shadows and relive it all again?'

There's a long silence.

'Then let me choose, love,' Eliza says. 'You need to do this.'

9. Tina: The Scent of His Skin

Eliza and Harry stay overnight with us on their way home from Port Victoria. Eliza has at last persuaded Harry to let Klara and Yvonne use his paintings in the book they're publishing. Although he says he's relaxed now after their holiday, he still seems a little tense.

Small Leo tells me solemnly, 'We saw barques, Aunty Tina, four-masted barques.' I kiss him and wonder why Harry and Eliza have always been mad for those decrepit old things. It's odd really, given the very modern world we now find ourselves in.

Not just those awful atomic bombs, but it seems the future is all the world is thinking about. Honestly, *rockets*? Nikos's sensible magazines now have shiny spaceships and men in silver suits on the covers, and they're talking about going to the moon, for heaven's sake!

The only moon I like to think about is in music: *Blue Moon, Moonlight and Shadows, Moonlight Serenade*. *Claire de Lune*, too. Steve's been playing that a lot lately and it makes me feel peaceful. Yes, Steve. Nikos agreed Stavros didn't have to use his Greek name all the time and the boy's been a different person since.

One day he gruffly admitted to me he wanted a piano. We had space for it and Nikos agreed, but we didn't show his grandfather until it was installed. Then Steve played him some of his favourite folk songs and even he was won over.

Steve's still a bad-tempered adolescent, but at times he's almost human, teasing Nikos with snatches of dance music and me with jazz pieces.

This is László's influence of course—László Richter, his new teacher, the piano player at the Starlight Lounge. One day I mentioned Steve's new instrument to Jimmy Kelso, and when László finished a tune Jimmy called him over.

'Now here's the very fella for you. Our man teaches music when he's not too busy mesmerising the ladies, and maybe he'd give your boy a hand tickling the ivories.'

László smiled politely—he does everything politely, in a European sort of way—and agreed to teach Steve. He's a DP, a displaced person, who settled here from Hungary after the war. His eyes are always sombre and the only time he relaxes is sometimes at the end of a piece, when he nods at the applauding audience.

He visits our house twice a week in the early evening. He's usually gone by the time I get home so we don't talk much, but I'm grateful for the change in Steve. It's such a relief and simply adds to how much I love my new life.

My mind buzzes happily day and night with the problems, the demands, the successes of the business. I have money to buy beautiful clothes and jewellery—fashionable, flattering, in the best of taste. Pearl, the restaurant manager, allows me a little grudging respect, and Jimmy doesn't even try to hide his admiration.

He takes me to meetings where sly, thick-necked men in rumpled suits sit up and straighten their ties and bring me tea in dainty porcelain cups. Jimmy says I'm the best thing that ever happened to the place, not simply for the rigour of my accounting but for my eye for secrets, my sharp, cynical, honed-by-war *eye*.

I know a lot more now about the world Jimmy inhabits. It took him some time to trust me enough to show me the real account books: one set for the taxman, the other with the true figures.

Along the way he's been teaching me about the swirling power struggles between the crime families (Italian, Jewish, Greek, Irish) that control Sydney business. That control whether or not Jimmy has a business at all.

Like everyone else, he buys policemen and bribes judges, juries and politicians. He pays 'insurance' to the Italian crime family currently at the top of the heap. As anyone who reads the paper knows, the Capellis are notorious for their links to mysterious bashings and discreet drug-dens and unsolved murders, but no one important ever seems to go to gaol.

I was shocked at first, of course I was. My mother was a school teacher and I was a well-behaved girl. Even during my service years I believed in the rules and followed them obediently.

But it was also in the army I discovered how blatant corruption could be and how widespread it actually was. How only the smallest fish were ever punished and the largest swam free.

Jimmy himself got his start as a quartermaster in some army unit that never left the country, handling supplies and hiving a small percentage off for his own profit. And once I was out of the service I could see the same corruption flourishing everywhere.

Jimmy's 'insurance' is the price he pays to survive. The shopkeepers, the builders, the madams, the accountants, the club owners: they all pay to keep the simmering violence no more than simmering. Not as it was before the war, with running battles between razor gangs and daylight executions on the streets.

The ordinary rest of us, the clerks and secretaries and doctors and housewives, we benefit too. We can keep going about our sunny, everyday lives with no idea of how close we might be to some unimaginable edge. Heavens, how melodramatic that sounds! But it's true.

The Cross—Kings Cross, a mile from the Starlight Lounge—is the centre of 'sin' (as the newspapers call it) and yes: there's an age-old, glamorous machine throbbing in the shadows of pretty harbourside Sydney, and it's nothing at all like Nikos's shiny silver engines.

It runs on money and sex and power, and draws people to the red-light clubs and glittering restaurants with promises of delight and oblivion. It's what keeps us in business.

And I find, after my first shock of recognition, it fascinates me.

In February 1950, a year after I started at the Starlight Lounge, Eliza rings. 'Tina, could I ask a favour? Remember Charlotte, Harry's ex-wife? She's visiting Sydney and wants to see us. Harry can't get away, but I was wondering if I could stay with you—'

'Of course. The spare room's always made up. Is Leo coming too?'

'No, he's fine, he'll stay with Harry.'

'When will you arrive? If Nikos isn't on a shift he can pick you up at the station.'

'Don't worry, I'll get a tram. Is tomorrow okay? About noon.'

'I'll leave the key under the mat. Eliza—is everything all right?'

'Yes, of course. See you then.'

I replace the receiver, wondering. *Is* everything all right?

My sister-in-law is bright, quick, fine-featured. Like me, she was in intelligence, but I was just a low-level signals bod in Australia, while she had heavy responsibilities in a Civil Service department in London.

One afternoon last year we were drinking a few cocktails while baby Leo was asleep, and she got surprisingly tiddly. It was fun, but somehow we ended up talking about the war and what haunts us in the early hours, even now.

For me it's the hospital ship *Centaur*, torpedoed off Queensland in 1943, despite being clearly marked with the red cross. Hundreds of doctors, sisters, orderlies and seamen died. But the worst of it is we might have been able to prevent it.

A friend in one of the other WAAAF sections reported a radar signal from an unknown vessel, but her superior told her sharply her job was to watch for aircraft, not ships. Then a second operator saw the same thing, and was threatened with discipline.

My friend said later, sobbing, 'It was the *sub*, Tina! And if they'd been warned—if I'd *insisted*—'

'If you'd insisted you'd have ended up on a charge,' I said. 'And you know radar was classified then. Reporting a sighting could have breached security.'

I barely convinced myself, and my friend went on to have a breakdown. I told Eliza about it as we drank in the late afternoon, and she nodded.

'Like that for me too,' she said quietly. 'We had top-secret devices, codes, intelligence. How could we act on what we knew without giving away how we knew it? So sometimes we didn't act, even

knowing ... Christ, it was hard. But harder for the poor bastards—'
She took another drink, and said bitterly, 'Bloody official *secrets.*'

She stopped then and we sat in silence.

She's crazy about her son but once I saw her watching him playing and tears were flowing down her face. I gave her a hankie and she joked it was just hormones, but I wondered—did Harry see how unhappy she was? How bored, how frustrated?

Certainly she appears more content after their trip to Port Victoria, but I think she needs a job as much as I do. Yet everyone else seems to assume her job is Leo and nothing but Leo.

I adore him, but couldn't bear, day after day, to never have a chance to use my mind. Still, perhaps with your own child things are different. How would I know?

Things are quiet at the restaurant on the day Eliza is due to arrive. Jimmy is out working on some deal, and Steve's piano teacher, László, is playing for the afternoon high tea.

I pause near the stage to listen, wishing the ladies in their furs and fashionable hats would just shut their gobs (as Jimmy would say) and let me hear the thoughtful music in the silence it deserves.

I murmur, 'Beautiful, László,' when he finishes.

He says, 'I need to see you, Mrs Loukas, about a document.' He follows me to my office, a dark haired, barrel-chested man with sensitive pianist's hands. We sit down and he lights up a thin cigarillo, then takes a folded paper from his pocket.

He opens it. 'As you know, I came here after the war. I was told my wife and son were dead. I had no proof, only the words of someone who thought he saw—' He clears his throat. 'I have wondered if it is so. The International Refugee Organisation has records and it is possible to apply to have them examined. But I need a witness to my declaration.'

'Of course I'll witness it. Show me.'

I scan the document, surprised to notice his date of birth.

'Oh, I didn't realise you were only—'

'Thirty-six, yes. The war had rather an ageing effect.' (My God, he's only Jimmy's age yet he looks a decade older.)

I read further. 'You were in … Auschwitz?' Even I know what that means. Lines bracket his mouth, lines that mark the faces of people who've suffered starvation. Harry has them, from Changi.

He nods, and breathes out smoke. 'I was extremely fortunate to survive. In some ways.'

'And you believe your family may also have survived?'

'I doubt it but I must be sure.'

'How long will it take for them to check their records?'

He shrugs. 'A long time I expect. Shall I sign now?'

I push the paper across the desk to him and he writes his name at the bottom and I witness it.

'László, what did you do before—?'

'I was a music teacher. Hungary collaborated with the Nazis, as you probably know—'

'No. No I don't.'

'Jews were taken away for labour, but not to the camps. We imagined we were safe, we thought Hungary was a civilised country. But in 1944 the Germans invaded us to impose their *solution*. Then it became a very difficult time.'

'It must have been terrible.' (Oh, how shamefully inadequate.)

'The Soviets liberated us, but still difficult times continued. When I gave up all hope for my family I escaped over the border. And finally—here.' He gazes around the room with a dry smile.

'Yet you play, despite … you play *beautiful* music.'

'It is a living,' he says, and stubs out his cigarillo and stands. 'Thank you, you are kind.'

'But I don't know enough—I should know more about it—'

'Too much knowledge is a burden that can never be set down, Mrs Loukas. Believe me.'

'No need to call me Mrs Loukas, you're the only one who does. Just Tina, please, László. And tell me what happens when you hear more.'

He nods with his usual grave politeness, and leaves.

*

When I get home, Eliza is sitting in the lounge room chatting to Billie, who's stopped by after work.

I make us coffee. Billie takes the cup with a quick smile and says to Eliza, 'Jeez, *Charlotte?*'

'She's only here for a couple of days,' says Eliza. 'The new husband had to go to Canberra, some sort of government briefing on Vietnam—and she wanted to see me and Harry. He's too busy, but I told her you were around and she said she'd love to see you.'

'Love? Come on, Lizzie. She barely tolerates me.'

'Well, you're always teasing her, Bill, be fair.'

'But it's fun. And she gives as good as she gets.'

'So, I've rather lost track of Charlotte's doings,' I say. 'I only met her once, ages ago, when she was married to Harry—'

'Indeed,' says Eliza dryly.

'So then she ran off with Pete and had his child—sorry, Billie—'

'Nah, I'd dumped him by then.'

'Redeemed herself working with war refugees—'

'Yeah,' says Billie. 'She was okay then.'

'And got engaged to Stefan, Toby's boyfriend?'

'Didn't last,' says Billie. 'So she found herself a French general and is apparently as happy as a lark again.'

'My God,' I say. 'You lot were running round playing musical beds with each other while the war was on—'

'Mostly before then,' says Eliza, smiling. 'It *was* the thirties, Tina, and we were a lot younger.'

'I was still at school in the thirties,' I say, sipping my coffee. 'But I suppose my friends and I had our own fun during the war. Had to, didn't we? Not to think about all the horrible stuff.' For a moment I remember what László told me today and feel chilled.

'How's Harry?' says Billie.

'Bit tired,' says Eliza. 'The book with Ned is taking more time than they thought. Yvonne is having problems with the printing equipment too, but hopefully it'll soon be done.'

'And you, Lizzie?'

Eliza smiles and leans forward. 'Well, it's amazing, I'm actually much better. I've no idea why I was unhappy for so long after Leo was born, but the gloom started lifting a few months ago and now I'm a new woman. Harry says this sometimes happens after babies, it takes a while for the hormones to work properly again.'

'That's wonderful,' I say. 'You're certainly looking brighter.'

'You've got the strength to cope with Charlie then,' says Billie. 'When are you seeing her?'

'Tomorrow afternoon. And she's suggested we all go out that night too, when the new husband's back from Canberra,' says Eliza. 'But I don't know any nice places.'

'Of course you do,' I say. 'The fabulous Starlight Lounge. The food is fine and the band, I promise, is excellent. My treat, as long as I can come too.'

The evening we're going out I wear my New Look dress, the height of fashion. The shantung jacket curves over my bust into a tiny waist and the silk chiffon skirt flares out from my hips, *twenty-five* yards of swaying fabric in a deep, dark turquoise that suits me.

I twirl on my high heels in front of the mirror and smile. My hair is shorter now, a strawberry blonde halo that shows off my slim neck and a pearl necklace Nikos gave me (well, not real pearls but it still looks good).

Downstairs I find Eliza has just returned from her meeting with Charlotte, and is looking stunned. She says, 'Charlotte had an ulterior motive for seeing me today. *Naturally.*'

'And?'

Eliza rubs her face for a moment. 'You know, of course, she was still Harry's wife when she became pregnant to Pete and had Vivian. Well, out of some bizarre sense of shame or morality or Christ knows *what*, Charlotte secretly put *Harry's* name, not Pete's, on Vivy's birth certificate.'

'But everyone knows Pete is Vivy's father, don't they?'

'Yes, but it means Harry is legally the poor girl's father, not Pete. It's all come out now because Vivy needs a passport.'

'Can't the name on the certificate be changed?' I say.

'There's some tedious process of statutory declarations of fatherhood and non-fatherhood and dates and places of conception and all sorts of rigmarole. It can be done, but oh—that bloody, *bloody* woman! She wants *me* to give Harry the declaration form and get the whole crazy circus under way.'

I hear the car. Nikos is bringing Billie here after work so we can all go together, and soon they enter.

Billie is in her evening dress, the slightly-dated jade one, but still looks elegant. Nikos goes upstairs to get ready and Eliza tells Billie about today's meeting with Charlotte.

Billie collapses laughing onto the sofa. 'Jeez, she's *unbelievable!* Poor old Harry, poor old Pete! Just when the scandal had faded away Charlie revives it single-handedly. Wonder how much the new husband knows?'

'Everything, I expect,' says Eliza. 'She may have kept this little secret under her hat but she's usually brutally honest.'

'Emphasis on brutally,' says Billie.

Pearl shows us to the best booth in the house, which has a view of the whole golden-lit room. The band is playing softly on the small stage, lights glittering from their instruments and the sequinned trim on the drapes behind. A few people are circling on the dance floor but most are at their tables, eating, drinking and laughing.

I'm admiring Eliza's dress—olive silk with a high open collar, quietly sophisticated like Eliza herself—when a hush comes over the restaurant.

At the door are Charlotte and her new husband.

She's in cornflower blue satin with a cowl neckline, a tiny waist, and a long skirt like the bell of a tulip. Along with every other woman in the room I realise this is exactly what we'll be wearing in two years' time, when the local dressmakers catch up with Paris.

I don't feel precisely dowdy but perhaps a little deflated. Of course that's what I'm supposed to feel, so I sit up straight again. What else? Ripples of golden hair, diamond earrings, a chiffon wrap like a wisp of mist. I nod in grudging respect.

The man beside her? Khaki uniform, a chest of decorations and a kepi cap with gold stars and a strip of brocade. A good-humoured face, large nose, dark grey moustache, a trim frame. Charlotte appears to have done well for herself.

Pearl shows them to our booth (giving me a raised-eyebrows look of awe behind their backs). Billie gets up and hugs her and says, 'You amazing *cow*, Charlie, just look at you.'

'Don't ever join the diplomatic service, sweetie,' says Charlotte, kissing her on both cheeks in the French manner. 'You're looking remarkably well yourself.'

She gazes around—Eliza just nods coolly—and Billie says, 'You might remember Harry's sister Tina, and this is her husband, Nikos Loukas. You two, this is Charlotte and—?'

'My husband, *Général* Louis de Ferrier.'

He shakes hands with Nikos, then bows to Eliza and kisses her hand, then Billie's, then mine. Billie can hardly contain her glee.

The head waiter takes their coats and they settle beside us. I discreetly beckon Jimmy, who looks sophisticated in a new suit.

'Everyone, this is our host, Jimmy Kelso,' I say.

Nikos and Billie greet him—we've had a few cheerful evenings together here by now—and Eliza says, 'At last we meet. Tina's told me how happy she is working for you.'

'Couldn't do a thing without her.' Jimmy waves at the hovering waiter. 'You'll have some champagne on me, I hope. French, naturally.'

He grins at Charlotte and her eyes twinkling, she says, 'Won't you join us, Mr Kelso?' (How does she *do* that? Teasing, sexy, dry, all at once?)

'Ah, I don't want to break up the party—' he says, and Billie says, 'Come on Jimmy, sit down.'

He shakes hands with the general and Nikos, then takes the seat beside me. Hoping this would happen I'd told Pearl to set the table for seven. The waiter brings over the special menus with the chef's finest dishes.

Jimmy puts his head close to mine and murmurs, 'Only the best for your friends.' I breathe the light spice of his cologne.

We order food, then drink and chat. The general has just returned from some political conference in Canberra, then he and Charlotte are planning to set up house in Vietnam. I don't even know where that is, but I vaguely remember Harry talking about it.

'Smothering a minor insurgency against French authority,' says the general. 'An irritant. I have been posted to our headquarters in Saigon and Charlotte insists she will come.' They glance lovingly at each other. 'Of course she will be safe, but she may tire of the heat.'

'*Nous verrons, cheri.* We'll see,' says Charlotte. 'You know I always enjoy a challenge.'

Waiters bring our dishes and no one says much for a while apart from sighs of appreciation. When we finish, the general says, '*Extraordinaire.* I have not eaten so well in this country!'

'*Mon chef de cuisine, Gaston, est francais, mon général,*' says Jimmy. (I only did French at school but even to my ear he's fluent.) '*Un immigrant—un nouvel australien, comme ils disent.*'

'*Alors, garde-le heureux, mon brave,*' says the general. '*Il est superbe.*'

Jimmy nods, then turns to the rest of us and says, 'I've actually got an announcement I'd like to make, concerning wee Tina here.'

'What?' I say, surprised.

'Signed the papers today.' He lifts his glass to me. 'I'm going to open a club at Kings Cross—a jazz club, and I'm hoping Tina will do us the honour of being the manager.'

'A *jazz* club? Jimmy, really? You don't even *like* jazz!'

'Ah, but I like a business opportunity and this city is crying out for somewhere modern. You tell me often enough about this grand new music—well, let's see if you can make a go of it. To Tina's club.'

Everyone toasts me, and I feel like laughing and crying with joy.

*

The evening is a delight. Charlotte (I hate to admit) is infuriatingly magnificent, Nikos is open and warm, Billie can't stop laughing, and Jimmy glitters with sophisticated wit.

I suddenly remember what Harry told me about Vietnam, and say to the general, 'But isn't Vietnam one of those colonies that was promised its freedom? Why are the French hanging on to it when even the British have let India go?'

He says, eyes twinkling, 'Ah, should anyone ask my opinion—which they do not because I am a soldier—I would say, let those people decide their destiny for themselves. But I must do what my country tells me to do.'

Charlotte smiles at me. 'It's just a nine-day wonder, sweetie. The Reds haven't a chance.'

'They're independence fighters, Charlotte, *not* Reds,' says Eliza coolly. 'Unless you force them to be.'

Charlotte shrugs. 'Don't take everything so seriously, Eliza.'

'Serious consequences often flow from the *silliest* little actions though, don't they, dear?' says Eliza, finishing her glass of champagne, and holding it out. Nikos refills it.

Charlotte rolls her eyes and luckily the band starts to play. Jimmy stands and says to her, '*Madame, voulez-vous danser?*'

Charlotte stubs out her cigarette and says, 'God, yes,' and they go onto the floor. She dances well but nothing like Billie, who's saying something to Nikos about 'that *bloody* pontoon.'

The pontoon is central to some tedious saga at the flying boat base, so I mentally tune them out (an essential radio-operator skill) and, intrigued by their voices, listen to Eliza and the general.

'I believe I know an old acquaintance of yours,' the general says quietly. 'I was in London with the Free French and we had many friends in the government.'

'Who?' says Eliza.

He mentions a name and there's a silence. I glance over and Eliza is gazing at the general. He nods. 'I was asked to give you the regards of your old section as well.'

'Thank you,' says Eliza coldly.

There's a burst of laughter from Billie and Nikos so I miss a bit.

'—northern border,' says the general. '*Certainement*, the victory of the Red Chinese has changed everything.'

'No. I'm not interested, I used to work on the Japanese, not—'

'But you have a connection. I believe your aunt is part-Chinese.'

'I would never ask Izabel to do anything of that kind, *never*,' says Eliza in quiet fury. 'What they did with her reports on the Singapore Chinese! How they let her husband abuse her! Are you *mad*? Leave her out of it.'

'Laurence Kuan is alive,' says the general.

There is silence then Eliza says, 'Unlikely. How do you know?'

'He studied in Paris, we have sources. His disability kept him from the worst of the civil war, his grasp of strategy made him invaluable, and his friends now control Red China. Perhaps your aunt might wish to know her lover is alive? She may also wish to know we would be delighted to help her get in touch with him.'

Eliza stands abruptly and says, 'Could I have the house keys, Tina? I'm getting a taxi back. Please don't say a word.'

I hand her the keys and she leaves. The general harumphs, gazes into the distance and drinks. Charlotte and Jimmy return, laughing. Charlotte takes her husband's hand, saying charmingly, '*Maintenant, cheri, on va danser*,' and leads him away as the next song begins.

Nikos says, 'Tina, would you like to—'

'No, you and Billie go.' They need no encouraging, and I watch them on the floor: they move beautifully.

Jimmy pours us fresh drinks. He waves his glass at Nikos and Billie and says, 'Ah now, say if I'm speaking out of turn but—you don't mind? They make a handsome couple.'

'They do, but no, I don't mind. They're just friends, Jimmy.' I gaze at him. 'Like us.'

'Not precisely like us, *a chuisle*.'

I smile. 'What does "acushla" mean?'

'Come for a trot around the floor and I'll explain.'

*

It had happened so imperceptibly I didn't protect myself, though I knew from my friends how easy it was to yearn for someone else. And how bitterly they came to regret giving in to that yearning.

And yet, and yet.

Perhaps it's my powerful sense of smell. Scents intoxicate me like wine: oranges, sea spray, apples, silk, passionfruit, cut grass. With people it's a mixture of odours that becomes simply *them*.

I've always liked Nikos's smell of woodsmoke, oregano and cinnamon, warm and comforting. But he's become so familiar I hardly notice now.

But Jimmy: leather, lemon, tarragon? I don't know, but it's unfamiliar and disquieting. My breath becomes short when he stands near me; my neck flushes, my nipples tighten.

He watches me too I know, his face still.

Again, I hardly noticed how my awareness grew, but now, whenever he passes, my nostrils open to breathe him in and I cannot think for desire.

Desire is so *ridiculous*, I tell myself crossly over and over. Jimmy is a hood, cunning and ruthless. My husband is clever, educated, thoughtful. I must be insane.

To our friends we're a package, Tina-and-Nikos: although I'm perfectly aware many of the women prefer the Nikos side of the equation, and if I weren't with him they might not be quite such good friends.

If I weren't with him? How can I even *think* such a thing?

I married Nikos forever and this is just a bumpy patch, every marriage has them. Jimmy will pass out of my life one day as simply as he entered it and I will thank God I didn't do anything stupid.

And yet, and yet, how sweet it is to follow him to the dance floor, to feel his hand clasping mine and his arm on my waist, his face so close, warm with the scent of his skin. His rough male skin.

I take a breath. 'Jimmy, I can't thank you enough for the jazz club. I'll work my heart out.'

'I know you will. Would you like László to help you out with organising the bands and music too?'

'A good idea,' I say. 'But don't you need him here?'

Jimmy's mouth quirks. 'The Lounge is going mainstream now, the afternoon ladies prefer to be soothed, not challenged. So László will be free to help you with your wild modern tunes.'

'That'll be wonderful.' I smile. 'Jimmy, you spoke French so fluently to the general. How come?'

'Ah. My mother was French, you see. I learnt it as a kid but just as quickly forgot.' He hesitates. 'She died a few years ago—hadn't seen her in a decade. So I took a course to refresh my memories. Of her.' He take a breath. 'There now, *a chuisle*, you know something about Jimmy Kelso no one else even suspects.'

The music becomes slower and we move close, my head in the curve of his neck, my nipples against his chest.

'Tell me why you call me "acushla"?'

He murmurs, close to my ear, '*A chuisle* means *my pulse*.'

'A bit clinical,' I say with difficulty. I can feel his thigh against mine and his hardness on my belly, and I cannot even pretend I am not throbbing with yearning.

'*A chuisle mo chroí*. Pulse of my heart, Tina. Ah, grand romantic that is.' He moves his face against my hair, his breath warm.

'Jimmy, no,' I whisper.

He murmurs, '*I drew him down to me so he could feel my breasts all perfume yes and his heart was going like mad and yes I said yes I will Yes.*'

I shake my head, but it feels as if I'm caressing his face.

'James Joyce wrote that, mountain flower,' he says. 'The Yanks call it obscene but what would they know?'

I look up. His grey eyes are gentle, his brows dark with longing. I want, I so desperately want to kiss his mouth: but I pull away and he slowly lets me go.

The music ends and we walk in silence to the table. I can feel Billie's eyes on me.

'There you are, sweetie,' says Charlotte. 'We must be on a plane at some ungodly hour tomorrow so we really should go now. Thank you *so* much for organising this, and Jimmy—you've been the perfect host.'

'*La cuisine était magnifique*,' says the general, 'This is the only place in Sydney worth coming to.'

'*Formidable*,' says Jimmy. '*Au revoir, madame, mon général. Je vous souhaite un bon voyage.*'

We're going to drop Billie off at her flat in Kings Cross on the way home. She's in the front seat beside Nikos, where there's room for her long legs, but I don't mind sitting in the back.

She turns to me and says, 'Is Lizzie all right? She just disappeared. Did she feel unwell?'

'She took a taxi back to our place,' I say. 'I think it was more that she didn't like something the general said. But you'd better talk to her about it, I'm not sure what was going on.'

We drive along Victoria Street to see where Jimmy said my new jazz club will be. It's a drab building, but it's near two restaurants, a pub and some small shops, and there seem to be people about even at this time of night.

'Not a bad position, Tina,' says Nikos.

'And my flat isn't far away so you can call round,' says Billie.

'I can't believe it,' I say. 'What a responsibility!'

'You'll be great, Teen. You were a sergeant, remember, you can organise *anything*.'

We stop at Billie's flat, which is upstairs in an old terrace. I get out of the car to sit in the front seat and she gives me a hug, then bends down and waves to Nikos at the wheel and says, 'Night, mate. See you tomorrow.'

Nikos and I chat a little, but most of the drive home is quiet. I breathe deeply but can't seem to catch the scent of my husband.

I find myself wondering about his friendship with Billie. They're about the same age, they get on well, they have the same interests. Why wouldn't they be fond of each other? And if Nikos had someone else, if he let me go, then—

The earth seems to tilt, and I feel terror and ecstasy: and hope.

PART II. IMPROVISATION

10. Billie: A Long, Lazy Day

What the *hell* was going on last night? There were so many strange cross-currents I could hardly stay afloat, and it certainly wasn't the booze. I bite into my sandwich.

Usually I eat in the lunchroom with everyone else, but today I've come to a favourite spot, a jumble of rocks, good for listening to the lapping water. And thinking.

Out on Rose Bay I hear an engine start, then one of the gleaming white Sunderlands from Trans Oceanic Airways begins to move. It's the daily flight to Lord Howe Island, five hundred miles away.

The massive plane looks as if it couldn't possibly leave the water but it goes faster and faster in a rush of spray, then it hits the step, that clever bit of engineering that breaks the water's grip on the boat-like hull, and up and away it lumbers, the great handsome beast. *Ah.*

Do I wish I were at the controls? Yes, because that moment of soaring free into the sky compares to nothing else. And no, because I'm as strangely happy earthbound as I've ever been.

Of course this isn't a bad place to spend your time—blue water, sunny skies, beach on one side, park on the other, distant green headlands scattered with houses. Almost everyone is easy to get on with and I seem to fit in, hardly an oddity at all compared (for instance) to the woman ground engineer who's also a pilot, dance teacher and racing-car driver.

I work in a building near the terminal, relaying radio and teletype messages back and forth to the planes—weather reports, flight plans, course changes, storm warnings—an interesting, vital job.

I don't see Nikos that much, as he's usually out on the water or in his office, but if we're on the same shift he'll sometimes pick me up or drop me off at my flat in King's Cross. Nice not having to wait for the tram, especially when it's raining.

I like my place, the upstairs of a scruffy terrace house on the side of a hill. Mrs Beatty, a quiet soul with a small suspicious dog, lives on the ground floor. Sometimes she needs help to change a fuse or open a jar but mostly we keep to ourselves.

The place was owned during the war by some American big-wig whose wife insisted on indoor plumbing upstairs and down. Bless her, and bless the late Mr Beatty who bought the place cheap when the Americans went home.

At one end of my large lounge room is a bench with cupboards beneath, a stove and an old refrigerator, which Mrs Beatty optimistically calls a kitchen. The lounge room has long French doors that lead to a balcony looking over rooftops to the harbour and the famous bridge.

I keep a couple of wicker armchairs out there and love to watch the indigo waters or city lights or drifting rain. I sat there last night after the Starlight Lounge but couldn't make sense of anything.

Now, today, focus. What was going on?

The much-decorated *général* said something to upset calm Eliza, who went off like a rocket and disappeared. Self-centred Charlie wants to live in a war-torn speck of Asia, genial host Jimmy revealed he was a calculating sophisticate, and no-nonsense Tina made it obvious she was flirting with disaster.

When she returned from dancing with Jimmy, her pupils dilated, her walk languid, it was almost amusing the way she avoided his gaze. I've noticed before that partners in lust usually don't look at each other—perhaps they know it's too revealing.

Everyone else was picking up coats and shaking hands and kiss-kissing and *au revoir*-ing. Everyone but Nikos. I wonder—

A shadow falls across my lap and I look up. There's Nikos with his sandwich in greaseproof paper and two apples. He throws me one and says, 'Can I have a rock?'

'Whichever you like. All pretty comfy, except that one. Nasty bit of goods, too pointy.'

He sits down and says, 'So what do you think?'

'Um.' I take a bite of apple. 'About what?'

He lifts one eyebrow at me. 'The farce last night.'

He unwraps his sandwich and takes a mouthful, and after a moment says, 'Eliza went back to Newcastle first thing this morning. She was already furious with Charlotte about Vivy's birth certificate, but she was incandescent about something the general said. Maybe give her a ring and find out?'

'Spy on your behalf?'

'Something wasn't right, Billie. Didn't you feel it?'

'You sure it's only Eliza worrying you?' I say, then think, *no, stupid, stupid.*

He smiles dryly. 'It's all right, of course I realise. Fascinating Jimmy, glittering with gifts. Mesmerised Tina, wanting the world.'

'Perhaps she just enjoys her work?'

Nikos gives me a patient look and I shut up.

'Tina doesn't want to be married to me any more, that's been clear for some time,' he says. 'It took me a while to accept, but if she'd found a decent man I'd let her go. I'd have to. She's free to love whoever she wants.'

'I used to believe in free love when I was young,' I say.

'How did that go?'

'About as badly as you'd expect.'

Nikos smiles, then says, 'Trouble is, Jimmy's a bastard and he's going to hurt her.'

'Maybe you can't prevent it.'

'I have to try. I made a promise to protect her.'

'And if she doesn't want protecting?'

'Don't know. But I do know I'm not going to let myself be crushed.' He takes another bite of sandwich. 'Not this time.'

After a moment I say, 'This time?'

'When ... when my first wife died, I didn't cope very well.'

'What happened? You've never told me.'

'Ah.' Nikos sighs. 'Pneumonia, a few months after Stavros' birth.'

'Steve's birth,' I say.

'He was baby Stavros then.' Nikos smiles a little. 'Such a grin, all big eyes and gingery hair.'

'Gingery? But he's as dark as you now.'

'His mother had reddish hair.' He glances at me. 'Browner than yours, but she was tall like you. The night you arrived—it was a bit of a shock. You're nothing like her really, but for a moment—'

'Oh. *That's* why your eyes were so sad.'

'Were they?'

'Why I tossed the champagne at you, mate. Reminded me a bit too much of my own misery ...'

I stop. We sit in silence for a time.

Seagulls land nearby and gaze hopefully at the last of Nikos's sandwich, so he breaks it into pieces and throws them to the squabbling birds, and starts eating his apple.

'Anyway, I've decided I'm going to do everything I can to stand by Tina, whether or not she wants me to.'

I nod. 'Perhaps things'll work out.'

'You wild-eyed optimist,' he says. 'Now—apart from discovering what's going on with Eliza, there's something else I wanted to ask. An old friend, Cliff, is coming sailing with me tomorrow. He's about our age, widowed, very nice bloke. How would you like a long, lazy day out on *Wind Rose*?'

I laugh. 'Are you trying to find me a boyfriend?'

He shrugs. 'Don't know if you're already seeing someone—sorry if I've put my foot in it.'

I've been in Sydney for over a year. I had a fling with a man I met six months ago but it didn't last. Might be nice to consider a relationship, especially now I'm completely over Pete.

'Go out on a boat?' I say. 'Are you *mad*?'

'Suppose it wasn't the best idea.'

'Okay.'

On the tram home I think, Tina would have be crazy to let Nikos go. He's a good man, attractive, kind—half her friends would give anything for a chance with him, yet despite all the flirting aimed his way he never responds with anything more than warm politeness.

Sometimes I wonder why I'm not drawn to him myself. I've always liked dark-haired men, Pete for instance—slim, broad-shouldered, straight black hair.

Nikos's hair is charcoal going grey, curly if it wasn't cut short. His beard is thick and I suppose his chest is furry too. I had a lover once like that ... I drift off in a pleasant reminiscence and almost miss my stop.

Walking along the street I think, but that's interesting: even when we dance Nikos maintains that distance. He doesn't impose his presence and his hands don't wander, pleasantly or otherwise. It's a kind of generosity that lets me forget my usual wariness and simply trust in our shared rhythm.

Is it the hands then? I like men's hands. Pete's were long, finely-muscled, delightful; Nikos's are square, strong, brown, capable. Nothing wrong there, but I suppose I just don't *respond* to them. Or to him, it seems.

But he's a dear man, comfortable and funny and—I realise with surprise—probably the closest friend I've made since coming to Sydney. I'm very fond of Tina too, and keep thinking, no, no, what are you *doing*, Teen?

I've tried to suggest she's too caught up in her job, and she just laughs and says, 'That's hilarious coming from you, Billie!'

I open the front door. Mrs Beatty has left my mail on the side table—good, there's a letter at last from Vivy. All the fuss about her birth certificate made me realise I haven't heard from her for ages.

Upstairs I make myself a cup of tea and sit on the balcony and watch the sun setting behind pink clouds. I open Vivy's letter, wondering idly why she needed a passport in the first place.

Dear Billie,

Sorry I haven't written for a while. I didn't know what to say. Everything here is very strange and horrid. Remember Spencie, who used to mind me after Charlie went away? She died*, Billie. She had a cancer in her stomach. I've never known anyone who died before and I feel so sad.*

Another thing I don't know what to say about either, but Daddy and Janet are going to get married. I hope that doesn't make you unhappy, but I expect Daddy doesn't matter much to you by now. Janet is nice but rather strict, and I don't love her as much as Spencie or Charlie or you.

But now here's something that's a bit good and a bit bad.

Janet comes from south of Sydney, the Illawarra region (I think that's how you spell it), where her parents have a dairy farm. Her father is old and wants her home in Australia, and for her and Daddy to take over his farm. They talked about it lots and Daddy has decided to do it.

Billie, he's sold our farm on the Downs, my <u>home</u>! And when we go to Australia my pony Taffy will have to stay behind, and so will the ducks and sheep and all my friends from school and I'll never see any of them again. The only good thing is that you and I will meet again, but it's awful really, <u>enormously</u> bad and awful, and I'm so miserable.

When the fuss about my silly birth certificate happened I was glad because it delayed everything. But that will be fixed up soon and then we'll have to go. And it turns out Janet doesn't really like jazz (what a hypocrite!) and now she's nabbed Daddy she doesn't want to teach me any more.

So you can see why I haven't sent a letter for a while, and writing it all down hasn't made me feel any better either. But I think you and Aunty Eliza will remember Spencie from the old days and be sad for her at least (Janet only pretends to care).

That's all my news, Billie. I'm sorry it's not much fun.

Love, Vivy

Oh, you poor little kid. What a rotten thing for Pete to do, no matter how wonderful the hypocritical Janet. And kindly Mrs Spencer, dead? Yes, Eliza will be sad for her, and I will too. I re-read the letter.

Oh, Vivy. You think Pete doesn't matter much to me by now? Yet a knife seems to have entered my chest and your words are blurry.

But do I feel sorrow or anger?

Pete wouldn't even *consider* coming back to Australia for me when Vivy was small and the move simpler. But on behalf of this Janet cow he's quite happy to uproot his daughter at an age when (thinking back) everything is at its most painfully overwrought.

Ah, Pete. You could be a stubborn bastard, but in the old days you were never careless with Vivy's feelings. So on the whole I'm feeling rage rather than regret. Good.

Wind Rose is moored a few hundred yards from the flying boat base and Nikos rows us out in a dinghy. I look back to the shore and think how pleasant it is to be here in the sunshine, not the office. Today is Saturday so the base is quieter, but some staff still have to be there every day.

We climb aboard and I sit down abruptly when everything rocks.

'Had much to do with boats, Billie?' says Cliff, sitting opposite.

'I know they have port and starboard sides,' I say. 'And sterns and bows, but that's about it.'

'Covers the essentials,' says Cliff, and we smile. He's nice enough, pleasant-looking.

Nikos, who's up on the cabin-top doing something with ropes, says, 'You'll know a lot more than that before the day's over.'

'Threat or promise?' I say.

'Both,' he says, leaping down with surprising agility. 'Within hours you'll be shamelessly flinging around terms like halyard and vang and topping lift.'

'You're clearly making those up. And I didn't realise shame was involved in this long, lazy day.'

'Absolutely,' he says, grinning. 'If you can't tell me the difference between a cringle and a grommet by the time we get back, you'll have to swim to land.'

'Hey, I can swim.'

'But you'll be so exhausted from the long, lazy day,' he says. 'To say nothing of the sharks that feed in the dusk near the shore.'

'Interesting. I don't recall you mentioning the sharks before.'

He laughs. 'Shark Island's just out there, so I didn't think I had to.'

Nikos walks around on the side of the boat (there's probably a name for that) to the rear, oops, the stern.

He unties the ropes, steps down into the open section where Cliff and I are sitting (probably a name for that too), and does something mysterious with switches, and I hear a motor start up.

'You've got an *engine?*' I say. 'Sorry, isn't that cheating? I thought yachting was about braving the elements, catching the wind, spray on your face, and other cliches I try hard to forget.'

'Of course I've got an engine,' says Nikos. 'Think I'm mad? Oh right, yes you do.'

We motor until we're away from the flying boat alighting paths, then Cliff and I undo the biggest sail and laughing, haul it up. After that we tackle a little triangular one at the front and that's fun too.

Then the yacht leans over with the breeze, Nikos switches off the motor and suddenly, apart from soft splashings along the hull, everything is silent.

I sit at the bow, the sea all greens and blues, and take a deep breath. Nikos and Cliff chat quietly while I watch the water, mesmerised, and feel completely pleased for no reason at all.

Cliff takes the tiller as we sail around a headland and Nikos comes forward and squats lightly beside me. He holds out a jar with reddish ointment in it.

'Use some of this RPV stuff—it'll stop your skin getting too much sun. It was standard on the life rafts during the war, and my crew used it too.'

I'm wearing a short-sleeved shirt and capri pants, so I rub some of the jelly on my exposed arms, face and feet, and it feels okay.

We sail on. Beaches, headlands, rock platforms and houses come into view, slowly and interestingly, then pass out of sight behind us.

Every now and then Nikos or Cliff pulls on various ropes to change the angle of the big sail to catch the wind, and I have to duck my head so the wooden boom doesn't knock it off. (I had no idea sailing was such a *fussy* sort of activity.)

Time passes peacefully, then we reach an almost hidden inlet with a small crescent of sand at the base of a golden cliff. The water is a pale glassy-green and I can see to the pebbles on the sea-floor.

When there's only six feet or so free under the boat we lower the sails, crumpling like concertinas, then Nikos lets down the anchor.

I put on my old swimsuit in the cabin below—my sensible blue one-piece—then the men get changed too and we jump into the delightfully lukewarm water and splash about.

We paddle to the small beach, perhaps fifty yards away, and sit in the sunny shallows as wavelets gurgle in and out and around us.

After a while Cliff says, 'Magical spot, mate. How'd you find it?'

'Just pottering around over the years.'

'And come on, who's this Rose—an old flame?'

'Sorry?' says Nikos.

'*Rose*. Wind Rose. Named your boat after her.'

'Oh,' says Nikos. 'Means a compass, Cliff. Not a person.'

Cliff winks. 'Whatever you say, mate.'

Nikos pauses. 'All right, lunch? Last one back has to serve it up.'

I put on a burst of speed swimming to the boat and Nikos isn't far behind, then Cliff arrives panting, but we all help out with the delicious lunch.

Then we sit in the cockpit and feast on Greek delicacies wrapped in vine-leaves, fresh buttery bread with ham and cheese, glasses of beer, and for dessert, sweet soft peaches, black Muscat grapes, and dripping red plums.

'My God, these plums are magnificent,' I say, wiping juice inelegantly from my mouth. 'The family warehouse?'

'Nothing but the best from Loukas Foods,' Nikos says.

'Business still going well?' asks Cliff.

'My father says they're expanding again this year, so I expect so. I stay out of it as much as I can or it'd take over my life. Greeks are famous for their produce, but I'd prefer to be famous for something else—my beautiful yacht for instance.'

'Well, you got my vote,' I say.

'A convert to the maritime life already?' says Cliff, chuckling.

'I'm an easy sell. Sunshine, water, good food. That'll do it.'

'Easy sell? Had to practically drag you out here,' says Nikos laughing, and turns to Cliff. 'Billie much prefers planes.'

'Oh, air hostess, were you?' says Cliff.

With a jolt I realise I don't want to explain myself again. Don't want to see the disbelief or dislike or outright fear at the thought of a woman working in a *man's job*. I'm so bloody sick of it.

'Got any more of that anti-sunburn stuff, Nikos?' I say. 'Some on my back, if you don't mind.'

Nikos rubs the jelly on my shoulders and back then I put it on my chest and arms and legs. He offers the jar to Cliff, who shakes his head and says, 'No, don't need it.'

'Here, Nikos,' I say. 'I'll do your back.' As I'm applying the jelly I think, Yeah, he is as hairy-chested as I thought, but his skin's nicely smooth and brown. I notice Cliff's skin, in contrast, is going an ominous shade of pink.

'Should do your shoulders, Cliff, or at least put on a hat,' says Nikos. 'Feet can burn as well.'

'She'll be right, mate.'

We sip beer and relax in silence in the seating area, which I've been informed is called the cockpit, though it's not like any cockpit I've ever known.

I gaze at our feet on the deck: mine with their jaunty scarlet toenails, Nikos's strong brown competent ones (absurd—how can feet look competent?) and Cliff's, which are going a horrible red.

'Cliff, you *really* need to protect your feet,' I say.

'Now, now, Billie, no one likes a girlie who nags,' he says, laughing. 'Want another beer?'

'Yeah, sure.' Okay mate, suffer.

We go for a second swim then get changed, raise the anchor, haul the canvas, and set off home in the golden afternoon. There isn't much wind, but we're not in a hurry.

The sun is setting by the time we near the base, then we wait for a time because one of the Solents from Tasman Empire Airways is about to arrive.

The control launches have set out the flares, four golden lamps marking the rectangle of the mile-long landing channel and, along one side, a row of eight green lights gently rising and falling in the pink rippled reflections of the sunset.

Nikos leans on the tiller, his eyes amused, and says, 'Got a friend at a base in Africa who told me they do their flarepath with lamps on small boats, but one night a storm sank some of the boats. So a bloke took a signal-lamp out on a launch and stood there flashing in Morse, *I'm a flare … I'm a flare …*'

I burst into laughter, and Cliff says puzzled, 'What's so funny?'

'It's just—if he already *had* a lamp … nah. Don't worry about it,' I say, wiping my eyes.

We hear the drone of the flying boat in the distance, then see it gliding pale above the water, closer and closer to the surface till it touches with a wave of spray, sparkling in the last light of the sun.

It passes behind the green flares, one by one, then gradually slows and comes wallowing to a halt, as wavelets expand and subside on the serene harbour.

There's always a little tension in any landing, and Nikos and I glance at each other with quick smiles of relief.

'Big bugger,' says Cliff, who's had rather a lot of beer by now. 'Where's it from?'

'That's *Awatere*, Auckland run,' I say.

'No, really, Nikos mate, where's it from?'

'It's *Awatere* from Auckland,' says Nikos dryly.

'Oh, yeah,' says Cliff, 'Secretary here, aren't you, Billie? You must pick up all sorts of things.'

I laugh. 'Listen, fella. Next time you're flying in a storm and your poor pilot doesn't know whether to go down, up or around, comfort yourself with the thought I'm the *secretary* on the other end guiding him.'

'They wouldn't—oh, pulling my leg,' says Cliff. 'Ah, when will we land? Not feeling too well.'

'You've probably got sunstroke,' says Nikos. 'And you really should see a doctor about your burns, they're going to be bad.'

We clean up and secure *Wind Rose* (Cliff watching morosely) and Nikos rows us back to shore. We drop Cliff off at his hotel, suggesting again he see a doctor, and drive on to Kings Cross.

'I never did figure out that whole cringle and grommet thing,' I say. 'Maybe next time.'

Nikos parks the car in front of my place. 'So you reckon there'll be a next time?'

'As long as Cliff isn't crewing. You're a dreadful matchmaker, you know that?' I say. 'But look, if you've got time, come up for a chat—something I'm dying to tell you. Bring the box with the food too, I want more of that amazing fruit.'

'All right, one glass,' says Nikos. 'Steve's out with his mates and Tina has some event at the restaurant, so I can stagger in late if I want.'

'Well,' I say, pouring wine, 'I rang Lizzie and she said what *really* happened with the general. But first you need some background.'

I hand Nikos a glass and sit down in the other armchair. The evening is heavy with the day's warmth, stars are wavering through the haze, and lights are glowing gold along the Harbour Bridge.

'You know Lizzie's aunt is the actress Izabel Malory?' I say.

Nikos nods. 'She was very good. Whatever happened to her?'

'Had to retire after her rotten husband Felix revealed she was actually part-Chinese.'

'Bastard.'

'So they went to live in Hong Kong, where Izabel fell in love with a man called Laurence Kuan. He was helping the Reds fight the Japanese, but was ambushed.'

'The Reds? You mean the communist Chinese?'

'Yeah. They were the only forces trying to stop the Japanese invading China.'

'And if they *had* been stopped then?' Nikos says slowly. 'Might have saved a few lives.'

'Lost bloody opportunities, eh?' I say. 'Anyway, Izabel was told Laurence was dead, so she adopted his young daughter, Nancy.'

Nikos sits back, smiling. 'This is amazing, Billie, but what on earth does it have to do with Eliza and the general?'

I sigh. 'Jeez, I used to think I wasn't interested in all this political argy-bargy either, but nowadays I'm less of an idiot.'

'All right, tell me at your own pace, I'll probably catch up one day,' he says. 'In the meantime, please feel free to refresh my glass.'

I pour us both more wine.

'Patience, *please*. So a few years later, Lizzie and Harry and Izabel's family were all in Singapore when it was invaded. Harry was captured, Felix got away, but Lizzie, Izabel and Nancy were left behind in the mess, with the looters and deserters—'

I stop. Don't go into the details, not fair to Izabel.

'Anyway, after a horrible time they got back to London. Felix was still a bastard, but he finally shot himself, much to everyone's relief.'

Nikos smiles and sips his wine.

'Then Izabel discovered that Felix had kept a letter hidden from her for six years. Laurence had written saying he *didn't* die in the ambush—he'd gone off to fight for the Red Chinese instead. But by then it was 1945 and there hadn't been another word from him.'

'Did she think he was dead?'

I nod. 'Seemed pretty likely. But she and Nancy still went back to Hong Kong, hoping to find out more when the civil war ended— and now it just has, of course, with the Reds winning.'

'But how does *mon général* come into it?' says Nikos.

'Well, the French are pretty cranky because the Chinese plan to help the *Vietnamese* rebels fight for their independence.'

'Aha, a connection at last!' says Nikos. 'You realise I'm half dead of suspense by now?'

'So the general told Lizzie that Laurence Kuan is alive, and the French'd be simply delighted to help Izabel contact him again. But *Lizzie* is convinced they want to use her aunt to get to Laurence, then force him to spy on his friends in the Red government.'

'But how could he force him?' says Nikos.

'Threats to Izabel and Nancy. Lizzie saw it often during the war.'

'Okay, I can see why she'd walk out furious.'

'Yes and no. She also had to leave before she laughed in his face.'

'Laughed?' says Nikos.

'Because the day before she'd received an ecstatic letter from Izabel. In the chaos of victory, Laurence had managed to get himself *out* of mainland China. He's back living with Izabel in Hong Kong and determined to stay there, so the French now have no hold over either of them.'

Nikos grins. 'Good job.'

'So was the story worth the wait?'

'It certainly was,' he says. 'And I'm glad it worked out so well for them both.'

'Me too.'

We finish our wine, then I say, 'Coffee, mate?'

'Yes, please.' Nikos yawns and stretches. 'Told you a long, lazy day'd be exhausting.'

Nikos is asleep, breathing deeply, when I return with a tray of coffee. I put it down, pour myself a cup, and sit back and watch the night sky.

Nikos murmurs and I look over at him. He has one arm above his turned-away head, his legs stretched out. I smile again at the memory of *'I'm a flare ... I'm a flare ...'*

He's wearing his moccasins now, but it wasn't really absurd to think of his bare feet as competent. In fact his whole frame radiates a sense of calm capability—his hips, his hands, his shoulders, even his dark beard.

Beards are less common now since the war, but I like the gleam of his teeth when he grins, his brows fierce, his eyes creased with pleasure. The hair at his temples is grey and his forehead is lined, and I wonder what sort of young man he was.

Probably quiet and intense and a little shy, like his son. But I'll never know that Nikos, and he'll never know me as I was either—lithe, pretty (although I couldn't see it), convinced I could take on the world. And that's all in the past now too.

Nikos sighs and turns his head to rest in the crook of his elbow, his sleeping face towards me. I admire his unfairly long eyelashes, his strong nose, his mouth curved in the trace of a smile, his lips, sculpted and wry ...

And deep within my chest my heart halts: and floods.

Then I know—every nerve of my body knows—what I've been denying.

Nikos opens his eyes and we gaze wordlessly at each other.

11. Yvonne: Different Skies

'Such a lovely night—can you smell the frangipani? A good omen,' I say to Klara, as we walk up the steep narrow road to Darling Street.

'I hope you are correct, Yvonne.'

'You look beautiful, you know that?'

Klara smiles. 'Eliza gave me this gown years ago. Silk velvet, and such a dashing crimson.'

'It feels soft, Klara,' says Claire. 'Like a kitten's fur.'

'Your dress is lovely too, darling,' I say.

'I know,' says Claire. 'Blue suits me and also makes me happy.' She gazes critically at me. 'Your hair is coming out of its bun again, Yvonne, but you look pretty as well.'

'Aren't we a handsome family, then?' I say. Ahead of us is the printery with its new sign, Watters Press, which still makes my heart lift. 'The lights are on—Reg must be here already.'

Reg Frisket greets us at the door. 'Just doing some final touches.'

The printery building has a large meeting room with a high ceiling and brass chandeliers. The windows glimmer in swirls of stained glass and the panelled walls gleam amber. Reg has pushed the big table to one side to make space, and set out chairs in rows.

'I can smell oranges,' says Claire.

'Furniture wax, princess,' says Reg.

'Oh, you've got the drinks trolley ready,' I say. 'Thank you, Reg.'

'Polished the glasses too,' he says. 'And there's a stack of books for the authors to sign.'

'You've thought of everything!' I say.

'My job,' says Reg. 'Foreman's got to be responsible and you two haven't had a spare moment.'

I sit down, overcome. 'Oh, I *know*. We've been talking and ringing and writing letters to columnists, critics, editors, everyone! I do hope we get a good turn-out.'

'Claire, here is some lemonade—Reg, please get yourself a drink, and this is for you,' says Klara, handing me a white wine. 'It is time for us all to relax.'

Reg pours himself a beer and gazes around with pleasure. He's a good foreman. When I bought the printery one of the workers left, muttering he wasn't taking no orders from no bloody woman, but the others stayed on, and we're blessed with clever Reg, apprentice Tom, and elderly compositor Mr Wilkins. I help them out too, when things are busy.

Nikos and Tina come in carrying covered plates. 'Brought you some canapés,' says Nikos.

'Wonderful!' I say. 'Better than our boring old cheese and biscuits.'

Tina is in a grey silk dress, flattering and expensive, with a heavy gold necklace. She's so much more *glossy* than the frustrated housewife we first met two years ago.

'Not late, am I?' says a voice.

'Billie, come in,' says Klara. 'Of course you are not late.'

Billie nods at everyone and says, 'Are the famous authors here yet?' She's in baggy slacks and an unusually drab shirt.

'They are getting a taxi from Central and should be here at any moment,' says Klara. 'Come and have a drink.'

Billie moves to the trolley and pours a glass of wine, but as she turns she and Nikos almost bump into each other. After some apologising and side-stepping she comes and sits with me.

'Cheers, Yvie,' she says, clinking my glass. 'You've done well.'

'Thanks, Billie. I'm worn out, but we're so happy the book's finished at last.'

I think, that's odd, her eyes are as subdued as her clothes. I go to say something, but hear Harry's voice, then he enters with Eliza and Ned, and the moment is lost in greetings. Eliza is glamorous in a flared golden evening coat.

'Did you bring that boy with the *slippery* eyes?' Claire asks Harry.

He laughs. 'No, Jessie's minding him.'

'Oh, is Mum over her cold now?' says Tina. 'She wasn't well when I rang the other day.'

'Much better,' says Harry. 'She sends you and Nikos her love.' Tina smiles and glances at Nikos, but he's staring at his glass.

Three or four other people arrive, friends of Tina's. I notice Klara looking at her wristwatch and check mine. We gaze at each other. Fifteen minutes past the starting time.

'Is that real gold?' says Claire pointing at Tina's necklace.

Tina smiles and says, 'Certainly is, young lady.'

'Nikos must be very rich to buy that,' says Claire.

'Oh,' says Tina casually, 'No, it's a gift from where I work.'

Nikos turns to the pile of books on the side table, but Billie is already there, flipping pages, so he quickly moves away again. They don't look at each other—in fact, they barely even said hello earlier. What on earth's going on?

Klara checks her watch again, and I do too. Thirty minutes past our start time. Oh dear.

'Have you been out on *Wind Rose* in this lovely weather, Nikos?' says Eliza. 'And tell me—despite all her protestations, is Billie a good sailor?'

'I've been yachting a few times,' says Nikos. 'But no, I think once was enough for Billie.'

'Bit hectic at work, Lizzie, not much time,' says Billie. 'Bought myself a car too, sporty little number, pretty useful.' She turns to me. 'What's happening, Yvie? Thought this started at seven?'

'We've been waiting for a few people,' I say. 'From the newspapers.'

'But it's past eight.'

'So it is.'

'Oh, hell,' says Billie. 'Bastards couldn't be bothered?'

I nod and pick up one of the books. We *did* do it well, I tell myself. The hard cover is dark teal linen, the title stamped in copper. Once we decided to concentrate on Ned's poetry alone, we added more of his and Harry's work, so it's a good size.

I look up and nod in resignation to Klara. She goes to the front, a pale-haired pixie in a shimmering crimson dress, and taps a spoon on her glass.

'Good evening,' she says calmly to the two-thirds-empty room. 'I wish to present a new book from the Watters Press, *Poems of Rage: a Memoir* by Edward Quest and Harry Bell. The searing clarity of Ned's words and Harry's art offers their personal perspective on historic times. This book owes everything to the tireless Yvonne Watters, who brought this printery into the twentieth century—'

Reg calls out, 'Hear, hear.'

'—and our foreman, Mr Reg Frisket, a source of strength and advice since we began this odyssey eighteen months ago.'

'Thank *you*, Reg,' I say and lead the applause.

Klara continues, 'This unique creation was forged from pain, yet begins and ends in peace. I give you *Poems of Rage.*'

We clap again, then Ned shyly waves Harry forward.

Harry says, 'Our thanks to Klara, who conceived of the book and wrote a generous introduction. Both Yvonne and Klara encouraged us when our spirits faltered, as they often did on re-examining times that may be in the past, but will probably never be truly behind us. So despite my often-expressed reluctance—'

Nikos says, 'Often and loudly expressed, mate,' and there's a ripple of laughter.

Harry smiles. 'Despite that, a fine book has been produced. Also, I could not have coped without the support of my wife Eliza, who has dealt with more in our lives than was reasonable or fair.'

He gazes at Eliza, seated in her golden evening coat, and she nods with a wry smile.

We applaud, then Edward and Harry sit and sign their book, and the few people present buy copies. Tina says brightly, 'Well, I *must* have several—for us, and Nikos's parents, Steve's school library, oh, and László from work wants one as well.'

After a time Tina's friends leave, and Reg says quietly to me, 'Valma's got a bit of a do on tonight—'

'You've helped so much, Reg, go. We can tidy up tomorrow. Thank you again.'

The rest of us eat canapés—there are plenty left over—and drink wine. Plenty there too.

Ned sighs. 'I really should be used to it by now ...'

'The world's indifference?' says Eliza. 'It's so unfair.'

'Not *one* person from the newspapers or radio?' says Tina. 'That's shocking. I'll have a chat to Jimmy and see if—'

Billie laughs. 'Not even Jimmy could nobble this particular horse, Teen.' She empties her glass and says, 'Gotta go. Anyone want a lift?'

I say, 'We'll walk home after we lock up, but thanks, Billie.'

She waves and abruptly leaves. Eliza and I glance at each other.

'Now, you're all invited to our place tomorrow for afternoon tea, to relax at last,' says Tina. 'So let's go home. You Newcastle folk must be exhausted.'

'God, yes,' says Eliza. She stands and her evening coat falls open and I see what its well-cut folds have been obscuring. She wraps the coat around herself, and gazes at me and shrugs.

Tina and Nikos's backyard has trees and flowers growing along the fence and they've put an old table, seats and deck-chairs beneath a pergola that's covered in a rampant grapevine. Today is another warm spring day, so it's perfect to sit in the dappled shade.

'Coffee, tea, how many?' asks Tina. She returns with a tray of cake, plates and cutlery, while Nikos brings another tray with cups, saucers, tea and coffee pots.

Ned adjusts his glasses. 'Strawberry and cream sponge—what a treat, Tina!'

Nikos pours and hands the cups around. 'Where's young Claire this afternoon?' he says.

'Visiting a kindergarten friend,' says Klara. 'She's had enough of grown-up parties for now.'

'And Eliza?' I ask.

'Resting,' says Tina.

'No, I'm here now,' says Eliza sleepily, coming through the kitchen door. 'What a lovely day.'

She sits down in a deck-chair, her cotton dress revealing her rounded belly.

'Have some cake,' says Tina, passing plates around, and we eat.

'Delicious,' says Harry.

'Mmm,' says Ned, cream on his lips.

Klara says, 'So, Eliza, are you feeling well? When is the baby due?'

'Yes, I'm fine,' Eliza says calmly. 'March next year.'

'Did you plan this baby or was it a surprise?' says Klara. 'I recall you saying one child was enough for you.'

'I did, didn't I?' says Eliza. 'Yes, something of a surprise.' She picks up her tea and sips.

'Leo is very happy at the thought of a brother or sister,' says Harry, gazing at his plate.

'Well, congratulations from us,' I say. 'That's—marvellous.'

Harry nods but he and Eliza don't look at each other.

Piano music flows from the house. Tina says, 'Steve's got an examination in a few weeks. Working surprisingly hard for it too.'

'We've never seen him as focussed as this,' says Nikos. 'László's been a very good influence.'

'László?' asks Ned.

'Steve's music teacher,' says Tina. 'My right-hand man at the club.'

'Your jazz club sounds terribly avant-garde,' says Ned. 'Do people have to wear berets and black roll-neck jumpers to be admitted?'

Tina smiles. 'Most people who like jazz in Sydney are rather unfashionable young men, although I see a few beatnik beards here and there. Our audiences are growing, but I wouldn't say the club's been an overnight success. Lot of hard work involved.'

'What did you end up calling it, Tina?' says Eliza.

'We had so many ideas, but I liked Tempo, so that's it.'

'Tempo,' says Ned thoughtfully. 'Time *and* rhythm—very nice. But is it true that clubs like yours aren't licensed?'

'Yes. The alcohol laws in Sydney would baffle anyone sane.' Tina says. 'Technically you can't get a drink, although we serve a lot of remarkably fortified tea when the police aren't around.'

'Doesn't that make you nervous?' I say. 'What if they raid you?'

'We pay them off, Yvonne, just like everyone else.' Tina's grey eyes are shrewd.

Nikos abruptly stands and takes the tea and coffee pots back to the kitchen. When he returns with refills, Harry says, 'Where's Billie on this lovely day? Working?'

Nikos says nothing, pouring fresh cups for everyone.

After a moment Tina says, 'We don't actually see a lot of her right now. She's been keeping to herself for—oh, the last six or seven months. I have no idea why.' She laughs. 'I reckon someone made a pass at her when they went sailing—'

'Enough, Tina,' says Nikos.

'More cake, anyone?' says Tina coolly.

Eliza says, 'Look, there *is* something Billie's probably unhappy about. You all know she and my brother Pete used to be close. Well, he and Vivy and his new wife Janet are coming to Australia to run a farm in the Illawarra.'

'What is the Illawarra?' says Klara.

'A region fifty miles south of Sydney,' says Harry. 'Apparently it's Janet's family property. Good land, so they should do well.'

'Has Pete *sold* the Hampshire farm?' I ask, and Eliza nods. 'I never thought he'd leave there. Poor Vivy, she loved the place.'

'We all did,' says Eliza. 'My darling grandfather left it to Pete, and I stayed there as a child. It was simply beautiful.'

'So that's why Billie's down in the dumps,' I say. 'Is she going to see them when they get here?'

Nikos is gazing at the trees along the fence, his face still.

'She'll see Vivy I expect, but probably wants to avoid Pete, might reopen old scars.'

'Was Vivy's birth certificate debacle finally resolved?' says Tina.

Harry groans. 'Dear God, finally. Statutory declarations regarding Charlotte's indiscretions were signed, sealed and delivered by both me and Pete, and finally His Majesty's Government was persuaded that Pete was the real father and issued Vivy with a passport.'

I laugh. 'How's Charlotte going over in Vietnam?'

'We get the odd letter,' says Eliza. 'She calls it charming, so I'm sure she hates it. But I don't care. She and her interfering general are out of our lives, and out of Izabel's too.'

Eliza smiles. 'Oh, and some good news from Hong Kong—Izabel and Laurence were quietly married a week ago.'

'What about Nancy?' I say. 'She must be all of twenty-one by now.'

'Izabel says she's not sure what to do with herself,' says Eliza. 'I'd hoped we could visit them, but that's unlikely, with …' she waves her hand at her belly.

Harry clears his throat. 'I believe the only real problem they have is with Laurence's health. His thigh was badly broken when he was shot some years ago, and it's never properly healed.'

'Oh?' says Ned. 'What's the medical opinion?'

'Not promising, according to the local doctors.'

'Tell them to send the X-rays to me if they want,' says Ned. 'I might see some possibilities.'

'Of course—you are a *bone* surgeon, Ned,' says Klara. 'I always think of you as a poet.'

'He's a bit of a poet in the operating theatre too.' Harry nods. 'Good idea.'

'Might be my only chance to meet the amazing Izabel Malory,' says Ned, laughing. 'Or no, she'd be Izabel Kuan now, wouldn't she? Still amazing.'

Eliza goes inside, and a little later I follow her and wait in the kitchen. She comes out of the bathroom saying, 'Not much fun having somebody tangoing on your bladder.'

'Klara used to say that when she was having Claire too. Eliza, are you all right—really?'

She runs water into a glass and takes a drink, and sighs.

'No, I suppose not.' She faces me. 'Six months ago everything was going so well, Yvie. My depression had lifted and I was really enjoying life with Leo. We were planning to visit Izabel and Laurence, and doing the book seemed to be helping Harry with his memories. I had high hopes for us all.'

She sits down beside me at the kitchen table. 'Then I became pregnant. Christ, I'm forty-*three*.'

She rubs her eyes. 'I don't know how I'll cope. Harry doesn't understand. It's the return of the greyness I'm terrified of, the *unfeeling*. The sadness so deep my whole life seems nothing else.'

I touch her hand. 'I'm sorry, love. We'll help however we can.'

There are tears on Eliza's face. 'We wanted a child so much and couldn't, and it made me sad for years. Then Harry came back from the war and I conceived and thought our problems were over. It's so unfair. I was young once, then my whole life was swallowed up by that *fucking* war, and now I'm old and broken.'

'Oh, Eliza.' I put my arm around her as she sobs.

After a time she gets a hanky from her pocket, saying, 'Came prepared. I've been embarrassing myself constantly. Bloody sick of it.' She wipes her eyes and sighs. 'Thanks, Yvie. Ah well, it'll all be over in a few months. And maybe … who knows? Other mothers tell me it's different with every child.'

She gets up and splashes water on her face at the sink, gives me a rueful smile and goes out to join the others. I sit and thoughtfully wind my hair back into its bun.

Nikos comes to the door with a stack of dirty plates, but can't get past the fly-screen with his hands full, so I get up and hold it open for him. We've had an easy rapport ever since we met, probably through our shared friendship with Billie, and I say, 'How're you going, Nikos? Haven't said much today.'

'Could hardly get a word in edgewise.' He puts the plates in the sink and runs water on them.

After a moment I ask, 'So—why was Tina needling you about Billie?'

'Guilt, probably.'

'Nikos.'

'Yes?'

'Guilt? What the hell?'

He turns to me. 'I don't know, Yvonne She spends most of her time with Jimmy.' He rubs his head. 'And given all those costly trinkets, he's either wildly appreciative of her skills or he's more involved with her than I'd prefer.'

'Okay,' I say. 'But why was Tina on about *Billie?*'

There's a long silence.

'Nikos?'

He says haltingly, looking down, 'I think ... I think Billie and I both recognised we were spending too much time together, more than was wise for two lonely people. So we stopped.'

'Oh, *Nikos*. And Tina assumes there's more to it than that?'

'That's how it usually is in her charming low-life world.'

'Don't you miss Billie, though?'

'Of course I do. But anything else could mean hurting her. She's got friends at work, and I hear through the grapevine she's seeing someone, so—' He shrugs hopelessly.

In the mild night Klara and I walk through the streets to our home near the scented green park.

'Everyone's in such *trouble,*' I say. 'Who could have imagined Eliza and Harry barely speaking? Billie and Nikos no longer friends? Tina discarding her marriage for feckless Jimmy?'

'Vivy dragged away from home?' says Klara sadly. 'Yvonne and Klara unable to sell the book that has consumed eighteen months of their life? Poor Charlotte forced to live in a war-torn Asian country?'

I laugh. 'Sympathy for Charlotte may be too much. But I suppose we can be glad Izabel is happy with Laurence, and young Steve is playing the music he loves. And Claire is content, and we have a business that will succeed, one day at least.'

'Speaking of which, Reg Frisket told me he has an idea that might help us sell the book. So all is not lost,' says Klara. 'Let us run!'

Hand-in-hand we dash along the narrow footpaths and through winding streets until, laughing, we reach the park.

'See, the first stars are out,' says Klara, pointing, 'and soon the moon will rise. Remember when we wished to live beneath different skies? Now we do, with a home that makes me so happy. And Yvonne—my nightmares have stopped.'

'My God,' I say. 'I've been so busy, so tired, so caught up, I didn't *notice*. Is it true?'

'I no longer wake up sobbing and you, my love—I clearly see—are no longer afraid.'

On Monday, we meet Reg in the office. Klara says, 'Now, what is your idea, Mr Frisket?'

'Well, as I once mentioned, Frisket is my *nom de plume*, although I don't actually have a *plume*.'

'Oh?' says Klara.

'Had a good job in the Education Department once, but blotted my copybook. A student, lovely lass, seventeen, we got fond of each other. Couldn't last of course, but I was a lot stupider than I realised. Poor girl.' He sighs. 'Well, the nipper was adopted out and the lass never spoke to me again and I reckoned I'd die of shame. So I hid away and took a new name.'

'Ah,' says Klara.

'Then the war began, everything changed. You had your mates, you were a Digger. You saw things, did things, suffered things.' He glances at his walking stick. 'But the army's a small world. Kept running into blokes I'd known before and we were all different by then. Rebuilt our friendships, and afterwards—we kept in touch.'

'Mmm,' says Klara.

'*Well*,' says Reg, leaning forward. 'The Department's always on the lookout for new books for the senior students, and a mate of mine does some of that looking out for them. He did his own hard time in a camp, and I reckon if he saw *Poems of Rage* he'd be knocked sideways. And—you never know—Ned and Harry's book might end up on the curriculum, and *then* we'd sell a few copies.'

'*Oh!*' says Klara.

12. Harry: Duty

It's only five o'clock when I leave the hospital, but in mid-winter it's dark already. I see Ned and say, 'Sure you won't drop by tonight?'

'No, when I'm operating I prefer to meet in a medical setting first. Time for chit-chat when all has gone well—I hope—afterwards.'

'I think you're just worried your head will be turned by Izabel.'

Ned smiles. 'Could be a factor.'

'But you think it will go well?'

'Reviewing Professor Kuan's X-rays, I think so, but it's going to depend on the scarring and how it heals afterwards.' He sighs. 'Lot of unknowns, Harry. I'll do my best.'

'I know you will. I'll say hello for you, anyway.'

'By the way, you may have a letter at home,' he says. 'I got mine today—a royalty cheque from Yvonne. Only pennies, but the book's starting to sell into a few schools now.'

'Excellent. You deserve the success.'

'And you too, mate.' He gazes at me. 'Regrets?'

'Not regrets, but I'll always feel ambivalent about the exposure.'

'Should have used a pseudonym.' Ned grins. 'What about Harold Crusade? It'd go well with Edward Quest.'

'Harold Crusade? Sounds very earnest,' I say. 'But who'd recognise my name, anyway? Common as muck.'

Ned laughs. 'See you tomorrow, Harry. Should be interesting.'

I'm still smiling when I get my bike, switch on the headlamp and set off for home. Harold Crusade? I didn't even think about a pseudonym when we were doing the book.

It doesn't matter though—not as it does to Ned, who wants to carry on his dual lives as poet and doctor. My artistic side is done for now, but I don't mind. I'm as happy working in the clinic as I've ever been. My home life however … I suppress a sigh. Well, time will improve things. It must.

Baby Jennifer is four months old and I'm besotted. Leo is proud of being a big brother, especially since the baby has no possible demand on his favourite toys.

But Eliza? The birth was hard. Unlike Leo, Jenny wouldn't suckle easily, so she went on the bottle. I can help Eliza with that at least, but I can't seem to help at all with the sadness that envelops her.

It's a cold evening, the last light of the day glowing pink behind Mount Sugarloaf. I bump along the road past Pacific Park, along Hunter Street and through Parnell Place, to Beach Street and home.

The road ends at the top of a small bluff and looks over the ocean. My mother's house is just a few blocks away, and the rush of breakers on the sands nearby has been a part of my whole life.

This afternoon Eliza picked up Izabel, Laurence and Nancy from the station. I've never met Laurence Kuan—none of us have—and I last saw Izabel nine years ago, just before the fall of Singapore. Nancy was twelve then, a quiet girl with a wry sense of humour.

I park the bike and go inside. Izabel is by the fire in the lounge room, listening to Leo describing his train set, laid out on the rug.

'Harry!' she says, looking up. 'Oh, *heavens!*'

We hug and say, laughing, how splendid the other is looking, and in her case it's perfectly true. When I last saw her she was thin and unhappy, married to the odious Felix and in secret mourning for Laurence. Now with a new serenity, her dark hair in waves to her shoulders, her eyes amused, she's as lovely as ever.

'And here's Nancy!' Izabel says, and sitting in an armchair is a young woman I barely recognise. She smiles coolly and says, 'Hello, Uncle Harry.' I shake her hand and say, 'I hardly recognised you, Nancy, all grown up.'

She's really Eliza's cousin, but as we're an older generation she's always called us aunt and uncle. Like Izabel, Nancy is Eurasian, her mother a Frenchwoman who died long ago. Her eyes are green and her dark brown hair is tied firmly back.

'Nancy and I are holding the fort,' says Izabel. 'Laurence is resting, and I told Eliza to lie down for a bit too while the baby's asleep. My goodness, Harry, *what* a charmer.'

'I know,' I say. 'Leo and Jenny both. We're very lucky.'

Leo says, 'Nancy, want to have a look through my telescope? You can see ships too.'

Nancy shrugs slightly and says, 'All right,' and they go upstairs.

'I'll make us tea, Izabel,' I say. When I return with the tray I ask, 'How was the trip?'

'Not bad. Three days—flying boat from Hong Kong to Singapore, then another to Sydney.'

'Did Billie meet you at Rose Bay?'

'Yes, and it was just lovely to see her. And Klara and Yvonne were there too—quite the reunion! Then Billie took us to Central, and here we finally are.' She sighs. 'A long trip but hopefully worth it.'

'Ned is a superb surgeon, Izabel. If anyone can help your husband he can, although it's been so long since the original injury there are no guarantees.'

'We have to try, Laurence is in such pain. He's returned to lecturing at the university so he's on his feet a great deal.'

'And you, Izabel—what have you been doing?'

'Teaching stagecraft to children again. It seems to be my strength and I do love it.'

'You certainly look happier than I've ever seen you.'

'Oh, Harry, I *am*. And you?'

'I work in an outpatient clinic at the hospital, more general practice than anything, but I enjoy it. Quite a change from my past as a researcher.'

'And Eliza?' says Izabel gently.

'Ah. Perhaps you noticed—'

She nods.

'It's a kind of depression that hits some women after giving birth. She had it to some extent with Leo, but now with Jenny it's worse.'

'Are there no treatments?'

'A few not very effective drugs. Some doctors suggest electro-convulsive therapy but I'd never give that to my worst enemy, let alone Eliza. I got her to see a psychiatrist a few times and I think it allowed her some relief, but he didn't have any solutions.'

I shake my head. 'All we can do is hope it passes, as with Leo.'

Izabel nods sympathetically. I hear slow steps from the downstairs guest bedroom, then Professor Kuan enters.

He's silver-haired, tall and well-built, wearing a white shirt and dark trousers, and I can see the resemblance to Nancy in the handsome bones of his face. We shake hands, then I pour us all pre-dinner sherries.

'I'll check the oven,' says Izabel. 'The roast should be nearly done.'

Laurence Kuan raises his glass to me. 'Cheers, Dr Bell. Thank you for having us here, we are most grateful. The Hong Kong doctors were so pessimistic, but Dr Caswell has given us new hope.'

'Do call me Harry, please—you're Eliza's uncle by marriage, after all. Family.'

'Oh yes, cheers to *family*,' says Izabel, returning from the kitchen and raising her glass.

'Izabel says you're teaching at the university,' I say. 'What subject?'

'History. It used to be Dutch exploration, but lately I have become something of a specialist in modern China. I saw rather a lot of change from the inside,' Laurence says dryly.

I smile. 'I imagine you did. But I was wondering—didn't your friends in the government want you to stay with them now the civil war is over?'

'I always made it clear I would do what I could to help the revolution, but when it was possible I would return to Hong Kong, to Izabel.' He gazes at her. 'If she would still have me.'

Izabel laughs. 'If?'

I hear footsteps on the stairs and Eliza comes in. She's rubbing her eyes, trying to smile, and wearing the same dress she was wearing yesterday.

Izabel says, 'Have a sherry, darling. I've checked the roast and another ten minutes should do it.'

'Thank you, Izabel.' Eliza sits and sips from her glass, saying nothing, watching the fire.

Nancy and Leo come downstairs, Nancy with baby Jenny in her arms. 'She woke up, so I think she probably wants a bottle.'

'I'll get it,' says Izabel. 'Harry, would you mind setting the dining table? Leo, you're a big boy, you can help your daddy. Laurence and Eliza can just sit back and take it easy tonight.'

'The fragments of bone visible in the X-ray are pressing on the sciatic nerve in your thigh, Professor Kuan, that's why you're suffering constant pain,' says Ned.

He points to the light-box. 'I can remove those fragments, which should help. However, if they've caused too much damage, the pain will never be completely gone.'

'And the scarring?' says Laurence.

'I've had a good look at the fibrous tissue, and can remove the worst of it and encourage it to heal cleanly. I believe the operation will improve the mobility and comfort of your leg, although I cannot claim we'll fix it completely.'

Laurence looks at Izabel. She says, 'When, Dr Caswell?'

'If you wish we could do the admission this afternoon and operate tomorrow.'

'*Oh,*' breathes Izabel. Laurence nods and says, 'I would be very happy to go ahead.'

We stand and Izabel takes Ned's hands. 'I'll never be able to thank you enough, Dr Caswell.'

Izabel and Laurence leave, and Ned murmurs, 'My knees are shaking, Harry. She's just *magnificent.*' He sighs. 'Hope I don't screw up the surgery.'

In the afternoon I take Laurence back to the hospital for admission. That evening, over dinner, Leo gazes solemnly at Izabel and says, 'I'm named after your daddy.'

'I know. Your mother promised me she'd do that. Thank you for carrying his name, Leo.'

Leo nods. 'That's all right, I like it. My grandma from Perth says it means I'm a lion.'

'Oh, yes,' says Izabel. 'Eliza, how is Rosa? I haven't seen her for years. Is she well?'

Eliza nods. 'She visited, with my aunt Lucy, soon after Jenny was born. That was nice.'

'You must miss them,' says Izabel. 'But your brother's here now, isn't he? At least some of the family's not too distant.'

'Yes, he arrived six months ago.'

'Pete's about a hundred and fifty miles away on the south coast,' I say. 'We haven't met up yet because of the baby. He's settling into a dairy property with Vivy and his new wife.'

'I remember Vivy from England, when we'd visit their farm,' says Nancy. 'She was only little then. She must be fourteen by now.'

Izabel says, 'Eliza, when you do see Pete and Vivy, please give them our love.'

'No idea when that will be,' says Eliza distantly.

'Still, it'd be interesting to meet the new wife at some time, love,' I say encouragingly.

Jenny starts crying, and in the soothing and feeding of the baby the conversation moves on. A thought occurs to me and I say, 'Nancy, I've been wondering how it was for you when your father reappeared in your lives again after so long.'

She looks up, flustered. 'Oh. Well—wonderful, but confusing too. In my mind *Ah-bah* had black hair, and now it's silver and he has wrinkles. But he feels the same and smells the same.' She smiles suddenly. 'No one's asked me that before, Uncle Harry. Yes, it's been strange but very sweet.'

Her smile lights up her face and I think, my goodness, she's a pretty lass when she comes out of her shell.

Next day I drive Izabel and Nancy to the hospital, and they wait while I catch up with some work. Our rooms have a fine outlook to Newcastle Beach, as do the general wards.

I firmly believe the seascape builds the morale of patients, but penny-pinching Dr Godfrey wants the wards with good views turned into well-paying private rooms. So far he hasn't been able to get his way and I'm determined he won't.

The operation started early and Ned said it wouldn't be over till noon, so at eleven I take Izabel and Nancy to the doctor's lounge for a cup of tea. I introduce them to the Medical Superintendent, who says, 'Oh, please, Mrs Kuan, do call me Chris,' and practically bows over her hand.

It must be odd to inspire such awe in grown men, but beautiful Izabel has had that power most of her life and it doesn't appear to be fading. Still, she's always been gracious with it, and she sits with the Super and chats about the hospital as if she hasn't a care in the world, and her beloved husband isn't deep under anaesthetic in an operating theatre.

Dr Godfrey comes into the lounge and stares at our little group. He started at the hospital more than two years ago, but to my relief he's stayed well out of my orbit unless there's some official matter to be discussed; and fortunately he never goes near Ned.

It wasn't easy seeing him around when we were working on *Poems of Rage*, but I seem to have mentally separated the traitor I once knew from the dusty-looking middle-aged man he's become.

To my annoyance Chris—perhaps proud of being in the company of the fabulous Izabel Malory—beckons him over and introduces him as Chief Administrator.

His colourless eyes sweep over Izabel and young Nancy in an almost crude manner. It leaves a sour taste and I take them back to my office as soon as I decently can.

'Is *that* the dreadful man you and Eliza mentioned?' Izabel murmurs. I nod and she shudders and says, 'Disgusting.'

Time passes slowly, then Ned finally turns up, tired and content. 'Mrs Kuan, the surgery appears successful. I removed the bone fragments and reduced the scar tissue. Of course, there can always be complications, but if all goes well Professor Kuan should recover nicely. I'll take you down to his room now to see him as he comes out of the anaesthetic.'

Izabel puts her hands on either side of Ned's face and solemnly kisses his forehead. 'You are my *hero*, Dr Caswell. Thank you.'

He blushes. 'Well, perhaps—ah, let's go and see the patient.'

'By the way, Ned,' I say, 'you didn't meet the Professor's daughter yesterday. Nancy, this is Dr Ned Caswell.'

Nancy holds out her hand and smiles like an angel. 'Thank you so much for helping my father.'

Ned takes her hand, gazing at her. I don't believe I have ever seen a man fall in love as suddenly and utterly as he does at that moment.

Four weeks later, poor Ned is in despair. 'They'll be *leaving* soon. What in God's name will I do?'

'Have you told Nancy how you feel?'

'Indirectly. We spend a lot of time talking about Chinese poetry versus Western poetry, and I'm certainly better educated, but that doesn't help.' He's silent for a moment. 'I kissed her, but she held back. I don't know if she was annoyed or glad, or even *what* she felt.'

'Has she ever spoken to you about Singapore?' I say.

'Only a little. I know she got out at the last moment and probably has the same godawful memories as the rest of us, but I don't see how that matters.'

'She was only twelve and she was exposed to … dreadful things,' I say. 'She may be reserved with any man for a long time. Are you certain you can deal with that?'

'I'd marry her in a heartbeat and gladly wait for as long as she wants me to wait.'

I smile. 'Then how can we get her to stay?'

'I had an idea,' says Ned. 'She was so good with her father after the operation, and Eliza said she's been very helpful with young Jenny too.'

'True. She's kind, but not sentimental. Are you thinking of nursing, perhaps?'

He nods. 'There'll be a new intake of students very soon.'

'You realise she'd have to live in the nurses' quarters under Matron's eye? And you know quite well nurses aren't allowed to go out with doctors.'

'I know, but at least she'd be *here*. And perhaps I could see her at your house. If you don't mind having us around, that is.'

'Of course we wouldn't mind. Eliza's very fond of both of you.'

Ned sighs. 'Naturally, I have other doubts. I'm a lot older and it's obvious I'm damaged goods.' He touches his scar briefly. 'She's only twenty-one and could have her pick of men.'

'You're still a young fellow to me, and I'm pretty sure Nancy hasn't been talking Chinese poetry with anyone else. And don't you know women find scars dashing? They do in books, anyway.'

'I'd miss her of course, but she'd have you and Eliza nearby. But then,' Izabel says dryly, 'how do you think Nancy would go, here in this very white Australia?'

'Quite a few of our nurses come from Commonwealth countries, so there wouldn't be official barriers. And Ned is simply head over heels,' I say. 'He understands, too, she's a complex girl. I mentioned that Singapore had left its mark, but didn't go into the details.'

'You can tell him what really happened, Harry. I've always refused to let it shame me, and none of it can hurt me now.' Izabel gazes at me, her head tilted.

'When—' I hesitate. 'When you and Laurence were reunited, did what happened in Singapore ... come between you?'

She slowly shakes her head. 'Oddly, no. I'd wondered myself, how things would be when—*if*—we were ever together again. But seeing him again, *alive*, after years of believing he'd died in Shanghai?'

She laughs in disbelief. 'Oh, Harry. All that horror simply *disappeared*. Evaporated. It meant nothing compared to the reality of Laurence's existence.'

'Really?' I say. 'I can't imagine the ... things I went through disappearing, no matter how happy I might feel.'

I feel suddenly anxious. How on earth did I get into such a personal discussion?

She nods. 'I can see it's been hard, for you and Eliza both.'

I clear my throat. 'Yes. It's a pity Eliza's still so—gloomy.'

'She's sad, Harry. And angry too, of course.'

I laugh abruptly. 'What on earth's she got to be *angry* about?'

Izabel looks taken aback. 'Well, Singapore left its mark on her, too. She had a responsible job for years and now she doesn't. She's depressed, and even when the children are older what can a woman as clever as Eliza do in this country town? She once had so much to absorb her and now she has nothing.'

'I'm not certain you quite understand, Izabel,' I say, my tension releasing into simple irritation at a lecture on my own *wife*. 'She's very happy in Newcastle, she says so. She adores the children. These difficulties will pass.'

Izabel stares at me, puzzled. 'Harry, do you actually know what work Eliza did after you were taken prisoner?'

'Of course. Signals intelligence, as before the war. She doesn't talk about it, though.'

'That's because, like me, she's bound by the Official Secrets Act. But I was just a lowly cog at the Government Code and Cypher School, while Eliza—'

'Izabel, I know *perfectly* well that's where she clerked. So?'

'By the end of the war, Harry, she was a high-level section head.'

I scoff. 'You mean those Civil Service fogies let a woman do something important?'

'Harry, you weren't *there* during the war, the world was different then, it *had* to be,' says Izabel, her eyes fierce. 'Women were doing all the jobs men did, and doing them damned well.'

'Then where are they now?' I say, trying for a light-hearted air. 'Don't see them around today.'

'No, you don't,' Izabel says bitterly. 'They were fired, got rid of, encouraged to move on. But even if you can't imagine Eliza in such a role, you must admit Billie and Yvonne were flying all sorts of planes, and Charlotte and Klara were helping refugees—'

'My selfish ex-wife Charlotte was doing real war work? Don't pull my leg, Izabel.'

She looks surprised. 'You didn't know?'

I shrug. 'I always pictured society-lady tea parties.'

'Much more than that! Look, women like Eliza *must* be allowed to use their skills, they can't be themselves otherwise.' Izabel hesitates. 'Harry, your thinking is a little old-fashioned. The forties was a different world for women. Of course it wasn't your fault you missed out, but perhaps you're a bit stuck in the past. You need to expand your horizons.'

'My horizons are *perfectly* adequate, thank you, Izabel.'

Silence. Oh God, when did I become such a ghastly stuffed shirt?

I rub my face and sigh. 'I'm sorry. I know you want the best for Eliza. Of course I'll let her do whatever she wants, once she's feeling better and the children are older.'

Something like pity flickers over Izabel's face, but I'm not sure who it's for.

After we farewell Izabel and Laurence at the railway station I walk into work feeling pleased. Laurence has recovered well for a man of fifty-two (although I don't see that as old now—just turned forty-nine myself). He's in almost no pain now, his limp minimal.

Nancy is happy, looking forward to her training, and Ned is miles away on Cloud Nine. It's been a bloody good few weeks, I think. As I turn the corner to my office I'm surprised to see Dr Godfrey.

'Well,' he snarls. 'You *bastard*. You've been waiting for your revenge, haven't you?'

'I'm sorry, Godfrey? What—?'

'*This*, you swine! My *niece* is studying this at her bloody *school*.' He waves a book at me and I recognise the dark teal cover, the incised copper title: *Poems of Rage*.

'The White *Jap*?' he says, incredulous. 'Last time I heard that little slur I sued the bastard for defamation! By God, he regretted it, and he's *still* bankrupt. Those daubs of yours? You won't have a shirt on your back by the time I'm through with you, Bell.'

'For Christ's sake, Godfrey, they're just impressions. You're the only person who knows it's you. Because you were *there*. If you don't like it, tough. Don't bullshit me.'

He stares, his face white. 'Bullshit you? Oh, I mean every word, Bell. And when I find out who this drivelling poet is—this, this— Edward bloody *Quest*, I'll sue the fucking shirt off him too.'

He pushes past me and disappears around the corner. I go to my office and sit down shakily at the desk. Christ. This never even occurred to me. *Have* we defamed him? But it's all true, surely that's a defence! But court? Oh, Jesus. I hold my head and try to think.

No wonder I always had that strange, sick fear of exposure. I didn't want the responsibility, I *never* bloody wanted it! How easy it was for everyone else to say just go ahead. Eliza *especially*.

But it's not her who's going to be sued. It's me.

Eliza serves me a dried-out dinner. 'Sorry. You were late.'

I eat a little then say, 'Think I'd prefer a gin right now.'

I pour us drinks, take a mouthful of mine and say, 'I've had rather an awful day.'

Eliza picks up a book and sips her drink and says, 'Oh?'

'Godfrey ambushed me at the hospital. He's got hold of *Poems of Rage* and he's furious, says he's going to sue us. He can't, can he?'

'Suppose you'd better ask Yvonne that,' says Eliza, turning a page.

'But what if he does, what then?'

'Then you'll stand up in court and prove it's all true.'

'But even if we're vindicated, mud will stick. And if we're not vindicated we could lose our savings. It might even affect my job.'

'Was what you saw true, Harry? Was what Ned experienced true? If so, then defend it. You can't let Godfrey browbeat you.'

'*Browbeat* me? I never wanted those bloody paintings published. You all nagged me until I agreed and I *knew* it would be a mistake.' I take another mouthful, surprised to find I've finished the glass.

'I've noticed lately,' Eliza says thoughtfully, 'how very timid you've become, Harry.'

I stare. 'What?'

'You seem terrified of the responsibility of standing up for the most honest work you've ever done in your life.' She sips her drink.

'As far as I can see, you had—and still have—a *duty* to bear witness to the world with your paintings.'

'But my memories are agonising. I could barely face them.'

'I've also come to realise there's rather a lot you've never been able to face, Harry.'

'I don't quite …?'

'In our early days together, you were kindly Harry in thrall to wild Charlotte,' says Eliza. 'But you couldn't face divorcing her, so you put me through hell for years.'

'That's not fair. She wouldn't divorce me and I dared not divorce her. You know my mother's got a weak heart—she couldn't have borne it and Charlotte took advantage of that.'

'Yet here we are,' says Eliza, 'and Jessie coped very well in the end.'

'In the end. I didn't know that then.'

Eliza gazes at me over her glass. 'And Singapore.' She laughs bitterly. 'It always comes back to Singapore, doesn't it? You couldn't face your duty there either.'

'I *did* my duty, Eliza. I stayed with my patients!'

'But if you'd done what our leaders said to do—and happily did themselves—you'd have left. With all your Socialist insight, Harry, you *knew* how incompetent and pointless that last stand of Empire was. Yet you stood there, stupid as a sheep in an abattoir, bleating about your duty to stay. What about your duty to *me*, to yourself, to our friends?'

'I thought it was the—the right thing …'

'And if I hadn't wasted that final morning begging you to come with us we'd have *all* got away. I wouldn't have suffered years of anguish over your fate. Poor Izabel wouldn't have been raped by a gang of deserters, and Nancy and I wouldn't have cowered for hours in a dark cupboard, terrified the rapists would find us too.'

Eliza puts down her glass and stands up. 'You talk about your fucking memories, Harry. Try a few of *mine*.'

13. Tina: The Glitter of Shadows

Determination? I've got determination. When I was promoted, the Captain (a nice old girl) said, 'Sergeant Bell, despite your tendency to daydreaming we all recognise your determination in the face of obstacles. Well done, dear.'

At the time all I could think about was Nikos, so no wonder I was daydreaming, but at least that determination has always been my strength. Without it I could never have held out for so long against Jimmy. Everyone assumes I'm already his mistress, but I'm not.

Yes, I take the jewellery he gives me and why shouldn't I? I damn-well deserve it. I've helped him make more money than he's ever seen before. As well as the restaurant and the jazz club, Jimmy's now got a betting-shop under his belt.

I've exploited loopholes and forged alliances and brought him real influence on the streets of Sydney, and it was me that saw the opportunities, did the planning, made it all fall into place.

Clever little Tina Loukas is worth a great deal to Jimmy Kelso, and he knows it. But if business was the only thing between us I'd be laughing. Unfortunately I'm not certain how much longer my determination will hold out against my desire.

Still, Tempo is my refuge. László has been a great help—he plays piano sets at the club, acts as watchman and lives in one of the two flats above it. I use the other flat as an office, and for the times I'm too tired to drive home (I have my own car now).

On those night Nikos seems to assume I'm with Jimmy, but I simply sleep better at Kings Cross. I don't mind the revellers from the pubs, the noisy cars, the yells of streetwalkers or their clients.

At home in our quiet comfortable bed, I can't relax. I lie on my side, my back to Nikos. I can feel his warmth and bulk and I hate myself for being so loveless, but I can't turn to him and reach out because I don't *want* him.

The only way I can fall asleep beside my kind, blameless husband is to think about Jimmy. To wonder how he'd feel, how he'd smell if, if … and more.

Sometimes so overwhelmingly more, I must get up quietly and go to the bathroom and lean against the door and stroke and caress and bring myself to the summit, that piercing summit of want (*yes I said yes I will Yes*), and tumble, gasping from the peak until I can breathe normally again.

But why *don't* I give way to my desire?

Determination, of course. I chose this path and want to follow it very carefully until I understand what I'm getting myself into. Fear too, fear of losing my familiar life.

Of course Jimmy could never give me the constancy, the open-hearted affection of Nikos, they're as different as a house pet and a wild animal. (Oh, but the skill needed to bring such wildness to heel: how intoxicating, how dangerous the fantasy.)

Doubts, then? Jimmy has his secrets, I accept that. He's mercurial too, switching in a moment from startling charm, to fierce insight, to unspoken menace.

But today I wonder if I know the slightest thing about the man.

When I'm staying in my small flat, László and I sometimes sit in his lounge room and share a joint, a reefer of marijuana. The musicians often smoke pot before playing, but László gets his own supply because it helps him sleep. I love the relaxation and enchanting ideas it brings.

I've grown fond of László, and glad his piano lessons have transformed my stepson Steve. I like his calmness and elegant cigarillos, and I especially like being with someone who doesn't make me ache with desire or feel shamefaced with regret.

I think he enjoys having me around too, although we don't talk much except about the club or music or what's in the paper. He rarely mention his past, apart from the so-far fruitless attempts to discover the fate of his family.

Tonight, as László is rolling up our joint, he passes me the newspaper. 'There is an interesting item on page two, Tina. Do you remember the bookkeeper whose job you took over?'

'Montague Truscott? Who could forget?' I say. 'I suppose I should be grateful—if he hadn't cooked the books and run off I'd never have got the job.'

I shake open the paper and read aloud: '*Numbers Man Found in Harbour. Body found floating near the Woolloomooloo wharf yesterday has been identified as Montague Truscott, an accountant for the Capelli family business, rumoured to be a front for a criminal enterprise.*'

I look up. 'Wow. Rumoured to be? Diplomatic of the reporter.'

'It is very dangerous to cross the Capellis now.' László licks the paper to seal the reefer. 'They are worried about the growing strength of the Adlers, and have become careless and vindictive.'

'Do you think he cooked the Capelli's books too, and that's why they killed him?'

'I expect so, poor man. You know, I met him on the ship coming here after the war, both of us refugees. He changed his name to something he thought would go unnoticed in Australia.' László smiles gravely, strikes a match to the joint and takes a deep hit.

'Montague? Oh dear.'

László passes me the reefer and I take a lungful. I hold my breath for a few moments, let it slowly flow and say huskily, 'Vaguely remember … Jimmy saying karma, fate, would sort that fella out, he'd more important things to do. Suppose it did. Sort him out … not Jimmy. Monty Truscott, I mean …' I hand back the joint.

'Not like Jimmy …' says László, drawing deeply, the paper crackling, then breathing out a plume of smoke, '—to leave things up to fate…'

We smoke for a little while longer then he says, 'I think I shall make some tea …' and drifts out to the kitchen.

Good. I need tea, my mouth is dry. I tap out the joint in the ashtray, and watch the fire. It's early spring and I envy László this fireplace, all cast iron and pretty green tiles. My little flat only has an electric heater.

I love the way the flames move. I sigh and stretch with pleasure. Hard to decide what colours they are. You could say yellow, or orange, but that's not it. Are there words? Vermilion? Amber? Scarlet? Saffron? Nikos uses saffron in his cooking.

There's a hint of turquoise on the edge of the embers and the rug's got turquoise in it too. Pretty. Mmm, I'm warm and cosy. But still thirsty. Where's László and the tea?

'Here you are,' he says. 'A biscuit too …'

We sit peacefully by the fire, chatting idly about the musicians playing next week, hiring another waiter for the club, a grog delivery we're expecting.

László puts a record on the gramophone, a new jazz quartet, and I'm entranced by the flow of the instruments as they swoop and entwine in a display of such careless, exquisite skill.

'*Ah,*' I sigh. László nods, smiling.

Finally I yawn and say goodnight, and wander across the cold corridor to my flat. It's raining outside so I turn the heater on, wash in my tiny bathroom and boil the kettle for a hot-water bottle.

Outside a woman calls out, 'Ya fuckin' bastard—' and a car swishes along the wet road.

The rain patters on the roof, and I shiver and snuggle under the blankets. Warm and sleepy, I remember László's words: 'Not like Jimmy … to leave things up to fate.'

In the morning I walk down to the Italian cafe. As I sip my coffee and eat a flaky apricot confection I wonder—why did that stick in my head? *Not like Jimmy … to leave things up to fate.*

Perfectly true. Jimmy controls everything in his small empire. To pretend he believed karma would catch up with Monty Truscott was a joke that went completely over my head at the time.

But that was two and a half years ago! Even Jimmy isn't patient enough to wait so long to take revenge for the theft of what was, really, a fairly petty sum.

And to suspect he could murder someone over it?

He's happy enough to break the absurd laws we must tolerate to make the business work, but I'm certain he'd never do anything so vile. Could his right-hand-man Davy have done it?

Hard to imagine too. Big Davy, against all the odds, has managed to get disdainful Pearl to agree to marry him. The wedding's in a few months and that's all either can talk about right now.

Yes, Jimmy's empire runs pretty close to a criminal enterprise, but it's nothing like the violent Capellis, who've done worse than this and openly too.

Still, I don't understand him. Jimmy's offered me crumbs of his past—his French mother, his angry Catholic father, leaving bitter northern Ireland. Living on his wits as a labourer, gathering a nest-egg in the profligacy of war, building up the Starlight Lounge.

But they're just crumbs. We're working side by side every day, but in the smothering of my desire for him I've also had to smother any hope of the intimacy that would reveal more of him to me.

And me to him. I sigh. Yes, me to him.

I'd love the chance to to talk freely, not to have to watch myself warily every moment. Perhaps the time is coming—perhaps it's come?—to be honest with myself and Jimmy. And then, then, perhaps to let my life with Nikos go?

It wouldn't be as I once imagined, he's not going to be comforted by falling into Billie's arms, but perhaps the truth would be kinder than deceiving him with every secret thought.

In the afternoon I drive from Tempo to the Starlight Lounge. Jimmy looks up, pleased. 'Come in, doll. Wasn't expecting you— what a treat to see your pretty face. Nothing wrong, is there?'

I shake my head. 'No. Just felt like seeing you.'

He stands up. 'That's what a man likes to hear.' He shows me to the couch, and goes to the door and calls to Pearl to bring us coffee.

She arrives with a tray, pours the coffee, sniffs disdainfully and leaves. Jimmy sits beside me as I add milk and sugar—I know how he likes it—then take my own cup, feeling suddenly shy.

'Ah, what is it, Tina?' Jimmy says gently. 'You're in a bit of a state, I think. Tell me.'

'Well—I read something in the paper. About your old bookkeeper, Montague Truscott.'

'Indeed,' Jimmy says. 'Poor bastard. I was furious at the fella, but wouldn't wish that on anyone.' He clears his throat. 'Actually— trouble is, wee Tina, I'm afraid I may be responsible for poor old Monty's fate.'

My scalp crawls. '*You?*'

'In the normal course of events, I'd have found him, thrashed him soundly and sent him on his way, telling him never to return to Sydney as long as he lives—if he wanted to keep on living.'

I gasp.

Jimmy sits beside me and says, 'No, no, doll, just a saying! What I mean is, I *should* have found Truscott and frightened him off for his own good. Trouble is, *you* starting here threw me completely, so I did nothing!'

He takes my hand. 'So he went to work for the Capellis, and imagined he could get away with doing to them what he did to me. Poor bloody fool.'

I sigh in relief. 'Oh, *Jimmy.* I thought you meant—'

He grins. 'Jesus, girl, I may be a bastard but I'm not a murderer.'

'No, you're not,' I say laughing.

'And here I am holding your pretty hand, and you're letting me.'

I withdraw it. 'Don't, Jimmy. Too complicated.'

'Telling me.' He hesitates. 'But enough of poor old Monty. More importantly, I was wondering if you'd be free to come back tonight and play hostess? I need you to knock some socks off.'

'Of course—but why is tonight important?'

'A meeting with the Adlers, Abe and his two sons. There's a chance of doing business.'

'The *Adlers?* My God! They're the biggest gang in town after the Capellis. Why?'

'Grog, Tina. Cheap, good quality, under the counter grog. Best deal I've ever seen.'

'But they're *criminals*. Maybe not as bad as the Capellis, but still—'

'You know we've got to be strategic, doll. We need friends, big, powerful friends, to stop the Capellis gobbling us up.'

I do know that, and I nod. 'All right, see you tonight. Dressed to knock socks off.'

This gown, *this* is the one. Black chiffon with tiny crystals all over, a strapless bodice and long skirt that sways with the weight of the beading, and glitters like eyes hidden in shadows.

I add cobweb-fine stocking and high heels, satin gloves that highlight my naked shoulders, and the strand of costume pearls Nikos gave me.

When I come downstairs he says, 'My God.'

'Is that approval?'

'You look magnificent, Tina. Pity it's not—' he stops and looks down at his book.

'For us? It's for work, Nikos, truly. We've got a special business meeting tonight and I have to impress the visitors.'

'You'll do that all right. I suppose you're staying at the flat again?'

'Yes, we'll be going pretty late and I'll be tired afterwards.'

'See you tomorrow, then,' says Nikos, without looking up.

I want to say, but it really *is* work!

Then I think of Jimmy, the two of us weaving a future together with our wit and cunning, the flash of white at his strong wrists, the quirk of his mouth, his dark eyebrows and grey eyes; and my throat goes moist. It's not work.

When I get to the Starlight Lounge it's closed to customers. Pearl is in the kitchen sorting out appetisers, so I pour myself a glass of wine and go to sit by the window.

I watch people scurrying home in the gloom from their work, thinking, this evening, this *moment*, I feel more alive, more real, more hopeful, than ever in my life.

I hear Jimmy coming lightly down the stairs in the office corridor.

His flat above the Lounge is all leather and mahogany and deep red velvet. Sometimes the staff are invited up, but I've never gone when it's just the two of us. I finish my wine, walk out to the corridor and meet him at the foot of the stairs.

'Ah, there you are, doll. Help me with this cuff-link, will you? The shirt's new and it's hard to get the bloody thing in.'

We stand there and I fasten the cuff-link. Jimmy smells—oh, like *Jimmy*—and I feel my nipples tightening.

'You look amazing, Tina. You *are* amazing, you know that?'

I shrug. 'Pretty clothes and make-up.'

He shakes his head. 'Just you. I've got something, later, to commemorate tonight—it's going to be important for us.'

I look up at him and he smiles and says, 'Ah, and those *eyes*. You know the two of us'd have the prettiest silver-eyed babies?'

I laugh. 'Not brown or green?'

He shakes his head. 'No, science says you and me could only have babies with grey eyes, and I reckon they'd be gorgeous too.'

'Guess we'll never know,' I say, the breath catching in my throat.

Pearl comes through from the kitchen. 'Jimmy, they're here.' She looks me up and down and says, 'Don't you *dare* wear anything like that to my wedding, Tina, I'm not sharing the limelight.'

Jimmy and I glance at each other.

'Let's go slay 'em, sweetheart,' he says.

'So you're Jimmy's little friend, ah, Tina?' says the man next to me, Sándor Adler. He's in his thirties, dark, slim, alert.

'I believe he introduced me as his business manager,' I say, smiling. 'Do have one of these canapés.'

'Connected to Loukas Foods?'

I nod. 'My husband's family.'

He looks impressed. 'Pretty straight for Greeks. Not like those Diakos bastards, too big for their boots.'

One of his legs is tapping slightly, he's flushed and his pupils are dilated. I think he's on speed.

'Giving you a bit of a run for your money aren't they, the Diakos gang?' I say, refilling his champagne glass.

'Not in the same league, babe.' He looks around. 'Thought my mate László'd be here tonight.'

'László Richter? No, he's minding the jazz club. You know him?'

'Came out on the same boat, bunch of Hungarian Jews heading for a new life.' He laughs. 'But László and Meyer didn't take advantage of what was on offer, not like us.'

'Meyer?'

'Meyer Tabori—called himself Montague Truscott. Should never have crossed the Capellis, the fucking fool.'

He gulps his champagne and gazes thoughtfully at my chest. I'm not wearing a bra because the gown has a kind of inbuilt support, the brainchild of my Parisienne dressmaker. '*Oh, cette poitrine,*' she said in admiration when fitting me. '*C'est magnifique.*'

I glance down. It certainly is *magnifique.*

'Jimmy mentioned your father's interested in a deal,' I say. 'It'd be good for us to have friends like you.'

Across the table is the patriarch, Abe Adler, famous for his piety and donations to good causes. He nods to me with wrinkled cynical eyes and raises his glass. He seems to like my chest too.

Sándor says, 'Moshe thinks we can work together. The Capellis are going downhill, too fucking careless, doing things the police can't turn a blind eye to. They're over.'

Moshe Adler is murmuring to Jimmy, their heads close together. Moshe is older and heavier than his brother. He runs the business side and I hear he's particularly clever and ruthless.

God, I hope Jimmy knows what he's doing. These blokes aren't amateurs.

Sándor sniffs, and says, 'Gotta go for a minute, babe. Keep my seat warm.' He heads for the toilets, presumably for more speed (perhaps he is a bit of an amateur after all).

I wonder what his father thinks about it and look up. The senior Adler is still more interested in my *poitrine* than his errant son, so I smile winningly and raise my glass to him.

A little later, Jimmy calls me over and says, 'Have a chat to Moshe here, doll. Work out some timing.'

Moshe nods and I sit down beside him. He couldn't be less interested in my body, thank heavens, as we decide on dates for the first grog deliveries to the Starlight Lounge and Tempo—and for our substantial payments in return.

At the end he glances at me and says, 'You understand this is quite a step for us. I would not normally permit association with—' He gazes around. I suppose he means a Gentile operation, not a restaurant, because his family's Eagle Club is the biggest and brassiest outfit at the Cross.

'We'll do our best to make it work, Mr Adler,' I say calmly. 'Could be valuable for us both.'

His smile doesn't quite reach his eyes. 'I expect the value will flow mostly in one direction, but we will see. We'll be going now. Good night, Mrs Loukas.'

The restaurant is dark and the staff have cleaned up and gone. Jimmy and I have been sitting in his office going over the details of the deal we've made with the Adlers. Finally he stretches and sighs. 'I need a whiskey. What about you?'

'Yes, please.'

Jimmy walks to his drinks trolley, then says, 'I've a brandy upstairs in my flat, Tina, and I swear it's made from angels' tears. Would you care for that instead?' He turns to me, his face still. 'I've a gift for you too. Perhaps—?'

I hesitate, all my arguments and fears and yearnings tumbling through my head in confusion, then the stream suddenly stops and my mind is crystal-clear.

I nod and stand. 'All right.'

We walk upstairs in silence, and Jimmy ushers me into his reception room. He turns on the lamps and closes the high velvet curtains. The fire has burnt low and he pokes the embers, and I stand there warming myself while he pours drinks.

He hands me a brandy balloon and I sip. 'Angels' tears, indeed.'

We're silent for a time, then Jimmy says, 'That little something, where did I—? Ah.'

He goes to an antique sideboard and brings back a small tissue-wrapped box.

'To thank you for everything, doll.'

I unwrap the ribbon and tissue to find a black leather box. Inside is a necklace, a fine chain of gold with a line of diamonds that glint and glimmer in the firelight.

Jimmy says huskily, 'For you, sweetheart.'

I lift it, my hand shaking. I have jewellery, but *nothing* like this.

'Allow me. Turn around.'

Jimmy removes Nikos's fake pearls, then drapes the chain around my neck and closes it. Still behind me, he lightly touches the diamonds, half-stroking the skin beneath.

I turn to face him, hardly breathing. 'How does it look?'

'There's a mirror in my room. Come and see for yourself.'

He holds out his hand and I take it. He leads me to the bedroom and I stand before the cheval glass in my glittering shadowy dress.

Jimmy looks over my shoulder. 'All right, then?'

'Oh, *Jimmy*.'

Light dazzles above the curves of my breasts. Behind me Jimmy strokes my arms, then bends his head and slowly kisses and nibbles the line of my shoulder. Then he looks up into the reflection of my half-closed eyes. I nod, very slightly.

His body is light and warm against my back. He reaches around to my hand, flicks apart the tiny satin buttons tight at the glove's wrist, then glides the silky covering down and off. I shudder with pleasure.

He removes the other glove, as I wonder how such a thing could feel like … *that*. Then one by one he undoes the buttons at the back of my bodice and slowly opens it, his breath warm on my spine. He pushes the bodice down and, as it slithers to my waist, the chiffon, with its tiny crystals, catches for a moment on my taut nipple.

And I am naked to the hips.

I am exposed, wanton and exposed, and *oh*, how it pleases me. Over my shoulder Jimmy watches me, his eyes narrow.

From behind he lifts the sweet weight of my breasts, still gazing, gazing, and runs his fingers back and forth across their tips, and I whimper. His hands go lower, caressing my waist and hips, then he pushes the folds of chiffon down and the gown falls into a shimmering heap.

'*Ah*,' he says, and takes a deep breath.

Under my dress I'm wearing nothing but a garter belt to hold up my wisps of stockings. Feather-light, Jimmy brushes my brazen bush of hair and I murmur at the stabbing pleasure. He strokes slowly down my cleft and moves, moves, moves against the sweet nub, then his fingers slip and curl inside me, and my knees buckle.

He whispers, 'We'd better lie down, sweetheart, I'm going weak at the knees myself.'

I turn and laugh in delight, and wrap my arms around his head, and pull his mouth to mine, and kiss it hard and deep, the mouth I've desired for so long.

He feels new, and different, and better than I'd ever imagined.

I kick away the dress at my ankles, and my high heels, and sit on the bed, unclasp my stockings and roll them off. Then I undo the garter belt and throw it away.

I lie back slowly, luxuriously, my arms above my head, and show myself to him, all of myself, dressed only in my new diamonds, and say lazily, 'Get your bloody clothes off, Jimmy.'

He chuckles in amazement, and sits down beside me, running his hand over my belly, and laughs again. He pulls off his shoes and socks, bow tie and shirt. Then he stands and removes his trousers and drawers, and he's every bit as fierce and fine a man as I imagined he'd be.

He lies down naked against me and kisses my breasts and my mouth, his fingers insistent, and whispers, 'Oh, *you*.'

I reach and stroke his balls and they lift, hard and tight, and I pull him on top of me and wrap my thighs around him and ease his heft deep inside.

Then I enjoy, and enjoy, and enjoy, climbing to that piercing summit, and yes, yes it's *real* now, so sweet and real; and I soar from the peak into rolling clouds of pleasure. I pause, breathing deeply, then enjoy and rise and soar again.

At some time during this exquisite tempest Jimmy groans in the release of his own. Then we roll to one side, panting and slippery, and he holds me against him, and sobs, 'You. *You.*'

During the night we turn to each other from the depths of sleep and take our violent pleasure once more, and again at dawn; but slowly then and deliberately.

Some time afterwards Jimmy gets out of bed and says, 'Think I need a restorative cup of tea, *a chuisle.*' He gazes at me and says, 'You truly are my pulse, you know.'

'I know.'

'And so you've been for a very long time.'

'I know that too.'

He makes the tea and we sit in bed and drink it, and it's exactly what I want at that moment. He strokes my fingers and I realise the gold ring he wears isn't a signet, but two hands holding a heart with a crown above it.

'My mother's wedding band,' Jimmy says. 'But my poor old broken pinkie's the only one it fits.'

I lift his hand and look closer (his nails are always beautifully manicured). 'It *is* a bit crooked, isn't it? What happened?'

'Ah, a fight over some foolish thing when I was a labourer.' He grins. 'Always imagined when I was rich I'd get it re-set, but hardly see the point of it now.'

I slide down in the bed, and Jimmy does the same. I prop my head on my hand and gaze at him and he runs his fingers along my diamond necklace, still the only thing I'm wearing.

'Well, mountain flower. That was one hell of a night.'

I laugh. 'Wasn't it just?'

'And now, wee Tina?'

I hesitate. 'I don't know.'

'You going back to Mr Loukas, pretending nothing's happened?'

'I've been married for six years, Jimmy.'

'Correct me if I'm wrong, but you don't seem to spend a lot of time with the hubby.'

'True.'

'So,' says Jimmy, and picks up my hand and kisses it.

'So?'

'So it sounds as if leaving all that behind wouldn't be the worst thing in the world.'

'What do you suggest as an alternative, then?' I say, my heart thumping.

'Well, just maybe you could stop being Mrs Loukas and become Mrs Kelso. Worth a thought.'

14. Billie: One Weakness

It's New Year's Eve 1950. Today's been hot, but I'm on my balcony watching the stars and the harbour, and the evening air is cooling me down. I get up and go inside to the fridge and refill my wine glass, then relax again in the wicker armchair.

Funny to think I've been at Rose Bay for two years now. Not sure I've ever stayed in a job that long, apart from flying during the war. Must be getting old and stuck in my ways. Jeez, I *am* old, who am I kidding? Forty-four a few months ago.

But I'm all right really—steady pay packet, interesting work, good friends. In fact, for a time there, I thought my life might actually be changing for the better.

Then I fell for Nikos.

Ten months ago we'd had that vivid, delightful day on the water, and afterwards, chatting on this balcony, at peace with each other, our eyes met in silence for a little too long. And suddenly we both understood: the stream of affection between us had opened out into a bottomless sea.

Haltingly, excruciatingly, we agreed we shouldn't spend any more time together. As friends we'd hugged in greeting and entwined on the dance floor, but when Nikos left he kissed me very softly on the cheek and nothing between us had ever seemed quite so intimate.

So I bought myself a fast car, put out the word I was seeing some non-existent man, and went to earth. The first time we spoke in ages was at the launch for Harry and Ned's book, and that was just momentarily.

The launch was a disaster in any case, but I was so mired in my own misery I didn't even notice poor old Lizzie was pregnant. Since then she's been doing it rough too, says Yvie.

Suddenly fireworks crackle and rockets flare into great silvery blossoms in the sky and I realise the new year of 1951 has begun.

I go and fill my wineglass again. Drinking alone probably isn't a good idea but then I'm careful, always have been. Hardly smoked either, apart from the war.

Nah, I've only ever had one weakness.

A month after that lonely New Year's Eve, Vivy, Pete and his new wife sail into Sydney on a luxury liner. Klara and Yvonne are old friends, so they plan a welcome dinner and gently suggest I attend.

I grit my teeth and decide we may as well meet up again in civilised circumstances. One hot night I drive over to Balmain and, despite myself, I'm wearing a nice dress, my hair flatteringly loose on my shoulders.

Pete's only ever seen me with a tomboy crop so I wonder if he'll notice? *Stop it.* I mentally slap myself.

Klara opens the door, then Vivy dashes down the hall, yelling, 'Billie!' I yell back, 'Kid!' and we hug. She's fourteen now, still with her mass of chestnut curls and brown eyes and infectious giggle.

In the lounge room I say hello to the famous Janet. She's blonde, pretty, in her late twenties—a lot younger than Pete—educated at some posh boarding school, and with a certain over-confidence in her own opinions. All right, perhaps I don't quite take to her.

She watches vigilantly as Pete gives me a peck on the cheek. Still a fine-looking man, a few more lines around the eyes, a little grey in his straight dark hair, but he's much the same. That's confusing. I'd expected Janet's husband to be a different person from the Pete I once knew.

The evening proceeds uncomfortably, probably because Pete can hardly bear to look at me (so much for the power of a new hairstyle). We get through the appetisers and into the main course with chit-chat about my job and their voyage and Janet's family.

I'm surprised to hear Vivy won't be living with them at the farm, but will start soon at a boarding school in Sydney. Janet's old one. The posh one.

I say, 'You okay with that, kid?'

'I know it won't be like Enid Blyton, Billie—though I hope it might be a *little* bit—but it has a good music department, so I'll get better voice training than before.' Vivy sighs. 'It was *awful* leaving Taffy behind, but he's got a new home now and I can have a horse at the farm too, so everything's turned out all right, really.'

'Well, if you're going to be here in Sydney, guess I could take you out occasionally.'

'Ooh, yes! And is it true Uncle Harry's sister has a *jazz* club here?'

'Tina runs a club called Tempo at King's Cross,' I say. 'It's not far from my flat, so maybe we can go out one evening, if Pete—if your parents—agree.'

'That's kind of you, Billie,' says Janet, smiling insincerely, 'but I'm not sure about Kings Cross. It has rather a *reputation*, after all.'

'Yeah,' I say. 'Look, I live there and it's really just an ordinary place. The bad stuff the papers talk about—it sells papers. I'm sure crime exists, but it's pretty well hidden.'

'Not so much the crime,' says Janet delicately. 'The *ladies*, Billie. Ladies of the night.'

'But if we only go in the evening,' says Vivy, 'we won't see any ladies of the night.'

Pete says, 'We'll discuss it later,' which sounds like a no.

We struggle through the evening, Klara and Yvonne doing their best to keep the conversation rolling, but it's awkward. Janet reminds me of Charlotte, but without any of the wit or charm. Her eyes are on me and I can almost hear her thinking, What on earth did he see in *her* all those years?

And it's true, I probably don't come off very well compared to a pretty young blonde with more unwarranted confidence than I've ever had in my life. At least *my* bloody confidence was earned the hard way.

Still, I survive the dreaded reunion, and off they go to their dairy farm. Vivy starts at her new school and sends me letters about how wonderful it all is, with unsubtle hints about the jazz club.

We go on a couple of happy outings to Taronga Zoo and Luna Park, then she tells me Pete has *finally* agreed I can take her to Tempo, as long as we go in the daytime.

Tina says a band is playing that Saturday afternoon, so I pick Vivy up and we drive to the Cross. She's disappointed not to see any glamorous ladies of the night, and I don't explain they're actually the tired, gap-toothed drabs on the street corners.

Tina is delighted to meet Vivy, and Vivy is equally delighted with sharp, stylish Tina. Since Harry is Vivy's uncle by marriage, they establish that Tina is a sort of an aunt, which pleases them both.

In the early evening, after the group has finished and the place is almost empty, Tina asks a quiet European man named László to play the piano so Vivy can sing for us.

She does so without any coyness, and she's amazing. She sounds confident and mature, her voice throaty, delicate, thoughtful, with what even I can tell is an acute feel for the jazz tempo.

Tina exchanges glances with László.

'You're only fourteen, Vivy?' she says.

'And a half.'

'Well, keep working at your lessons, sweetheart, I think you've got a great deal of promise. And look, if you want advice—about music or anything at all—just talk to me.'

As we're leaving Tina murmurs, 'She's very, very good, and at *that* age? Gave me goosebumps.'

She stops and looks at me. 'Haven't seen you for ages, Billie. I miss you, always loved going shopping with you.'

'Ah, Teen. Don't get out much, don't need new clothes.'

Tina's shocked. '*Everyone* needs new clothes. But, tell me, are you seeing anyone?'

'Oh, now and again.'

She kisses me goodbye. 'Well, take care of yourself, doll.'

I take an ecstatic Vivy back to school, and wonder about Tina. Is she really sleeping with Jimmy (doll) as everyone else seems to assume? She has the air—and I should bloody know—of a woman who isn't actually getting much in the way of satisfying sex.

*

Next morning I hear the door-knocker banging. The suspicious little dog is yapping and Mrs Beatty is at church, so I go downstairs in my kimono and open the door, half-yawning.

Pete is standing there, scowling, black-browed. 'Something we need to sort out, Billie.'

'Do come in,' I say, and we go upstairs.

I put the kettle on and turn. 'What's the problem, mate?'

'I tried to ring Vivy at school yesterday and they told me you'd taken her to Tempo. But Janet *specifically* said she wasn't to go there. She's insisted I come up to Sydney this morning and make things *very* clear to you, Billie.'

'What things, Pete?'

'Well—first of all, that you've got no relationship to Vivy, you're not her mother.'

'I wasn't aware I'd actually applied for the job.'

'And, ah, second, you can't just waltz in and do whatever you like with her.'

'That's it?'

After a while he says, 'Suppose so.'

'As it happens, Vivy brazenly told me to my face you'd agreed she could go to the club in the daytime.'

'*Did* she?'

'She did. So I wasn't precisely waltzing in, Pete. I was being—you know—helpful.'

He sits down. 'That little *brat*. Sorry, Billie. Should have known you wouldn't ...'

I laugh shortly. 'Disobey the fair Janet? I'm perfectly aware I have no relationship to either you or your daughter.'

'You know that's not true.'

'Still take one sugar? Or has Janet got an opinion on that too?'

'I *said* I'm sorry, Billie.'

'For what? Accusing me of crap? Ruining my Sunday morning? Ruining my fucking *life*?'

He stands up again. 'You can't say that—*you* left me, remember?'

'There was no work for me in England, my mother was sick and I *had* to come home! What the bloody hell could I have done if I'd stayed there, Pete?'

After a long pause, he says, 'Lived with me. Loved me.'

'You didn't love *me* enough to come back with me then! Yet for *Janet*—' My throat closes in grief.

'No, listen Billie! After you'd gone I started to realise I'd done as much as I wanted to in England. Then I got involved with Janet and it turned out the Illawarra farm's a great opportunity. Suddenly it was the right time to move.'

'Wow. The love story of the ages.'

'Of course I should have done it before. My family's here and after all, you are too.'

'*Me?*' I say scathingly.

Pete laughs, shamefaced. 'I'm a fucking fool, aren't I? I didn't even realise it at first. But when I saw you again I understood, properly, why I had to come home—and it wasn't about farming at all.'

'Yeah?'

'That night I hardly dared even *look* at you, not with Janet in the same room. Ah, Billie. You know you always were, you always will be, the very air in my lungs.'

He holds out his arms and slowly I move towards him, and we embrace for a long, long time.

I've only ever had one weakness.

After a scolding, Vivy is allowed to visit Tempo again with her father, as long as she writes essays about the music for school. Pete comes to Sydney every few weeks on business or to see Vivy, and at night he stays with me.

No one knows he's here apart from Mrs Beatty and her little dog, who's taken to him, like most creatures. Like me. When we fall into bed it's a homecoming for us both, made more intense by the brief times we have together.

And, oh, the comfort, the glorious comfort of Pete's familiar heartbeat beneath my ear, my head on his smooth warm chest, his arms real and solid around me.

I'm content enough after he's gone too, but there's always a moment when he's dressing and leaving me behind that hurts a little. Still, that doesn't compare to the sweetness of his company when we're immersed in our passion and laughter and memories.

The year that had begun so glumly now opens up into joy, although perhaps it's seasoned with a touch of guilt. When Lizzie has her baby in March I send her a toy and a card, but don't make any plans to visit Newcastle, and probably won't. Lizzie might see more than I want her to.

I briefly meet our old friends Izabel and Nancy and—at last— Izabel's impressive husband Laurence Kuan. They're on a trip to Harry's hospital to see if Laurence's leg can be fixed up, and I hear it goes well.

Soon after that, Yvie rings to give me the bizarre news that she and Harry and Ned are being sued by some mad doctor who didn't like his portrayal in their book. The case isn't till next year but Yvie's not worried—she thinks they have a good defence.

Now and then I go to Tina's club, just a couple of streets away. The atmosphere is easy and you can get a drink if you don't mind having it in a mug.

Encouraged by Vivy's enthusiasm I find I'm enjoying jazz more as well. It's not all all wild discordant swooping, but often fascinating and dreamy. László, with his cynical eyes, is a good musician and explains some of the subtleties to me.

He looks after Tina too, and backs her up if there's any trouble, but compared to most places at the Cross there's almost never any trouble at Tempo. The police are comfortably compensated.

Towards the end of this extraordinary year, Tina herself goes through an amazing change. From her usual crisp style she blooms overnight like a sultry flower. It's obvious that, like me, she's now getting rather a lot in the way of satisfying sex. Jimmy becomes very cheerful as well, so I assume the sex is with him.

It makes me wonder how Nikos is going. I see him at a distance at Rose Bay but he avoids me. That may be a good thing. I feel embarrassed now to realise I was probably attracted to him because of loneliness and my long separation from Pete.

Tina sits down beside me at the club in a music break and says 'Want to go to a wedding?'

'Yours, Teen?'

She laughs and waggles her hand with its new, large diamond ring. 'Just a dress ring, dear. For now.'

'So whose wedding?'

'Pearl and Big Davy's, remember?'

'Oh yeah. Why?'

'Nikos refuses to come and I don't want to sit by myself.'

'What about Jimmy?'

'He'll be busy being best man—and besides, in public we try to keep a professional distance.'

'Not fooling anyone.'

'Perhaps not, but will you? I'll shout you a dress.'

The dress we buy is emerald silk, three-quarter sleeves, wide neckline and a flared skirt and, sitting in the church, I feel gorgeous. Greens suit me. I remember an olive dress I wore at some wedding—wow, *eighteen* years ago, when Pete and I first became lovers.

We'd had a row, then the Anson I was flying got an oil leak and the engine stopped. I parachuted out but was then stuck in the countryside. Pete thought I was dead and had to face the depth of his feelings. I had to face mine too, and that was the start of our affair. Ah, *Pete*.

The organ blasts into the Wedding March, and we look around at Pearl on the arm of an elderly gent, and she's smiling for what may be the only time in her life. Big Davy is waiting nervously at the alter with Jimmy, both of them formal in dark suits. All goes according to plan and soon Pearl and Davy are wed.

We shuffle out of the pews and Tina wipes her eyes. 'Having fun, Teen?' I say and she sniffles.

Fortunately we're soon at the reception in the Starlight Lounge being plied with champagne. László is nearby, lighting a cigarillo. Tina once said he's the same age as Jimmy, but he seems older. Still, he's a nice-looking man, olive skin, cool smile, dark hair.

I say, 'Went without a hitch, eh? Every time I hope someone will object, but sadly—'

László nods gravely. 'I, too, always hope for that. Are you here with a friend, Billie?'

'Technically I'm Tina's date, but she's cast me off already.'

We glance over at Tina, seated beside Jimmy. They're smiling radiantly at each other.

'She says they keep a professional distance, so I'd be curious to see them when they're not,' I say. 'You here with your wife, then?'

'No. I have no family here. Anywhere.' László shrugs. 'The war.'

'Ah. Apart from a nutty father I don't have any family either, but it was natural causes did for our lot.'

He smiles a little. 'Tina was helping me make enquiries. There was a possibility my wife and son had survived, but I have heard nothing, so I think it is time to let it all go.'

My eyes suddenly sting. '*Oh.* I'm so sorry, László.'

'I apologise, Billie, I did not mean to make you sad.'

'It's all right. Think I've been to too many damned weddings.'

'Indeed. Such relentless hope is exhausting.'

'Reckon they'll get there?' I nod at Tina and Jimmy.

'I believe the divorce court must have its say first. But then—'

'More relentless hope?'

He nods dryly, then we go over to congratulate Pearl and Davy.

A week later I'm heading for the lunchroom at work, when I nearly bump into Nikos, carrying his sandwich-bag. 'Oh, sorry,' he mutters, and I can't stand it a moment longer.

'For fuck's sake, Nikos, *talk* to me.'

He laughs and I remember how much I like the sight of his white teeth and dark beard and smiling eyes.

'Come on,' I say. 'Let's sit on the rocks, I haven't for ages. The seagulls have probably starved to death without us feeding them.'

'They're smarter than that,' he says. 'Anyway, how do you know I haven't been going down and feeding them every day—for—'

'Twenty-one months.'

'Twenty-one months. Yes.'

'I've missed you,' I say.

'And I you.'

We walk to the rocks by the water, shaded by trees, make ourselves comfortable and start eating.

'Tina said you went to a wedding with her last week,' says Nikos. 'She told me you looked wonderful, but that was because she bought you the dress.'

'She might have bought it, but it was me carried it off with such elegance,' I say. 'Sounds like you're on speaking terms, at least.'

'Sometimes. She's usually in a daydream.' He hesitates. 'She wants a divorce. I've tried to get her to wait, to find out what she's flinging herself into, but she won't listen, so I guess that's that.'

'Will you sue her for adultery or be found by a detective having breakfast with some helpful lady?'

'Probably the latter. The noble thing to do.' He shrugs. 'Makes it easier on Steve. One thing to have a father who's a bit of a devil, another to have a stepmother the subject of gossip.'

'How's he going, anyway?'

'Studying music at the Conservatorium, and very happy. No arguments from his grandfather either, not since Steve did so well in his Leaving Certificate.' Nikos looks at me. 'Should thank you for that. Helped me see how much he needed music in his life.'

'Can't take all the credit, it was Tina got him the piano,' I say. 'Here, seagulls, try a bit of this.' I throw a crust and the usual squabbling begins.

After a time Nikos says, 'And you? Tina says you're seeing someone. I hope you're happy.'

I keep my eyes on the seagulls. 'He doesn't live in Sydney so—well, early days.'

Nikos nods. 'You're welcome to come out on *Wind Rose* sometime. Both of you. If you want.'

'Thanks,' I say, ashamed. 'Must be nice on the water right now.'

'Only place to be.'

I gaze at him. 'Sounds as if you're pretty resigned to everything.'

'Sometimes.' His dark-lashed eyes meet mine, then he looks down and crumples his lunch-bag in his hands. His capable hands. 'But it's a long hard business falling out of love with someone.'

Now it's New Years Eve again, and tomorrow is 1952. Another year gone, but at least this time I'm not drinking alone on my balcony. I'm at Tempo, drinking with Tina and Jimmy and László and, if nothing else, I'm enjoying the music.

Vivy is on summer holidays at the dairy farm and, her Christmas card informs me, she *adores* her new horse. Apparently Pete and Janet are holding a party tonight, with Janet's parents and their wealthy friends.

How *boring*, says Vivy, and I suppose it is. Except Pete will be there and I am here.

The thing I hate, I tell myself as I swig my booze, the thing I fucking hate, is my own self-pity.

15. Yvonne: Ridicule, Hatred, Contempt

The solicitor's name is Mr Roderick, Ronald Roderick. With his fringe of white hair and rimless glasses, he looks as if he's just popped out of a Dickens novel. We're at his office, waiting for Ned to arrive from Newcastle (Harry's too busy to come).

A secretary ushers in not just Ned, but Nancy too. We caught up with her briefly some months ago, when Izabel and Laurence were on their way to Newcastle for Laurence's operation, but I've no idea why she's here today.

They're introduced and seated beside us around a polished table. Mr Roderick looks at me over his glasses and says, 'Let us begin. Miss Watters, I'm rather concerned you've left it so long to get advice in this matter when the trial is only four weeks away.'

'I suppose we thought it was—well, almost absurd,' I say. 'This Dr Godfrey has taken exception to a few poems and watercolours. Only a few people who were in the camp might realise who they referred to, but most wouldn't have the faintest idea. *If* they opened an obscure book of poetry in the first place.'

'Without even one review in the papers,' says Klara mournfully.

Ned says, 'Surely he should let sleeping dogs lie rather than make such a fuss about some supposed slander?'

'You have not slandered Dr Godfrey: such would be the case if you had defamed him in speech,' says Mr Roderick. 'No, he is charging you with libel, that is, with defaming him in print.'

'But *why*?' I say.

'I take it you haven't read the suit in detail?' Mr Roderick gazes around the table. 'Dear me. I shall clarify a few points. Dr Godfrey is suing you as publisher, Miss Watters, for exposing him to public ridicule, hatred and contempt, and seeks damages to the sum of ten thousand pounds. Similarly, he is suing Dr Bell and Dr Caswell for the same amounts.'

'But the poems and paintings are *true*,' I say.

'Certainly, truth and public benefit are mitigating circumstances, but I must ask what *proof* you have of Dr Godfrey's actions, other than Doctors Caswell and Bell's strongly-held beliefs? Convictions in a court of law—perhaps a post-war tribunal? Government records? Sworn statements from senior prisoner hierarchy?'

I shake my head.

Mr Roderick continues. 'You see, in many people's eyes, even to hint of favourable association with the Japanese is regarded *prima facie* as defamation. A few years ago a woman was awarded two hundred pounds against a newspaper which had mistakenly suggested she was married to a Japanese man.'

Nancy gasps. 'But that's a nurse's wage for a year!'

'Indeed,' says Mr Roderick. 'And for ten thousand pound you could buy yourself three fine houses. So irrespective of any injury, Dr Godfrey's suit may have its own rationale. Should he win, a jury probably won't award him thirty thousand, but he'd probably get a good proportion of it. Sydney juries are notoriously generous in awarding damages for defamation.'

There's a silence. Mr Roderick sighs. 'If truth cannot be proved, your motivations may also have bearing. Now, the suit claims Dr Bell is a Communist who wishes to destroy a devout Christian—'

'What?' Ned says, laughing.

'That Dr Bell's paintings are recent works and are not from the period in the prison camp—'

'Nonsense,' says Ned.

'That you, Dr Caswell, are a Communist sympathiser because you gave treatment to Professor Kuan, a Chinese revolutionary—'

'Absurd.'

'That you, Miss Watters, also wish to destroy a devout Christian, but that is because you are a lesbian rather than a Communist.'

'Good God,' I say weakly.

'And finally that Watters Press wishes to whip up a controversy with the book, and make Dr Godfrey a scapegoat in order to sell more copies.'

'We only wanted to publish fine *poetry*.' My chest is tight with anxiety.

'And you're saying we have to go to court in a month?' says Ned. 'But Godfrey only knows my pen-name, he doesn't know I'm actually Edward Quest. And if I have to face him in court—I don't know if I can.'

'I'm sorry, Dr Caswell, but before the trial begins we shall be required to inform Dr Godfrey's solicitor of your true identity. Your poetry is fundamental to the case. For instance, in the lines, '*Free from God's kindness, White Jap's betrayal*'—you hint at the man's name and use a term he has already sued someone for and, sadly, very successfully too.'

'And if—if Godfrey wins, and a jury says we must pay him the money, then what?' says Ned.

'Then, Dr Caswell, you must pay it or go to gaol.'

'But if you don't *have* the money?' says Nancy.

'The usual course is to declare bankruptcy. That means your property becomes the legal property of a trustee, who will sell it so the proceeds may be paid to Dr Godfrey. If he wins, of course.'

'Property?' Klara whispers. 'The printery? Our *home*?'

'Indeed. And if you are employed, sums are recovered from your wages until the debt is met.'

We sit in horrified silence, while Mr Roderick scratches notes with his pen. After a time he looks up and says, 'Do you still have friends from that time? More witnesses might strengthen the case.'

Ned shakes his head. 'It's been seven years, we've all scattered. We were civilian prisoners, don't forget. We don't join the Returned Servicemen's League, there's nothing that brings us together. Harry —and Godfrey—are the only people I still know from that time.'

As we walk back to the printery I say, 'We didn't greet you properly before, Nancy, but how lovely to see you. Is your father still well?'

Nancy nods. 'Almost completely better, thanks to Ned.' They smile at each other.

'And have you come to Sydney to see the sights?' I say.

'Sort of.' Nancy pauses. 'Since Ned was here for the weekend, we though it might be nice for both of us ...' She trails off.

'Of course,' I say. 'We've prepared the basement flat for Ned, but it's got several bedrooms, so just make yourselves comfortable.'

'We wish to marry,' says Nancy shyly, 'but it is impossible to be alone together in Newcastle—'

'Congratulations!' says Klara.

'But you see, I've been afraid of men since Singapore. Since what happened to my mother. I don't know if I'll be able to be a wife, a real wife to Ned—'

'Oh, my *dear*, I've said it doesn't matter,' Ned says. 'I may be older but I'm almost as inexperienced. That's how it is for many people, yet things seem to work out in the end.'

She shakes her head. 'I won't marry you, Ned, unless I know for certain we can both be happy.'

There's a silence as they gaze soulfully at each other.

'Well,' I say. 'That's wonderful. You two go and have as much peace and quiet as you want, while Klara and I have a think about this crazy lawsuit.'

I rummage in my handbag. 'Here's a front door key—Ned, you remember how to get to the house from here, don't you?—and we'll see you at dinner tonight.'

At the printery, Klara and I sit in my office and smile at each other. 'Poor things,' I say. 'I wouldn't be that confused and untouched again for a thousand pounds.'

'Nor me, my love,' she says. 'But we may need a thousand pounds and more if we lose this case.'

'Oh God, I can hardly believe it! How could our *beautiful* book trigger such a disaster?'

Klara shakes her head and opens a folder Mr Roderick gave us. 'He says we must find answers to many questions. One, what proof do we have that Dr Godfrey was collaborating with the Japanese?

Two, who called him 'White Jap' and why? Three, is Dr Bell certain that when Dr Caswell was arrested, Godfrey was genuinely pleased? Four, are Dr Bell's portraits of Dr Godfrey in friendly conversation with Japanese officers an accurate likeness?'

'Gosh, *stop*,' I say. 'For the first we have to find other people to testify. Might help with the second question as well. Number three, we can ask Harry if he's certain. Um, what was four, again?'

'Harry's portraits,' says Klara.

'We've never met this awful man so we have no idea how good the likenesses are—but I suppose Ned could tell us.' I sigh and pin my bun back into place.

Klara smiles and tucks a strand of hair behind my ear. I kiss her and say, 'What else?'

'The charge that Harry is a Communist—surely, he is a Socialist?'

'I believe so, but I've no idea of the difference—' I say.

There's a tap at the door. Reg Frisket says, 'Got that proof copy you wanted, Yvonne.'

'Reg, come and talk to us. You're in the union—what's the difference between a Communist and a Socialist?'

He laughs and sits down. 'Give me a month and I'll explain, and the next bloke'd tell you I've got it all wrong. But they both want people to have a fair share of the proceeds of workers' labour, but with Communism the state owns and controls everything. Socialism's less extreme, so private property's all right. What else? Communism won't have a bar of religion, wants to close all the churches. Not like that with Socialism, more tolerant.'

'Ah, so *that's* why Harry the Socialist is alleged to be a Communist who wants to destroy the devout Dr Godfrey,' I say.

'And what a fine bloke Harry is, too,' says Reg. 'Look at Britain now and their new National Health Service! In this country people die because they're too bloody poor to afford a doctor. Wouldn't happen in a Socialist state, I tell you!' He stops. 'Getting a bit cranky there. Sorry.'

'Why is this country so obsessed with hating Communism?' says Klara. 'Did not the Prime Minister try to *ban* it last year?'

'The old sod certainly did,' says Reg earnestly. 'Tried to ban the Communist Party and failed, then pulled a referendum about it as well. But the whole country decided you could join whatever party you liked. I was proud to be Australian that day, I can tell you.'

'But to be called a Communist is still a problem, isn't it?' I say.

'Oh, yeah. People are always suing each other for defamation right, left and centre.'

'You mean it's defamation to call someone a Communist if they're not?' I say. 'Gosh. We might be able to turn that back on Godfrey. Marvellous, Reg!'

'Glad to be of service,' he says grinning.

'Service,' says Klara. '*Service*. Reg, you were in the army. We must find people who were civilian prisoners at Changi to back up Ned and Harry's story. But those men do not gather at the Returned Servicemen's League. How we would locate them today?'

Reg is puzzled. 'Why do you think they don't gather at the RSL?'

'That is what Ned said.'

'Ned and Harry, bless them, they're too posh—wouldn't go to the RSL in a fit. But yeah, as it happens, some of the civilian internees do. Only place they can be with other blokes who understand. Look, I'll put out the word and see what we can dig up.'

'There,' I say, closing the oven door. 'Should be ready in about forty-five minutes.'

We hear footsteps on the stairs. 'In here,' I call out and Nancy and Ned arrive at the kitchen door. Klara makes everyone gin and tonics, then we go into the lounge room where, as usual, Claire is curled up reading in an armchair.

I notice Nancy's hair is looser and her cheeks are flushed. By the look of it she and Ned are starting to enjoy their time together.

'Everything all right down in the flat?' I say.

'Perfect, Yvonne,' says Nancy, and Ned goes a little pink.

'Did you say earlier you cannot spend time together in Newcastle?' says Klara.

'I live in the accommodation for doctors,' says Ned, 'and Nancy's in the Nurses' Home, but doctors and nurses aren't permitted to go out together. If we were even seen in a cafe, Nancy would lose her job and I'd be reprimanded. I don't think we realised how restrictive it would be.'

'What about Eliza and Harry's house?' I say.

'We're welcome there,' says Nancy, 'but—'

She gazes at Ned and he shakes his head. 'Actually, it's awful. Eliza and Harry are so unhappy. They snipe at each other all the time. That's why Harry didn't come today. He doesn't care about the case. He doesn't care about anything at the moment.'

Klara and I glance at each other. 'On the phone it was not obvious,' she says. 'That is bad news.'

'So we may have to fight this case without much help from Harry,' says Ned. 'Did you come up with any ideas this afternoon?'

'It seems the RSL might be useful, even for civilians,' I say. 'And Mr Roderick wants to know how accurate Harry's depictions of Godfrey are.'

'They appear dashed off, but if you know Godfrey they're unmistakable—the posture, the smirk,' says Ned. 'But if you don't, it could be anybody.'

'I thought of something else,' says Nancy hesitantly. 'In law there's something called *consciousness of guilt*. Why is Godfrey seeing himself in a few paintings that, if you didn't know him, could be anyone?' She looks around at us. 'I think he can't stop himself suing because he *knows* he's guilty. But I don't know how we prove it.'

After dinner I go out to the phone in the hall and ring Harry. Eliza answers and says, 'No, he's not home yet. How did your talk with the solicitor go this morning?'

'He didn't have very good news. Eliza, I'm sorry to tell you, but if Godfrey wins this case—and that's looking not impossible—we may lose our house. You may lose yours.'

'The *house*? But Harry didn't think it was as serious as that.'

'Nor did we. You see, in the end we have no *proof* of Godfrey's culpability. The lawyer asked if we had—oh, convictions in another court, post-war tribunal, government records, statements from senior prisoners, that sort of thing.'

'No.' Eliza sighs. 'I don't think so. Harry and Ned were so certain in themselves—but that doesn't count, does it? And without that sort of proof, then perhaps we *have* libelled him.'

I hear her moving the phone. 'Sorry, feeling a bit shaky. Just sitting down.'

I say, 'So you see we have to find other people who were in the camp, senior people if possible.'

'But Harry's lost track of everyone he knew then,' she says.

'Perhaps we can find some ex-prisoners through the RSL. Reg is working on it.'

Eliza laughs bleakly. 'That's good, but I still can't … oh, Christ. Our *house*?'

'I'm afraid so.' I take a breath. 'Also, Nancy mentioned things were a little difficult for you and Harry right now.'

She hesitates. 'Could say that. Actually we're barely on speaking terms. It's escalated from a couple of quarrels to …' After a time she swallows and says, 'Yvie, I can't understand it.'

'I'm *so* sorry, love,' I say gently. 'I expect this lawsuit's eating away at him, making him feel terrible. Would you ask him to ring me back when he can?'

'Of course.' Eliza clears her throat. 'Oh, I meant to tell you—have you seen Tina?'

'No, not lately. Why?'

'She's divorcing Nikos,' says Eliza. 'Going to marry Jimmy Kelso.'

'Oh that *silly* girl!'

'I know. And poor old Nikos is playing the guilty party, so it won't take long, she says.'

'Talk about from frying pan into fire,' I say. 'Does she really imagine a lounge lizard is going to be a kinder, better husband than Nikos?'

'Don't think she's looking for kindness, Yvie. Excitement, I suppose. I've tried to talk sense, get her to slow down a little, but she's so *certain* about Jimmy she just shrugs it off. Still, she's a grown woman, nothing we can do about it.'

'True,' I say. 'And have you heard from Billie lately?'

'No. That's something else I don't understand. Jenny's nearly a year old and Bill's never even come to see her.' Eliza's voice changes. 'To see *me*, and we used to be so close. Sorry, I'm such a maudlin cow lately. But I miss her so terribly—'

'I haven't seen her either, not for ages. I think she's avoiding us all for some reason, not just you.'

She laughs sadly. 'A small comfort. Oh, wait on—sounds like Harry's just coming in. You can give him all the ghastly news yourself.'

16. Harry: The Letter

We're here in a courtroom, all dark timber, ornate plaster and red carpet—the Supreme Court of New South Wales, for God's sake—and I'm about to lose everything because of this stupid, bloody scheme by Klara and Ned and Yvonne and my own *wife*.

My paintings, my memories, they were private! Why the hell did I give in and let them be published? I'm sick with with foreboding. And now the whole damned tribe is turning up as well—as if *that's* going to help.

Nikos and Tina enter and sit in the public gallery, chatting amicably. I'm surprised to see them together given the divorce—and amazed they got it through the courts so quickly as well. What on earth is society coming to? Though Nikos always was a little offbeat—reads science fiction, cowboys in space, rockets going to the moon, for Christ's sake.

He also looks older than before, poor sod, while my sister is groomed and content. No sign of the new man Jimmy. I haven't met him yet, though Eliza says he's attractive and cunning. Hope Tina'll be all right. But she's become quite the little perfumed steam-roller, so I'm sure she'll be fine.

Billie's next, with some cynical-looking bloke. They sit down beside Eliza and Billie says, 'Oh, Lizzie love, I've been such an idiot, I'm sorry I haven't been to see you, I've missed you *terribly*,' and they hug. God knows why that affects Eliza so much, but she has to get out her handkerchief.

'Harry this is László, who works at Tina's club,' says Billie. 'Good drinking mate.'

László and I shake hands. He must be the refugee musician Tina sometimes mentions. I must say Billie's looking better than at our book launch, eighteen months ago. And what a bloody abyss between then and now.

Ah, there's Reg Frisket. What a godsend he's been. Through some mates at the RSL he managed to track down Frank Foster and Maurie Johnson to be witnesses. All three sit behind me, and I turn and shake their hands, feeling like weeping.

Frank was a hospital orderly, while Maurie was a chemist who made pigments for the camp artists out of berries and all sorts of odd things. He's here to testify my paintings are original and from wartime. Of *course* they bloody-well are. Who'd paint those nightmares if they had better things to do with their lives?

I rub my face. I'm so tired and the circus hasn't even begun. My throat is dry and I desperately want a piss, although I went before we came in. Just nerves, keep calm.

I gaze around. To my right is the jury section, in front are the barristers' tables, then beyond them are the high leather chairs of the bench. A few people are seating themselves, court officials. Our lawyer is at the front—not the solicitor Mr Roderick, but our barrister, Mr Barrington. He's Barrister Barrington. I almost laugh. Stop it, you fucking fool.

'Harry?' says Eliza, her face anxious. My wife's face. My wife, the woman I hardly know any more, the mother of my children. She takes my hand, which surprises me as she so rarely touches me nowadays. I withdraw it and say, 'I'm all right'. Eliza blinks and turns forward again.

I don't know how this is supposed to work, I'm a *doctor*. How the hell did I end up here?

Godfrey comes in. That bastard Godfrey, who's so spectacularly torpedoed all our lives. He sits beside his barrister and they murmur to each other. Mr Barrington turns and beckons. It's time for us defendants to sit with him. I feel exhausted.

The judge comes in, bewigged and black-robed. Someone says, 'All rise.' We do, and bow, then the judge sits. There's some palaver about the jury, apparently you only have four people for defamation cases, not twelve, Christ knows why. The four jurors sit down, one of them a woman. I didn't even know they *let* women onto juries.

I think of Izabel's fury at my lack of respect for all the supposedly clever things women did in the war. She said I was old-fashioned, stuck in the past, but it's not the bloody past right now!

It's the agonising present, and my oh-so modern wife Eliza has only helped blow this disaster up in our faces.

The judge says, 'We meet to hear the claim for alleged libel brought by the plaintiff Dr Aylwen Godfrey against the defendants, Dr Edward Caswell, Dr Harold Bell and Miss Yvonne Watters. Mr Jones is acting for the plaintiff and Mr Barrington for the defendants. Now, Mr Jones, I believe you and Mr Barrington have met and agreed to withdrawn some of the plaintiff's claims?'

Mr Jones bobs to his feet. 'Yes, your Honour, we've agreed the charges of Communist bias made against Doctors Caswell and Bell are unable to be sustained—'

'I'm glad to hear that, Mr Jones. As we all know from the referendum, political beliefs are a personal matter. And the accusation of sexual prejudice on the part of Miss Watters?'

'Again, your Honour, we agreed that has no standing in the case.'

'Very good Mr Jones. I'm surprised you permitted your instruction to rest upon such shaky ground. Now where are we?'

'Perhaps we may consider the motivation of Miss Watters, principal of the Watters Press, to cause a swell of controversy in order to sell more copies of the book?'

'Perhaps we may, Mr Jones. Is there the slightest evidence a controversy has arisen from the book, apart from the ripple engendered by this very action brought by Dr Godfrey? I believe, in fact, the book has passed unnoticed in the greater literary world.'

Klara sighs to herself.

'Yes, your Honour,' says Mr Jones, with a touch of desperation.

'Let us move on, shall we? The issue of belief, Mr Jones. In discussion with Mr Barrington, did you come to any decision about Doctors Caswell and Bell's strongly-held beliefs that Dr Godfrey— to put it at its most brutal—collaborated with the Japanese?'

'There's certainly no question they are sincerely-held beliefs,' says Mr Jones in despair.

'Speak up, Mr Jones. So the defendants believe their depictions are the truth, and nothing has been advanced that might support a defamatory motivation either, would you agree?'

'Mmm, yes, your Honour,' says Mr Jones. 'But the *proof*, we must question what is the proof behind these groundless accusations of collaboration with the enemy—accusations that have left my client open to ridicule, hatred and contempt.'

'The trouble is, Mr Jones, I'm puzzled why your client assumes that these poems and watercolours apply to him in the first place? One of the fundamentals of defamation is that the defamed party is *identifiable*—in fact it is almost dogma that the party be *named*.'

The judge rubs his forehead. 'Your client is not named, and were he not before me today I would never have been able to identify him from these paintings. What on earth is going on, Mr Jones?'

Mr Jones gathers his dignity. 'Your Honour, while we today may not identify my client from this libellous publication—'

'Mr Jones.'

'—this publication there were, however, thousands of civilians in Changi Prison who would be able to identify him through that despicable phrase, White Jap.'

'A broad reach,' says the judge. 'But the phrase, Mr Jones? The phrase in the poem—' he flips through the copy of our book on his desk, '—*Games of Betrayal*, which I believe is the crux of your client's suit? Let me quote—'

> *'Free from God's kindness*
> *White Jap's betrayal*
> *Broke all the rules as*
> *Pawns are discarded*
> *In endgame's despair'*

Mr Jones says, 'I would point out, your Honour, that *Free from God's kindness* does indeed convey Dr Godfrey's name.'

'Hmm,' says the judge. 'It may suggest. Continue.'

'*White Jap* was a calumny thrown at anyone who tried to deal with the enemy captors in perhaps a more—ah, devious manner than outright aggression. But its use does not mean my client was *actually* a traitor and, your Honour, any assertion to the contrary is plainly defamatory.'

He sits down. Mr Barrington—who has probably been enjoying the sight of Mr Jones being roasted on the judicial spit as much as the rest of us—gets to his feet.

'Your Honour, one assertion of the plaintiff is that Dr Bell's paintings are a recent attempt to smear him and did not originate from the period in Changi Prison. I would like to call Mr Maurice Johnson to the stand.'

Dear old Maurie comes up and testifies he used to make me pigments and he'd seen my paintings and they were the originals, done in the prison camp. Cut and dried.

The judge looks over his glasses. 'Continue, Mr Barrington.'

'I'd like to call Mr Francis Foster to the stand.'

Frank is greyer but still the solid, reliable bloke I used to know. Mr Barrington says, 'You were an orderly at Singapore General Hospital, were you not, Mr Foster?'

'Yes sir, and I was marched off to Changi alongside Doctor Bell and the others.'

'What was your perception of Dr Godfrey before the days of the Double Tenth in October 1943?'

'He was a penny-pincher at the hospital, and in the camp he'd go out of his way to brown-nose the Japanese. They gave him extra food. He was the only bloke getting fat that year, I can tell you.'

Mr Barrington smiles. 'By brown-nose, you mean—cultivate?'

'Yeah.'

'And your perceptions of Dr Godfrey *after* the Double Tenth?'

Frank looks at Godfrey with contempt. 'Didn't help out at the hospital when all the poor bastards came back tortured and broken by the secret police, that's for sure. He also had a stash of drugs from the Japs we'd have killed for, but just kept them for himself.'

'And how do you know that, Mr Foster?'

'Ah—a mate got into his room and found them. Wrapped up in Jap packaging, but we knew what they were: antimalarials, antiseptics, pain-killers. But we put them to bloody good use.' He stares steadily at Godfrey, who gazes away, expressionless.

'And were you aware of the usage of the term *White Jap* in the camp?'

'Yeah, started after the Double Tenth. Before that you could say, oh, maybe he's trying to get on their good side, spy on them. But afterwards? He loved the attention, loved them calling him Godfrey-san. Mark of respect for Japs, you know, your Honour.'

'Thank you, Mr Foster,' says the judge. 'Carry on.'

'Godfrey'd strut around, and the guards'd even bow now and then, *bow* to him! Look, I can't prove what he told them, but they certainly liked it. Most of us thought it was because of *who* he fingered. Not just innocents like Dr Caswell, but I know for a fact they collared a couple of our radio blokes straight after Godfrey was seen whispering in the guards' ears.'

'Thank you, Mr Foster,' says Mr Barrington.

The judge says, 'Do you have questions for the witness, Mr Jones?'

'Ah, no, your Honour.'

'Please stand down, Mr Foster.' Frank winks at me as he takes his seat in the gallery again.

Mr Barrington says, 'Now, we know from Mr Foster's testimony that Dr Godfrey flaunted his friendships with the Japanese guards, also born out by Dr Bell's paintings, exhibits four, six and seven, in which Dr Bell recorded Dr Godfrey's pleasure—and implicit culpability—at the arrest of Dr Caswell. Dr Godfrey obtained food and medicine from guards and did not share them for the benefit of all. It was believed he helped choose suspects for torture by the secret police, so the appellation "White Jap" became widespread.'

He leans forward. 'But here, your Honour, let us come to the essence of the matter. Dr Godfrey has made no effort *whatsoever* to present the slightest rationale for his behaviour. He has simply insisted my clients are wrong and have thus defamed him!'

He turns to the jury. 'In the absence of the slightest evidence to the contrary, my clients' beliefs are perfectly appropriate. The defence of truth in this case was a belief sincerely held by the defendants, and by extension, their publisher, Watters Press. For them to express those beliefs in a work of the higher arts cannot, and should not, be regarded as libel.'

I notice the jurors are nodding a little as if they agree, and my hopes rise. Then the judge tells us to break for lunch and meet back here at two o'clock. I can't believe a whole morning has passed already.

Mr Willoughby shakes our hands and leaves, while Ned and Nancy wander off to a park to murmur sweet nothings to each other. The rest of us go to a cafe. The women sit at one table, no doubt to admire my sister's enormous engagement ring, while we men are at another and hoe into sandwiches.

Maurie tells me he's a chemist in a paint factory now.

'Happy as a pig in mud, Harry, but still can't make a deep red like that one I did for you. Squashed bugs, alum, piss, damar gum—just can't replicate it.'

'Not bloody surprising, mate,' I say.

Maurie laughs and says, 'See any of the other boys nowadays?'

I shake my head. 'Couldn't believe how Reg here managed to track you down. Do you?'

'Not very often, but I saw old Sly Sammy in the street last week.'

'Sly Sammy?' says Frank. '*There's* a man who lived up to his name.'

I turn to Nikos, who's still eating, and László, lighting up a thin cigarillo.

'Sammy was an engraver, fantastic eye. Used to do forgeries of official documents in the camp, fooled the guards every time. So what's he doing, Maurie?'

Maurie grins. 'Keeping *very* quiet about his current job, which suggests—along with a certain twitchiness—he's still engaged in the noble art.'

I chuckle. 'And you, Frank? How's tricks?'

'Great, Harry. Married, couple of nippers, living like a king. Still work at a hospital but I'm a paper-pusher now, can you believe it?'

'You were always a crafty bugger. How the hell could you tell that judge straight-faced it was a *mate* nicked the medical supplies from Godfrey's room? Good one, Frank.'

We laugh, and then Nikos asks about my youngsters. I tell him they're fighting fit, and enquire after Steve. Nikos says, pleased, 'In his second year of music at the Conservatorium.'

László nods. 'He is doing very well, too.' That reminds me he was teaching Steve the piano.

I joke, 'Going to get him playing at the jazz club?'

László nods. 'He is already sitting in on sessions with bands for the experience.'

I glance at Nikos, wondering what he thinks of that. After all, the jazz club is Tina's territory and linked to Jimmy, the man who broke up his marriage.

Nikos shrugs and says, 'Whatever Steve wants to do is all right by me. I had enough of being told what to do by my own father. He'll find his own feet.'

He and László glance at each other. Allies against the all-conquering Jimmy, perhaps? Good, means they'll keep an eye out for my sister. I know she thinks the world of László and, despite the divorce, she and Nikos are still close.

That puzzles me yet again. *Women.*

All too soon it's time to reassemble. I'm feeling optimistic after this morning's arguments, then a clerk comes in quietly and gives Godfrey's barrister an envelope.

He looks at the contents and gets to his feet. 'Your Honour, I apologise, but this very important evidence has only just arrived. May I present it?'

'Very well, Mr Jones. Let me see,' says the judge. A clerk hands him the letter and he reads, looking up at Dr Godfrey at one point.

After a time he says, 'I will submit this into evidence. It is a communication from Dr Everett—now Sir Hugh Everett—whom those of you from the civilian prison will, of course, recognise was the elected leader of your camp.'

Ned and I look at each other, puzzled. Everett was certainly the camp leader and did most of the negotiations with the Japanese— much to our advantage too, as he spoke some of the lingo.

He was a fine old chap, always puffing away on his pipe. I'd believe anything he put his name to, but can't imagine what he'd have to say about Godfrey.

The judge clears his throat and reads:

To Whom it May Concern,

It has come to my attention that Dr Aylwen Godfrey has been defamed as a "White Jap" who betrayed his fellow prisoners to the Japanese during the imprisonment of civilians in Singapore from 1942 to 1945. Nothing could be further from the truth.

Now, long past the events of those difficult days, I have been given official dispensation to reveal a closely-held secret. Dr Godfrey was personally assigned by me to cultivate friendships among the Japanese guards, to make it appear he was a traitor, to bear the painful appellation of "White Jap", and to consistently work, despite appearances, for the success of the Allied effort against the Japanese.

On the terrible day of the Double Tenth, his skills as an intelligence agent saved almost all of the men maintaining our vital radio communications from certain torture by the secret police.

Tragically, that meant a number of innocent prisoners were taken away. There was nothing the camp hierarchy could do to ameliorate this, as the greater good had to prevail in wartime.

After Dr Caswell returned from his imprisonment I must emphasise I went out of my way to explain to both him and Dr Bell that the situation was more complex than they realised, and that Dr Godfrey was acting in a covert role under my instructions.

I wish to make it clear at this time that Dr Godfrey is entirely irreproachable in this matter, and that any communication to the

*contrary by Doctors Bell and Caswell, who were perfectly aware of
the true situation, is most certainly defamatory.*
   Yours faithfully,
   Sir Hugh Everett KBE

The judge passes the letter to a clerk, who shows it to us then places
it with the other evidence. Ned and I stare at each other,
astonished. It's clearly Everett's distinctive handwriting.

I vaguely remember him making some statement at the time
about sacrifice in war, but I didn't realise he was talking about
Godfrey! Was I so oblivious? Did my dislike of the man mean I'd
defamed him, just as he was claiming? Sweat chills my spine.

Mr Jones rises, smiling. 'Your Honour, we now have *proof* that Dr
Godfrey's actions were at the direct instruction of the camp leader
and also, damningly, that the defendants themselves knew this.
Still, they published this web of lies, well aware of what an
accusation of treachery might mean to a man as irreproachable—I
repeat, in the words of Sir Hugh Everett—as *irreproachable* as Dr
Godfrey. As compensation for this malicious libel I call upon this
court to award him the maximum in damages.'

Mr Barrington says something, but his words are like the rushing
of wind in my brain, airy and insubstantial. The jurors are
frowning, then the judge sends them to consider their verdict.

Mr Barrington murmurs, 'I suggest you go out, have a break, get a
cup of tea.' He doesn't have to say this is a fucking disaster, it
obviously is.

As we file out of the court, busybody Eliza lingers at the evidence
table to read the damning letter. We sit slumped on benches and
time passes. Someone finds a tea trolley and I get a welcome brew,
then I have to piss again. My heart is thumping, my skull hurts.

Eliza sits silently beside me, then says, 'Hugh Everett was a
Japanese speaker, wasn't he?'

I nod.

'Interesting,' she says. 'I think he was a friend of Mr Kingsley.'

'Who?'

'Mr Kingsley. Worked with me. Authority on the Taishō poets.'

'Eliza, this isn't the time or place for a trip down memory lane.'

She glances at me. 'Probably not.'

I fall into a semi-stupor. Eventually an usher comes and we troop back to the courtroom.

The judge says, 'Has the jury reached a verdict?'

The foreman says, 'Yes, your Honour.'

'What is your verdict?'

'We find the defendants guilty of defamation.'

Guilty? I feel as if the ground has given way. But—but—

'And have you determined the extent of damages?'

'Yes, your Honour. The defendants must each pay the plaintiff three thousand pounds.'

The judge's face is bland, calm. It's nothing to him but this is my *life*, and it's suddenly in chaos, suddenly incomprehensible.

I hear gavel-banging and legalistic mumbling, and 'All rise' and people going here and there and saying words, words, words, and I don't know what's going on. I want to put my head on my arms and block it all out, but I have to wait, stiff-faced, and desperately try not to weep.

Godfrey, grinning ghoul-like, pushes past us with his barrister.

Reg Frisket and our old mates come over and thump our shoulders in commiseration and talk about getting a beer some time. Ned and I nod and shake their hands, as dazed as men awaiting execution.

17. Tina: The Shimmering Wedding

As the courtroom empties we gather around Mr Barrington. He taps his papers together and slides them into his fine leather briefcase, and says, 'Now, we'll get started soon on the appeal, as there's rather a backlog and it could be a year before it's heard.'

'Appeal?' says Harry slowly.

'Of course. That letter was a brilliant move, but we can tear a dozen holes in the story. What was this Sir Hugh Everett told about the case and by whom? How reliable is the fellow in the first place? Producing the letter so late stopped us investigating it properly, and impressed the jury far more than it should have. Of course we'll appeal.'

My brother shakes his head. 'We don't have the money—'

'Yes, you do,' I say. 'I'll help. That little toad isn't going to get away with this.'

'Thanks, Tina, you're a gem,' says Harry, his shoulder slumped. He looks at the barrister. 'But our *house*? When do we have to sell it?'

'Sell it?' says Mr Barrington, closing the briefcase with an expensive click. 'You don't have to sell anything.' He shrugs. 'If we lose the appeal you may have to consider your options, but that's a long way into the future.' He gazes around at us. 'This is only the beginning, don't despair.'

That sounds promising. As Yvonne and Klara say goodbye and leave with Nancy and Ned, I overhear Eliza speaking to Mr Barrington.

'Will you be given a true copy of that letter?' she says. 'A photographic copy?'

'Usually we get just a typed transcript, but I suppose we could ask for a copy.'

'I'd like one as well,' she says evenly.

'Certainly, Mrs Bell. I'll see about it as soon as possible.'

I murmur, 'You're amazing, Eliza. That look of steel—in the army you'd have made Brigadier.'

She smiles. 'Oh, Tina. Couldn't show an instant's weakness running a Civil Service department or they'd have been onto me like vultures.'

'Why the copy?'

Eliza shakes her head. 'Something about it was slightly off. I met Hugh Everett a few time in Singapore before the invasion—he was a friend of one of my colleagues. Probably nothing, but worth a second look.'

I nod, and turn to the others. 'Listen everyone. Come back to Rozelle—we've already got food and drink ready. We'd hoped for a happier outcome, but we can still cheer ourselves up. I've got a surprise as well. I'll take Eliza in my car because I want to gossip, Nikos can take Harry, and Billie, you bring László with you.'

'Oh, not sure I can come—' says Billie.

'Yes you can. Both of you. We need your brains and his cynicism.'

Billie laughs. 'I'll come if I'm the cynicism and László the brains.'

'We will see you there, Tina,' says László, smiling.

As we walk out to the cars I think, Who *is* Billie sleeping with? Could it be László? I've never seen her at his place, but nowadays I only use my rooms at Tempo when I stay late after busy nights, otherwise I'm with Jimmy at his opulent flat above the Lounge.

I suppose if Billie and László were having an affair he could go to her place, but he always seems to be at Tempo. It's odd. She must be involved with *someone*—some days she's glowing and sleepy-eyed, and others she's pale and distracted. She's clearly in a relationship, and by the look of it a difficult one.

Married man, perhaps? Hope not. Only a stupid cow would go down that path.

'*You* want to gossip?' says Eliza, as I turn into George Street.

'I can gossip. I'm just a ruthless business dynamo part of the time.'

Eliza smiles. 'So what about?'

'Your brother Pete brings Vivy to Tempo now and then. The other day he said he hasn't seen you at all since coming to Australia, though he's been here for over a year. Why?'

Eliza shrugs. 'They arrived just before I had Jenny, and afterwards I was so low I didn't want to meet anyone. Newcastle's a hundred miles further away from him than Sydney and Janet doesn't like to travel.' She sighs. 'We talk on the phone, and I'd love to see him, but Pete's very busy.'

I nod and stop at a red light. 'And now Jenny's turned a year old, how are you feeling?'

'A little better, but it's not her, she's a darling—it's just that *everything* seems grey. This court case is the most interesting thing to happen in my life for ages. Which is a bit sad, really.'

I laugh. 'Well, let's get home, I have a surprise that might interest you there.'

'You talk as if you still live in Rozelle,' says Eliza, puzzled. 'How does Nikos feel about that?'

'He's been so kind, Eliza. I hurt him terribly, but now we're divorced we talk more easily than we have for years. He says I can stay at Rozelle any time I want—in the guest room, of course.'

'But what does Jimmy think about your ex-husband offering you a cosy bolthole?'

'Jimmy understands.' I smile. 'He knows he's the only man I want.'

I park the car. I still have my own key so we enter, and I open the champagne just as Billie and László arrive, followed closely by Nikos and Harry.

Harry seems a bit more himself again. 'My God, I'm so *naive*. I had no idea we could appeal, and the barrister seems optimistic too. So I'm not going to worry, at least for tonight.'

The doorbell rings and I go out saying, 'Ah, my surprise, I hope.'

It is, and I usher my visitors to the lounge room. 'And here we *are* —it's Pete and Janet!'

I've met Pete at Tempo before but not Janet, who apparently thinks the club is a den of sin. He's a good-looking man in his early forties and she's a blonde in her late twenties with a cool smile.

Amid a babble of welcome, Eliza and Harry jump to their feet.
Eliza hugs him, crying, 'Oh, *Pete!*' and Harry thumps him on the
back. Nikos shakes Pete's hand, grinning, and László waves genially
from his seat—they've met previously at Tempo.

Billie has known him for ages too, so I'm sure she'll be glad. But
she's staring in ... consternation, delight, horror?

She flushes pink and gulps the contents of her glass and gazes at
the floor. Pete looks everywhere but at her, and it hits me: they
used to be lovers.

And they still are.

As the evening continues Billie recovers. She's quiet, but not
noticeably so. Pete glances at her from the corners of his eyes, again
not noticeably.

Janet watches them both, but she's too young to recognise the
awareness flowing between them like a long, mellow note on the
saxophone.

I can see why Klara and Yvonne said they hadn't quite taken to
Janet. With a meeting of family and old friends there's always lots
of 'do you remember?' and 'whatever happened to?' but the silly
woman doesn't know when to shut up.

She may have fascinating things to say about their large property,
Vivy's posh school, her rich friends, but now is not the moment. I
do my best but she keeps dropping clangers, and I almost feel sorry
for her.

Billie joked once that Janet reminded her of a second-rate
Charlotte, and I agree. I recall (with fresh envy) Charlotte's blue
satin gown: Janet seems like a cheap cotton copy in comparison.
That's unkind I suppose, but I wish she'd let Eliza finish a sentence.
The dear girl is animated for the first time in ages.

But poor Billie! Surely she can't expect it to end well? Janet's not
the sort to let her husband go even if he wanted to. But would he
want to? No, I get the feeling Pete is hooked on her pert blondness,
just as Eliza told me he was with Charlotte.

And perhaps Pete, for all his dark good looks, pretty wife, clever mistress and prosperous life, seems even now … dissatisfied?

I shake my head. Silly Tina, you've had enough to drink. While the conversation bubbles along I get up and take plates out to the kitchen, and Nikos follows me with empty glasses.

'What a good idea of yours,' he says. 'Pete seems a nice bloke, Harry's almost forgotten about the court case, and Eliza—I haven't seen her so happy in ages.'

I start running hot water in the sink and laugh. 'I *know*. Despite all the bizarre undercurrents I'm feeling very pleased with myself.'

Nikos brings the glasses over to the sink. 'Undercurrents?'

'Come on,' I say. 'I can't be the only one to see it. Billie and *Pete*. Obvious as the neon sign outside Tempo. But you'd have to be crazy to get involved with a married man. Poor old Billie.'

I put the plates in the hot water and turn.

Oh, foolish Tina.

At the sight of his face I realise for the first time why, when other men might have blustered and lashed out, Nikos let me drift away so easily from this marriage. The beating core of his passionate, sensible heart is no longer me.

I leave soon afterwards and drive to the Starlight Lounge. I find Jimmy on the sofa in his flat, listening to dance music on the radio and sipping brandy: the beating core of my own passionate and far-from-sensible heart.

'You're back, sweetheart. Had a good night, then?'

'Oh, Jimmy, I've made such a *faux pas*!'

He laughs. 'Come and tell me about it, and the court case too. Coffee or brandy?'

'No, just put your arms around me.'

'Easily accommodated, doll. Now what's going on?'

'Well, the court case was lost, but they're taking it to appeal so it might be all right in the end.'

'Good. No *faux pas* so far.'

'And tonight, Pete and his wife turned up just as I planned and it was all going swimmingly, except I suddenly realised Pete and Billie are having an *affair*, so she didn't know where to look, poor thing. And what's worse, I blurted it out to Nikos and it was if I'd gutted him. He loves Billie, you see, that's why he's been so civilised about you and me.'

Jimmy nods. 'Always thought it was on the cards from the way they danced.' He grins. 'Sure your feelings aren't hurt because Nikos has moved on so quickly?'

I look at him indignantly. 'Not at all. Well, perhaps a little.'

Jimmy strokes my cheek. 'I'm pretty sure he'll always have a soft spot for you, anyway.'

'You don't mind?'

He shakes his head. 'We've all got our pasts, the people we're linked to forever. I know you love me and that's all that matters.'

'Oh I *do*, Jimmy, you're all that matters to me too.'

He kisses me, his mouth brandy-tasting and warm, and I sigh and rest my head on his shoulder.

He clears his throat. 'Actually, something I need to tell you about in that general direction, sweetheart. You know how it's taking a bit of time before we can get hitched—'

'Yes, and I still don't understand why.'

'Well, wee Tina, it's like this. I was a silly young fool before the war—' He scratches his chin. 'What I mean is, I got myself involved with a woman, a barmaid. Ah, Dimple.'

'Dimple? Dimple who?'

'Dimple Dorsey. Hard to believe, but her real name.'

'All right. You and Dimple Dorsey. So?'

He takes a breath. 'Fact is, sweetheart, we went and got married.'

'*Married*? But—surely you're divorced by now?'

'Doll, it took a ton of time and money to even *find* the bitch. But at last it's done.' Jimmy smiles. 'The decree absolute came though today. We can tie the knot whenever you want.'

I don't understand the pit in my belly, but then I do: only a stupid cow would let herself get involved with a married man.

My heart hammers. 'But Jimmy, you lied, you told me to my face you were single.'

'Was how I felt, sweetheart. Don't be cross. Look, I was a fool but I was terrified of losing you, smart little Mrs Loukas. You could have returned to your marriage at any time and no one would have blamed you. But I couldn't take the risk, don't you see?'

I nod stiffly. 'But if you lied about that, what else is there?'

'Nothing, I swear it, Tina. Look at me, baby, look into my eyes, I swear it. And it was only to get you, to be sure of you. Come on, you fibbed to me too.'

'Me?'

'Those early days. *Don't touch me, Jimmy, I don't want you.* But you did, Christ how you wanted me. And how I wanted you, your scent, your body, your laugh—you drove me mad and I know you were driving yourself mad.'

Jimmy strokes my knee. 'I *know* when a woman is wet, sweetheart, even though she's sitting up brightly and doing the accounts, and I know when her nipples are throbbing and she's aching, aching, just here ... and here. Oh, yes ... and especially here.'

His sly hand moves higher, past my stocking-top. He caresses me, and I sigh.

He pushes up my skirt and pulls off my panties and buries his face between my thighs, breathing, kissing, licking. I watch, wide open to him, relishing him there, his brown hair against my ruffled red-blonde.

After a time—*such* a time—he lifts his head and we gaze helplessly at each other. He whispers, 'By Christ, I'm not lying now, Tina, and neither are you.'

I groan and urge his head down again and move against his clever, clever mouth.

So the plans for our wedding proceed, and I enjoy every moment of organising it. It's going to be a registry office ceremony, with a luxurious reception at the Starlight Lounge afterwards.

I want Billie to be my bridesmaid but when I tell her, as we're out shopping, she laughs.

'Nah, Teen, I'm no bloody maid.'

'Something of honour? I know, aviator-of-honour.'

'What about Lizzie? She's your sister-in-law.'

'She said she couldn't guarantee being here on the day, what with the kids and Harry's work. So it's got to be you. I'll buy you a gorgeous dress.'

'You can't go bribing me with a dress *every* time you want me to do something,' says Billie.

'Of course not, doll. But what do you think of this coppery silk?'

So that's settled. We buy my dress too, a strapless silver shantung with a built-in corset, tulip skirt, and a dainty jacket to keep my naked shoulders warm. Jimmy loves the sound of it.

László is going to be his best man. I thought it might be Big Davy, but he's gone away to Brisbane.

Pearl's eyes are red and when I ask she says bitterly, 'Those Capelli bastards—they have it in for Davy. Jimmy sent him off for his own good and I don't know when he'll be back.'

'True,' says Jimmy later, frowning a little. 'Had to get the poor bugger away from here. Picked a fight at the betting-shop with Enzo Capelli, not the brightest of moves.'

'But when can he return? Pearl's distraught.'

Jimmy grins. 'Might be sooner that she thinks. The Adlers are making a move, Moshe tells me. The Capellis have lost their grip and a lot of people want them gone.'

'Not a *shooting* war, Jimmy?'

'God no, sweetheart. But the police are going to be very helpful indeed—you can't annoy both the Commissioner and the Adlers without repercussions.'

The weeks go flying by, till it's only days, then hours to the wedding. The night before I stay at my flat above Tempo, wondering how I'll feel when Jimmy and I are finally joined for life.

I remember the modest ceremony with Nikos, seven years ago at the Newcastle registry office. Guess I'll never have the big church wedding, the parade down the aisle, but I don't care. Tomorrow I'll be Mrs Jimmy Kelso.

In the morning Billie comes over, and Pearl a little later. She rarely gives anything away about her past but she was once a hairdresser, so she helps me and Billie get ourselves ready. Pearl is done up to the nines herself, and has resumed her usual feline demeanour—Jimmy has told her Big Davy will soon be home.

Finally we're ready. I stand in front of the mirror, my bouquet in my hands, a little hat with a silvery veil over my eyes, my dress shimmering like moonlight.

'Jeez, you scrub up well, Teen,' says Billie.

'Not so bad yourself, aviator-of-honour,' I say. 'And you too, Pearl —what a gorgeous bunch of ladies we are.' I turn around and take a deep breath. 'Let's go.'

Gaston is waiting downstairs. He's the French chef at the Starlight Lounge and he's going to chauffeur us to the registry office in a rented limousine.

His eyebrows rise and he says, '*Superbe*! How beautiful you are, all of you,' but he's gazing at Pearl. He's always has a fondness for her. Pearl adores the attention, but they'd better be careful once Davy's back in town.

We drive through the city to the impressive old sandstone building of the Registry Office, opposite Hyde Park. Gaston stops the car and we emerge into winter sunlight and climb the stairs.

My mother Jessie, Eliza and Harry can't attend today (they and the kids are all sick with colds), but Yvonne and Klara and friends from the club welcome us in the foyer and someone points us down a corridor to the Marriage Room.

My heart is thumping madly then I see Jimmy and László waiting, and feel a flood of relief. Jimmy takes my hand and whispers, 'My God, you're an angel, *a chuisle*, an *angel*.'

The previous marriage party emerges laughing, then an usher calls out 'Kelso wedding?'

The Marriage Room is pleasant enough, with carved timber and ornate curtains. Our friends sit down in the rows of seats.

With László and Billie beside us, Jimmy and I stand before the registrar as he reads a speech on the sanctity of marriage. Jimmy holds my hand and I can feel his trembling. My heart swells—he's as nervous as me.

The rest is a blur. We promise to love, honour and (in my case) obey. Jimmy puts the ring on my finger and we vow and kiss. We go to one side to fill in the registry, with Billie and László our witnesses, then we turn and our friends smile and applaud.

We stand there dazed, then Billie says, 'Let's get out of here, we've got a party to go to!'

On the registry staircase László takes photos of us with a box camera, and our friends throw confetti and the tiny pieces of coloured tissue flutter and drift up to the clouds.

Jimmy says, 'Come on, baby,' and with Billie and László we dash down to the limousine and jump in, laughing, and drive to the Starlight Lounge a few blocks away.

Jimmy murmurs privately, fiercely, 'My *wife*,' and buries his head against my neck.

The others are walking or driving here from the registry, so when we enter the Starlight Lounge it's empty. I gasp. Everywhere I look are silvery streamers, balloons and banners, glinting and bobbing and shimmering.

'It's starlight, you see—starlight for you, Tina,' Jimmy says shyly, and I sob for a single breath.

Then I say, 'My husband, my *wonderful* husband—give me champagne!' and Jimmy pours me a glass full to overflowing, and says, 'Anything for you, my love. Anything.'

Next morning we wake in Jimmy's bedroom—*my* bedroom now —sunlight glimmering through a gap in the red velvet curtains. He gazes at me, his face still, and says, 'I may have mentioned this before, but that was one hell of a night, Mrs Kelso.'

'It was, but you didn't call me Mrs Kelso that time.'

'Foolish of me. That's who you were in my heart, even then.'

'Not Dimples McGee, or whoever she was?'

Jimmy throws his head back laughing. 'By God, you're fearless. Since the moment you walked into my office that first day, I knew you were mine.'

I nod. 'Took me a while to see it, but here I am, love.'

Later we take baths and wrap ourselves in dressing gowns and sit by the fire, Jimmy's head on my lap.

He chuckles, and I say, 'What is it?'

'Ah, just thinking how I used to tease you about your grey eyes and mine, the beautiful silver-eyed babies we'd make.'

'I remember.' I pause. 'Jimmy? Is that something you want?'

'Is it what I *want*? Oh, Christ.' He takes a breath. 'Yes, always. You?'

'Not with Nikos, we grew apart too quickly. But your baby? I'd have yours in a heartbeat.'

'Takes a bit longer than that, or so I'm told,' he says, grinning.

'Did you want a child … before?'

There's a silence.

'I did, as it happens. But the first wife, she had something of a past and girls like that, they get—damaged, you know.' He sighs. 'She used to say I was shooting blanks, Tina, when it was bloody obvious it was her. It's what ended it for us, I reckon.'

I stroke his face. 'Must have been hard.'

'Funny—most young fellows don't want kids, but I always did. It'd be a family, you see, a family for me here in this country.'

'Sounds good to me, love.'

'You mean we can ditch the French letters and give it a go?'

I laugh. 'My God, *yes*. Let's make a baby.'

Life slowly returns to normal, though it's lit up with the sweetness of being Jimmy's woman, not just as his clever little business manager, but his *wife*. We talk and talk about what's in our hearts, what we've felt and experienced, what we dream of for the future.

I open up to him as never before with anyone, and Jimmy loves me, loves me, loves me, no matter what.

The Adlers send us a handsome wedding present, an antique jewel-box, while several of the thick-necked business associates offer us elegant, expensive gifts: I think László has dropped a quiet word about what would be appropriate.

Every day we seem surrounded by good news. Pearl is happy again, although Gaston the chef isn't, when Big Davy comes home from Brisbane.

László gets news that makes him almost giddy with hope—a possible sighting of the wife and son he feared had died at Auschwitz—and letters are dispatched to Europe to find out more.

Even when a gang war breaks out, it subsides quickly after a few subordinates are shot or beaten or dispatched to gaol—and the fearsome Capellis move their operations to the countryside to reinvent themselves as marijuana, sorry, fruit farmers.

The Adlers, our suppliers, become the new kingpins. Their main business is grog, illegal betting shops, and baccarat casinos in the back-rooms of various clubs. Government officials and policemen of the most exalted rank attend the casinos in droves, so they're well-protected. The Adlers leave drugs to the other dealers, but of course they take their cut.

Old Abe Adler tells me one night they would never deal in drugs because they cloud the mind against *Hashem*—he points solemnly to the heavens—but that stricture clearly doesn't apply to women, for whom he has an elderly, unabashed relish. I sometimes wonder if he even knows what I look like above the neck.

I mostly work on grog deliveries with clever Moshe Adler, the older son. Heavy-set and ruthless, Moshe is happy with our cash flow and even grudgingly admits one day the deal with us turned out surprisingly well.

I hear the other son Sándor—who obviously doesn't appreciate what the heavens require of him—spends a lot of time in clinics coming down from drug binges.

The only problem I have is babies: specifically the lack of one.

Months of disappointment pass, and during a phone call I haltingly tell Eliza about it and burst into tears.

'Tina, love,' she says. 'Don't worry, I had to wait forever. I didn't get pregnant before the war and almost gave up. Then when Harry came back from Singapore it happened instantly. There's no rhyme or reason. Keep trying, don't lose hope.'

Jimmy nods when I tell him, and cuddles me. 'She's absolutely right. And look what she's got now, two beautiful kids. We'll get there, sweetheart, and worrying's the worst possible thing.'

He grins slyly. 'But any advice to keep trying sounds pretty smart to me, what do you think, mountain flower?' And I laugh through my tears and kiss him.

I don't see much of Billie nowadays. I suppose her spare time is taken up with Pete and their affair. I've never spoken about it to her and don't know if I should, but in any case I'm suddenly busy: Tempo starts doing very well.

Of course jazz is now more popular overseas but I hadn't expected it to take off so quickly here too, especially at my club, such an odd little fish in the murky waters of Kings Cross.

Our takings don't compare to the gambling and prostitution joints, and the only drugs I permit around the place are marijuana and alcohol. We may be protected by the Adlers, but I don't want to attract the attention of the sorts of sharks who think they can get away with a quick shotgun raid or a stand-over bashing.

Still, Tempo's new prosperity means we can redecorate the place at last. We start in early 1953, and László and I are kept busy trying to keep Tempo open and cope with the builders as well.

I work in my flat above the club, but rarely sleep there now as I only want to be with Jimmy. My desk and office are in the flat's lounge room, and off the corridor behind is a small bedroom and even smaller kitchen and bathroom. It's a scruffy little place, but it always feels cosy.

László's larger rooms are across the landing, and we have a standing joke about doing up both flats like palaces one day, but of course there's never time.

I'm usually in my office first thing—László is in and out on errands—and mid-mornings he brings us pastries from the European cafe to share over coffee. Then it's back to the paperwork. Afternoons are more practical, sorting out the staff and stores and arrangements downstairs.

The club is closed on Mondays and Tuesdays, then the rest of the week it's open from evening to the early hours, with extra gigs on weekend afternoons. László still plays piano of course, sometimes in a trio with double bass and drums, and they're very good.

I love the *busyness* of Tempo, but I also love the peace late at night, sitting back in the audience and drifting away on a river of glorious music: daring, intricate, perfect.

One summer night we don't close till almost dawn, so I stay at the flat and share a reefer with László. We sit in his lounge room and I gaze at the fascinating pattern on the rug and let the evening drift through my head.

'We do this, you know ... you and me,' I say. 'In this place we built ... we bring them together, musicians and audiences, and create this magic ... this incomparable magic.'

László nods, his eyes heavy-lidded with contentment.

'Here is the mail and the paper,' says László, coming into the office. 'And no apricot pastry today, but I am told the peach is very good.'

The kettle whistles from the kitchen and I go to make our coffee. When I bring the tray back and set it down, László is sitting on the couch, reading the paper. He looks up.

'Problems, perhaps. Police have found two bodies near the wharves, well hidden for perhaps eight months. It is bad enough that one was Enzo Capelli, but the other was a woman named Dimple Kelso.'

He gazes at me, troubled. 'Surely not related to Jimmy?'

'Dimple?' I say, dread in my guts. 'Dimple *Kelso*? And she's *dead*?'

'Tina, are you going to be sick?' Practical László grabs the waste-paper bin.

I shake my head. 'No, no, I'm all right. She ... was Jimmy's wife, his first wife.'

'I had no idea he had been married before.'

'No one does,' I say, breathing heavily. 'They were divorced. My God, I hope Jimmy doesn't go to war with the Capellis. They might have left the city but they're still powerful.'

'But surely it would not have been them. Enzo was a favourite son. It must have been someone else, someone with a grudge against the Capellis.'

He stops and we stare at each other, horrified. 'The *Adlers?*' I whisper.

László stands, rubbing his forehead. 'We cannot jump to conclusions. And I *know* the Adlers, we came out to Australia on the same ship. They are criminals, of course, but above all they are clever, and this is not a clever crime.'

'A jealous boyfriend?' I say. 'He found her with Enzo and killed them both?'

László shrugs. 'It happens.' He sighs and sits down again and says carefully, 'Tina, it is most important we do not say anything of this. No one else knows of this connection to Jimmy and it is very, *very* important they do not.'

'You don't think *Jimmy*—' I can't breathe.

'Not even for a moment. Tina, please.'

I take a shuddering breath.

'But no one must know of the *connection*.' László shakes his head. 'It may be nothing, but I do not like it in the slightest. It is also important that Jimmy himself does not get the wrong idea. That could be the most dangerous thing of all.'

I jump up. 'I'll go—'

'No, no, Tina. You must not.' László stands and grabs my shoulders. 'Anyone seeing you would know instantly there is a big problem. Go later when you are calm, talk to Jimmy.'

László gazes away, blinking rapidly. 'Tell him, tell him, you believe it was a jealous boyfriend, get *Jimmy* to believe that, to believe *you*. If he decides, even for a moment, it was the Adlers ...'

I sit down again, and rub my face. 'Oh, Christ. Disaster.'

László sits too and picks up his coffee, his hand shaking slightly. He laughs bitterly. 'You are fortunate that, if nothing else, the camp gave me a fine sense of self-preservation.'

We drink coffee and eat pastries, and I start to feel a little better.

'I'll just work for a while till I've settled down,' I say. As László nods and goes to the door I start sorting the mail. 'Oh, wait on, here's one for you.'

He opens the envelope, unfolds a letter, then stands very still, staring at it.

'László?'

He waves his hand dismissively and swallows. After a long pause he says, 'Precisely as I expected. The possible lead on my family comes to nothing. A dead end, you might say.'

He turns and leaves, his steps heavy on the stairs.

18. Billie: Starlight Tango

Tina does it again, bribes me with a dress. But oh, what a dress—a copper silk that highlights my hair—and among the multitude of bloody weddings I've been forced to attend, *what* a wedding.

The Starlight Lounge glitters in silver and platinum, with candles, glass and mirrors flickering sparkles of light back and forth. And dear Teen, with her shimmering gown and ecstatic eyes, is a comet whirling in Jimmy's arms. Despite my misgivings about the man, I love him then for how happy he is and how he delights her.

I feel pretty good myself. I flirt with the sexy head chef, Gaston— all Gallic charm and flashing black eyes—and force László chuckling and protesting onto the dance floor for a tango, and he's a far better mover than he claims.

I drink and dance, and dance and drink with all sorts of clumsy thugs and smooth operators. Half a dozen men want me to go home with them, but I go home alone.

It's a wonderful night: only thing missing, as usual, is Pete.

Living at the Cross it's hard to avoid the junkies, thin, broken-toothed, grey-faced, worn beyond their years. At first it astonished me that people could possibly fall into such a trap, let themselves become addicted to something to the point that, beyond all sanity, they crave and crave and crave for another hit.

Silly old Billie, eh? I'm not astonished any more.

Pete comes to Sydney every month to see Vivy at her school and take her out for the day. At night he comes to me. Every month, twelve times a year, although it's not really twelve because sometimes Vivy's at home on holidays.

So perhaps he's here ten nights in a year. Oddly, I don't sleep well on those nights, despite being limp with satisfied lust.

I'm so unused to having another body in my bed, even Pete's murmuring in his sleep brings me awake, as alert as if an air raid siren's gone off.

I stare at the dim ceiling and try to fall into the deep easy sleep of the other three-hundred and fifty-five nights of the year, but often, too often, I lie watching the dawn outline the ornate cornices of the old room.

We have a quick breakfast then, bacon and eggs, which Pete adores because Janet never cooks them—she's watching her weight and watching his, too. And yes, greyhound-elegant Pete is getting heavier. I don't care: it's still him.

But then he goes home to his little kingdom, and I'm left restless and tired and craving something beyond sex, beyond even love. And if I look in the mirror I'm surprised I'm not broken-toothed and grey in the face myself because, jeez, that's how I feel.

A few weeks ago I broke down after dinner at Klara and Yvie's place, sick with despair at witnessing the serene domestic life of people who get to sleep beside each other every night.

They've known Pete for years and love him as an old friend, but they were horrified for me. I swore them to silence, convincing them it would all soon end. It sounded good at the time.

Now, after a hot day at work, I'm sitting on my balcony with a cup of tea. I might go to Tempo tonight—it's ages since I've seen Teen or László.

I hear a knocking downstairs and my heart leaps. Pete is the only person who ever visits me here, and I dash to the door and stop, amazed.

'*Vivy*? What on earth?'

'Oh, Billie, you're here!'

'But –? Come inside.'

She's carrying a small suitcase and has been crying. Upstairs I get her a fresh handkerchief and she wipes her eyes.

'I'm *never* going back, Billie, *never*.'

'To school? But you've just done your Leaving Certificate, you're finished for good.'

'No. To the *farm*. I hate her so much. She wants me to go to a typing academy in Wollongong and get a job in a bank.'

'Janet does?'

'She wants me to call her *Mummy*, and I don't even call Charlie that. And all she does is play bridge or golf with her horrible friends, and they make *jokes* about me being a singer.'

'Would you like tea? Or I've got some lemonade.'

'Lemonade, please,' she says in a small voice.

'When does term end and you go home?'

'Today,' she says in an even smaller voice.

'But won't Pete be picking you up?'

'Mm-hmm.'

'Vivy, is Pete at the school *now*, looking for you?'

'Suppose so.'

'Oh, Christ.'

'I don't *want* to go home, Billie.' She sighs dramatically. 'I want to to stay with you. I want to be a jazz singer and live in Sydney. Here, with you.'

I hear another banging on the door-knocker, and dash downstairs.

'Pete. Good to see you,' I say carefully. 'It's all right, Vivy's here in my flat. She's rather upset.'

'Upset?' he says. 'I'll give that little brat *upset*.' I follow him, and even before he's reached the top of the stairs he's saying, 'Do you *know* how long I waited at the school before one of those idiots told me you weren't there and they hadn't the faintest bloody idea where you were?'

'No, Dad.'

'Did you wonder even for an instant what I'd think? That you were lost, hurt, *kidnapped*—'

'Taken by the white slave trade?' says Vivy helpfully.

'*God*.' Pete sits down, holding his head. I put the kettle on.

'Glad you thought to check here first, Pete,' I say. 'Before you went to the police.'

'Police?' says Vivy.

'Of course, police,' says Pete heavily. 'Jesus, Vivy.'

'I'm sorry, Dad.'

'Come here and give me a hug,' says Pete. Vivy does, and sits down beside him.

'But are you all *right?*' says Pete. 'How did you get here?'

'The tram. Easy.'

'Have a cuppa,' I say, and Pete takes the mug.

'But *why?* Why didn't you wait for me to pick you up at school? Why did you run off?'

'I was just telling Billie,' she says. 'I'm sixteen and I want to be a jazz singer and live here with her, in Sydney. I'm not going home to be a typist like *Janet* wants.'

'Vivy,' I say gently, 'I don't have any space.'

'Yes, you do. You've got that little room at the back.'

'That's where the landlady puts all her old furniture.'

'Then I'll sleep on the couch.'

Pete's horrified expression probably echoes mine.

'No, kid, I need my privacy,' I say. 'It's just not possible.'

'What about Klara and Yvonne's then? They've got space, and I could babysit Claire.'

I shrug. 'You'd have to ask them. Might be possible.'

'There, you see?' she says. 'I *can* do that and stay in Sydney and be a jazz singer.'

'Vivy, you *can't*, don't be silly,' says Pete. 'Tempo's about the only jazz club in Sydney. Even if Tina was good enough to let you sing there occasionally you couldn't make a living at it.'

'But I could be a waitress as well, or work in a shop.' Vivy takes Pete's hand. '*Truly*, Dad. I'd be safe at Yvonne and Klara's. And Billie would keep an eye on me, wouldn't you, Billie?'

'I don't ... Pete?'

After a long pause he sighs. 'Well, perhaps you could have a sort of holiday here, see how it goes. But if there's *one* problem, young lady, you'll be back home so fast you won't know what's hit you. And nothing's settled till we talk to Klara and Yvonne, so don't go getting your hopes up.'

'I'm going to live in *Sydney!*' crows Vivy, whirling around the room, arms raised, chestnut curls flying. 'Thank you Dad, thank you Billie! I'll behave myself, I *promise.*'

Pete shakes his head and we smile. Like me, he's probably thinking this gives him an excuse to visit me more often.

Vivy spends that Christmas at home and at the start of 1953 comes to live in Sydney. Klara and Yvie are glad to have her with them: they have enough room and they do need someone to help mind eight-year-old Claire. But Vivy's so volatile and Claire so sensible I'm not certain who's going to be the one in charge.

Overcome by a rare bout of shyness, Vivy persuades me to ask Tina about singing at Tempo, so I go over to the club one morning. The place is a bit of a mess. Chairs and tables are pushed to the side of the room, builders are plastering a wall and an electrician is up a ladder doing some wiring. I see László as I head towards the stairs, but he just nods formally.

In Tina's office I say, 'What's up with old László? He's a bit reserved for someone I've danced the Argentine tango with.'

'He had high hopes of a lead on his family, but just a few days ago got a letter, it was a dead end. He's pretty sad.'

'Poor bastard,' I say, then notice Tina has her arm in a sling.

'What's happened to you, Teen? Broken arm?'

She laughs briefly. 'No, just tripped over and sprained my wrist. Clumsy fool.'

'Poor you as well. Is it still sore?'

'Almost better,' she says. 'So what brings you to Tempo? Haven't seen you since the wedding.'

'I've been despatched by an uncharacteristically shy Vivy. She's left school, staying with Klara and Yvie, and was wondering if she might perform here some time.'

'Of course,' says Tina. 'Hmm. She'd need backing musicians. Does she know any?'

'Don't think so.'

'Wait on—Steve, my stepson, might help out. He'd have mates from the Conservatorium too. She'd need a bassist, drummer—maybe a saxophonist, too. Let me talk to Steve. And tell the silly girl to come and see me herself, she doesn't need to be shy.'

'Thanks. She'll be all over you like a puppy given half a chance.'

Tina laughs. After a moment she says, 'Look, Billie, something I wanted to mention. Last year, the party at Rozelle—I didn't realise I'd put you on the spot by inviting Pete. I'm sorry.'

'Oh.' I hesitate. 'It was okay. We'd met up before that, at Yvie and Klara's. All very civilised.'

Tina gives me something like Nikos's patient look. 'Not quite what I meant.'

I sigh and sit down.

'Are you still seeing him?' says Tina gently.

I nod.

'What's going to happen?'

I shake my head. My throat aches and I can't speak.

'Oh, love.' Tina gets up from her desk and sits on the couch beside me. 'I'm sorry.'

I wipe my eyes with my sleeve. 'Just—fell into it, imagined I could walk away like before. But this time I can't *bear* it when he goes back to his bloody wife.' I look up. '*I* could have been his wife you know, but I thought—oh, Christ knows *what* I thought.'

'If you'd married Pete, I'm not so sure ...' Tina laughs shortly. 'Then again, what do I know about marriage?' She opens a drawer. 'Here's a hanky, give your poor sleeve a chance. You're just a complete savage, Billie Quinn.'

I smile tearily. 'I'll be all right. Not getting enough sex, that's the problem.'

'Plenty of men would have you in an instant.' She stops and says carefully, 'Have you ever considered, perhaps—Nikos?'

'Nikos? No, he's seeing some woman at Rose Bay now. There was a possibility ages ago ... but that's long gone. Trouble is, Pete just looms so large I can't even imagine another man in my life.'

'Well,' says Tina dryly, 'with a bit of luck that'll pass.'

'Ah, well.' I say as I stand up. 'Thanks for the kind words, Teen.'

'Let's go shopping again some time, Billie. Promise I won't try to bribe you with a dress.'

I give her a hug. 'Go ahead, bribe away. I love it.'

I'm half-way out the door when I remember, and turn around. 'Oh, I meant to ask you about a story in the paper a few days ago. That poor woman found dead at the wharves—she had the same surname as Jimmy. Not a relation, was she?'

Tina is gazing out to the street, nursing her hurt wrist. 'No,' she says distantly. 'Just a coincidence.'

And I think, she's not clumsy. Tripped over?

When I get home there's a letter from Charlotte on the sideboard. I think she's lonely in Vietnam, despite the reports of *charming* locals, *marvellous* food and *divine* colonial parties.

She's adept at alienating other women, so Eliza and I are among the few she's built a prickly friendship with, both of us linked through Pete and Vivy.

The first time Pete and I separated, I knew in his fantasies he was already in Charlie's bed. They began an affair, had Vivy and got married (in that order), but a few years later she drifted away and they divorced. When Pete and I were together again in the war he'd say I was the love of his life, but I think it's always been Charlie.

I open her letter. She and her general were here three years ago, and since then his 'minor insurgency' in Indochina has flared into war. The Vietminh are covertly supported by the Chinese, the French by the Americans (also floundering in their own own Korean quagmire), and both sides are struggling back and forth, with many casualties and little progress.

Sweetie,

At last we're having a few cool nights in Saigon and the humidity is down, so it's glorious weather. Maurice and Jeanne held a Roaring Twenties party last week, Les Années Folles, and it was such fun doing the Charleston and Foxtrot and Shimmy again after all these years. But, oh, to have my seventeen-year-old stamina once again! My maid had to spend most of next day massaging the kinks out of my muscles.

It's impossible to believe little Vivy's left school already, she must be so grown up. Tell Klara and Yvonne I'm very grateful they're having her to stay. I do miss Vivy more as she gets older, rather than less. Is that odd?

(Why I'm asking you is beyond me, you've never even mothered a kitten.) Still, I was such a hopeless parent Vivy was probably better off without me.

But perhaps next year I'll come and visit—I'd love to see her again. This ghastly war should be over by then, too. Despite the setbacks the French, naturally, are prevailing.

I'm a touch on edge because Louis has been posted north to take charge of a garrison. He tells me it's a backwater far from the fighting, so I'm being terribly brave and helping him pack. He'll be gone before the Vietnamese New Year which is usually such fun, but I'm sure the cocktails au château Leclerc will ease the pain.

Tell me when (if?) Vivy gets any singing jobs. I hope she does but if not, I'm sure everyday labour in a shop will be good for her character. As a secretary, you'd know all about that.

Je t'embrasse, Charlotte

You cow, Charlie. I laugh and shake my head. Still, her anxiety's showing—she was shocked eighteen months ago when one of her husband's fellow generals in Vietnam was assassinated, and from her too-casual words it's long been obvious she feared Louis would have do his duty on a battlefield rather than at headquarters.

She's probably right about her parenting too. She was so unhappy when Vivy was small it's not surprising she left the marriage. Little Vivy still had a good life on the farm, more than many other kids had then. Charlie's always kept a bond alive with Vivy through letters and phone calls, but I think it's dawning on her at last what she's missed.

Still, what would I know? I've never even mothered a kitten.

It was Nikos who helped Vivy get a job. Some cousins of his run a delicatessen in Balmain and she was taken on to serve at the counter. After a few days she rang me. 'Billie, there's so *many* kinds of cheese and they all have funny names. And they even sell sausages made out of pig's *blood*. It's a very strange place.'

Still, she likes the shop, the shop-people like her, and she adores their sweet pastries with nuts and honey, the baklava Nikos's mum would send over when I lived with him and Tina.

That was a long time ago, over four years. I suppose I'm completely settled in Sydney now. Dad died last May and I went back to Western Australia for the funeral, but I doubt I'll ever live there again.

But is Sydney my home? Is this where I'll spend the rest of my life? And is this *how*? Waiting like a beaten bitch for an occasional moment of joy with Pete? I groan.

Time to get ready for work. It's Saturday but I'm doing the evening shift—one of the radio blokes wanted to swap so he could go dancing with his girlfriend.

I put on a light cotton dress, perfect for the weather. When I come out to my car the day is still heavy and humid, but I'm glad the radio says a cool change is on the way: a southerly buster is roaring up the coast and will bring us some blessed relief.

We've got three flights due—*Ararangi* from Wellington at 4.50 pm, *Star of Papua* from Port Moresby at 7.00 pm, and *Awatere* from Auckland at 11.00 pm.

I'm at my desk checking today's reports when Nikos comes into the radio room. He nods hullo to me and asks Stan, the meteorologist, 'How's the weather?'

Stan shakes his head. 'Southerly buster just hit Wollongong, so it'll be here in about an hour.'

'That should be after *Ararangi* lands,' I say. 'How's the flarepath?'

'South-east to north-west,' says Nikos.

'*Star of Papua*'s in at seven. Guess you'd better plan for hard north-south by then.'

Nikos laughs. 'I'll say. Stan, how strong are those leading winds?'

'Only thirty knots according to Wollongong, but you know how fronts can accelerate.'

'Well, keep me updated, I'm out on the launch.'

'Jeez,' I say. 'I thought only the lowliest minions got to enjoy Saturday night on the launch with a southerly coming in.'

'I'm a minion this evening,' says Nikos. 'One of the blokes is sick, or so he claims.'

'What a pathetic bunch we are,' says Stan morosely. 'Should be dancing the night away at the Starlight Lounge or the Trocadero, not getting rained on. You like dancing, Billie?'

'Oh, now and again. Anyway, it's the poor sods on the launch who'll get drenched. Hope you've got a thermos of coffee, Nikos.'

'We've raided the kitchen, we'll be fine. See you both later.'

Ararangi alights on time, but isn't brought up beside the jetty because the winds are rising. Her crew moor the wallowing boat-plane to storm buoys, and launches bring the passengers ashore.

I go outside to watch the southerly buster approaching, a long, dark rolling cloud flickering with lightning. Turning to look in the opposite direction the scene is idyllic, the harbour shimmering in the late afternoon sun.

Then within minutes the light fades, the sky darkens and the storm hits. The temperature drops ten degrees and I can't even see the water for a grey blur of rain and small hailstones. I return to the stuffy office and Stan opens a window: the cool air is delicious.

'Stan, is it true the sky goes *green* with southerly busters?' I say. 'Sydney people are always telling me that, as if they reckon I should be impressed, but I've never seen it.'

'Only the biggest storms, Billie—maybe once in a decade. But yeah, they can look like that from all the hail in the clouds. Spectacular but scary, that's for sure.'

Star of Papua is due, but it'll be delayed. After I sent the pilot the weather report he detoured out to sea to miss the storm front.

Later, restless, I walk to the landing stage and gaze at the mile-long flarepath, with its twinkling lights rising and falling in a fluid rhythm. A distant drone becomes louder as the flying boat approaches. *Star of Papua* slows, and descends lower and lower, then there's a pale rush of waves, and it's down.

Now the storm has passed the water is calmer, so the pilot manoeuvres the great beast beside the landing stage. The thirty or so passengers from Port Moresby—public servants, planters, wives —step onto the jetty.

They walk just a few yards into the bright terminal, where stewardesses bring them cups of tea while the suitcases and mail bags are unloaded. Half an hour later they're all through customs and heading off, and the place is quiet again.

The final flight that night, *Awatere* from Auckland, comes in at eleven. I do some paperwork, then leave when the midnight shift arrives. Outside the night sky is clear, the air scented with rain.

The cicadas are rasping their summer songs and puddles reflect the rows of hangar lights in wavering ripples. On the water the green and gold flarelamps move gently in the swell.

As other staff call out 'good-night' and drive away, I lean against my car and gaze at the stars, brilliant in the fresh air.

I hear footsteps and Nikos says, 'Long night?'

'At your end, probably. Mine was much as usual.'

'I should get out on the launches more often, better than being stuck in the office.' He stretches, then says, 'Ouch. Maybe not.'

He leans against my car and we gaze companionably at the sky.

'Can you navigate by the stars, Nikos?' I ask.

'Of course, I'm a sailor. What about you?'

'Of course, I'm a pilot.' I laugh. 'Well, not any more.'

'Is that a sore point?'

'A little, but really, my reflexes aren't as sharp as they were.'

'But you don't have to fly Spits any more either,' he says. 'What about something less demanding? Myself, I've always fancied the idea of being flown in a seaplane to the Hawkesbury River, to visit my uncle Georgios on his oyster farm.'

'And in this particular fancy, what sort of seaplane did you have in mind?'

'A bloke I know has a nice little DHC-3 Otter.'

'Otter? They're new,' I say. 'Haven't been in one.'

'But Steve informs me, wide-eyed, you can fly anything.'

'I may have over-impressed him.'

'I doubt it,' he says.

'But why don't you just drive to the Hawkesbury with Doreen from Accounts to read the map?'

'Doreen from Accounts thinks only men are able to read maps,' says Nikos. 'And she doesn't like sailing or Greek food.'

'Not even baklava?'

'I know,' he says. 'Unbelievable.'

'So it's all going swimmingly then?'

'She doesn't like dancing either,' he says. 'What do you reckon?'

'Run for your life, mate.'

He laughs. 'What about you?'

I hesitate and the silence lengthens.

Nikos says gently, 'Tina told me in her usual diplomatic manner you're spending time with Pete.'

I swallow. 'Not the smartest move, but—' I shrug. 'Probably won't end too well.'

'Perhaps it'll work out.'

'I said that once about you and Tina, so I don't think either of us are very good oracles. Strange, isn't it? Whenever one of us is footloose the other's involved with somebody else. Guess we'll never be in sync.'

'Are you *kidding*?' says Nikos.

He stands up straight, then steps out and gazes formally at me in the *mirada*, the request to dance.

I laugh. 'Honestly, *here*?'

'Where better? Come on, Billie.'

I meet his eyes and nod, the *cabeceo*, and he steps forward and hums the start of my favourite *vals*, the fluid blend of tango and waltz. I hum it too, and smile as I rest my wrist lightly on his back.

He holds my waist and lifts my other hand high, as if it's something precious. Then we step, step, step into the slinky, playful, seductive moves, to the rear, the side, around and through.

Our hips and shoulders turn, flashing precisely, dramatically, perfectly together beneath the stars. We hum the familiar melody together all the way to the end: to the lovers' sweeping embrace, to the moment the dance is complete.

Then the only music in the night is the soft rasp of cicadas and the swish of distant cars. Nikos kisses my mouth very lightly and whispers, 'Oh, we're in sync, Billie. No matter where we are or who we're with, we're in sync.'

I fling myself back in his arms, my hair flying, and laugh aloud in delight.

I drive home, still smiling. Dear Nikos—what an unusual, touching moment. It's been far too long since we've danced together.

Then all thoughts of the evening disappear as I park outside my place and see Pete's car is there. Mrs Beatty usually lets him in if I'm not around, so I go inside and run upstairs.

'Pete?'

'Here.' He's lounging on my bed reading a magazine, and he opens his arms to me. We snuggle together, warm and familiar, and I sigh with relief at the easing of my craving, my fathomless craving for his voice and smell and touch.

After a while I murmur, 'What's the special occasion, then?'

'I was meeting some business mates today and had to see you. Got some news, excellent news.' Pete leans up on one elbow. 'I know I've been a bastard, coming and going, putting you in such a rotten position, Billie. But it's all going to change now.'

'Is it?'

He nods. 'I can't stand the bloody marriage any more, I've been a complete fool. Janet and I fight all the time. She nags me to play golf or bridge when I'm flat out working, and she doesn't even *pretend* to like Vivy! It's a total disaster.'

He lies back against the pillow, rubbing his dark brows. 'Trouble is, my money's tied up in the property. But I've found an accountant who can disentangle it without causing a fuss. In about a year I'll be able to pry myself out of the whole godawful mess and get a divorce.'

'Oh, Pete. *Truly?* What—what would you do then?'

'I know a lot about farming here now, provisioning, moving produce—and the mates I saw today are in logistics.' He grins. 'Billie, they've just offered me a bloody good job. I'd stay at the farm but work one day a week in Sydney. And when I'm divorced and free to move here it'd be a full-time job.'

'You'd move to *Sydney?*' My heart is thumping.

'Where else! I love the place, my two favourite girls are here, after all. And then—'

He rolls off the bed and kneels theatrically, hands on heart. 'This would have to be the *fourth* time I've asked you to marry me, Billie Quinn, and I reckon you should get off your bloody arse and snap me up quick smart.'

I laugh and lean over and pull him back on the bed, and hold his dear body against mine, two beings entangled through the light and dark of a lifetime's passion for each other.

'Nah, not the fourth,' I say. 'Only the third, Pete. You haven't really been trying.'

PART III. ALTERED CHORDS

19. Yvonne: The Minutiae of the Law

'Is this all right, Yvonne?'

I look up. 'Gosh, Vivy, that's amazing. Klara, come and see!'

Vivy is in black, a boat-neck top, slim trousers, flat shoes. Her curly chestnut hair cascades down her back and her brown eyes are enormous.

'You look like a beatnik,' says Claire from her usual spot beneath the reading lamp. 'But that's all right. Beatniks are cool.'

'You will fit in very well, Vivy,' says Klara. 'I hope you have a wonderful time.'

Vivy shivers. 'It should be all right, we've rehearsed so much.' She turns. 'Yvonne? I'm ready.'

When we get into my little Morris Minor it starts first time, thank heavens. I let out the clutch and off we go to Kings Cross and Vivy's first show at Tempo.

The club's entrance is unobtrusive and 'cool' (Claire's latest word). We go upstairs to Tina's office, and she's sitting at her desk, head on her hands. She looks up and smiles quickly.

'Oh, don't you look *marvellous*, Vivy? You're going to be a real drawcard. So remember, if anyone bothers you at all, speak to me or László immediately. Well—are you ready?'

Vivy nods.

'Start off quietly,' says Tina. 'If you need a break, take it, don't struggle to the end of the set or you'll hurt your voice and your confidence as well. Understand?'

Vivy nods again and says steadily, 'Let's go.'

Vivy is a revelation. Billie had said she was good, but here in a room with nice acoustics, her small band smooth and tight behind her, she's superb.

I'd feared there'd be missteps, first night nerves, forgotten lines, wrong notes, but she sings as if she's worked clubs for years, with quiet confidence, direct eyes, perfect phrasing.

She's bright and teasing in the brash songs, and in the slow ones, touched by a single spotlight in the dark, she's heartbreaking.

The room gradually fills, and the applause is loud by the end of the first set. Tina brings Vivy a lemonade, saying, 'Let's go upstairs, darling. We'll keep you a bit of a mystery for now. You were very good, though you should swing more in that last number.'

'I *know*,' says Vivy. 'Got distracted. Next time.' She turns. 'Yvonne, are you coming?'

'I'll just stay here and sip my gin.' (The gin is in a teacup but still tastes nice.)

Near the stage László is offering Vivy's band a tray of drinks, then he beckons me over and kisses me politely on the cheek. 'How good to see you, Yvonne. Please let me introduce the band. You would know Steve Loukas, the pianist, of course—'

'Steve? Gosh, thought you looked familiar but didn't realise. It must be *years*!'

Once a gawky adolescent duckling, Nikos's son is now a dashing swan, all dark smouldering eyes and dramatic cheekbones— although the most dramatic change of all is the smile.

'Hey, Yvonne,' he says. 'It's so cool you could come. Guys, Yvonne is a friend of Dad and Tina's—and this is Jeff, on drums, Bill's the bassist, and Col the sax player. He wants us to call him Bird but we reckon Dodo's better.'

The sax player elbows Steve and says to me shyly, 'Hey, man.'

'But you're *wonderful*! How long have you been playing together?'

'A while,' says Steve, 'but having a vocalist has made us a lot tighter. This is our first real gig with Vivy.'

He suddenly looks very young when he says her name. Ah.

A couple of men in turtle-neck jumpers come over to enthuse with the band, so László nods his head at my table and we sit.

I say, 'Did you realise Vivy'd be so *good*? I didn't.'

László lights a cigarillo. 'I have heard her before, so indeed I did.

And how are you, Yvonne? Will the appeal in your libel case be heard soon?'

'In a few weeks. Our barrister thinks the sudden appearance of the letter prejudiced the jury, but we don't have any new evidence as yet. Still, here's hoping.'

'Indeed, here is hoping.'

'And you, László? Last time we chatted you were expecting to hear from the refugee organisation. Any news?'

He breathes out smoke and shakes his head. 'The promising lead went nowhere in the end.'

'I'm so sorry. Is there anything else you can do?'

He shrugs. 'I was going to stop looking, you know, but then I discovered something I was not aware of. When we were rounded up and put on trains for Auschwitz, I was separated from my wife Éva and son Róbert.' He looks up. 'I am so sorry, of course you do not want to hear—'

'László, the Hungarian side of Klara's family died at Auschwitz. You can tell me.'

He nods gravely. 'Ah, so you understand. Well, what I did not know was that some of the trains did not go to Auschwitz at all. Many women and children were diverted to Austria, to become slave labour.'

'And what happened to them?'

'Towards the end they were marched to Mauthausen, to the granite quarries.' He nods sadly. 'I see you know what that means. Still, *some* survived.' He ashes the cigarillo. 'I am a fool, but I have started making enquiries in Austria. Who knows?'

I squeeze his hand. 'Who knows? Good luck, László.'

He clears his throat and says, 'Now, there is something I wish to ask of you, Yvonne.'

'Me?'

'You will perhaps be here more often with Vivy at future shows?'

'I expect so.'

He sighs. 'There is a matter I am concerned about and I fear I cannot be involved. Jimmy is a very jealous man.'

'Jimmy?'

'You have noticed perhaps Tina is not as happy as she once was?'

'Yes. She seems—subdued.'

'Her husband is under pressure, and such things can make him difficult. She says nothing, she is a very loyal woman and I cannot ask, it might make things worse. Would you talk to her, Yvonne? It probably is nothing, but—' he shrugs. 'I would hate her to be sad. She has been very good to me.'

'Of course I will.'

During Vivy's second set, Jimmy himself arrives. His henchman Big Davy pushes people aside to let him through like someone who's seen too many gangster films.

Jimmy beams at Tina, murmurs to her for a time and kisses her before leaving. Tina smiles to herself then returns to listening to Vivy. They seem fine. I wonder why László is concerned.

A fortnight later Vivy has another show at Tempo and it goes as well as the first. In the interval shes sits, laughing with her band and a small group of fans, László keeping a careful eye on things.

I notice Tina go upstairs to her office and a few minutes later follow her. I tap on the half-closed door and it swings open. Tina is sitting on her sofa, hands over her eyes.

'Are you all right?' I say quietly.

'Oh, Yvonne. Just a bit of a headache. Come in, I'll boil the kettle.'

I can see Tina's been crying, but when she returns with the tea-tray she's wiped her eyes. 'Well,' she says brightly. 'What a *lovely* evening. I think Vivy'll build up a following easily.'

'There's a small crowd hanging onto her every word right now.'

Tina smiles and pours the tea. 'Milk? Of course you do, silly me.'

She sits down beside me. 'And how *are* you, Yvonne? Is Claire well? She must be getting big by now.'

'Eight this year, and yes, she's good, doing well at school. Vivy's been a great help with her, especially when Klara wants to write.'

'How's that going now?'

I sigh. 'Still difficult. The trial and the threat of losing our home had hit her very badly. She's becoming depressed again ... though she *says* she's not. Oh Tina, the truth is I'm so *worried* and don't know what to do! How I *wish* Klara was happier.'

Tears trickle down and Tina says gently, 'It's all right, Yvonne.'

I laugh weakly. 'Oh dear. I should be comforting you, not the other way around.'

'Should you?'

'Had a feeling you were a little down yourself.'

'Did László say something?'

I hesitate, then nod.

'Honestly, that man fusses like a maiden aunt.' Tina takes a cigarette out of a gold case, lights it and blows a plume of smoke.

'A couple of months ago—you might have seen it in the paper— two bodies were found down at the wharves,' she says, her eyes narrow. 'A man from a crime family and a woman. The police thought they'd been killed by a jealous lover, but never arrested anyone.' She laughs shortly. 'Par for the course for our perceptive constabulary.'

She sits forward. 'Anyway, the woman was ... distantly connected to Jimmy. When we talked about it he was upset and shrugged off my arm. I slipped and sprained my wrist. Truly, Yvonne, you've never seen *anyone* as contrite. But dear old László thinks Jimmy's been mistreating me.'

After a pause I say, 'Then why were you crying tonight?'

'I've just discovered I'm not pregnant. *Again.*'

'Honestly? Tina, it's not only László who's concerned. You're involved with some very dodgy people and you're living on the edge of the criminal world. Dead *bodies*, for heaven's sake! Aren't you worried, just a little?'

She slowly blows out smoke. 'Sometimes. But what I really worry about is Jimmy. We've talked and talked, you wouldn't believe how deeply, but I feel I don't know him as well as I want to. Of course it's silly—isn't that how it is? You can't know another person completely, can you?'

I shake my head. 'Of course you can't. But you need to listen to your instinct too, Tina. And if something's making you cry—'

'*Truly*, that's just disappointment about babies. Jimmy is the best of husbands.' She sighs. 'I suppose it's just reality hitting home. You think when you find the love of your life that somehow your souls will merge, but it doesn't happen like that, of course it doesn't.'

'No, I think not,' I say. 'But we all dream of it.'

Tina smiles ruefully. 'I'm so glad you dropped by, Yvonne. I *did* need to talk to someone—and just hearing my own words shows me what a fool I am. Apart from a baby I've got everything in the world and I should damned-well appreciate it.'

'And you'll get to understand Jimmy better too, I'm sure of it, but that'll probably take years not months.'

Tina kisses me and says, 'Come on, Dr Freud, let's go downstairs and see what little Vivy's up to. And you can reassure László I'm absolutely fine.'

Next morning Vivy is sleeping in and Klara has retreated to her office. I'm doing the washing up and Claire is at the kitchen table, leafing through a magazine.

I empty the sink and sit down. 'What's the magazine, love?'

'It's Vivy's, all about modern music,' says Claire. 'It's very hip.'

'Is *hip* your new word?'

'Suppose so. I was getting sick of *cool*.'

I laugh and re-pin my bun, which is falling down, as usual. Claire gazes at me, then looks at the magazine, then back to me.

'Yvonne? See?'

'She's pretty. Who is she?'

'Juliette Greco—a French *chanteuse*. That means she's a singer. But *look*, Yvonne.'

'At what?'

'Her hair, the latest style, all long and straight. It would suit you.'

'Me? Gosh. But a *fringe*—isn't that terribly Roaring Twenties?'

'What's the Roaring Twenties? No, fringes are hip.'

'A bit too hip for middle-aged me. Can't even remember last time I had my hair cut.'

Claire laughs excitedly. 'No, come *on*, Yvonne. My friend's mum works in the hairdresser near the printery. Let's get your hair done.'

'Oh, but—' I can't think of a good reason not to, so within a short time Claire and I are walking to Darling Street. Well, she's tugging my hand and I'm following.

I'd hoped the salon wouldn't have an appointment but there's been a cancellation, so I soon find myself in a chair unable to avoid the sight of my very ordinary face in a very large mirror. I look so washed-out and unemphatic compared to Claire, with her blue eyes and halo of platinum curls, and the crisply made-up face of Mrs Bellamy, the hairdresser.

She runs a comb though my hair and holds out a long limp hank. 'Been a while?'

'Afraid so.' I want to cringe as she lifts clumps of hair here and there, then she says, 'Can't believe it, you lucky, *lucky* girl. Not a single grey. Look at that, Claire, not *one* grey on her head. Do you know how lucky you are, Miss Watters?'

'Am I?' I say, relieved.

She nods, her lips pursed. 'I know women who'd give their right arms to have your hair. That soft brown? *Exact* shade of a dye called cinnamon, all the rage. Now how do you want it?'

Claire holds out the magazine. 'Like this, Mrs Bellamy.'

'My goodness, Claire. That's daring.'

'*Too* daring?' I ask hopefully.

She gazes at the picture of the beautiful young woman, then at my ghastly reflection, then at the picture again, and says, 'I can do it. Over to the basin, please.'

She washes my hair then sits me in a cape before the unforgiving mirror again. I look like a drowned rat.

'Don't be such a *sook*, Yvonne,' says Claire.

Mrs Bellamy assembles an array of sharp instruments and starts combing and cutting. After a time she dries my hair with a noisy machine, unties the cape, shakes it out and says, 'There.'

I open my eyes—my suddenly large, definite eyes—which are outlined by a soft fringe and sitting above a new set of cheekbones. Shiny brown hair (*cinnamon*, I murmur to myself) falls to just below my shoulders, and shifts like raw silk as I turn my head, astonished, from side to side.

'Said I could do it,' says Mrs Bellamy.

'I knew you could,' says Claire.

'Mrs Bellamy—that's amazing,' I finally manage.

'I'll book you in for a trim, six week's time,' she says firmly. 'Needs maintenance, of course.'

'Of course,' I say, and pay the three shillings (that's all for such a miracle?) and float out of the salon with a smug Claire, and glance awestruck at my reflection in windows all the way home.

'I had no idea I even *had* cheekbones,' I say. 'And how did my eyes get so big? Did Mrs Bellamy put a spell on me?'

Claire laughs. 'There's no magic, Yvonne. She cut the hair like a picture frame, and now it's the right shape for your face.'

At home I go upstairs to the office and tap on the door. I open it to see Klara, crouched down in a corner, her arms over her head. My heart lurches.

'Oh, love, are you all *right?*'

Klara lowers her arms and gazes at me dazed, and then bursts into tears.

'I am so sorry,' she says later, as we sit together, damp-eyed. 'I was somewhere else in my thoughts. You looked like a stranger, and then you looked like yourself, and back and forth it went, and I could not bear the *dissonance*. I am so sorry, my love.'

I say helplessly, 'Claire insisted—I'd never have dared to myself.'

'But it is wonderful. So very pretty.' She runs her fingers through the strands. 'Like tassels from a palace, silken and swaying.' She smiles. 'You are Queen Nefertiti, your eyes so large and luminous. How did I not see that before?'

'Claire says it's because it's like a picture frame, no magic to it.'

'The magic is in your changing yourself, I think. When I cut my hair short in the war it made me feel brave and resolute.'

'Is it all right, though?'

Klara nods, her eyes still sad. 'Yes. Hug me, Nefertiti.'

And I hug her and whisper, 'What's wrong, Klara, what's *wrong?*'

I feel her shake her head slightly. 'I do not know.'

All at once it's time to go back to court for the appeal, where a judge is to decide if there are any reasons to re-examine the defamation case. Everything hinges on this. If not, then that's it. We must sell everything to pay for Godfrey's award.

What then? Where will we *live*, where will we work? How will Claire continue at school?

Klara loves this house more than any in her life, she says, and I'm sure the fear of losing it is eating away at her sanity. Yes, her sanity, my poor, poor love.

Ned and Nancy come for the hearing and stay in our basement flat, as they have a few times over the last year. It's obvious they're now a contented couple. Over dinner with them that evening Claire says, 'Can I come to the courthouse with you tomorrow? I might want to be a lawyer one day.'

Klara and I glance at each other, both thinking she'd handle the minutiae of the law with ease. Klara says, 'If you miss school, you must write an essay about the court in your best handwriting.'

Claire nods. She'd probably do it anyway for her own pleasure.

Next morning we cram into my Morris Minor and drive into the city to the Supreme Court. Most of our friends can't be here today because of work, but Eliza and Harry stayed overnight with Nikos and have already arrived.

'Well, don't *you* look marvellous?' Eliza says, hugging me.

'Claire made me do it,' I say, 'but I certainly feel marvellous. You're looking well yourself.'

'I found out something. You'll hear later,' she says.

We sit down behind Mr Barrington, not far from Godfrey's barrister, Mr Jones. A few minutes later Godfrey rushes in and says to him, 'Sorry. Bloody train was late.'

He glances at us. Klara is anxiously grasping my hand and Godfrey's pale eyes look us over, slowly and crudely. He smirks and murmurs, 'Fucking dykes,' then turns his back.

Such language, sadly, is not new to Claire, and she whispers, 'I hope that horrible man goes to gaol for twenty years.'

'Me too,' I say, 'but sadly it's not that kind of trial.'

The room fills with court officials then the judge arrives, a different man from the earlier case, his face severe. He summarises the case and I feel overwhelmed by the familiar phrases—ridicule, hatred and contempt, Harry's paintings, Ned's poems, Changi prison camp, defence of truth, White Jap, bias, Double Tenth, collaboration and on and on and *on*.

'I believe the appellants seek to appeal on several grounds,' the judge says. My mind races for a moment, then I remember we are the appellants and Godfrey the respondent. 'Mr Barrington?'

Our barrister launches into a speech about aspects of the case, with reference to other cases, so-and-so versus so-and-so, dates, judgements, arguments, until my head is whirling.

At last we come to something I recognise, the letter from Sir Hugh Everett that exonerated Godfrey. Mr Barrington argues that its late submission was unfair and unduly influenced the jury.

The judge says, 'But the respondent's counsel did not have this evidence until then, so while irregularly submitted, this was not necessarily a deliberate attempt to sway the jury.'

'I would direct your Honour to the letter,' says Mr Barrington, undaunted. 'Please note the date and the sender's Melbourne address. It was written one *month* before the trial. No one could pretend it was not able to reach us well before the trial began. It did not need to be rushed into court, and should have been submitted as usual, with enough time for all parties to consider it.'

The judge nods thoughtfully as Mr Barrington sits, smiling.

Mr Jones says, 'Your Honour, this letter was sent by air mail. Sir Hugh Everett, in London, used his Melbourne address and dated it for his receipt of official approval to reveal Dr Godfrey's role. But he was slow to post it, so it only reached us on the day of the trial.'

Godfrey looks around, smirking. The judge's eyebrows lift. 'That would appear to remove the basis of your argument, Mr Barrington. Do you have anything else?'

The barrister stands. 'I do, your Honour, and it is a little ironic that similar circumstances have arisen with *our* new evidence, which arrived via air mail from England just this morning.'

'Indeed, Mr Barrington. Please submit it.'

Mr Barrington passes papers to a clerk, who takes some to the judge and others to Mr Jones. Godfrey reads over his shoulder then looks up, his face red, and notices me watching him. I smile sweetly and he turns away, furious.

The judge finishes reading and looks up. 'I believe you have a new witness, Mr Barrington?'

'I do, your Honour. Would Mrs Eliza Bell please take the stand?'

Eliza stands and walks calmly to the witness box. Harry stares, seemingly as much in the dark as the rest of us.

She swears on the Bible, then Mr Barrington says, 'Mrs Bell, please tell the court your position in the British Civil Service at the end of the war.'

Eliza takes a breath. 'The court will understand I am constrained by the Official Secrets Act, but within those limits I can state I worked for the Secret Intelligence Service and was head of a small department in GC&CS, the Government Code and Cypher School.'

'And four years before that, at the fall of Singapore?'

'I was a Senior Clerk in the Far East Combined Bureau, a section of GC&CS. We were stationed at the Naval Base at Sembawang, interpreting intelligence on the Japanese.'

'Were you acquainted with Hugh Everett, as he was then?'

'Yes. He had a position in the Colonial Secretary's Office and we met reasonably often on the social circuit. He was a good friend of one of my colleagues at the Bureau—they shared an enthusiasm for Japanese poetry of the Taishō style.'

Mr Barrington smiles. 'Indeed, poetry does seem to be the crux of this case. Now, Mrs Bell, would you tell us your thoughts on the letter submitted as coming from Sir Hugh Everett?'

'It greatly puzzled me. Hugh Everett was not employed by the intelligence services,' Eliza says evenly. 'As leader at Changi Prison he was free to ask anyone to gather intelligence. He did not need dispensation from anyone to discuss such a matter.'

Mr Jones jumps to his feet. 'Your Honour, are we expected to believe a *housewife* knew everyone in Singapore intelligence?'

'Not relevant,' says the judge. 'Continue, Mr Barrington.'

He turns again to Eliza. 'What did you do then, Mrs Bell?'

'I wrote to my old department many times, a rather long and frustrating exercise, as most of the people I knew had left or moved on. After a tortuous process'—Eliza's mouth takes on a surprisingly bitter line—'someone gave me the address of my retired colleague, and he finally put me in contact with Sir Hugh in London.'

'You are saying, Mrs Bell, you have had direct communication with Sir Hugh Everett yourself?'

'Yes.'

'And what did he tell you?'

'He said he did not write the letter purported to come from him.'

There's a murmur of surprise around the room.

Eliza continues, 'He also gave me samples in his own handwriting to compare to the letter, copies of which are in the documents we have just submitted to the court. Sir Hugh has also sent his statutory declaration that the letter is a forgery.'

Mr Jones stands. 'Given this talk of forgeries, Mrs Bell, an extraordinarily serious claim, can you prove that the documents *allegedly* sent by Sir Hugh are also free from any such suspicion?'

'Yes I can,' says Eliza calmly. 'I have a letter for the judge's eyes only, from an acquaintance of his at the highest level in intelligence. It testifies to the truth of our documents.'

Mr Barrington passes a sealed letter to the clerk who takes it to the judge. He tears it open and reads it, his face expressionless.

After a time he says, 'Thank you, Mrs Bell. You may stand down.'

Eliza sits and the judge says, 'For the record I will state that the documents submitted by the appellants today are accepted by this court as true in their entirety.'

There's another murmur around the room.

The judge continues, 'Which of course, Mr Jones, leads us to the question of the provenance of the letter you submitted on behalf of your client, Dr Godfrey. Would you care to explain?'

Mr Jones glances at Godfrey, aghast. 'I will have to consult with my client, your Honour.'

'Please do, Mr Jones. As you yourself stated, submitting a forgery in evidence is an extraordinarily serious matter.'

The judge looks up. 'Well. Putting aside the letter, we are left with the rather compelling testimony of the previous trial. According to those who knew him at Changi, Dr Godfrey was generally held in low esteem, hence it was not unreasonable for him to be portrayed in that light in the appellants' artistic renderings of their lives as prisoners.'

He frowns. 'But they *are* only artistic renderings, and what I find extraordinary is that Dr Godfrey claims he is defamed by works that no reasonable person would associate with him, unless they were both fellow prisoners and avid readers of modern poetry.' He smiles dryly. 'Perhaps a rather small population.'

He stops smiling. 'Yet Dr Godfrey has been willing to litigate to the point of submitting a *forged* letter to this court. Is he perhaps driven by guilt or by hope of financial gain? Guilt regarding the letter is yet to be explored: however, in the case of the latter, my determination today is that there will be *no* financial gain.'

He leans forward. 'The damages awarded by the trial court are reduced by me to zero. I also award costs to the appellants. Finally, given the seriousness of such a forgery, I also refuse the respondent leave to appeal this matter in future. Understood, Mr Jones?'

Mr Jones says, 'Understood, your Honour. No further appeal. Thank you, your Honour.'

The judge raps his hammer, we stand and bow, then he leaves.

Ned says, dazed, 'Is that it? Is it over?'

Mr Barrington laughs. 'It's over. Mrs Bell, you saved the day! And you've all been awarded costs too, some recompense at least for this painful episode. My congratulations.'

Mr Jones and Dr Godfrey are furiously whispering to each other, then Mr Jones grabs his briefcase and walks out. Godfrey looks after him, red-faced, then scuttles away with his shoulders hunched.

I turn to the others, who are happily chatting, and feel dizzy with relief. My God, our homes are safe, our lives are safe, this dreadful time is *over*!

Then I glance at the woman who saved the day, and I'm shocked at the bitter set of Eliza's mouth. And beside her, Harry is blank-faced with confusion.

20. Harry: For a Lifetime

On the Flyer back to Newcastle after the appeal, I say I'm tired and turn away and pretend to sleep. At my mother's we pick up the children and tell her everything is all right, and Jessie is delighted. We get back to the house and Eliza cooks a light meal and the children finally go to bed.

In the lounge room I open a bottle of good whiskey and pour two glasses. I hand one to Eliza and say, 'Got this especially, hoping we'd have something to celebrate.'

'Thanks. Suppose we do,' says Eliza.

There's a silence. I sit on the sofa opposite my wife. 'So. Were you ever going to tell me?'

'We're not supposed to talk to anyone about what we did, official secrets and all that. But if you'd asked, Harry, of course I'd have explained as much as I could. But you never asked.'

'Izabel once said you'd worked at some exalted level in intelligence, but it all seemed rather unlikely.'

'Did it?' says Eliza.

The whiskey burns my gullet. 'And now I discover you've been writing to London for a year behind my back, wrestling with bureaucracy to find your old mate who loves Japanese poetry.'

'I *did* mention Mr Kingsley at the first trial, but you brushed me off. Not the time for a trip down memory lane, you said. So I decided to work on it myself.'

'Well, congratulations are in order, Eliza. Saved my bacon.'

'I saved our bacon *and* Ned's and Yvonne's. But you don't seem very happy about it.'

'Embarrassed, I suppose.' I laugh shortly. 'The oblivious fool with no idea his wife was such a bigwig. A woman who can conjure up missives from intelligence mandarins that make even a Supreme Court judge roll over and wag his tail.'

'Are you under the impression it was *easy*, Harry?'

'I've no idea. I expect it was for someone as high-level as you.' My gut is clenched.

Eliza stares at me. 'It wasn't, and as it happens it may cost me rather a lot.'

'Cost?'

'The intelligence services are ruthless, Harry, especially with anyone who's worked for them—they don't have to explain the rules, you see. Since the war I've had to wriggle out of several bids to enlist me as an informant, for patriotic reasons of course.'

I shrug. 'So?'

'So when patriotism fails they go for blackmail. And needing their assistance, as I did for that *missive*, gave them just what they wanted. A hold over me.'

'You mean you've got to do something for British intelligence in exchange?'

'Not British,' she says. 'No, I believe they'll hand me over me to their mates in Canberra. You know, the ones obsessed with banning Socialists.'

'But what on earth would they want *you* to do?'

'Probably get a job in a sensitive workplace and send them titbits about unionists.'

'That's absurd. And surely illegal.'

'Don't be so naive, Harry. The government decides what's legal, and they've got their informants everywhere. And how do you think we'd go in a union town like Newcastle if it became known your wife was betraying worker confidences?'

I think of my outpatient clinic, set up in cooperation with local unions and industry, and feel a chill of dismay.

'But if that's—for how long?'

'Oh, indefinitely. Every compromise is leverage for the next task.'

The whiskey is burning my gut but I take another drink.

'Of course I've read the espionage novels, Ambler, MacInnes, Greene, but that's *fiction*. I can't believe—'

Eliza says dryly, 'Helen MacInnes' husband used to work for us.'

She sighs. 'A pity, really. I'd have loved a job doing what I want, not what someone else finds politically convenient.'

Yet another shock. 'Eliza, how could you *possibly* go to work? You're a mother, you've got a job.'

'Izabel's always worked and looked after Nancy as well.'

'Don't be disingenuous,' I say. 'Nancy was eight when Izabel adopted her. No comparison.'

'My goodness, Harry—how old-fashioned you sound.'

'Well, I *am* old-fashioned, and this spying nonsense is certainly beyond me. But what's almost incomprehensible is that it involves my own bloody wife.'

She says coolly, 'That I was once someone *more* than your wife, Harry, is probably what you find most incomprehensible.'

I feel as if I've been drinking battery acid.

'Christ, Eliza. What's *incomprehensible* is that one moment we're happy in Singapore, the next you're gone and I'm a caged animal fighting for my life.'

I put down my glass and rub my face. 'Somehow I survive, we have the miracle of Leo, then this bloody book blows up in my face. And now I find out you're some exalted cloak-and-dagger spy? *My entire—fucking—life—is—incomprehensible!*'

And I cannot contain my misery a moment longer. It explodes out of me, a volcano of grief and fear and anguish. To my horror I sob like a soul trapped in hell who's lost everything he ever loved: as it seems I certainly have.

And most terribly, I cannot, *cannot*, stop myself.

After a time, Eliza comes to sit beside me. She puts her arm around me in comfort, as she has not done for a long time. I lean into that comfort, as I have not for a long time, either.

Finally, after a shameful eternity, my sobs slow. I fumble for my handkerchief and wipe my face, my breath coming in hiccoughs.

Eliza says gently, 'You sound like Leo did when he lost his teddy bear on the tram.'

'Exactly how I feel, too.' I try to smile and fail. 'But, Eliza, I thought you were *happy* when we were together again.'

'Dear God, to have you home, to have a baby, of *course* I was. But I was also the woman I'd been all those years you were away, the woman you never knew. And it hurt, terribly, that you never wanted to know.'

'But ... after the camp none of us liked to look back.' I clear my throat. 'And—oh Christ ...'

'Harry?'

I sigh. 'One of the guards' favourite pastimes was describing, crudely, what our women were doing while we were prisoners. And who they were doing it with. Americans were a favourite.'

Eliza stares. 'Did you think I'd had an *affair*—?'

'Look, love, I thought—if you had I wouldn't have blamed you in the slightest, wouldn't have begrudged you that kindness, the comfort of it, I *swear*. I never doubted your feelings for me, Eliza, never. But it seemed wiser to let it go. Not to pry.'

Now Eliza sobs, half-laughing, and I hold her.

After a time she says, 'I'll tell you everything about those days, Harry, just not now. But I was so tired and overworked all I wanted in bed was sleep, and once there I only ever thought about *you*.'

I kiss her head—how long has it been since I've done such a simple, loving thing?—and say, 'You state that with all the authority of a woman who gets Supreme Court judges to wag their tails, so I'll have to accept it into evidence.'

Eliza smiles and leans against me.

'I didn't really doubt you,' I say, my face against her scented hair. 'But I didn't even want to admit I might have. And there's something else—'

'Not more revelations?'

'You'll enjoy this one, love,' I say ruefully. 'You were right, absolutely right. I *should* have left Singapore with you when I had the chance, but I was stuck in some old-fashioned fantasy of what a man should do. So I stood, as you so accurately put it, bleating about my duty like a sheep in the abattoir, and brought disaster down upon our heads.'

'Not certain you get all the credit for the fall of Singapore, love.'

Eliza sighs. 'And even if you'd come with us you might still have died in a dozen nasty ways, and you wouldn't be here today.'

'Going a bit far to suggest Changi might have done us a favour,' I say. 'But yes, we *did* survive, both of us. And we're here, we have our children and we're safe.'

'And we've still got a roof over our heads, despite Godfrey's best efforts to the contrary.'

We hold each other silently, in a kind of peace, then Eliza says hesitantly, 'Something else I've never quite understood, Harry. Yes, the book had repercussions, but when we started we didn't know that. Yet you were so vehemently opposed to anyone seeing your paintings. I've always wondered—why?'

My heart thumps. 'It was just ...' I falter and lick my lips.

Eliza waits.

I try again. 'Such difficult times ...'

Silence.

I swallow convulsively and take a deep breath. 'Something I didn't want anyone to know.'

'A secret?'

I nod. 'I was ashamed.' I close my eyes. 'You see, in the war it's not just women are raped, like poor Izabel. It's rarely spoken of, except in obscene jokes, but ...'

Eliza breathes carefully. 'You, Harry?'

I laugh weakly. 'No, too old and ugly. But a nice young lad, Leadenhall—the guards would mock him, say they'd get him. Then one night I was coming back from the latrine, and he was cornered by five of them. All I could hear were his whimpers. And their grunts.'

Eliza nods slowly. 'And?'

'They were armed guards and I had dysentery, could barely stand. So I hid myself in my bunk and in a sick, helpless rage sketched that picture, the last one in the book. The attack.'

'Ah.'

'When I gave Yvonne the art for the book I kept that one. Then I burnt it, hoping it meant I'd forget my cowardice.'

'Not cowardice, Harry. You couldn't have stopped the guards.'

I shake my head. 'Logic doesn't work and I'll never forgive myself. Later that night the poor lad crept off and killed himself.'

Eliza holds me close and I let myself fall into the comfort of her warmth. 'Did you tell anyone why he did it?' she says.

I shake my head. 'No. And I reported his death as from illness.'

'You kept those secrets for him then, Harry. That was kind.'

'*Kind?*'

'To him. And to his family.'

'I never ... thought of it like that.'

'You protected him in a different way.'

I didn't think I had any more tears left to weep, but that takes me to the edge once again. After a time I wipe my eyes and sigh deeply.

Eliza says, 'How are you feeling?'

I think for a moment. 'Odd. Relaxed for the first time in ages.'

I can hear the smile in her voice. 'Letting go of secrets is very good for the emotions.'

I look up. 'Oh, love, what did you do to me? You must have been clever at interrogation.'

'I certainly was.'

I gaze at her bright eyes, her gentle mouth. 'Dear God, I've missed you, Eliza. How did we let ourselves get into such a ludicrous state?'

'Suppose it felt safer hidden away in our shells. I'm sorry I've been so distant, Harry.'

'I'm sorry I've been such a short-tempered, oblivious idiot.'

'Grumpy and preoccupied perhaps, but far from an idiot,' Eliza says. 'Come on, we're exhausted. Let's go up to bed.'

That night is the start of a new phase in our lives, although it doesn't ease everything, of course. The main problem, still unresolved, is the difficulty with physical connection Eliza has felt since Jenny was born.

To be fair I find it difficult too. Perhaps I'm simply anxious the baby will wake up any moment or Leo come to our bedroom door.

And while I'm no adherent of Dr Freud's theories, I occasionally wonder if my distress at poor Leadenhall's fate could somehow be a factor. Thankfully I've had far more peace of mind in that regard since telling Eliza about it.

But I think I mostly fear that Eliza might not welcome my embraces. For a year we've had this court case hanging over us and in that time we've withdrawn from each other. I see now that was mostly my own fault but Eliza's reticence has been obvious too.

I'm no longer the vigorous young man she loved before the war and, even if she showed she wanted me, would I be able to respond as she deserves? I suspect we're both afraid to find out.

Still, at last we're free to talk openly about the years of each other's lives we missed, which eases my heart and Eliza's, too. The gloom she's felt since the birth starts to lift, and our life together becomes better than it's been for a long time.

As if in reflection of our good mood the early autumn is lovely, and Jenny's second birthday arrives. We take my mother and the children to the park and watch the sea and eat fairy bread and chocolate crackles, and light two candles on a cake Jessie made for the birthday girl.

Afterwards Jenny falls asleep and Leo plays on a swing. He's six and already coming home from school with wide-eyed tales of the feats of bigger boys.

He wriggles off our laps now when we want to cuddle him, which makes Eliza sigh. But Jenny still nestles into us like a koala, so that eases the pangs of first separation from our boy. They're so very different. Tawny-haired Leo is outgoing, his hazel eyes alight with enthusiasm, while Jenny is quiet and curious.

She climbs the furniture to stare at ornaments that Leo never notices. If she can, she grabs what she sees and gazes, gazes with her aqua eyes, as if it holds some invisible design. Then she replaces it and sits down, smiling to herself.

My heart aches with love for them both, but I suppose that's how it is with children: fear and hope mingled together is a painful business.

Stretched out on the picnic blanket, Eliza says, 'Had a letter from Billie. She's fine, but little detail as usual. I think she's with some man. She's gone so quiet.'

'When Billie goes quiet doesn't it mean she's not happy?' I say.

'Very true.'

'I met the lass in London, did I not?' asks Jessie.

'When you and Tina came over in 1936?' says Eliza.

'Aye, when you and Harry were play-acting you were just best mates. That'd be it.'

Eliza laughs. 'Yes, I introduced you briefly. A tall, slim woman with auburn hair.'

'Had a tongue on her sharp as a razor. Funny bairn, but melancholy too.'

'She'd just broken up with my brother Pete. Eventually got over him, though.'

'That time,' I say. 'What about their second fling? She was still very unhappy, remember Tina and Nikos's welcome party?'

Eliza nods. 'Hit her pretty hard. But at least *this* time it can't be Pete—'

She stops and we gaze at each other in disbelief.

'Oh, no,' says Eliza. 'Surely not.'

'But he's married now,' I say. 'He wouldn't be that stupid.'

We both sigh.

Godfrey is charged with submitting a forgery in evidence, but sadly doesn't go to gaol. His lawyer claims some intermediary offered to contact Sir Hugh for a letter, then produced the forgery himself.

Of course this phantom intermediary has vanished, but presumably to save face all round the tissue of lies is accepted. At least Godfrey has to pay a large fine for his misdeed, and we try to put the whole sorry business behind us.

Our contentment at home grows, so it comes as a horrible shock when Eliza gets an official letter telling her to meet a Mr White at the Astoria Cafe in Hunter Street, at ten on Saturday morning.

Eliza refuses to let me accompany her, but goes alone, dressed in a neat suit and hat, her face calm. She's back by eleven.

'Short and sweet. Mr White didn't waste any time, but I've fobbed him off.' She smiles wryly. 'Told him I was so busy being a mother to my dear little children that I couldn't possibly think of helping the intelligence service for years yet.'

'Rather cheeky of you, love.'

'I told him my mind has been all *mushy* since the baby was born. For once in my life feminine frailty has worked in my favour.'

I laugh. 'Mushy? You're as sharp as a sword.'

'Before he realised I'd be useless to him, he started saying something interesting about leftists at the State Dockyard. What's the State Dockyard?'

'A ship-building site across the harbour at Carrington. Some of the workers are patients at our clinic. But from what I've heard it's a model of industrial harmony, hardly a nest of radicals.'

'I suppose the government sees Reds under the beds everywhere. Ah well, danger averted for now.'

Life follows peacefully, then around the middle of the year Ned drops by my office with an envelope, saying shyly as I open it, 'Nancy wants it in a church in Sydney, and her parents will come over from Hong Kong.'

'Congratulations!' I say. 'Eliza and I will certainly be there— when?—February 1954? A while yet, Ned.'

He shakes his head. 'Apparently it takes forever to make dresses and bake cakes and all the other paraphernalia. I'm leaving it up to Nancy.'

Eliza is delighted. 'I know Billie always says she's been to too many damned weddings, but we'll see everyone and dress up, and eat and drink and dance. What a lovely thing to look forward to.'

Doe-eyed Vivy and angelic Claire are Nancy's bridesmaids. In pink, crowned with flowers and lit by the church's high coloured windows, they solemnly follow her down the aisle.

Nancy is dressed in white lace and the three of them are such a picture of beauty it makes my eyes sting. When Ned lifts Nancy's veil the look on his face tightens my throat even further. After everything he's been through, how he deserves this happiness.

When Eliza and I were married it was in a registry office, not a handsome old church. Her veil was the netting on a little blue hat, but I'll always remember that moment of lifting it and seeing her amber eyes full of such joy. My dear.

I swallow, and luckily the ceremony's all done and dusted before I make a public exhibition of myself. As we assemble outside of the church for photographs I greet our friends, who are done up to the nines. Even Yvonne, who usually looks as if she's put on whatever's in the laundry basket, appears surprisingly stylish.

Izabel, the mother of the bride, is wearing a long red silk coat covered with embroidered flowers and birds, while Laurence is also in a full-length robe. They look magnificent.

We hug Izabel and shake hands with Laurence, who jokes, 'I have recovered well, Harry, although my daughter bringing Ned into the family is fine insurance for the future.'

I notice Pete arm in arm with a woman, but it isn't his little blonde wife, it's *Billie*. I nudge Eliza, who waves and murmurs, 'My God, we were right.'

After the obligatory snaps are done, Nikos and Steve drives us to the reception. Steve's become a fine-looking boy, still keen on music and plays at Tina's club.

Tina herself isn't here. She and the new husband Jimmy aren't really close to Ned or Nancy. Nikos doesn't seem in very good spirits, though. He smiles, but his eyes are sad. Perhaps he's still not over the divorce.

At the reception there's lots of catching up and laughter. As we eat and drink I let the gossip drift over my head—Eliza will fill me in on the important bits later.

Yvonne is beside me and I compliment her on her attractive new hairstyle, quite a departure from her usual bird's-nest mode.

'It seems I have cinnamon-hued hair, Harry, and it's all the rage.'

'But isn't that just your normal colour?' I say, puzzled.

'I know. Who'd have *imagined* I could be so fashionable?'

We're both laughing, when Eliza nudges me and I turn. Pete is saying something, and the whole table is listening intently.

'—so it's almost final,' he says. 'Got pretty ugly. Janet cited Billie when she could have done the usual thing, blamed some stranger. And, ah, she's taken quite a lot. Thought I'd managed to separate our finances, but her lawyer got around that.' He shrugs and smiles. 'Still, I've got some damned good news as well.'

He gazes at Billie, and she says wryly, 'I've spent half a lifetime running away from this bloke, but looks like he's caught me now.' She holds out her left hand, with a modest diamond on her ring finger, and all the women express their admiration.

I glance at Nikos, but he's gazing away bleakly. Ah, perhaps it's not Tina making him low, Eliza says he cares a lot for Billie.

I've always been fond of her too, but if I'm honest her forthrightness is sometimes a little *too* bracing. Still, tonight I've never seen her so happy and I'm glad.

The evening turns into one of the best ever. Eliza is relaxed, leaning into me and murmuring snippets of gossip in my ear, and during Ned's shy speech to his bride she squeezes my hand.

The children are at home in Newcastle with my mother. We're staying with Nikos and, as well as being a welcome change from our usual situation, his comfortable spare room holds many happy memories for us.

That night, as she's at the dressing-table taking off her makeup, Eliza says, 'Had a chat to Billie. Apparently the divorce was nastier than Pete said, and pert little Janet has taken him for every penny. He's got a job with some logistics firm so he won't starve, but it's been painful.'

I pull back the sheet and get into bed. 'Are they living together?'

'No, Pete's taken a small flat not far from Billie's place.'

'Odd. Perhaps he doesn't want to upset Vivy?'

'Unlikely,' says Eliza. 'Yvonne said she loathes Janet so much she wanted to throw a party.'

'Did you see Nikos's face when Billie was showing off her ring?'

Eliza gets into bed. 'He cares a lot for her, I think.'

We snuggle down, facing each other, and I stroke her cheek. 'In the church I was recalling when we got married. You with your little blue hat and veil and your lovely eyes. Haven't changed a bit.'

She smiles. 'I was thinking about Ned and Nancy. They're the sort who'll fit each other for a lifetime, riding out the roadbumps and growing old together. But Billie and Pete? All that passion and drama, highs and lows—sometimes my heart quails for her.'

'And us? What about ...?' I stop, suddenly afraid.

Eliza says gently, 'We're the sort for a lifetime, love.'

She puts her hand to my head and draws my face to hers and kisses me softly, then deeply, in a way she hasn't for so long.

It's intoxicating. It may just be the drinks, the joyous evening, the celebration with friends, but it doesn't matter, it's *her*, my beloved, pressed against me.

We breathe each other in and suddenly, suddenly we're *ourselves* again, the selves I feared we'd lost forever, the Harry and Eliza who know every response, every texture and murmuring, every turning and rising up and folding together, every fierce delight of our long, sweet coupling.

And what is new, what allows us an abandon I've never known before, is the certainty of how precious is our bond, and how stupidly close we came to losing it.

A couple of months later a letter arrives from Charlotte in Vietnam. Eliza sits down slowly.

'Oh, Harry. *Otto's* died. How awful.'

Otto is—was—Charlotte's father, a professor and bearded bear of a man, and long ago I was very taken with his Socialist ideals and alluring daughter. He helped Eliza get her first job as a clerk in intelligence; and he grew stooped and white-haired working with the *Kindertransport* children in those hard times when (as Izabel so briskly pointed out) even feckless Charlotte was at her best.

I sit beside Eliza and scan the page. 'Ah, heart attack, very sudden. Well, at least he didn't suffer a long decline, poor old Otto. Does he have any other close family?'

'No, only Charlotte and Vivy.'

I put my arm around Eliza. 'I feel surprisingly sad. A good man. I was just thinking of how he affected us all.'

She nods. 'Me too. But I just had a silly thought. Charlotte's got no relatives in England now, and her daughter's in Sydney. Let's hope her French general keeps her busy in Vietnam or God knows what sort of havoc she'd wreak if she came here.'

We both laugh, a little unkindly.

But things aren't going as well in Vietnam as Charlotte's breezy letters would have us believe. In particular there's a valley called Dien Bien Phu, with an airstrip the French are using to attack Vietminh supply routes.

The swaggering jargon of the newspapers slowly gives way to terms like *heroic garrison, blitz, besieged* and *desperate*, as the French are outgunned and outmanoeuvred by the clever Reds. In May 1954 the French are forced to surrender.

A few days later Eliza calls me into the kitchen, the paper spread out, and points to a grainy photo of six officers looking fraternal, fierce and battle-weary.

'Harry, look—commanders at Dien Bien Phu, fate unknown, it says. I think one may be Charlotte's husband. I only saw him briefly four years ago, and he's labelled General Louis de Fermer—but perhaps that's a misprint for de Ferrier.'

'Let's hope they survived, then.'

Eliza scans the article. 'The Vietminh have taken nearly twelve thousand prisoners. No casualty lists yet. Oh, God, I hope it's not really him.'

But four weeks later a black-bordered envelope arrives from Charlotte. The man in the photograph was indeed her husband, and he died in the final days at Dien Bien Phu. He shouldn't even have been there, she says bitterly. He was on a routine inspection and became stranded when hostilities suddenly escalated.

She'll stay in Saigon, it has such happy memories of Louis, she says. He's left her wealthy, so she'll fund an institute for war orphans in his name.

But when the formalities are over she wants to come to Sydney for a few days, to see her daughter Vivy and at last hear her sing.

Four months later Jessie again comes to our rescue and minds the children and we take the familiar train trip to Sydney, to meet Charlotte and watch Vivy perform.

We're staying with Nikos but he doesn't want to come that night, so we take a taxi by ourselves to Kings Cross. Eliza is wearing a red dress that not only suits her delightfully but is, I am told, stylish enough to stand muster in the demanding presence of Charlotte.

Eliza says, laughing, 'I'm so looking forward to this. I've known Vivy since the moment she was born, and now she's *eighteen*. Unbelievable.'

The neon sign above the club announces *Tempo* in a dashing blue script, while posters of a glamorous Vivy line the doorway, emblazoned *Sydney's Own Jazz Songbird, Miss Vivian McKee*.

Tina, wearing a silver gown, greets us at the cloakroom. 'Welcome, you two! Harry, you haven't met Jimmy before—darling, here's Harry and Eliza.'

A man in a dinner suit turns to us. He's a pleasant-looking fellow, slim, mid-height, half-grin, not at all the lounge lizard I'd expected.

'I'll be blessed,' Jimmy Kelso says, firmly shaking my hand. 'My new brother-in-law! What a treat to meet you at last, Harry Bell. And Mrs Eliza—how fine you're looking tonight. Give the girl your coats and come and make yourselves comfortable.'

Tina stays in the lobby to greet people and we follow Jimmy into the club. He says, 'Billie and Pete brought Vivy in earlier—here we are. I'll go get us some drinks.'

Billie, seated beside Pete at a big table, looks like a fashion model in a sparkly green gown. She says, 'Vivy's out the back with the band. You'll love the performance.'

'Speaking of performances,' says Eliza, sitting down, 'where's Charlotte?'

Billie laughs. 'At some very posh hotel, so maybe she can't find her way to seedy Kings Cross.'

Jimmy returns with a bottle of French champagne and László follows with a tray of glasses.

I joke, 'What's this? Thought we had to drink from tea-cups.'

Jimmy grins. 'I gave the police commissioner over there a bottle too, so we'll be fine.'

Eliza and I chat happily with the others, then Tina brings Charlotte in to join us. They're quite a contrast, Tina in her slinky silver gown and Charlotte in subdued black, her eyes sad, her compelling face framed by waves of golden hair.

For a moment I'm flung into the past, to a part of my life closed off, although not quite forgotten: when Charlotte was my wife, both of us young and passionate and (me at least) innocent.

She was magnificent, a blonde lioness—careless, shameless, cruel. I doubt she's any different today and I think, thank God I'm with Eliza. But Charlotte is so obviously wounded everyone hugs her, even me.

She sits and touches her eyes with a handkerchief.

'*Toutes mes condoléances, Madame de Ferrier,*' says Jimmy, passing her a glass of champagne.

'*Merci beaucoup, Monsieur Kelso.* How marvellous to see you all,' she says. 'What a *ghastly* few months it's been.' She takes a deep breath and raises her glass. 'To darling Louis. And to the joy of seeing you again, my dearest friends.'

The lights dim, the chatter goes quiet. Vivy's band appears and tunes up, then Vivy walks out and stands relaxed at the microphone. She's in flat shoes, slim trousers, her chestnut waves loose, her face pale in the spotlight. And then she sings.

After a few minutes I whisper to Eliza, 'My God, she's extraordinary!' and Eliza smiles and nods, and the interval comes far too soon. People go to the stage and ask Vivy for autographs, then after a few minutes László clears a path for her to our table.

'Oh *Charlie!*' she says, hugging her mother. 'How *are* you?'

Charlotte wipes tears away and says, 'All the better for seeing you, my darling.'

Vivy sits down next to her and leans past to say, 'Hello, Dad, Billie. Did you like that?'

'You joking, kid? It was great,' says Billie. 'And look who's here from Newcastle to see you.'

'Aunt Eliza, Uncle Harry!'

'That was just wonderful, darling,' says Eliza. 'And I reckon you've even converted Harry to jazz, quite an achievement.'

'It's true,' I say. 'I'm growing a little beard as we speak.'

Vivy laughs and Charlotte takes her hands. 'I can't even *tell* you, sweetheart—I'm so *proud*, and I'm sure your father is too.'

'I see those expensive vocal lessons didn't go to waste after all, young lady,' says Pete.

Vivy says, '*Dad*. Honestly.'

Pete grins and turns to Charlotte, and they gaze at each other. She reaches out and cups his cheek. 'Who could ever have imagined? *Our* daughter, Pete. Our beautiful, beautiful daughter.'

I feel Eliza beside me go very still.

21. Tina: The Besamim

What a bloody disaster of a night. Jimmy's come along to Tempo as he's curious to meet Harry at last, but he's anxious too because he's got a temporary chef in at the Starlight Lounge.

Gaston, the head chef, is indisposed after some unpleasantness with Big Davy over Pearl. After Vivy's first set I ring the Lounge and Pearl tells me the new man is coping, though he's not as good as Gaston, she says sulkily.

I give Jimmy the news at the table, and Charlotte says, 'Gaston? Wasn't he the *chef de cuisine* Louis appreciated so much? Will he come back?'

'Ah, your man's gone,' Jimmy says. 'Bit of a lady-killer. Got too fond of one of the girls and her husband took against him, so he's done a flit. We'll survive.'

I must say I admire how well Charlotte's playing the grieving widow. At first glance she seems subdued, broken-hearted, then a closer look reveals the 'modest' black dress is a Balenciaga *haute couture* masterpiece.

It frames her face and shoulders like a cameo, and showcases every voluptuous contour of her body without exposing an inch of skin. Jimmy gazes at her in the half-light, and turns to me, eyes wicked, and silently whistles.

I smile back, then notice Eliza is giving me a curious look—alert, dismayed. Something's up, there's an odd atmosphere.

I'm seated next to Charlotte, Pete is on her far side. When the lights on Vivy become brighter for an upbeat number, I'm at just the right angle to see that beneath the table Charlotte's hand is on Pete's thigh. She's moving her fingers very slightly in a circular motion close to his groin. It must be both agonising and delicious.

Billie has shifted her chair so there's space between her and Pete, and from the set of her shoulders I don't believe it's accidental.

She mentioned once ages ago, a little too casually, that Pete has always been the proverbial putty in Charlotte's hands. I recall my original sense of him as dissatisfied, and now he doesn't even have the pretty young wife and big farm to show off.

He's engaged to Billie, a woman he's apparently pushed into leaving him before, a woman with a quiet life and a modest job, while the glamorous, wealthy mother of his child has her hand very near something that's probably far from putty by now.

Pete breathes deeply, his eyes a little unfocused. Billie glances at him, grabs her purse, and says, 'Feeling sick. See you later.'

She's out the door, a streak of shimmering green, before any of us even realise what she's said. Pete stays beside Charlotte and doesn't follow her.

Next morning I drop by Billie's place. She's still in her dressing-gown. We sit down with coffee and she says dryly, 'To what do I owe the pleasure?'

'You know perfectly well, Billie. But look, you're taking it too hard. Charlotte tries to lure every man—you should have seen Jimmy's response to that bloody dress!'

'Come on, Teen. I know Pete's face. She had her hand on his prick, didn't she?'

'Well—not precisely *on*.'

Billie nods wearily.

'But listen, doll, last night I thought of something. When you two separated before, what actually *happened*? I've heard bits from Eliza, but—'

Billie shrugs. 'First time he was falling for Charlie, got drunk, crashed a very expensive plane, and ended our plans for a flying school. The second? War was over, I had no prospects as a pilot, my mother was ill and I needed to come home. Pete flatly refused.'

'Exactly as I thought! When you've parted before, Billie, it wasn't *you* who decided. Pete *goaded* you to leave him. He put you in such a bind you simply had no choice but to go.'

Billie looks as if I've slapped her. After a time she takes a shuddering breath.

'Christ, you're right. He's always pushed me away, and I never let myself see it.' She slowly shakes her head. 'Charlie didn't lure him last night—Pete *chose*, the bastard. He chose her.'

She covers her face and sobs in wrenching groans, and I put my arm around her. Finally she stops and fiercely rubs her eyes. 'I'm such a blind, fucking *fool*.'

'Perhaps you need some time off, Billie. Take a holiday.'

'Yeah,' she says bleakly. 'Dunno. Could visit Lizzie and Harry. Hop on the train, see Nikos's famous Hawkesbury, meet the sprogs, walk on the beach. Change of bloody scenery'll work wonders, won't it?'

When I get to Tempo that morning Moshe Adler is there. He's smiling and speaking to László in Hungarian. László thumps him on the back and they shake hands.

He's still smiling when we get to my office, and I say, 'You're in a good mood today, Mr Adler.'

He nods. 'Last night my wife had a daughter, our first. I have three sons but I always wished for a girl. In a week I will have the honour of reading a blessing at the Synagogue and pronouncing her name to the congregation. It is a time of great joy.'

'That's wonderful, how lucky you are. I'd *love* a child, but so far—' I stop, my throat tight.

'One day you will be so blessed, Mrs Kelso.'

'I hope so. What are you calling her?'

'Devorah.' He smiles to himself.

A few days later I'm walking past an antique shop and halt at the sight of a toy. A fish made of silver, with intricate filigreed scales, the length of my hand with small sparkling emeralds for eyes.

The man behind the counter says gruffly, 'Very old.' He passes it to me and I realise it's articulated into sections and moves almost like a real fish. The man names a ludicrous sum and I pay it.

When I get to Tempo, I call László to the office and show him the ornate silver fish.

'It's a toy for Moshe Adler's new baby, Devorah. Will she like it?'

He picks up the beautiful thing in his sensitive pianist's hands and says nothing.

'László?'

He sits down, opens a tiny hinge at the head of the fish and sniffs deeply. 'Here, Tina, smell.'

I sniff, then sit too, dizzy at the ghostly scents of cloves, oranges, spices. 'That's lovely. So it's not a toy?'

László shakes his head. 'It is a *besamim*. At the close of Shabbat there are candles and wine, and the besamim is passed around, full of spices. The sweetness consoles us for the necessary return to the everyday world.'

His eyes glint with tears. 'It is not a toy, but a fine gift for a girl who will have her own household one day.'

'László, what's wrong?'

'I have not smelt the besamim for many years.'

'Why not?'

He looks at me. 'Tina, I have no family beside me to celebrate Shabbat. I have no wife or son or candles or wine or besamim. And, you see … I no longer believe.'

He puts the silver fish into my hands and the haunting scent rises again.

'But isn't there still some hope? New information from Austria?'

He sighs. 'If and when it finally arrives, I will know. One way or the other.'

He bends his head to the filigree scales once more and takes a deep breath. I hold it to his face, gazing at his closed eyes and his mouth bracketed by privation. Oh, László.

Moshe Adler is just as deeply touched. 'It is much like my own grandmother's, from the days *before*. My daughter is fortunate to have such a handsome gift. Thank you, indeed.'

'I'm glad you like it, Mr Adler. László explained to me what it really is. I'm afraid I had no idea, I just loved it because it was beautiful.'

'You loved it. That is what matters.' He runs his fingers over the silver scales and gazes at me.

'You have been good to work with, Mrs Kelso. I had my doubts, of course—a Gentile, a woman; hot-headed Jimmy Kelso's woman. He is so careless, but you are not. I appreciate that.'

My breath catches. 'Careless?'

'Oh yes. He talks too much. I do not blame him for Meyer's fate, but he must at least share in the guilt.'

'Meyer? Monty Truscott? But Jimmy feels bad he didn't warn him away from the Capellis, you can't blame him for what *they* did.'

Moshe looks at me curiously. 'Jimmy would joke often about Meyer embezzling him, but it was just foolish chatter to pass the time. As it happens Meyer was not cheating, but the Capellis felt they needed to make an example.' His mouth is bitter. 'Hence our good friend ended up dead. Were you not aware?'

I shake my head.

He sighs. 'I read a great deal, you know. I enjoy books about explorers, especially in cold remote places, the Arctic and Antarctic. Do you find that odd?'

'A little. You're a man of the city.'

'Perhaps that is why.' He shrugs. 'Those cold places have creatures called elephant seals. The males weigh perhaps four tons. They fight constantly with each other on the icy beaches—lumbering, crushing, destroying everything around them.'

He pauses. 'Mrs Kelso, I think of you as someone admiring seashells on the beach, blissfully unaware that the elephant seals are all around you.'

I drive to the Starlight Lounge. Surely Moshe is mistaken, surely Jimmy can explain, surely this sense of anxiety in my gut will lift. Yes, my husband is careless and hot-headed.

And a few times—but *only* a few—I've felt the brunt of it. Asking about the death of Dimple brought me a sprained wrist, but that was practically an accident. Fussing about finances when he was hungover got me a slap in the face, but I probably deserved it.

And a stupid joke about Monty Truscott, on a day Jimmy was at his wit's end, earned me a punch in the ribs—but now I understand the terrible guilt he was suffering.

His remorse afterwards has been heartbreaking. He was beaten without mercy as a boy, so I'm amazed he can still be so patient and loving towards me.

I'm desperate, today, to be reassured of that, but when I get to the restaurant he's not there.

Pearl, behind the counter, says lazily, 'Went out. New waitress, Sharon, needed someone to sign for a flat, so he's helping.'

I'm suddenly irritated by Pearl, by her feline smile, by her air that she knows something I don't.

'How's the latest chef going, Pearl?' I say tightly.

'Okay,' she says, wiping down the counter.

'Better than poor old Gaston?'

'No.'

'What does Big Davy think?'

Her nostrils flare with annoyance. 'Doesn't mind.'

'Had it off with him yet?'

'Bitch,' she mutters.

'Actually, Pearl, it'd be helpful if you don't lead *this* poor guy on. It'd be nice not to have Davy beat him to a pulp just because your knickers fell down. Again. I can't imagine, myself, why Jimmy's kept you on. Must have gone through a lot of chefs in your day.'

Pearl stops, her cat's eyes cold. 'Can't you, Tina? Really? And who do you think Jimmy was screwing while you were playing the coy little married woman?'

She leans forward, her cleavage sharp. 'He liked it in your office, you know. Remember your hat on the coat-stand? He'd get me to wear it and lie on your desk naked—not a *stitch*, Tina—and he'd fuck me and fuck me and fuck me. Oh, I loved it, and so did he.'

Her mouth is contemptuous. 'And he still does, our Jimmy. But he's got Sharon now. Always liked a bit of variety.'

Somehow I get myself back to Tempo. It's quiet, Monday, and we're closed. I manage to climb the stairs without collapsing. At the top I hear sobbing. Is it me?

But my face is rigid and dry, and I realise it's coming from László's flat. The door is ajar and I go in. László is standing in the centre of the room, a letter in his hand.

'Ah, Tina,' he says, taking a gulp of air. 'The letter has arrived and at last I know. Such laudable bureaucrats, the Germans. There, in Austria, all this time, are the records I have sought for so long.'

'Oh, *László—*'

'Here, you see. Richter Róbert, aged four, dead of starvation. Richter Éva, twenty-five, shot for insolence.' He groans. 'My courageous wife. My hungry little boy.'

He drops the letter, his face agonised, his body swaying. I lead him into his bedroom.

'Please, László, you should rest—'

He turns and takes my hands, his eyes tormented. His knees give way and he falls onto the bed. I lie down beside him, and put my arms around him and hold his head to my breast.

We cry together. And then, to my utter amazement, I take off his clothes and my own, and we make love.

The hurricane of grief and desire passes and we lie there, shipwrecked, holding each other.

László strokes my hair. 'I suspected what was between Jimmy and Pearl, but it was before you were with him. Tina, he was a single man and we are all jealous of the lovers who came before.'

'But what about anyone else—since?'

'I think Pearl was simply lying to hurt you.' He laughs wryly. 'Did you do this in revenge, perhaps? That was very hasty of you.'

'I only wanted to hold you, László. You've always been so good to me. That's all.'

'Thank you, Tina. For me it has been a very long time. You see, I cannot bear too much closeness, not with anyone. I only ever wanted my Éva, my Róbert, in my life.'

'I like the way you say their names. Róbert especially. *Roe*-bert. A sort of growly *r*.'

'*Rrr*,' László says, and smiling, I try to copy him, and we hug and kiss and then we're making love again: slowly, sweetly, generously. How I like his sensitive hands, his scent of tobacco and paprika, his brown eyes and deep, quiet laugh.

He's always dressed formally and never rolls up his sleeves, so for the first time I see on his arm the marks of a tattoo, a number. I kiss it and he sighs and holds me close.

We sleep, and when we wake it's mid-afternoon.

I gaze at him. 'I have to go.'

László nods, his face serious. 'Tina, listen. This has been a moment out of time. But no one can know, and we can never, *never*, be lovers again. Do you understand?' He takes a breath. 'You must shower, and then you must go to Jimmy and take him to bed.'

I'm surprised. 'But I'm still angry about Pearl.'

'You do not understand, Tina. We did not take any precautions.'

'But I don't, I've been trying—*oh*.'

'You see? And should you conceive in this month, there must be no doubt in Jimmy's mind about the child, and none in yours. This did not happen. You are Jimmy's woman.'

'You'd forget me so easily?' I feel oddly hurt.

'Never. But think, Tina, *think*. If Jimmy suspects for one moment that we have slept together, I am dead, and probably you are too.'

'He's not like that, László, he *wouldn't*.'

He strokes the hair back from my face. 'Jimmy starts things off, then they fly out of his control. His petty gossip gets a man murdered. He orders a beating and it goes too far.'

'Too far?'

'I heard earlier. Gaston has died in hospital.'

My scalp crawls. 'But—that was Big Davy, jealous about Pearl. How is that Jimmy's fault?'

'One night Gaston was very tired and spoke rudely to Jimmy. So Jimmy told Davy to *punish* him, just a little. But Davy does not know when to stop.'

I'm stunned. After a time I say, 'Moshe Adler said he thinks of me as someone admiring the seashells on a beach, unaware of the rampaging beasts all around me.'

László kisses me. 'Leave me now, Tina. Go back to Jimmy and be happy. But yes, you should occasionally look up from your pretty shells.'

After that astonishing interlude with László I shower at my flat, then go to the Starlight Lounge and delight Jimmy by enticing him upstairs to bed.

As he dozes I stare at the ceiling and think, I am the sort of woman who would screw two men on the same day without the slightest shame. Little Tina Bell of Newcastle would be very surprised at that. But no matter how I try to shock myself, all I feel is a sense of contentment.

László and I continue as always. We never refer to what happened between us, not with glance or pause, or the slightest change to our easy amicability.

Life returns to its normal flow, organising bands and staff and booze, and delighting in the intense, brilliant music we create together at Tempo. Nothing is different, except one day I realise everything is.

22. Billie: Wind Rose Cove

In my shimmering green gown I dash to the door at Tempo, but it's so cold I go back to get my coat from the cloakroom. I try not to look inside the club, but the briefest of glances is enough to show Pete is still cosied up to Charlotte. In the street my dress flaps against my legs in the wind, my coat no protection at all.

Where should I *go*? Not to my flat, too many memories. Just this afternoon we'd made love, then I'd showered and dressed, full of anticipation for the evening.

Why didn't I even suspect this might happen? I know how ruthless Charlie can be! But I'd assumed the heartbroken widow might wait a few months between men, and in any case I thought she'd finished with Pete long ago.

I'd let my wariness fade, trusting that Pete and I were happy at last. I did feel a twinge of unease when he rented his own flat, but it was easy to rationalise: uncertain circumstances, extra belongings, Vivy sometimes staying.

But I let it go and we'd talk instead about living together when we were married. *Married*!

What now? I'll just go somewhere, see someone. Who? Most of my friends are sitting in the club with Charlie and Pete.

Wait on, I can visit Yvonne and Klara. I walk to my car, high-heels clicking on the footpath, and drive to Balmain. I'm freezing by then, I've never coped easily with the cold, let alone shock as well.

Yvie opens the door. 'Oh, Billie, come in, you're shivering! What's happened?'

'Not now. Just let me sit in the warm for a bit, will you?'

'Of course. The fire's going, Claire's in bed—it's just us and Nikos. He came over to help us make something delicious for dinner.'

In the lounge I nod hello and sit down, and hold out my hands to the glorious fire.

Yvie says, 'Bill, your fingers have turned *blue*.'

'I can't bear the cold—remember how I could hardly move after those long flights?'

'It is because you are tall, and your feet and hands are so far from your heart, Billie,' says Klara.

I smile a little. 'Nikos is tall too, but the cold doesn't affect him.'

'Good Greek food, that's the secret,' says Nikos. 'I thought everyone knew that.'

As I warm up Klara says, 'You are looking very glamorous in your green dress, Billie. Were you not going to Tempo tonight to welcome Charlotte?'

'Yes, I went. But I didn't feel like hanging around. Restless.'

'How was Vivy?' says Nikos.

'Marvellous, as always.'

'It must be confusing for her to be around Pete and Charlotte, when they are together,' says Klara thoughtfully. 'Confusing for everyone, I expect.'

I start feeling short of breath. 'Actually, I think I'll go now. Just a silly whim to drop in.'

'Can I hitch a ride home?' says Nikos. 'I walked over, but now I'm feeling lazy.'

I nod and kiss Klara and Yvie goodbye, my teeth clenched at the effort of being polite.

We get in the car and I ram it into gear and roar along beneath the streetlights.

'Are you all right?' says Nikos. 'Hey, watch out for the kids skipping, the puppy dogs romping. Slow the hell *down*, Billie.'

'There's no one about.'

'We can't see them because we're going at the speed of light.'

I laugh, despite myself. Soon we turn into Nikos's street and stop. 'Goodnight,' I say.

Nikos gives me his patient look. 'What's up?'

'Nothing. Don't want to talk.'

'All right.' He leans back in the seat and crosses his arms.

'Nikos, I mean I don't want to *talk*.'

'I'm not talking.'

I bury my face in my hands and groan.

'All right, I'll go.' He leans over and lightly kisses my bowed head. 'But drive slowly, please, Billie?'

'Good*night.*' I say. But I make my way home carefully, feeling numb and lost. Still chilled, I huddle beside the fire for a time, then get ready for bed.

My diamond ring catches my eye, small because Pete lost so much money to Janet. I'd told him honestly I loved it because it was his, but in my heart I always knew it had a mean look.

I put it in a drawer and sleep well, considering. Perhaps I just prefer to be unconscious.

Tina drops around next morning and confirms what I already knew from Pete's face and Charlie's hidden hand. Then she says something extraordinary about how in the past he's always *goaded* me to leave him.

It's as if a flare lights up in my head. Pete has ruthlessly chosen me over the years and then not chosen me, and I've never let myself see it. Finally I can no longer postpone the anguish.

When I emerge from the depths I make a weak joke to Tina about taking a holiday, and suddenly that doesn't seem the worst idea I've ever had. So I ring Lizzie and organise leave from work.

A few days later I'm sitting on the Flyer as it huffs and puffs towards Newcastle. Once we're out of Sydney, the bushland flows away over the blue hills and deep gorges with distant glimpses of water. Soon we're clattering over a long steel bridge.

The river—Nikos's beloved Hawkesbury—is broad and grey-green, slow and magnificent. Past the bridge the train-tracks run along just yards away from the shoreline. Out on the water are the rows of narrow timbers marking the oyster farms (I love oysters).

The day has warmed up and I open the window and breathe the dusty tang of eucalyptus. I wish I'd done this before—both Harry and Nikos have enthused about this part of the world often enough.

It's wild and uncompromising and scruffy. A bit like me, I suppose.

In Newcastle, Lizzie's kids are as nice as I'd expect. Leo is eight, bright and confident, while three-year-old Jenny is laughing and large-eyed.

'How are you and Harry going?' I ask Lizzie. 'Didn't have a chance to talk that night at Tempo—too bloody much happening—but you both looked happy.'

'Oh, Bill, we've rediscovered our old selves, thank God,' she says. 'Everything between us is wonderful. The only problem is that I want a job and Harry wants me to wait till Jenny's in school, and I think he means high school!'

She laughs. 'But I've got plans. There's a kindergarten around the corner, and a nice woman nearby who'd love to babysit.'

'What will you do?'

'Just an office job I expect. A couple of years ago some horrid little man mentioned the State Dockyard. I know a bit more about it now and they advertise occasionally for staff.'

'Why there?'

'It's on the water, they build ships.' She grins. 'Not four-masters, but you can't have everything.'

'Sounds *perfect*. Hope it works out, Lizzie.'

'And you, Bill? I'm sorry Pete behaved so appallingly.'

I shrug. 'He's always done whatever he wanted. I expect Charlie'll throw him over again eventually, but that's his problem, not mine. It'll never be mine again.'

'Yvonne rang to say Vivy's upset,' Eliza says. 'She's furious at him for hurting you.'

'Ah well. Maybe all that passion and heartbreak'll be good for her singing.' We laugh affectionately.

During this time away I sleep a lot, and in the spring warmth I like to wander along the beach to Nobbys Head, with its lighthouse and the weather station I've often contacted from Rose Bay.

I'm taking a final walk now—tomorrow I return to Sydney. The sky is blue and I splash in the sandy shallows, while the breakers further out collapse into floods of lacy foam.

They rush up and around my ankles and flow out again, as fluid and peaceful as white noise on the radio. When I reach the cliffs at the base of Nobbys I turn and start back.

On the horizon to the south is a storm, a rolling cloud-front of charcoal, with rumbles of thunder pushing through the heavy air. Lovely, a southerly buster to cool everything down.

But by the time I'm half-way back along the beach the winds are strong and the storm almost upon me. An open stretch of sand isn't a good place to be right now, so I look around for shelter.

There's only a grassy dune, so I press myself low against it as the skies open up. I watch, amazed, my teeth chattering, as the rain flows like rivers over the beach and lightning explodes around me.

Just when I decide I'm more-or-less done for, the stormfront throws a final peevish thunderbolt at Nobbys Head and moves northwards. *Wow.* I sit up, drenched, and shake my head.

On the way back to Lizzie's, the roads are steaming in eerie tendrils and water is gushing along the kerbing. But the sky is blue again, the air is warm, and I take a deep breath.

I think I feel all right.

Back in Sydney there are easy days and difficult days, but I find a certain calmness. I ruefully remember Nikos saying, *It's a long hard business falling out of love with someone.*

I promise myself I'll never again care about a man who still wants the woman who came before me: but in any case I'm not much interested in men right now.

I don't hear a word from Pete. He and Charlie get re-married in a silly rush and head off to Vietnam, but poor Vivy, emotionally torn, refuses to go with them. I think they could have tried harder with her, but I'm a non-motherer of kittens, so what would I know?

Vivy stays with Klara and Yvie. She still works at the delicatessen, but she's better-known now in Sydney's expanding jazz scene. As well as Tempo, she sings at the city's Ironworkers Club or Criterion Hotel, or Mocambo in Newtown, or El Rocco at the Cross.

Tina isn't worried about the competition. She says there's more than enough business to go around and it's true, sometimes there are long queues outside Tempo.

But she's probably more focused on her own situation—at last she's pregnant and utterly content. I see her now and then, but I spend more time with Klara and Yvie, and sometimes Nikos, who comes over because he's teaching Yvie Greek cooking.

Nowadays he and I are comfortable with each other. I can't imagine feeling desire for any man again and he's also a bit shell-shocked. Hid girlfriend Doreen, the one who didn't like baklava, suddenly went off to Brisbane with one of the mechanics.

Nikos says he's philosophic about it, but he still seems sad. I wonder if Tina's pregnancy is also weighing him down—he said once he wanted more children.

At work we eat in the lunchroom with everyone else, but sometimes in good weather we sit on our favourite rocks by the water and chat about friends or work or the perennial topic, the future of what's now called Rose Bay Water Airport.

Two years ago Trans Oceanic Airways closed down, although Ansett Flying Boats took over their Lord Howe Island flights. But Qantas has been moving its Pacific services onto long-distance DC4s and DC6s, so it'll be leaving the base in a few months, while New Zealand's TEAL is also phasing out flying boats.

Two or three hundred people used to work her at the base, but now there are only half that, and we're all wondering what lies ahead.

This warm autumn day Nikos and I are sitting on the rocks, offering the seagulls our scraps.

'Tina's asked me to be with her at the birth,' I say, curious to see if that's what's bothering him.

He just nods absently and says, 'When's it due?'

'In six weeks, June. She's as big as a blimp, but very cheerful.'

'Did she bribe you with a dress this time?'

'She offered, but I said I'd do it anyway. I'll call in the debt one day, though.'

'I'm sure you will. Oh, nearly forgot to tell you,' says Nikos. 'Remember my old grey cat, Shadow? Poor thing died, but it was fairly quick. I buried her under the grapevine and the house is pretty quiet without her.'

'She was stunningly unfriendly for a pet.'

'I still carry the scars,' he says. 'She liked you, though. I remember she was purring away on your lap the first day we ever talked.'

'That's right. I'd just been telling her my litany of woes.'

'I overheard you say straight-faced all I *can* do is dance and fly, and it made me laugh,' he says.

'Is that why you brought me baklava?'

'You always had good taste in desserts.'

'Yeah, I know, just not in men.'

He smiles. 'Actually I have a favour to ask, so I'll have to be in your debt as well. You know young Ron from the engineering section and Beryl, the secretary?'

'Yeah, he's been making eyes at her for a while now.'

'Well, he's had a breakthrough—she's agreed to go for a romantic cruise on *Wind Rose*. But sadly he can't sail, so I have to go to keep them afloat. But *she* feels shy at braving the ocean wave alone with ruffians like Ron and me, so she wants another woman along.'

'And that's where I come in?'

'I know you're not wild about sailing, but he's a good kid. And true love's pretty hard work at the best of times.'

'Who said I'm not wild about sailing?' I say. 'Like any half-sane landlubber, I simply have my reservations. When are you going?'

'This Saturday, about ten.'

'Okay, I'll meet you down here. But you've got to bring some of that great food again.'

It's a gorgeous day for sailing—warm, sunny, a light breeze—but it looks as if it's not going to happen, as by ten-thirty neither Ron nor Beryl has turned up. I sit on the shore beside the alluringly scented picnic basket, while Nikos goes to his office and rings Ron.

He comes back grinning.

'They're on the way?' I say.

'No. Seems they went out last night to celebrate the prospect of a day on the water, and kept on celebrating. Ron can't believe his luck, says he's never letting her out of his bed again.'

I laugh. 'True love triumphs after all. But what a pity, that picnic basket smells damned good.'

Nikos shrugs. 'We can still go.'

'But don't you need two people to sail that thing?'

'We have two people.'

'What, you mean *I'd* have to do all the running around hoisting things and saying 'Aye, aye, Cap'n?'

'The 'Aye, aye' bit, certainly. But only a small amount of hoisting is required. You had fun when you and Cliff were doing it.'

'Be still, my beating heart,' I say. 'Whatever happened to the poor guy, anyway?'

'Never went sailing again, that's for sure.'

'I seem to have that effect on men. Okay, can't waste this perfect day, um, Cap'n.'

'All right, First. Grab the basket and I'll haul the dingy closer.'

'First what?'

He takes off his moccasins and splashes out to the dinghy. 'How could you *possibly* have spent all these years around Eliza and Harry and not know—?' He shakes his head.

'Are we doomed, like the *Titanic?*'

'Probably.'

Nikos rows us out to *Wind Rose*. I climb the ladder at the stern and he hands me the basket, ties the dinghy to the mooring and comes aboard.

The boat rocks pleasingly beneath my bare feet as we take the covers off the sails. Nikos starts the engine and we motor out past Shark Island.

'Did you check the weather report with Stan?' I say.

'A southerly's on the way but it shouldn't be here till this evening. Otherwise perfect.'

I rub some of the anti-sunburn jelly on myself, then sigh with contentment and lean back in the cockpit.

'Don't get too comfortable, First,' Nikos says. 'Need you to hoist the mainsail in a minute.'

'Hoist the *mainsail*? Honestly, who even says that in real life?'

He gives me his patient look. 'Jump to it, First.'

'Aye, aye, Cap'n.'

With altogether too much hauling and tying and untying of little ropes ('*lines*, First') we potter along in the sunny morning. I love the slow unfolding of the foreshores, the small beaches and rocky outcrops, the old boathouses and modern villas, the trees and water in the quiet day.

By early afternoon we reach the little cove I remember so well from my first sail. The beach itself is barely fifty feet long, enclosed by tall rocks at either end, backed with a steep golden cliff behind. Wavelets splash and sparkle on the shoreline.

'Nice, isn't it?' I say. 'Does it have a name?'

'Not on the charts.'

'I reckon we should call it Wind Rose Cove. Do you like that?'

Nikos is pleased. 'Wind Rose Cove it is. Let's get the sails down and put out the anchor.'

Once that's done he finds a rubber float to tow the picnic basket and towels ashore, and we swim to the tiny beach. We spread out the towels and share a feast of savouries and cheese and fruit, and drink beer from a bottle we keep cool in a rock pool.

'Poor old Ron and Beryl,' I say. 'Fancy swapping all this for a day of lust in a rumpled bed.'

'Can't believe you just said that,' says Nikos, laughing.

'Ah, who am I kidding? Pass the beer, please.'

Nikos has another swim while I curl up on a towel in the shade and snooze off my lunch. When I wake up, Nikos is also dozing on his towel. I hear a noise again—whatever it was that woke me—and rub my eyes.

I nudge Nikos with my foot.

'Did you hear that?'

'Mmm?'

'That noise.'

He sits up, yawning. The bright shimmering harbour stretches before us, the North Shore hazy and distant, the sun lower in the sky. It must be three in the afternoon by now.

The temperature drops and the noise comes again, a rumble.

Nikos says, 'Can't be thunder. The cold front's not due for ages.'

We walk to the shore, as far as possible from the overhang of the cliff, and turn to see what's behind us.

My throat goes suddenly dry.

The sky is filled with charcoal-green clouds, towering and tumbling. Lightning flickers back and forth between the billows and the thunder growls. As we watch, astonished, the rolling clouds pour above and over us.

We're hit by a blast of freezing wind, everything becomes dim, and a lightning bolt explodes.

'Come *on!*' says Nikos and grabs my hand and we run back to the shelter of the cliff. Lightning strikes again on the water, a few hundred yards away. I cry out in shock but can hardly hear myself for the noise.

'Should we try to get to the boat?' I yell.

'No, too dangerous, squeeze back in here.'

We huddle beneath the overhang, which is hardly any protection at all, then after half a dozen more blinding lightning strikes the heavens open up.

At first I think it's rain, then realise it's hail. But not hail like the usual tidy little peas: it's hail like bloody great cricket balls.

'Jeez, I heard you get bad weather in Sydney but this is *insane*,' I scream. I have to scream because the racket of thunder plus clattering hail is also insane, as if we're trapped inside a cauldron of noise.

The storm covers the whole sky and lightning strikes in every direction. After an endless time the cricket-ball hail becomes plum-sized hail, and pea-sized, then turns into torrents of pelting rain so heavy I can't even see the yacht fifty yards away.

By now I'm saturated and desperately cold. Even Nikos starts shivering and we huddle together for warmth, but it's a losing battle. My hands and feet are numb and blue, and my jaw aches from the tremors.

Then slowly, slowly, the time between flashes and thunderclaps grows longer. The rain becomes lighter and the front draws away, out over the harbour towards the city and the North Shore.

Nikos stands and lifts me, groaning, to my feet. I'm frozen.

'We've got to get back to the yacht now, Billie, get you dry and warmed up, or—'

I nod. I can't speak. This kind of exposure is terribly dangerous. I'm already half-asleep and yearning for unconsciousness.

Nikos helps me limp to the water, warm compared to the air, but I can't possibly swim so he wraps his arm over me in a lifesaver's hold and hauls us both out to *Wind Rose*.

He pushes me up the ladder and I slip and fall down in the cockpit—slip because every bloody surface is covered in hailstones as smooth as ball bearings.

Nikos helps me up and gets the cabin door open and I slither down inside, groaning.

There's a little retained heat from the day, just enough to unclench my jaw and start it chattering convulsively, but I can only stand rigid, dripping, frozen. Nikos rummages through cupboards and finds towels and rubs me briskly as I drag off my painfully icy swimsuit.

'Christ, Billie, your poor *feet*. Here—' He rubs them dry then pulls back the covers on the bunk. 'Get in.'

He grabs a fresh towel, takes off his dripping swimmers and dries himself quickly, then gets into the bunk and wraps the blankets around us both.

'Turn your back to me.' He holds me from behind, his large body pressed against my frozen shuddering flesh, and I sob in gratitude at the warmth. He takes my hands and massages them, and slowly and painfully my fingers thaw a little.

'Thank you, thank you,' I say through my chattering teeth.

'Press your feet against mine.'

'Even they're hot,' I manage to whisper. 'How come?'

'I told you, good Greek food,' he says. 'Other side now.'

I turn and cling to him, and gradually the shivering stops. He wraps his arms and legs around me, and the blood returns to my feet and hands, and I never, never want to get out of this bunk again for as long as I live.

Some hours later I wake up. The clouds are gone and moonlight softens the lines of the cabin. Nikos is breathing deeply beside me and I'm astonishingly comfortable, but I need a pee. I try to wriggle out without disturbing him, but it's a small bunk.

'You okay?' he murmurs.

'Just want to—'

He sits up sleepily and I swing my legs behind him and emerge. The yacht has a tiny bathroom in the bow and I manage to work all the little levers in the right order, then scurry back to the cabin. Nikos moves over to the far side of the bunk and opens the blankets for me.

We snuggle down. He puts his arm beneath my head, and I nestle into his cosy shoulder. We wrap ourselves around each other again, only this time I'm not frozen. I'm warm and getting warmer.

After a time Nikos says thoughtfully, 'Well. Not quite what I'd expected for today.'

'Nor me.' I snuggle closer.

'Is it possible we're actually in sync at last?' he says. 'No fiancés, wives, boyfriends or girlfriends hanging around? I'd hate to make any rash assumptions.'

I look up, and the moonlight is shimmering on his long-lashed eyes. I run my fingers along his cheekbones and through his beard.

'You can make rash assumptions if you like.' I wrap my arm around his neck and pull him close and we kiss, slowly and sweetly.

After a time I murmur, 'So is this one of the duties of the crew, Cap'n?'

'Certainly is, First. It's in the Ship's Articles.'

'Oh, good. First *what*, anyway?'

'Mate.' He grins. 'First Mate.'

I wrap one leg around his hips in a smooth tango move, and stroke the texture of his chest and belly. 'At last I discover the secret of your amazing warmth,' I say. 'Fur.'

'Keep going. You're almost at the auxiliary heating unit.'

I laugh. 'Really?'

'Of course. For emergencies only.'

We caress each other and he whispers, 'Oh, Billie.'

'Call me First. Maintain that ship's discipline.'

'I'm pretty sure you're the one in command now.'

'Is that so?' I say in delight.

He rolls onto his back and pulls me over him. I clasp his hips with my thighs and move against him till I'm soft and slick, then rise and ease him into me, sighing at the glorious warmth.

'Told you,' he says. 'Heating unit.'

'But emergencies *only*?' I say. 'That's a pity.'

'And special occasions.'

'How special?'

'Any time I'm with you.'

We wake at dawn, make a cup of tea and sit in the cockpit, watching the sun rise between wispy pink-gold clouds. Ripples shimmer on the water, a breeze ruffles our hair, and I lean on Nikos's shoulder, a blanket around us as we gaze at the morning.

When the day warms up I set our wet things out to dry, while Nikos swims to Wind Rose Cove to retrieve the picnic basket, still half-full of food, and tows it back to the yacht.

As he steps into the cockpit and sets down the basket I admire his body, amazed that only yesterday I thought I was indifferent to it.

'You look like one of those statues of Poseidon rising from the sea,' I say. 'Bearded, mature, muscular, with those sexy narrow hips. Very nice.'

'Comparing me to a Greek god?' he says. 'I can live with that. But you certainly don't remind me of an Aphrodite, all plump and submissive.' He sits beside me. 'Don't think they make statues of women like you.'

'Like me?' I say dryly. 'No, I suppose women like Tina are the ideal. Curvy, adorable, petite.'

Nikos turns to me and cups my face in his large hand, but I'm suddenly sad and fearful, and can't meet his eyes.

'Do you imagine Tina's my ideal?' he says.

'You mourned for ages after she left,' I say, swallowing. 'But look, Nikos, I have to tell you—I'm not getting involved with a man who's still yearning after a previous woman.'

He's silent, then says wryly, 'Billie, I was in mourning because I wanted you and couldn't have you.'

'But you had other girlfriends.'

'You had other boyfriends.'

Sunlight twinkles on the water but I don't think it's the dazzle making my eyes sting.

'You wanted *me*?' I say. 'But when did you decide that?'

'The night you threw champagne in my face.'

'No, I mean *really* wanted.'

'The night you threw champagne in my face.'

'But you couldn't, we'd only just met,' I say. 'And I was a mess.'

'You once said you did it because my eyes were so sad. But yours were so stunning I was simply knocked out.' He laughs. 'When you started working at Rose Bay, I thought—Christ, I had no idea, except I was so bloody pleased. And whenever we'd dance together I still couldn't believe my luck.'

'But you were always so *restrained* when we danced,' I say.

'I had to be restrained or I'd have ravished you, there and then on the dance-floor.'

'I'm such an idiot. I didn't even realise I fancied you till that night on my balcony, and I still managed to talk myself out of it.' I look up. 'All this time—*me*?'

'You.'

'Oh.' My body floods with joy. 'Well, if you'd like you can ravish me on the cabin floor.'

'I prefer the bunk. But I can make it wider, there's an extension.'

'Why didn't you make it wider last night?'

'And take the chance you wouldn't press yourself against me?' He shakes his head. 'You've got a lot to learn about sailors, First.'

23. Tina: The Cuckoo

Jimmy is beyond joy about my pregnancy, and brings me gifts and acts as if I'm made of glass. Apart from a little nausea I'm well and happy. The baby is due in June 1955, and Jimmy and I make plans and chatter and laugh about names for boys and girls.

Haltingly, one night I tell him what Pearl said, and he frowns.

'Aye, she's a nasty bitch,' he says. 'Look, sweetheart, it's true, we'd have a go every now and then.'

He strokes back my hair. 'Jesus, it was nearly three *years* before you let me touch you, and I expect Mr Loukas had a little more joy of you over that time than I ever did. True?'

I nod. 'He was my husband.'

'And I was alone.'

'And—my desk? Did you—?'

'Did I *nothing*. We never did it on your desk. What, with my back? And the shite about your hat—she caught me holding it, dreaming about you. Just jealousy.' He grins. 'But, Christ, what an idea. You want it with the hat, but on a comfy bed?'

I laugh. 'Maybe. And you haven't, with anyone else, since us—?'

He shakes his head solemnly. 'Never. Only you, love.' He clears his throat. 'Will I fire her?'

I think. 'No. Pearl runs the restaurant very well, she always has. And Big Davy—he's a nasty piece of work but he knows too much to be let go.'

Jimmy stares. 'You're amazing, Tina. Any other woman would have said fire them both, but you think, you plan, you look ahead. Sometimes, *a chuisle*, I'm flat out in awe of you.' He kisses me. 'I'm such a lucky bastard.'

Eliza sends me the softest baby blanket and Jessie churns out tiny cardigans like a whirling dervish who's taken to knitting.

Billie brings me flowers and says, 'Couldn't think of a present.

What would I know about kids? Never even mothered a kitten, as Charlie so kindly pointed out.'

I fill a vase with water. 'How are you feeling about Pete now?'

Billie nods. 'The holiday in Newcastle helped. I'm not over him yet, but I'm getting there.'

'Good. So where are they now?'

'Saigon. Charlie's playing the gracious lady, setting up her orphanage in the dead husband's name. Must be a bunch of laughs for the new husband.'

'They really rushed into it, didn't they?' I step back and adjust a couple of flowers.

'Charlie hated being alone, Pete hated being poor. Marriage made in heaven, I'd say.'

I laugh. 'You're my heroine, Billie. I plan to develop an attitude just like you.'

'Study of a lifetime, Teen, trust me.'

In the new year, when I'm five months along, Yvonne and Klara visit me. Yvonne says, 'Here's the latest in child-rearing manuals. It's got everything, diagrams of foetuses—'

'Oh,' I say, gazing at a gargoyle crossed with a broad bean. 'Is it *really* like that?'

'How to cope with colic—'

'Colic? But that's what horses get.'

Klara sighs and pats me kindly on the back.

Yvonne continues, '—eye-colours, growth, feeding. Everything.'

After they're gone I sit down and flip through the book. So much I need to know, *especially* about eye colour.

Half an hour later I sigh in relief. Jimmy's wrong. Two grey-eyed parents don't always have a baby with grey eyes. Sometimes the eyes can be brown if a grandparent's are too.

Thank God, an explanation. Just in case.

Of *course* the baby is Jimmy's, we made love all the time. It was only that once—well, twice—with László. For a moment I recall the scent of paprika and tobacco, and sigh.

That night I tell Jimmy about Yvonne's book and eye colours.

'Baby's grandparents, eh?' he says. 'My mother's eyes were blue, my father's as grey as the North Sea. Yours?'

'Well, you met Mum on that trip to Newcastle, hers are like mine. But Dad, now his were brown. He died when I was young and I haven't got any photos. All I remember is how kind he was.'

I sigh at the memory, almost believing it myself, of a dark man who had held me as tenderly as my blue-eyed father once had.

The months pass and I grow stouter and happier every day. And finally in June, when it seems nothing will ever change, in a few hours everything does.

The nurses tell me it's an easy birth, but in that case I'd prefer not to know the alternative. At one stage I say deliriously and firmly, I've had enough today, let's do this tomorrow, and Billie, holding my hand, laughs and says, sorry Teen, no way out now.

But a little later the fierce pangs ease and suddenly I want to catch the irresistible wave that's flowing through me, so definite and right and *good*, and everyone's telling me to stop, Mrs Kelso, hold on, when all I want to do is push and *push*. So I do.

And in a hot, wet, glorious slither, the most beautiful being in the world arrives in my life. They take him to be weighed and I crane my head until they give him back, and I open the towel and see for the first time his damp-dark head and small crumpled face, his snub nose and rosepetal mouth.

The doctor fusses and I have to push again for the afterbirth, then the nurses wash me and take me to a room, and finally they leave me alone with my baby.

And he opens his slate-grey eyes and gazes placidly at me, as if he knows me very well but can't quite recall the name.

Jimmy arrives and says, 'Sweetheart, I was pacing like a fool wearing a hole in the carpet. Oh, let me see him. Christ, what a beauty he is, what a clever, clever girl you are.'

He returns that night with armfuls of hothouse flowers. The baby sleeps as the nurses scurry around finding vases.

'He's already suckling,' I say, pleased but tired. It's beyond belief that this extraordinary being was not beside me yesterday: yet today here he is.

'I've thought of a name since I saw that fine little face,' says Jimmy. 'Reminds me of an uncle I loved, a good man, my uncle Robert. What do you say, sweetheart, is it a Robert we have here?'

'*Ró*-bert?' I say, dazed.

Jimmy laughs. '*Rob*-ert, got to give it that Irish lilt. Do you like it?'

I nod.

The baby wakes and whimpers and I take him to my breast, and Jimmy sits beside me, smiling, his arm around my shoulders, and I think, What have I done?

All too soon Robert's newborn slate-grey eyes deepen, and it becomes apparent they're as brown as his hair. But my mythical dark and long-departed father is called upon so often to account for it I almost forget the truth myself.

Jimmy adores him. He says one night, lying on the bed beside the baby, 'Who'd have imagined my little brown boy would be so much finer than that grey-eyed nipper I used to dream about, eh, sweetheart?'

I smile and nod. After all, only Harry and Mum know the truth about my father. Why would they even mention it? No one will know, and my beautiful baby will grow up loved and protected.

My time with Robert is a delight, but soon I want to catch up with a few jobs in my office at the Lounge. I'm also itching to know what's going on at Tempo, so to Jimmy's surprise I decide to work there for a few hours a week. I buy a cot and Robert comes with me.

The staff adore him and one day a waitress teasingly places him in startled László's arms. He stands stock-still, gazing at the dark-eyed baby with his gummy, heartbreaking smile.

I say quickly, 'Jimmy named him Robert for his uncle.' László glances at me in fleeting anguish. After that he keeps his distance.

After several weeks everything is ticking over nicely at the club.

One evening I drive home, feeling pleased at how it's all working out. I carry sleeping Robert upstairs and put him in his room.

Jimmy is nursing a drink on the sofa, so I pour myself a watered whiskey and say, 'How were things here today, love?'

'Oh,' says Jimmy. 'Jessie sent us a present.'

'Not more bootees?'

'Thank Christ, no. But very thoughtful, your mother. She's had an old photo enlarged, you as a little girl. I can certainly see the resemblance between you and the baby.'

'Really? Show me.' I sit down beside him and he hands me a carved wooden frame. Smiling, I gaze at the photo and the hair at the back of my neck rises.

'When was that taken?' Jimmy says. 'You're pretty young.'

I swallow a mouthful of whiskey. 'Um, nineteen twenty-two, I think. I was four, Harry's twenty, about to leave for medical school in London. Mum looks pretty, doesn't she?'

'And your Dad? That *is* your Dad, not some blond boyo who's dropped by? Strong similarity there, too.' He takes a slug of drink. 'Thought you said your man was dark?'

'The lighting's deceptive—'

Jimmy laughs. 'Not the only thing then, is it?'

He walks to the fireplace and gazes at the empty grate, then turns. 'So I got to wondering why our little darling is so very *different* from his grandparents. My goodness, says I, has someone *else* been a-climbing in the family tree?'

He sits and takes the photo from my icy hands and gazes at it.

'Fair racked my brains, I did. Who *does* the wee doll spends her days with, and quite a lot of her nights too? Made lists. Rubbed them out. Wrote them again. Who could possibly have fathered a little cuckoo in my own warm nest, since it clearly wasn't me?'

'Jimmy—'

'Shut your gob.' He drinks again. 'Finally, like some Irish Einstein, the mystery of the universe revealed itself to me. Of course! Must have been that brown-eyed wog, the one who's clearly been tinkling a little bit more than the ivories.'

I gasp, 'No!'

'What did I *fucking—tell—you?*'

With each word he smashes the frame on the edge of the table and glass sprays over the rug. He pulls out the photograph, crumples it into a ball and throws it in the grate.

'After you've cleaned up the glass, sweetheart, set a fire will you and burn that thing?'

He turns to me and I flinch. 'Oh, I won't hit you, doll. If I started I wouldn't stop. But we'll not speak of this again. You'll be the perfect wife, and no one will ever know how Jimmy Kelso's been shamed.'

'And—Robert?' I whisper.

'Ah, the bonny little angel. Image of his grandfather, or so I'm told. Of course, should anyone try to take him from me, or even *whisper* he's not my son, I can't guarantee how bonny he'd remain.'

I whimper.

'And your piano fella? I sent Big Davy round to have a word. He won't bother us again.'

I retch. *'No—'*

'Get the dustpan and clean up. Don't want splinters of glass in our little cuckoo, do we?'

Jimmy stands. 'Just so's you know, Sharon and me—rest assured we've never done it downstairs on your desk. But just last week she was straddling me on your chair and that was mighty pleasant.'

The threat to Robert is enough to keep me obedient so I have the freedom to come and go. At Tempo it's as if László never existed. No one has the faintest idea where he went, but they may be lying because of Big Davy. He's taken up residence in a corner of the club, drinking and annoying the waitresses.

I go into László's flat, dreading what I might find. Signs of a struggle, spilt blood? I even sniff the air, terrified his body might be there, but all I can smell is paprika and tobacco.

His things are gone—comb, razor, passport—and a few books he loved, one of them the copy of *Poems of Rage* I bought for him.

I lie on the bed for a time, my face in his pillow.

That night Jimmy says, 'Any sign of your chum?'

Davy's been spying on me. I shake my head.

Jimmy smiles. 'Now I'll tell you, wee Tina, stop worrying. I've only been playing with you. Davy didn't lay a *finger*. He just persuaded that fella to get himself onto a ship and leave the country, and that's what he did that very night.'

'Where did he go?' I say evenly.

'Tahiti. Dusky maidens, palm trees, beaches, he'll have a *lovely* time. Won't be back here though, that's for sure.'

I nod.

László didn't get on a ship. There's been a wharf strike for weeks and none have come in or out of Sydney.

Next day, Robert is asleep in his cot and I'm trying to concentrate in my office at Tempo, when I hear noises in László's flat.

My heart thumping, I go out to the landing and discover it's only Pearl and a couple of the waitresses with buckets and mops.

'Jimmy told us to clean the hell out of the place,' says Pearl, sly-eyed. 'Wants to rent it out.'

A few hours later they leave. In László's flat the kitchen is empty, the bed stripped, and the pillow and mattress gone. The air reeks of ammonia, erasing forever the perfume of paprika and tobacco.

That night I say carefully, 'Planning to rent out the flat, Jimmy? Could interfere with my business.'

'Not your business, sweetheart. *Mine.*' He shrugs. 'But you just keep pulling in a profit there and I'll let you go on playing that godawful racket. For now.'

He screws me every night. After he hits me a few times I stop resisting and now try to do what he wants. Like most women, I've sometimes wondered what it feels like to be a prostitute, to have to smile and pretend to lust.

I've discovered you can do it if you think of another man. A kind man with a deep, quiet laugh.

*

Moshe Adler comes to see me to organise the usual deliveries. Sly grog is still booming, but profits will fall if the laws are relaxed, and there's talk about that happening next year.

Still, the Adlers make most of their money from casinos, so they're safe from any legalisation that might stop the flow of cash into the pockets of the premier and police commissioner.

'Mrs Kelso,' says Moshe, 'I have a gift to celebrate your son.'

'That's kind of you.' I don't much care.

Inside the parcel is a carved wooden cube on a shaft with a pointed base.

'Is it a spinning top?' I ask.

'Yes, a dreidel. A traditional toy.'

'It's lovely.'

But I'm puzzled. The criminal world is meticulous at balancing the value of gifts exchanged. Although charming, this is not in the same league as the besamim I gave his daughter.

Moshe smiles. 'I have another gift for you of greater worth. But first, let me see your son.'

Robert is a placid child, and has woken, murmuring, as we speak. We lean over his cradle and I show him his new toy. He closes his small fist around it.

'It's a dreidel—is that how you say it, Mr Adler?—a dreidel for you, sweetheart.'

Robert gazes at Moshe's face and mine and smiles joyfully. He puts the new toy in his mouth and sucks it, then stares at it, beaming again.

'Ah, *boychick*,' says Moshe. He watches Robert for a time, then sits down and looks at me.

'Will you raise him in his father's faith?'

I take a breath. 'Catholic? When he's older, I'll—let him choose.'

Moshe smiles. 'But I know such eyes and skin and hair. He could be any child on the streets of Budapest. He could even be my son, Mrs Kelso.'

'How extraordinary,' I say. 'Yet he's my son, Mr Adler.'

'Some weeks ago László came to me and told me everything.'

I stare, shocked.

'He was afraid for his life, but more than that he was afraid for you and Róbert.'

'Robert,' I say.

'*Róbert.*'

After a pause I say, my voice shaking, 'What's *happened* to him?'

'I do not know, but of course your disgusting mamzer of a husband is responsible. Sadly, I cannot yet express the full extent of my displeasure—a greater problem has arisen. Remember the Capellis?'

'Haven't they retired to the country?'

'They've decided they prefer the city. Do you remember also the deaths of Enzo Capelli and Dimple Kelso, Jimmy's first wife?'

'László told you about her too?'

He nods. 'To hide their incompetence the police blamed a jealous boyfriend, and lately I have indeed discovered the woman had a boyfriend. Sadly, it was my unreliable brother, Sándor.'

'Did he do it?'

'I know for certain he did not. But now the Capellis think Sándor killed Enzo from jealousy, and Jimmy killed Dimple to be free to marry you. They believe we collaborated on those murders.'

'But Jimmy and Dimple were *divorced,*' I say. 'I remember when the decree absolute arrived.'

'Ah.' He nods. 'That is useful to know. Still, the Capellis are threatening war against both our operations, and for a time we must stick together.'

'For a time?'

He pauses. 'I did not know László in the camp. It was—a large place.' His mouth twists bitterly. 'We first became friends on the refugee ship coming to Australia. One night I was attacked by thieves and he saved me.'

Moshe leans forward. 'Because of László, today I am alive to take joy in my own children. Here is my true gift, Mrs Kelso. Come and speak to me when you wish to be free.'

24. Yvonne: Consolation

In March 1955 Klara and I visit Tina, who's five months pregnant and happily rotund, and take her books. (What else would Klara and I give anyone?)

That night we reminisce about Klara's own pregnancy and Toby's brave sacrifice: Klara and Claire's lives for his. We salute Toby in wine and celebrate in lovemaking.

Our everyday life continues. The printery is doing well, with almost more work than we can cope with, and Reg and I discuss how we might expand the business.

Oddly, we don't see as much of Billie or Nikos as we used to, then they visit us on a still day in May with a bottle of wine that tastes of summer fruit, and we drink it in the garden.

'Oh, that's lovely!' I say. 'Are we celebrating anything?'

Nikos gazes at Billie, smiling.

'My goodness, at last!' says Klara. 'We thought you two would never see the light.'

'Took us a while to find ourselves in sync, that's all,' says Billie.

I say, delighted, 'And do you have any—plans?'

'Well, there'll be no bloody weddings, that's for sure.'

Nikos laughs. 'Billie's discovered how enormous my family is—all the aunts, uncles, first, second and third cousins—and they love a marriage celebration. The pressure is unrelenting, but I'm standing firm despite threats of disinheritance.'

'We're getting a kitten, though,' says Billie, content.

A few weeks after that I'm late coming home. I usually pick up the mail and check it quickly before Klara sees it, even though I've started to relax—it's been months since the last letter arrived and I've never said anything about it to Klara.

But when I go into the kitchen she's sitting at the table in the dusk, holding a piece of paper. She looks up at me, her face shocked, tears in her eyes. I take it from from her trembling fingers and read the familiar, nauseating phrases.

STINKING COWS SHOULD BE ASHAMED ... POOR CHILD WITNESSING YOUR FUCKING ... TIE YOU UP AND AND SHOVE ... UNTIL YOU SCREAM ... SLIT YOUR LOATHSOME ... NAZIS HAD THE RIGHT IDEA ... GASSING AND BURNING TOO GOOD ... SHIT LIKE YOU ... REPORT TO CHILD WELFARE ... NEGLECT ... TAKEN AWAY

I drop it on the table and sit down heavily.

'I think you have seen something like this before,' Klara whispers.

I nod. 'The first was a year and a half ago. Then a few others arrived after that.'

'Why did you not tell me?'

'I didn't want you to know,' I say. 'And I thought they'd stopped.'

I go to put the aluminium kettle on the stove, but it slips from my hand and drops with a clatter on the floor.

As I'm picking it up, Ned comes to the kitchen door. He's staying with us for a few days so he can attend a medical conference.

He says, 'All right? I heard something crash.' He gazes from Klara to me. 'What's up?'

'A poison-pen letter,' says Klara. 'Yvonne has had others like this before, but she did not tell me.'

He sits and reads it. 'Good *God*, that's horrible.'

I say, 'They can't take Claire away from us, can they, Ned?'

He shakes his head. 'I don't see how. Klara is her mother and she was legally married to her father. Claire isn't a truant from school, she's healthy and well-cared for.'

'But what about *us*, Ned?' I say, panic in my chest. 'Could they say I'm a bad influence on her?'

He says gently, 'No one sane could call you a bad influence, Yvonne.'

'I do not think this letter-writer is sane,' says Klara.

She stands and pulls down the kitchen blind against the dark evening, and turns on the overhead light. 'But our life together is not illegal. We are safe, we must be. Claire is safe.'

'Did you say there have been others?' asks Ned.

I clear my throat. 'They started eighteen months ago, followed by three more, always different writing. The first was a week after we won the case, so of course I thought it was Dr Godfrey. In court he snarled about us being perverts who hadn't heard the last of it.'

Ned nods. 'Did you keep the other letters?'

I shake my head. 'Burnt them, they were disgusting. But they weren't postmarked Newcastle, I checked. All were sent from the Martin Place GPO in the centre of Sydney.'

Klara says, 'Could Godfrey be visiting Sydney to post them so we don't suspect it's him?'

Ned thinks. 'He went back to Newcastle straight after the court case, so if he'd posted it in Sydney first it'd have arrived in a single day, not after a whole week. And I know he hasn't left Newcastle for ages, he used up all his leave for the court case.'

Klara shrugs. 'He could have had a friend posting them for him.'

I laugh bitterly. 'Who'd be friends with him?'

'Is there anyone else who might hold a grudge against you?' says Ned. 'Even absurd niggles?'

I look at Klara and shrug. 'A man at the printery walked out when I took over, said he wouldn't work for a bloody woman. And there was that poet you rejected for *Poems of Rage*. He was pretty cross.'

'I heard he went to Europe,' says Klara. 'What about the horrid mother of that boy who bullied Claire?'

'They moved to Brisbane ten months ago,' I say, and sigh. 'But—I feel terrible saying this—could it possibly be Valma?'

'Reg Frisket's Valma?' says Ned.

I nod. 'She's often cranky about how helpful he is to us.'

Klara shakes her head. 'She is very fond of Claire and I think she is perfectly aware we offer no romantic threat to her relationship with Reg.'

Ned says, 'Look, this is truly appalling. I'll take the letter and get the opinion of some psychiatrists I know. If anyone can diagnose what might be going on, they should be able to.'

Soon another letter arrives, and then another. The handwriting is *different* every time, the paper, the envelopes, always different. Only the threats are the same. The authorities should take Claire away, and Klara and I should be violated and tortured and murdered in the most appalling ways.

Klara starts having nightmares again. The last time that happened, in London after the war, she had a complete breakdown. Ned is a wonderful support and talks to her on the phone for hours. Sometimes I think she'll be all right, then I find her in her office weeping softly, her arms over her head.

Ned speaks to his psychiatrist colleagues, but they aren't very reassuring. He'd hoped they might dismiss the letters as simply childish malice, but they use terms like *schizophrenia* and *pathological mania* and *psychotic delusion*, and frown and say, 'You should take these to the police.'

We take the letters to the police. They look Klara and me up and down, and snigger, and send us away saying we should see a psychiatrist, and snigger again.

And another letter arrives.

It's been one and a half years since we won the appeal against Dr Godfrey's libel suit. *Poems of Rage* is now a standard on the school curriculum and it sells well.

Klara has edited other books since then, but without the consolation of poetry she still battles for her peace of mind: and these letters have become one burden too many.

Tonight she wakes up sobbing. She whispers, 'We were forced from our home at gunpoint by Godfrey's forger and some Japanese soldiers—'

'Godfrey's *forger*? You mean whoever it was wrote the fake letter for the trial?'

'Yes. Godfrey is obviously evil. But his forger? I have never dreamt of him before, but I *know* he must be an artist. He must possess great creativity and passion, something even a secular Jew like myself understands is inspired by Hashem.'

'God, you mean?'

She shrugs and nods. 'Art does not simply happen, Yvonne. It grows out of love and connection to life. How could a *true* artist do something as destructive as the forger did?'

'Perhaps you're being too idealistic, love.'

'Perhaps, but still it haunts me.' She laughs bitterly. 'And of course, if I cannot express art myself, what does that reveal about my own connection to Hashem?'

'Oh, *please* don't say that, Klara.'

She shakes her head and slowly falls asleep again. I settle too, my thoughts going around and around.

Why did Klara dream about Godfrey's forger, of all people? We'd ruled Godfrey out as a suspect for the poison-pen letters because of his continued remoteness from Sydney.

But if his forger lived here that would explain a lot. He must be skilful too, so he's probably not some random criminal—I recall Harry and Ned's amazement at the perfect rendition of Sir Hugh Everett's hand.

My eyes suddenly open.

Could Klara's dream of Godfrey's forger and the Japanese soldiers be telling us the writer is known to both Godfrey and Everett? Someone who was an inmate of Changi?

I ring Harry next day to see what he thinks.

'My God, Yvonne—let me sit down. At the trial I was so relieved the bloody thing was a lie I didn't stop to wonder how Everett's hand was so authentic,' he says.

'And now? Is there anyone you knew in those days who might have been capable—?'

'Of course, of *course*!'

'Harry?'

'I know exactly who—Sly Sammy! Our camp forger, he worked closely with Everett making fake Japanese documents. *He* could copy Everett's hand perfectly, and of course Godfrey knew him. And Sammy's in Sydney as well—at the trial Maurie Johnson said he'd actually run across him somewhere!'

But if this Sammy is our poison-pen writer he's not so easily found. We talk to Maurie, but he only remembers meeting him briefly in central Sydney. We contact everyone else we know from Changi, but no one's seen him in ages.

The cruel letters still arrive every couple of months, but I always manage to intercept them, and half a year passes. That her own dream showed us this possible connection gives Klara heart that her own creativity must still exist. She cannot write but her nightmares ease off.

By early 1956 I've almost give up, but dear Reg Frisket hasn't, and someone tells him, 'Old Sammy? Yeah, met him at the Cross couple of years ago. He's crazy about those baccarat games.'

'The Cross?' I say to Klara. 'Perhaps *Tina* can help us. And her baby must be nearly six months by now. Let's go and see them again.'

We'd sent her flowers when Robert was born, and visited when he was tiny but now, unusually, whenever we ring her Tina never rings back. So next day we get in the car and drive to Tempo.

Tina seems flustered to see us, but says, 'Lovely! Come in. Haven't been keeping up as I should.'

Jimmy puts his head around the office door.

'Just be downstairs with Big Davy, doll. By the way, girls, know anyone who might want the next-door flat? Haven't been able to find a tenant yet.'

'If the flat is empty,' says Klara, 'where is László?'

'He left rather suddenly a few months ago,' says Tina evenly.

'And he didn't even *tell* us!' I say. 'Where did he go?'

'Tahiti, I believe,' says Jimmy. 'A happy man, wherever he is.' He looks at Tina. 'Maybe you should come back to the Starlight Lounge, sweetheart, get some rest.'

'I'm fine, darling.'

Jimmy leaves. 'And how are *you*?' Tina says brightly. She's pale, with dark circles under her eyes. 'Oh, don't even look at me. Robert hardly ever sleeps.'

Robert, dozing in his cot, gives no sign of stirring. I try gently to find out what's bothering her, but Tina keeps the subject firmly on baby chit-chat.

Finally Klara and I glance at each other and I say, 'Actually, Tina, we were hoping you could help us track down a man who's a regular at baccarat games. He's named Sammy, and he's short, with glasses and a thin moustache.'

'Really? I've got a friend in the baccarat business,' she says. 'Come back next Tuesday. We're meeting at twelve and you can ask him.'

On Tuesday a dark, heavyset man is waiting in Tina's office.

She says, 'Mr Moshe Adler—my good friends, Miss Yvonne Watters and Mrs Klara Fenn.'

Mr Adler gazes coolly at us, then Klara greets him in Yiddish. Surprised, he replies in Yiddish, then Klara switches to English. 'From Finland originally. The Budapest cousins were named Pólya.'

Mr Adler nods. 'Ah yes. László told me of you.'

The atmosphere lightens.

Robert stirs in his cot. Mr Adler lifts him out, murmuring to him in what I think is Hungarian. He looks up. 'Róbert needs a broad education, do you not agree, Mrs Kelso?'

Tina laughs, tired.

'I *do* like your way of pronouncing his name,' I say. 'So gentle.'

There's an odd silence, then Tina says, 'Now, Mr Adler, have you seen anyone like the man I described in the casinos?'

Mr Adler pauses. 'It is possible.'

Klara says intently, 'We think he is the forger who almost ruined us in court.' She hands him one of the letters. 'And who may now be sending us anti-Semitic threats.'

Mr Adler takes a deep breath through his nostrils as he reads the letter. He looks at Klara, narrow-eyed. 'And you wish to speak to this mamzer?'

She nods.

'I do not know you from the synagogue.'

'I no longer believe.'

'Who does?' he says. 'Who, today, would believe in anything? But your people are there.'

'My people are the friends in my life,' says Klara.

Mr Adler glances at me and says, 'Do your friends light the Shabbat candles with you? Do they celebrate the havdalah?'

Klara shakes her head. 'They celebrate other things.'

Mr Adler hands back the letter, stands and puts Robert in his cot. He turns and gazes at Klara. 'Pólya, you say? I knew them in the camp. For a time.'

'Help us then,' she says.

As I negotiate the traffic around the Cross I say, 'Was something strange going on back there?'

Klara nods. 'Yes. I think Robert is not Jimmy's child.'

'Not what I meant, but—*really?*'

'You have not travelled as I have, Yvonne. That is not an Irish baby. His looks are middle-European.'

'Gosh, *László?*'

'Probably.'

'Where is he, then?'

Klara shakes her head, frowning. 'If Jimmy knows about the baby, I imagine he is dead.'

'Oh, poor László, poor Tina!'

Later, over dinner, I say, 'Mr Adler seems a very religious man. Is he really a gangster?'

'Being observant does not stop him breaking the law,' says Klara dryly. 'Who, today, would believe in anything? he said, and quite correctly. Laws mean nothing.'

She sighs. 'At Auschwitz they would tell the prisoners, *The healthy survive three months here, priests one month, Jews two weeks*. That was in 1940, you know, when I was still so innocent I could be a poet.'

'You can be a poet today, love.'

'No. I know too much. I have lost too much.'

My heart aches, and I change the subject. 'What did Mr Adler mean about Shabbat candles and—havda-something?'

'Candles are lit before sunset on Fridays, the start of the Sabbath, then loved ones celebrate and share feasts. On Saturday evening the havdalah marks the return to everyday life.'

'Oh, what sort of feasts?'

'Wonderful food. Braided bread and wine, roasts, rich soups, sweet pastries—sumptuous meals that go on and on.'

'So why don't *we* ever cook Jewish dishes?' I say.

'I could not bear it.' Klara stands and leaves.

Tina rings a week later. 'Mr Adler's found Sly Sammy for you. Come over tomorrow.'

Next morning I drive us to the Cross, my spirits low. Perhaps we've got it all wrong.

Even if we've found Godfrey's forger he doesn't have to be the poison-pen writer too: there are plenty of people around who simply hate women and Jews.

I park outside Tempo, and when we pass through the club that horrible Big Davy man is sitting at a corner table, trimming his fingernails. I don't know how anyone can stand him.

We find Tina in her office with Mr Adler and a little man with glasses, who's sitting in a chair, his hands anxiously clasped.

'Good morning, Miss Watters, Mrs Fenn,' says Mr Adler. 'I believe we have found your forger. Sammy, do tell us your tale.'

The little man says, 'Look, I'm sorry, had *no* idea you were friends of—' he nods to Moshe Adler. 'I'd never, God's truth, if I'd *known*.'

I sit down, but Klara remains standing, staring at him.

'Were you the forger working for Dr Godfrey?' My throat is dry.

'He had me over a barrel!' says Sammy. 'Did him a favour when we got home—helping a fellow prisoner, wasn't I? Then he said he'd go to the cops for *that* job if I didn't do the letter for the court case. Wasn't till the last minute he said to put Ned and Harry's names in. Felt terrible, they were good mates.'

'Not good enough, apparently,' says Tina, her face unmoved.

'So you *admit* it?' I say, furious. 'It was *you* did the Everett letter? You rotten little worm, you nearly lost us our house and livelihood!'

'Sammy has kindly put all of this in writing for you. In his true hand,' says Mr Adler dryly.

'And—the poison-pen letters?' I say, my throat dry.

The little man gulps. 'Geez, I'm so *sorry*. Godfrey swore you and the other lady were cruel old bitches, tormenting a kid. He'd ring me and dictate the words. I did say, Steady on, mate, that language is a bit strong, but he didn't pay much attention. None, really.'

'Strong language indeed, especially to use towards a Jew,' says Mr Adler thoughtfully.

Sammy shakes his head. 'Honestly, Mr Adler, if I'd *known*!'

'But you should not need to *know* to whom you are addressing anti-Semitic filth, should you?'

'No, Mr Adler.'

'Bastard! You You almost destroyed us!' I say. 'What are you going to do about it?'

The little man shakes his head. 'No more letters, that's for sure.'

Klara makes a strangled noise.

I turn to Mr Adler. 'Can we *get* Godfrey for this now?'

'Sadly, no. He has already admitted the Everett letter was forged but claimed it was without his knowledge. He would not be tried again for the same offence.'

'So he's just going to get away with it?' I say, outraged.

'Not necessarily,' says Mr Adler. 'Sammy, tell us about the first job you did for Dr Godfrey.'

'Look, it was only a parchment with some gobbledegook, and a letter saying he'd done some work somewhere.'

'Where?' I say.

'Ah, well, Oxford. Some degree. I mean, he was already a doctor with a lot of experience, so I reckoned if he wanted to gild the lily a bit—remember, jobs were a bit scarce after the war.'

'He lied about his qualifications?' I say.

Tina says, 'Godfrey owes his position at Harry's hospital to that supposed degree. If it became known, he'd have to leave in disgrace. He'd probably never work again at any hospital.'

'I would, in fact, make certain he never again worked at any hospital in this country. And in most other countries,' says Mr Adler, thin-lipped. I believe him completely.

'But what about me?' whispers Sammy. 'What will you do to me?'

Suddenly Klara screams in rage.

She leaps towards him, hitting him with her fists, the thuds loud as the man is too shocked to respond. Then his glasses go flying and he wails and holds his arms over his head as she beats him.

'*Do to you?*' Her voice cracks. 'You—an *artist* who should be silent with *shame* before Hashem! I would *do* what they *did* to my aunt and her baby—and my nieces and nephews—so you know *exactly* what—*things* shoved into screaming bodies feels like—and I would make you *suffer* the desolation of *infinite* loss—and when you are broken—*utterly* broken—I swear I would do it all—*again!*'

The little man weeps and drops his arms and lets Klara hit him, but finally she slows and stands there, gasping for breath, tears pouring down her face. I draw her beside me on the sofa, and put my arms around her as she sobs.

Mr Adler picks up Sammy's glasses and hands them to him.

'Do to you, Sammy? Let us see. How much do you owe us?'

Sammy whispers, 'Passed some notes at Paddys Market, Mr Adler, paid off the debt.'

'But don't you owe the Capellis quite a large amount? They are less forgiving than us.'

Sammy moans and I feel suddenly sick.

'Send the little bastard away.' I look Mr Adler in the face. 'Send him to Perth or Darwin or anywhere, but don't you *dare* hand him over to the Capellis. That would be murder.'

Mr Adler's eyes are scornful. 'Compassion for *this?*'

'He's told us everything. It's *over*,' I say, my heart thumping. 'Please, Mr Adler.'

Tina's face is as pained as mine. Mr Adler glances at her and takes a deep breathe. After a few moments he opens his wallet and hands the little man some folded notes.

'That will get you a fair distance. Take a taxi to Central. *Now.* Leave your engraving tools, Sammy, your plates, your inks, your special papers, and go. Never, *never* come back to Sydney. *Do you understand me?'*

Sammy sobs and grabs the money. 'Yes, yes. Tell Harry and Ned I'm sorry, really sorry.'

He scuttles away. I breathe again and say, 'We'll deal with Godfrey ourselves from here and, trust me, it *won't* be with compassion.'

Mr Adler and Tina gaze at each other and for the first time I realise how sad they both are. Their friend László? He can't *really* have been killed, that's beyond belief, even for Jimmy.

I'm so exhausted. 'Thank you for this, both of you. Come on, Klara love, let's go home.'

'Wait,' says Mr Adler. 'There is something I require in exchange for this service. For finding that menuval and letting him leave here without punishment.'

'In exchange?' I ask.

'The giving of gifts is a finely calibrated art among criminals. Is that not so, Mrs Kelso?'

'Indeed,' says Tina dryly. 'But not at precisely the same time.'

He smiles a little. 'I require a gift of Mrs Fenn, although you are welcome to partake as well, Miss Watters.'

Klara says, her voice ragged, 'What do you want of me?'

'You will attend Shabbat this week with my family. My wife Ilona will make you welcome.'

'I do not wish to attend Shabbat.'

'But you shall. László himself asked me to do this.' Tina lifts her head and stares at him.

'László? Why?' says Klara.

'Because he and I lost everything and believe in nothing, but still we have the consolation of custom and friendship. I am told you have lost your poetry, your voice. Perhaps, unlike our forger, you have been silent in the face of Hashem for too long.'

'You imagine *that* is why I cannot write?' says Klara contemptuously.

He shrugs. 'I do not care, your reasons are your own. But this I promised László.'

She gazes at her hands, grazed and slightly bleeding. 'How often?'

'Again, I do not care. To invite you is my gift. To attend is yours.'

I post Eliza and Harry a copy of Sly Sammy's confession, then ring them to give them the good news. Then I start looking in my wardrobe for something to wear tomorrow at this mysterious Shabbat.

'Do I wear a veil? Or a *wig*?' I ask Klara, who's lying on the bed.

She sighs. 'No veil, no wig, just normal clothes. Nice clothes, to be respectful.'

I sit down beside her. 'It'll be all right, love.'

'That little man's eyes were quite empty, Yvonne,' she says sadly. 'It was clear his art was not inspired by holiness after all. Perhaps one day I will feel happy that I beat him, but today I am tired and ashamed. Still ... Mr Adler helped us, so I must do as he asks.'

Next day Klara prepares half a dozen superb dishes without even reading a recipe (for Saturday, she says). Enticing scents waft though the house, and Claire and Vivy stand at the kitchen door wailing, 'We're *hungry*.'

'You may have some at lunch tomorrow,' says Klara firmly.

In the afternoon we bathe and dress and drive to the Adlers' place at Rose Bay, past the flying boat base. Klara holds the bottle of wine we're taking for a gift, but doesn't say much.

I must admit I'm curious to see the private life of a notorious gangster. But while the house is large it's not lavish, and Mrs Adler, Ilona, is pretty and plump and seems perfectly normal.

Her little girl Devorah is eighteen months old, and she has three sons, the eldest a teenager. We're introduced to other family members, but I can't keep track of who's who and there's lots of Hungarian and Yiddish being spoken.

I'm almost disappointed at the ordinariness of it all, but I do notice Mr Adler's younger brother Sándor, who's flushed and talkative, and their father, the famous Abe Adler (or infamous, says Tina), who seems a genial old gentleman.

Everyone gathers and Ilona lights candles and swirls her hands over them, then covers her eyes and chants a prayer. Of course I don't understand, but I see Klara's lips move slightly. A melodious song is sung, and more prayers, then we have small cups of wine.

In the kitchen we wash our hands, right then left. At the table Moshe breaks loaves of braided bread and we eat the crusty pieces. The food is brought in, course after course, rich and delicious.

Klara talks to an older woman beside her in Yiddish—which, apart from her words to Mr Adler the other day I've never heard her speak before. More laughter, songs and prayers follow. It's a little overwhelming but I do rather enjoy it all.

'Not quite what I was expecting,' I say, driving home. Klara sighs.

Next day we have a marvellous lunch with Claire, Vivy and Nikos' son Steve, and in the afternoon relax in our bedroom and make lazy love.

In the evening we drive again to Rose Bay for the havdalah blessing—the separation, Klara tells me, between the Sabbath and everyday life.

The candles this time are unusual braided ones with multiple wicks, and a silver container is passed around, the besamim Tina gave the little Adler girl.

It is to *console* us, a nice old lady whispers to me. I take a deep breath of its tangy spices, and pass it on, feeling wonderfully consoled. Moshe blesses the wine, we sip it, then he pours a few drops over the bright candle to extinguish it.

More prayers and again Klara's lips move. On the way home, I say, 'That was okay, wasn't it?' but she doesn't reply.

*

That night in bed, Klara says, 'Yvonne, do you remember the poetry I used to write?'

'Of course I do. I loved it before I even met you. It—*glimmered*, almost eerily, it was shifting, dreamy—like landscapes built out of water or clouds.'

She nods. 'It was a wonderful world to discover, to experience. For years I have tried to find my way back to it again but it is gone from me. I am in exile.'

She turns to me. 'Mr Adler was correct. I told Sammy he should be silent from shame, but now I see that is why I am silent too.'

'What on earth have *you* got to be ashamed of?' I say, horrified.

'My old dreamscapes are lost, and all I can imagine are the wartime hells that followed. But I am *terrified* that if I write of those things they will destroy me. I feel shame at being alive, when those who died could have done so much more with my life. My silence is my shame, my shame makes me silent.'

'Oh, love, we all want to forget. Why shouldn't you too?'

'You are not a poet, Yvonne. You do not have a duty to remember and to transmute.'

'If you *could* write about that time would you find your voice again?' I ask.

'Perhaps,' she says sadly. 'Yet I do not have the courage.'

'But what of the good things, like the *Kindertransport* children?'

'Yes, there were moments of goodness.' She turns on her back, gazing at the ceiling. 'Tonight, I was reminded of one boy I cared deeply for. Mr Adler's oldest son, Tibor—the tall, shy one—has the same eyes.'

'I wonder how he survived the war,' I say. 'He must have been very young then.'

'He told me. After Moshe was taken, Tibor and his mother were hidden by friends on a farm.' Klara smiles a little. 'To him it was the happiest time of his life. Now he is not so happy, because he must study to be a lawyer as his father once was.'

'Moshe was a *lawyer*? But why on earth is he now a gangster?'

Klara is amused at my naivety. 'My dear, a refugee is not permitted to practise a profession, no matter how well qualified—it might threaten the livelihoods of fine upstanding Australians.'

'Really? That's not very fair.'

'Tibor came over to speak to me tonight, to ask me to tutor him. You see, he wants to write.' Her voice catches. 'Poor child. He wants to be a poet.'

25. Harry: The Conference

Eliza, on the phone, squeals and calls out, 'Harry, come here!'

I dash out to the hall, relieved to see she's smiling. She hands me the phone and Yvonne says, 'Harry? We've *found* him, we've found the bloody forger who did the Everett letter and he's the same man who's been sending us poison-pen messages!'

'Well *done*! Who is he, who's been paying him?'

'Just as you thought, it *was* Sly Sammy. And Godfrey's been behind it all, dictating letters on the phone to Sammy—and he'd send them via the Sydney post office so they weren't traceable.'

'But how on earth did you *find* him?'

'Remember Reg got a lead about Sammy being seen around the Cross? We went to see Tina, and Tina asked one of her gangster mates. He dragged Sammy in by the scruff of his neck, got a written confession and sent him on his way, saying never to return. Sammy said to tell you he's sorry.'

'Fat lot of use now, the stupid bastard. Still, what a relief for you and Klara! But how do we nobble bloody Godfrey for this?'

'Oh, that was the *best* bit!' Yvonne laughs. 'We have it in writing that Dr Godfrey's famous higher degree from Oxford is a complete *fraud* as well, courtesy of Sly Sammy. I've posted you a copy of his confession, then I expect you can have the enormous satisfaction of telling Godfrey yourself we're on to him. He'll never work in a hospital again.'

'*Marvellous*! Thank you for this, Yvonne, I'd quite lost hope. '

We hang up and turn to Eliza and lift her and swing her around, both of us laughing. 'We've *got* the bastard!' I say.

'Who have you got, Dad?' says Leo.

'Oh, an old mate, Leo my lad. I have plans to make his life very difficult indeed.'

'Why, Daddy?' says Jenny.

'Because he's been a very bad man, darling,' I say, and she nods sagely.

Eliza laughs. 'Oh my God, this is fantastic! I'd almost given up too. How clever of Yvonne and Klara—and Tina as well.'

'*And* the criminal friend,' I say. 'Wonder if he's a mate of Jimmy's?'

'No, Yvonne said it was Moshe Adler, and Tina once mentioned how much he dislikes Jimmy.'

We've been a little concerned about my sister. We saw her a few months ago, and she seemed under the weather—apparently László left very suddenly, so she's had a lot on her plate. She's still working at the club as well, which seems like madness to me, but Eliza says it's the only thing outside the baby that makes Tina happy.

Whenever we ring up Jimmy hangs around, so we can hardly even have a private word with her. His genial patter always seems over the top, while Tina herself sounds surprisingly stiff.

But they both insist they're happy and the baby is flourishing. I'd go to Sydney to check except we're a bit short-handed at the hospital. Perhaps later in the year.

I can hardly restrain myself until Yvonne's letter arrives with the copy of Sly Sammy's confession. It's gratifying to read, and even more gratifying to be outside Godfrey's office next day, knocking on the door.

Godfrey says, 'Bell. What do you want?'

His pale little eyes, his weak chin: what this loathsome creature has put us through.

I sit down. 'Godfrey, I've got a letter, a confession from an old mate of ours.'

'What rubbish is this?'

'Sly Sammy,' I say. 'How could you forget *Sammy*?'

'Get out, Bell.'

'Now—you told the judge the forger created the letter on his own initiative, then disappeared. Yet Sammy says he wrote it under your direct instruction, and you knew all the time how to find him.'

Godfrey shrugs. 'It's over, Bell. I was acquitted of wrongdoing and paid a fine for my lapse of judgement. I can't be tried again.'

'Not for that, sadly. But perhaps you could be tried for sending vicious threats to Miss Watters and Mrs Fenn on a regular basis—what do you think?'

'On whose say-so? *Sammy's?*' Godfrey smirks. 'Who'd take the word of a forger and lawbreaker over mine? He'd say anything to save his own skin.' He gazes at me coldly. 'I really hope you haven't mentioned this to anyone else: could be the basis of another defamation suit.'

I gaze at him through a mist of loathing.

After a silence he says, 'Don't waste my time, Bell.'

'Sammy's been useful to you for a while, I hear. He says you looked him up after Changi, asked him to do a job for an old mate.' I smile coldly. 'Oh yes, we know all about that too, the post-graduate degree at Oxford. Surprised you didn't give yourself a Nobel Prize as well.'

Godfrey is suddenly pale. He swallows and mutters, 'Get *out*.'

'I'm going, mate. Just dropped in on my way to see the Superintendent.' I stand. 'You malevolent, treacherous *prick*. If you'd admitted you screwed up like plenty of others in the war, it'd be forgotten by now. But you chose to drag us through hell.'

I stare into his mean little eyes, and say deliberately, 'Still, you'll pay, Godfrey. After you're fired from here I have it on good authority you'll never get a job in any hospital ever again.'

Godfrey wipes his forehead. 'Let me resign, get out with a shred of dignity. *Please.*'

I laugh. 'The old Harry Bell might have said yes. He still had notions of fair play, duty, all those dusty fantasies. But you, you contemptible bastard, you almost destroyed everything I love. Sadly for you I'm not that man any more.'

I go to the Medical Superintendent and show him Sly Sammy's confession. We compare a genuine Oxford degree with the Xerox copy in Godfrey's personnel file and, although cleverly done, it's soon undeniable that Godfrey's qualification is a fake.

'That bastard,' Chris says. '*And* he's put our patients at risk. I'm going to rip his ears off.'

But when we get to Godfrey's office he's gone, and when I ask at his lodgings he's fled from there too. He's simply vanished, and the relief is extraordinary.

A few weeks later my delight at his absence is redoubled when the Super appoints me as the new head of our outpatient clinic. He tells me, shame-faced, he wanted me in this role before, but Godfrey always vetoed it.

One Saturday Eliza goes shopping while I mind Leo and Jenny. When she returns she nods for me to come into the kitchen for a chat while the children are busy with a game.

'What is it?' I ask, as Eliza boils the kettle and puts tea in the pot.

'I met Mr White at the Astoria Cafe again this morning.'

'Who?' I set out the cups and saucers and sit down.

'Our friend from the intelligence service—remember, three years ago? He rang me yesterday to arrange a meeting. He assumed my mushy brain from motherhood had passed and I'd now want to be of service to my country.'

'My God, Eliza. What happened?'

'Something rather extraordinary. Walking towards the cafe I found myself becoming angry. Very, *very* angry. It's not just you or Ned or Klara left damaged by the war, it's me too. I suffered—' She stops and laughs. 'I suffered *obedience.*'

'I don't quite—?'

'The war was such an emergency, we had to do whatever was necessary for survival. I worked so diligently I learnt a habit of profound obedience. And I'm still suffering from it.'

She pours hot water into the teapot and turns to me.

'But it's *over*, Harry. The bloody war's been over for eleven years, and I will not submit to obedience any more. I looked Mr White in the eye and said, No, I won't do it, and if he contacts me again I'll go to the newspapers.'

'But would they print something that might embarrass the government?'

Eliza shrugs. 'Circulation went through the roof when they reported on the Petrov affair. A dear little housewife being harassed into becoming a spy? It'd be ludicrous, and I said as much to Mr White. And left him there, astonished.'

She sits down and crosses her arms, gazing at me. 'For so long I believed I had to be obedient for the greater good, but no more. And that goes for us too, love.'

I pour the tea. 'Us?'

'I know a woman who's a secretary at the State Dockyard, and a clerical job has come up. They need someone to look after the ship's records, and I'd be perfect for it. I'm going to apply.'

'But what about the children?'

'Leo's ten and Jenny's five. Mrs Collins down the road adores them. She's itching to babysit and she'll do cooking and cleaning as well.' She grins. 'You've just had a promotion, Harry, and I'll soon be bringing in a paypacket. We can afford it.'

She picks up her teacup and clinks mine. 'Cheers, love.'

For an instant I feel the old, familiar terror of being overwhelmed by forces outside my control. Then, like Eliza, I think *no*. The past is gone and I refuse to be stick-in-the-mud Harry Bell any longer.

I lift my teacup and touch hers in return. 'Cheers. And good luck with the job.'

Everything falls into place. Eliza gets the job at the State Dockyard and loves it. Every morning she catches the tram to Civic, then takes the company launch across the harbour to the offices and slipways at Dyke End. Mrs Collins is wonderful with the children, and to my surprise our home life is as peaceful as it's ever been.

My work is going rather nicely too. I gather statistics on our procedures in the clinic, and the results are fascinating. They lead us to several practical improvements, and the Super is delighted. 'Excellent, Harry. I want you to write me a research paper.'

'Come off it, Chris. I haven't done research in fifteen years.'

'Time you did some more then. I want you to present these results at a conference in October. This is important stuff, Harry, things other hospitals *need* to know. Go on, make us proud.'

I smile. 'All right, then. Where's the conference—Sydney?'

'No, it's being organised by the university and hospital in Melbourne.'

'Melbourne? Oh.' I swallow. 'Suppose I can arrange it. That's a little overwhelming.'

'Just start writing, man.'

So I do. It's hard to get back into the discipline, but half-way through the paper everything comes together. October arrives and, still half-amazed at events, I kiss Eliza and the children goodbye and get on the Sydney train.

This time I'm staying overnight with Klara and Yvonne. I'm in Vivy's old room—she lives in the basement flat now and is keeping company with Nikos's son Steve. Yvonne says it's all rather tumultuous and a lot of door-slamming takes place.

But I'm pleased to hear Klara's good news. She's discovered a new vocation, teaching poetry and writing together, and says shyly she may be finding her voice again as well. One of her pupils is Tibor, the son of Tina's rather sinister mate, Moshe Adler.

I visit Tina at Tempo. My nephew Robert is sixteen months old, a dark-eyed boy with a gentle smile who oddly doesn't resemble anyone in the family. I'm uneasy at the sight of my sister, pale and thin, with bruises on her arm, but she laughs and says she slipped.

The more I see him the more I dislike Jimmy. He keeps popping in with his genial, insincere patter, and I swear he's checking up on her, though Tina says calmly, 'Jimmy's such an attentive father.' Finally he goes downstairs and we can chat.

'So when did old László leave here, anyway?' I ask.

'Oh, a year ago now.' Tina's face is suddenly drawn with pain.

'My God, Tina, what's wrong?'

'Actually, Harry—László didn't leave.' She swallows. 'He died.'

'Died? How?'

'The elephant seals crushed him.' She flatly refuses to say more.

Back at Balmain I talk about it with Yvonne and Klara, but they don't know what's to be done either: just as she did today, my sister resists any attempt to discuss her situation.

We're diverted when Billie and Nikos turn up in the late afternoon, both looking remarkably well. (Eliza is amazed those two finally sorted themselves out but I'm hardly surprised. I always thought they'd settled on each other ages ago.)

'I expected you'd be out sailing somewhere,' I say.

Nikos smiles. 'And miss Shabbat with Klara? Not on your life.'

'Shabbat—here?' I say. 'But isn't that a Jewish ceremony?'

Klara smiles ruefully. 'You may remember I was not observant before. But now I find joy in celebrating with my friends.'

'It'll soon be sunset,' says Yvonne. 'It's time.'

I follow them curiously to the dining room, where the table is set with candlesticks, braided bread covered with a cloth, and glasses and wine. Klara strikes a match and lights the candles.

She brings her hands towards herself a few times over the flames, and covers her eyes and sings a prayer. Everyone else acts as if this is perfectly normal, and I think—well, given the bizarre twists in all our lives over the last few years it probably isn't that odd.

We sip the wine, then eat bread (with a bit more chanting), and at last some excellent food appears.

Billie leans over and says, 'Took me a while to cope with the hocus-pocus too.'

'Hocus-*pocus*?' says Nikos. 'Wait till we go to a Greek Orthodox ceremony. You have no idea. This is sheer amateur territory.'

Klara laughs and offers me more food. Feeling content, I gaze around at these dear friends, and decide this is a bloody good way to spend a Friday night after all.

Yvonne drives me to Central next afternoon to catch the train to Melbourne. She says, 'What a pity you'll miss out on the consolation tonight. I love the ceremony.'

'Well, Klara's certainly more at peace than I've seen her in years. If those traditions are helping her, that's wonderful.'

'It's not just the traditions, Harry, but at last she's started writing again—and in new ways too.' Yvonne says. 'It's as if teaching someone else has opened up some of the pathways that were blocked for her. I don't understand it, but I'm so grateful.'

'I'm glad for you both. And there's something I should have said a long time ago, Yvonne. Thank you for pushing me to do *Poems of Rage*. I know I sulked and dragged my heels, but in the end it offered me so much. It was the right thing to do.'

She nods. 'It was. It'll never be our biggest seller, but in the end it may well be the most important book Watters Press ever does.'

Her clear eyes gaze at me from beneath her fringe, and I think of her kind, constant support of us all through the dramas of the recent years.

'And you? What about you, Yvonne?'

'Oh, Harry, what else could I want?' she says. 'I've got my printery and young Claire and a contented Klara at last.'

'*And* your fabulously stylish hairstyle, don't forget.'

We laugh and I kiss her farewell.

In Central Station I buy a paper and get on the Melbourne train. I've got a sleeper booked so the trip won't be too arduous. A whistle blows and we're off.

I settle back and think, right now, at this moment, I'm nobody's father or husband or employee. No one knows where I am or what I'm doing. It's rather a pleasant feeling.

After a time we're rattling through the country, and I shake open my paper. On page 4 there's an article with a photo of a vast ship's hull that catches my eye:

Four-Master in Dry Dock: West Germany's 6,000-ton four-master Pamir at Hamburg. The old-timer will resume regular voyages to South America after the overhaul. Beside carrying freight, Pamir and sister ship Passat serve as training vessels for German merchant marine cadets.

Since we farewelled *Passat* and *Pamir* seven years ago at Port Victoria, Eliza and I have followed the chequered careers of both square-riggers. They've passed from owner to owner, usually always on the edge of bankruptcy. But it's good to see they may have a future yet.

And dear old *Inverley*? After the war she was donated to the town of Mariehamn in the Åland Islands. There's talk about making her a museum ship, to preserve the memories of a way of life that's quickly passing from the world's awareness. I hope it happens.

That night I lie awake in my sleeper. The last time I took this train I was (unbelievably) just twenty-seven. I had left my widowed mother and young Tina in Newcastle and was returning to London to continue my medical studies.

I was penniless, off to Port Lincoln to work my way to England on *Inverley*. It was there, on that passage, that Eliza and I first met and my life changed. I sigh in contentment and fall asleep.

At dawn the train arrive at Melbourne and I take a taxi to the hotel, unpack and bathe. I'm a day early so I meet some colleagues at the Royal Melbourne Hospital, then in the evening go over my work.

Next morning at the conference I enjoy the other presentations, but feel nervous too as my own talk is just after lunch. Far too soon I'm up on the stage and introduced: the auditorium is full of blurred faces, and I feel very alone.

But I seem to settle into it, and the lad running the projector gets the slides in the right order, so I survive. At afternoon tea I speak to some interesting people, and at last start feeling relaxed.

Tonight there's a dinner at a restaurant, more talks tomorrow, then back to Sydney on the evening train. At the dinner I sit with some friendly colleagues, and soon we're happily chatting.

The waitresses bring the first course and it's not bad, then in the break I drink and gaze around the room. The staff are busily coming and going through the kitchen doors, watched by the restaurant manager.

I realise Tina's words must be still weighing on my mind, because in the dimness the man somehow reminds me of László. Poor bastard. *Dead?* But why on earth would she say he was crushed by elephant seals, of all things!

I once saw a story in National Geographic on the lumbering, gigantic beasts. Did she mean László was crushed by the criminals of her shady world? Makes sense, but Christ, Tina, what are you *doing* with your life?

Then the manager turns, silhouetted by light from the kitchen doors, and I stare in shock.

I get up, thinking I must be mad, and sidle behind the tables until I can see him properly. He's only a few feet away and I hear him speak to one of the waiters: then I know.

Someone taps on a microphone, the room quietens and a speech about the conference begins. The manager looks around and nods, satisfied, then I step forward and touch his arm.

He stares, then quickly pulls me into a corridor and closes the door behind us. 'Hello, Harry,' he says quietly.

'*László*! What the hell? Tina thinks you're *dead*!'

He rubs his brow. 'Jimmy sent Big Davy to murder me because of the baby, but the fool went for a drink first. He said something and a friend heard and warned me in time. I got away.'

With a shock I recall Robert's brown eyes and gentle smile. Of course.

László's voice is anguished. 'I had to leave. Tina and Róbert were safe as long as Jimmy could pretend I was gone forever.'

'But Tina's in trouble. Jimmy's taunting her, punishing her. She's being so brave. László, you've got to go back.'

'Harry, *listen*. If I go back he will kill her and Róbert. I must never go near them again.' He groans quietly. 'Recently I met a man who knew me in Sydney, so now I must leave even this place. Next week I am sailing to Europe. Then Tina will be completely safe.'

'But is there anything for you in Europe?'

László shakes his head wearily. 'At least there, Harry, they don't call me a fucking wog.'

'No, they put a number on your fucking arm instead and kill you. László, you must see her again!'

'But Tina needs to believe, utterly, I am gone,' he says sadly. 'She could not hide it if she knew.'

'This is insane,' I say in disbelief. 'I'll tell her, I can't lie to her.'

'Do you not *hear* me, Harry, you fool?' László grabs my shoulders and shakes me. 'Do you love Tina? Do you want her alive? Then tell her *nothing!*'

He stops and leans his head on the wall, his eyes closed.

After a time he whispers, 'Please, Harry. Be kind to us both and let her believe I am dead. It is the truth. I died years ago.'

26. Tina: Paprika and Tobacco

Harry rings me from Central on the way home from his Melbourne conference. He seems hesitant and keeps asking how I am, so I tell him the usual lies. He says Eliza and Mum would love to see the baby again, I should visit them.

I say I will when things are quieter. More lies: Jimmy says he'll burn Robert with cigarettes if I take him anywhere.

My husband's in a bad mood lately. As Moshe Adler predicted, the Capellis have returned to the Cross. They beat up the boys at Jimmy's betting shop and told the customers to gamble with them now. They did worse to the Adlers, robbing a baccarat joint and killing a guard.

It's not all-out war yet, but not far off. Jimmy knows that without the Adlers' protection he'd be crushed by the Capellis, but he also knows Moshe will never forgive him for László.

A few months ago Jimmy decided he didn't want me meeting Moshe—meeting anyone—so he took over the grog arrangements. But Moshe refuses to talk to him, so now he has to work with Sándor instead.

'Course that speed-freak Sándor did it,' Jimmy says, drunk, sitting on the bed and taking off his shoes. 'Hated Enzo. Both of them screwing Dimple, the cow, and so was Big Davy. But it's me gets the blame. *Told* Marco, wasn't *me* wanted that bitch dead.'

'Marco Capelli?' I say. He's a young hothead.

Jimmy looks at me hazily. 'Forget I said that.' He grabs and twists my wrist viciously. 'One word to the Adlers and you'll be sorry. Won't you be *sorry*?'

'Yes, Jimmy. Yes, *yes*—I'll be sorry.' I try not to whimper.

He snickers. 'That old perve, you know, with the cravats and the boyfriends, heard he's fond of them *very* young. Pays well too. What do you reckon? Will I send our brown-eyed cuckoo out to work?'

I smother a scream and push myself away in revulsion.

Jimmy laughs. 'Got you there, didn't I?' He clambers into bed beside me.

'Take that fucking nightgown off and put this in your mouth.' He slaps my head. 'Stop whingeing and smile, sweetheart. Smile.'

When I wake up, Jimmy's gone and I'm aching all over. I don't know why he bothers with me—he's got his own small stable of prostitutes now.

He calls them his *good girls* and Pearl keeps them in line. They screw favoured customers in what used to be my office at the Starlight Lounge, garishly redecorated in red velvet.

I still do the accounts for the business, but now I work at a small desk in the corner of Jimmy's office. 'Got to keep an eye on this one, don't we?' he likes to say jovially.

At breakfast I gaze at my beautiful Robert, eighteen months old. I'm sickened by Jimmy's words last night and afraid too. Despite the banter, he doesn't actually joke about anything.

I take the baby down to Jimmy's office—I've got some work to do before going over to Tempo. Robert plays happily with a toy train, chattering to himself. I finish off the real monthly accounts, then go to the filing cabinet to get the taxman's version of the books.

Jimmy's a vicious thug, but one bizarre secret of his success is his tidiness. When I came to work here I was surprised at how neatly he kept all his papers in this cabinet.

Our bloody wedding certificate's probably just as carefully filed inside there too, I think bitterly, lined up with Dimple's marriage and divorce papers.

Ah—Dimple's divorce.

Moshe Adler wants to know the actual date, but I only recall it was a few months before my wedding. He still hopes to head off a gang war by convincing the Capellis the deaths of Enzo and Dimple are not connected to us, so it's important to show that Jimmy had no reason to want Dimple dead.

I've got time now to check—Jimmy's out for a few hours, meeting Sándor at a cafe. I kneel and open the bottom drawer, Jimmy's personal papers. I riffle through the folders—letters from family, old mates, papers from army days—and stop for a moment at the file marked 'Tina'.

He's drawn a heart around my name. Christ. I flick past a few more files and see 'Dimple'. I laugh bitterly. She scored a heart too, once upon a time.

Dimple's file has just a few letters and cards, their marriage certificate and, poor cow, her death certificate. But then—nothing? I check it all again. No legal or divorce documents, no *decree nisi*, and most certainly, no *decree absolute*.

I hunt through all the other files in the bottom drawer then, my heart pounding, through those in every drawer. Twice. Absolutely nothing. They never divorced, but Jimmy was desperate to be free to marry me.

He needed Dimple dead after all, and dead in a hurry.

Robert says, 'Mama?'

'Just a minute, darling. Put your train away now.' I carefully replace the files exactly as they were and look around quickly. Everything is as it should be.

'Come on,' I say. 'Let's go to Tempo and get pastry from the cafe.'

'Pastry,' says Robert, laughing and waving his arms.

In the hall outside I meet Pearl. She looks at me with contempt and says, 'Jimmy rang. Said to tell you he's gone to see Doris. Some problem with the plumbing.'

She smirks, knowing as well as I do that Doris is his latest girl and the plumbing is probably Jimmy's own. I can't imagine how he'd have the energy after last night.

'Thought he'd gone to see Sándor,' I say. 'There's an urgent delivery we've got to arrange.'

She smiles with a kind of glittering anticipation. 'Oh, Big Davy'll sort that one out.'

I can't bear the sight of her and brush past, then stop and turn to face her.

'Pearl, you and Big Davy were married in late '51, weren't you?'

'Yeah. So?'

'Ever meet Dimple Kelso?' I say. 'Died maybe six months after your wedding.'

'Once. Smug cow. Imagined everyone fancied her.'

'Oh? Apparently everyone did. Jimmy told me that before she died she was having it off with Sándor Adler, Enzo Capelli *and* your husband. Smug, but clearly versatile.'

'Bitch. You'll be laughing on the other side of your face when your wog mates get theirs.'

As I put Robert in the car I think, yes, it all fits. Big Davy was sent off to Brisbane before my wedding, supposedly after a fight with Enzo Capelli, and that was the last anyone saw of Enzo or Dimple.

Jimmy wanted Dimple dead and Davy loathed Enzo: Davy murdered them both.

As I'm driving to Tempo I realise, with a thump in my guts, what Pearl had actually said. Why would *Davy* be arranging grog deliveries with Sándor? He couldn't organise the proverbial root in a brothel. And Jimmy's been talking privately with the Capellis.

At Tempo I ring Moshe immediately.

'Mr Adler, we have a serious problem. Has Sándor left to meet Jimmy at the Espresso Cafe?'

'Indeed, Mrs Kelso. Ten minutes ago. Why?'

'Because Big Davy will be waiting for him instead, and I think he's going to try to kill him.'

'Oy *gevalt*,' he says in exasperation. He turns from the phone and yells what sounds like instructions, then I hear running feet and doors slamming.

He turns back to the phone. 'Thank you for that, Mrs Kelso. You've been very helpful.'

'But will they be in time?'

'I expect so. You do realise, after this, Big Davy will not be returning to your employ?'

'Good. I've just found out—' I take a breath. 'I think it was *him* who killed both Dimple and Enzo. It turns out Jimmy and Dimple were never divorced after all. Jimmy wanted to be free, Davy hated Enzo, so he murdered them both.'

'Ah. That makes a great deal of sense.'

'And Jimmy's been talking secretly to the Capellis, too.'

'Why am I not surprised? But now we know Big Davy is the culprit I think we can force the Capellis to a truce. Thank you again, Mrs Kelso. I will speak to you later.'

'Please don't go, not just yet.' I'm suddenly shaking with shock and feeling forlorn. 'How's your little girl, Devorah?'

'She is very well, already two years old.'

'Is she? Goodness! I don't see people very often now, so I'm a bit out of touch.'

'Ah. You might like to know that Mrs Fenn is teaching writing of a sorts to my son, Tibor. He tells me it will make him a better lawyer. I have my doubts, but he is happy, so what can I do?'

'I'm sure Klara will be a wonderful tutor,' I say. 'And do you see Yvonne, Miss Watters?'

'I do indeed. She appears to have taken up residence in my kitchen—she plans to publish a cook-book of my wife's recipes. Again, what can I do?'

I laugh, my voice catching. 'Oh, that's *lovely.*'

He hesitates. 'Mrs Kelso. With the Capellis no longer a threat, I am free at last to express my outrage over László's fate. Has the time come for my gift?'

It's a Monday, so Tempo is closed. In the early evening, while Robert is asleep in my office, I ring the Starlight Lounge.

'Jimmy? Listen, Big Davy's here at Tempo. He's wounded, but not badly, and he's dozing now. But he wants to see you urgently. He said to tell you things are fine, but there's something important you need to know. What's going on?'

'None of your business. I'll be there, ten minutes.'

I hang up and go downstairs, carefully closing the doors to the office and the bottom of the stairwell. I pour myself a gin and tonic, and sit at the best table in the house.

The blinds are drawn and, apart from a spotlight shining on the bar, the room is in shadows. Soon afterwards I hear Jimmy's key in the door and go to meet him.

'Davy's lying behind the bar,' I say. 'Couldn't get upstairs so I gave him a pillow and blanket.'

'Poor bastard. But he said things are fine, didn't he?' Jimmy walks around the end of the bar. 'Wait on, he's not—'

'No, he's not,' says Moshe Adler, moving out of the shadows.

Two other men step forward and I hear the click of a revolver.

'Ah, you right bastard, you can't do this to *me!*' says Jimmy, indignant. 'We're fucking allies.'

'We were allies until you tried to kill Sándor,' says Moshe. 'Come along with us.'

'Where's my man Davy?' says Jimmy. 'Tina! Don't let them take me, doll!'

I say quietly to Moshe, 'Make it fast and painless.'

He stares. 'This scum ordered the death of his first wife, tried to kill my brother, and murdered my close friend. My informants tell me he rapes you and makes vile threats towards your son. And you do not want him to *suffer?*'

'Just end it as cleanly as possible.' I think quickly. 'Make it look like an accident, no shooting. Please, let Robert grown up without any more ugly memories.'

Moshe gazes at me. 'Róbert, then, from now on.'

'Róbert, I promise.'

'Very well.' He looks up. 'Take him to the car.'

His men grab Jimmy's arms and lead him to the door. He yells, 'Tina, no! I didn't kill your piano fella, I was lying, lying, I *swear!*'

I shake my head.

'Stop whingeing and smile, sweetheart. Smile.'

*

Moshe Adler is as good as his word. Jimmy's car, with Jimmy inside, is found at the bottom of a cliff on a winding road he sometimes uses. Thankfully, when I go to identify his body at the Morgue, it's almost unmarked.

The attendant gives me a paper bag with all his possessions—his wallet and keys, and the old signet ring he wore on his crooked little finger. Ah, Jimmy.

The funeral goes well. It's a glorious day and I wear a new black dress with the diamond necklace Jimmy gave me so long ago. Black always suited me: I remember my chiffon gown with the tiny beads, glittering in the shadows.

At the reception Moshe Adler introduces me to his wife Ilona, who's tough and pretty and seems more than a match for him. Sándor Adler, flushed and twitchy, murmurs, 'I owe you one, Mrs Kelso, won't ever forget.' Old Abe Adler conveys his sincere good wishes to my bosom.

The Capelli, Diakos and Finnegan families all solemnly shake my hand, one by one, then the police commissioner and half a dozen smaller gangs line up to commiserate. (The state premier regrets his other pressing engagement, but sends a handsome wreath instead.)

To my joy Klara, Yvonne, Billie and Nikos also turn up. I'm dizzy at the prospect of being able to talk freely with my friends again, to visit anyone whenever I want, and most of all to think, and talk, and sleep unmolested.

I hire Annie, one of the waitresses who's always been fond of Robert—*Róbert*—to babysit him, while I spend time sorting out Jimmy's business dealings.

I fire his *good girls* and terminate the leases on their flats. And Pearl? She's red-eyed over Big Davy's disappearance—he's unlikely ever to be found, says Mr Adler—but I don't care.

I call her into the office and say, 'Suppose I must be laughing on the other side of my face at last, Pearl. So fuck off now and never come back.'

Perhaps I enjoy that more than I should have.

*

A few days after the funeral Moshe Adler visits me. We sit in the office, the desk piled with papers.

'Well,' he says. 'Do you intend to carry on with the businesses, Mrs Kelso? Tempo, the Starlight Lounge, the betting shop, the discreet enterprises?'

'I've already terminated the discreet enterprises, Mr Adler, but if you happen to know someone who wants a nasty little betting shop or the extremely well-regarded Starlight Lounge, I'm sure you'll point them in my direction.'

He smiles. 'The Capellis would like to buy the betting shop. The Starlight Lounge? I was seeking a new outlet myself. The restaurant would remain, but upstairs I believe there is a flat that would make a fine casino. If, of course, you could bear to part with it.'

'I think so. On three conditions. The first is that after I move out, the place is erased. Every rug and tile, every sofa and chandelier, every velvet curtain and gold tassel—*everything*—must be stripped out and completely destroyed.'

'Everything,' he says and nods. 'The second?'

'I plan to keep running Tempo myself, but naturally will need the continued protection of the Adler family.'

'Sándor's future gratitude is assured, as is mine. The third?'

'I want a good market price for the Starlight Lounge.'

'Of course.'

'Plus ten percent extra for Róbert.'

He mentally calculates. 'Very well. For Róbert.'

'Thank you, Moshe.'

'Thank you, Tina.'

At the start of 1957 my brother Harry comes down from Newcastle for a week to help me move. Róbert and I are going to live in the flat next to my office at Tempo, the one that used to be László's.

It's still empty because Jimmy, to his surprise, was never able to rent it out. Every time someone would look at it I'd regretfully mention the 'bedbug problem,' and they'd never return.

I buy new furniture and decorate the tall, graceful rooms. Tempo is so familiar to Róbert he settles in immediately, and Annie the waitress is happy to continue as his babysitter.

To thank Harry for his hard work helping me, I take him to dinner at the nearby Italian restaurant. Marco Capelli nods respectfully to me when we enter, but I don't point him out. Harry's had to deal with enough shocks about gangsters recently.

Over our antipasto he says hesitantly, 'Tina, there's something I wanted to tell you.'

'What? Mmm, try the mushrooms.'

'But I don't know how to,' he says helplessly. 'I swore I wouldn't for your sake, but now Jimmy's gone, everything's changed.'

I spear an olive with my fork. 'What, Harry?'

'Well—it was about two years ago László disappeared, wasn't it?'

I eat the olive and sigh. 'Nearly two and a half now.'

'Did you ever find out what happened?'

I shake my head. 'Jimmy used to pretend he'd gone to Tahiti, but it was obvious Big Davy murdered him. What's this about?'

He takes a breath. 'Tina, László's not dead. Or he wasn't when I was in Melbourne a few months ago. He got away from here just ahead of Big Davy.'

My fork drops with a clatter.

'He made me swear not to tell you. He was terrified if you knew then you and the baby would be in danger from Jimmy. And from what I've heard lately, he was absolutely right.'

My hand to my mouth, tears in my eyes, I say, 'László's *alive*? He's in *Melbourne*?'

'Not any more. I'm sorry. When we met he was just about to leave Melbourne for Europe, so he's long gone by now.'

'Oh God, Harry. Can we go home? Please.'

Back at my new flat I pay Annie for babysitting, then she leaves and Harry makes me a cup of tea.

I say, desolate, 'Pity to interrupt our meal. You should have waited till dessert to tell me.'

He sits down and takes my hand. 'I'm so sorry, Sis. I really am.'

'How did he look?'

'Healthy, prosperous. He was managing a fine restaurant.'

'He wasn't playing his music, then.'

'No.'

For some reason that makes me weep again.

After a time I say, 'Don't know why I'm crying at such good news. Relief, I suppose—I've always felt so *guilty*. It was my fault, you see. I was upset about Jimmy, and László was broken-hearted about something far worse. We both needed to be held.'

'At least you have Róbert now,' Harry says gently.

My beautiful boy. I look up. 'Did László give you an address?'

Harry shakes his head.

'Did he say where he was going?'

'No. Just Europe.'

'Oh, *Christ*. There's no way to find him now, is there?'

'I'm sorry, Tina.'

I breathe a shuddering sigh. 'At least he's alive.'

Harry returns to Newcastle next day. I kiss him and reassure him I'm over the shock, that he brought me wonderful news, something to be grateful about—and it's perfectly true.

Slowly I return to normal. Róbert grows confident now we're out of Jimmy's malevolent shadow, and I find comfort in the everyday routine of my business. And, as always, I take pleasure in the soaring, brilliant music we bring to life at Tempo.

But I was wrong when I thought the odour of paprika and tobacco had been erased forever from this flat. Sometimes late at night a scent wafts past me and I turn, smiling. But it's only a phantom, drifting perhaps from the woodwork.

Róbert loves music already and his small plump fingers are growing. One day he'll have his father's long sensitive hands.

27. Billie: Sputnik

'What do you think?' says Nikos.

'It's ghastly,' I say. 'Pink stucco? Reminds me of a dance palace.'

'The agent calls it terracotta.'

'He would, wouldn't he?'

'He says it has good views,' says Nikos.

'Anywhere round here has good views. The place is practically on the side of a mountain.'

Nikos unlocks the front door.

I recoil. 'Phew. Rats?'

'Possums in the roof. See the urine stains on the ceiling?'

'Possum pee *and* stucco. Can't imagine why it hasn't sold.'

I follow Nikos down the corridor and through a pair of doors, their glass etched with sailing ships.

Beyond is a sitting room with a wall of dusty windows. They display a panorama of the flying boat base, Shark Island, the Harbour Bridge and green Bradleys Head, laid out on a sweep of ruffled sapphire and indigo waters.

'Not bad,' I say.

Nikos nods. 'Not bad.'

'Can we afford it?'

'Just.'

'I could get to like pink stucco.'

Nikos sells the Rozelle house and I've got my own savings, so we put about the same amount into buying the place, although the solicitor nearly has a breakdown working out how two unmarried people could possibly become co-owners.

We rip up lino and carpet (there were rats, after all) and varnish the floor. The possums move out and a painter covers the stains.

Nikos, with his capable hands, does clever things with nails and bits of wood and after a while the place is definitely not bad.

We cut back the jungle round the house for the grey kitten. She started out as Shadow-Two, but she's nicer than her bad-tempered namesake, so she's just called Two now. We repair the fence and get a small cheerful mongrel from the dog pound and name him Three. (I reckon I've got this motherhood lark all figured out.)

Our bedroom has scintillating views over the water, and as I open the curtains one night to see the stars I say, 'You know, this is my first *real* house, the first I've ever owned.'

I get into bed and Nikos says, 'Do you like being an owner?'

'I'll say.' I snuggle close. 'The deeds arrived today from the solicitor and I sat gloating over them for ages. But I noticed you didn't get as much for the Rozelle place as you expected.'

'I did get more, but I've put some aside for a project. Remember my mate with the small seaplane, the DHC-3 Otter? He's looking to sell, and we could buy it if you want.'

'And then what would we do?' I run my fingers down his pleasingly-muscled back.

'Do you also remember my uncle Georgios with the oyster farm on the Hawkesbury?'

'Uh-huh.'

'The faster he can get his oysters to the Sydney fish market, the fresher they are and the better the price. Do you see where I might be going with this?'

'So you need a pilot.'

'And why do you reckon I've been chasing you since 1948—nine bloody years?'

'They only started selling the Otter four years ago,' I say. 'But I like a man who thinks ahead.'

Nikos laughs. 'Anyway, we could go for a test flight, find out more. We need to plan for the future, they're cutting back our hours at the base again.'

'Oysters, eh?' I say. 'I like oysters.'

'So do I.'

*

Nikos's mate Geoff takes us for us a spin in his Otter on a clear spring day. The seaplane is forty feet long, fifteen feet high, and able to land and take off over short distances. It fits ten passengers or lots of cargo, and is already well-known as a workhorse.

Geoff motors it to the landing jetty at the flying boat base and we step aboard the handsome little thing. Given the last time I flew a plane was ten years ago, the modern instruments and comfortable seats are a revelation. I take the co-pilot position and Nikos sits behind me.

'Strap in,' says Geoff, a middle-aged ex-RAAF pilot with a large moustache. He speaks to the radio room at the base, gets the okay, turns the Otter towards the open bay and opens the throttle. In just a few seconds we're airborne.

'Holy *hell*,' I say.

'Top speed's around one-thirty miles an hour, range eight hundred miles, and ceiling, oh, nineteen thousand feet,' says Geoff.

'But why would anyone want to go to nineteen thousand feet?' says Nikos.

Geoff and I look at each other and say, 'Fun,' at the same time. We're clearly going to get on.

He talks me through the instruments and handling characteristics as we circle over the harbour, then says, 'Rightio, off to the Hawkesbury.'

We're above the railway bridge over the river in about fifteen minutes and Geoff explains the landing sequence to me as we descend. Soon we're bobbing on the khaki-green Hawkesbury, and tie up to a mooring not far from shore.

Before we left Sydney, Nikos rang his uncle to tell him to watch out for the plane, and soon a motorboat near a blue shack starts up and heads towards us.

It comes alongside and we step down and greet Uncle Georgios, who's affable, tanned and grey-haired, and has an even larger moustache than Geoff.

Back at the shack we we sit in the sunlight and chat about the possibility of a seaplane service to some of the remoter stretches of the river. Then we share a long lunch of—what else?—oysters, and a salad with olives and cheese and some excellent red wine. It's a good afternoon.

In the evening Georgios motors us back to the Otter, and with thanks and farewells we get in the little plane.

'Your turn,' says Geoff.

'Okay.' I sit in the pilot's seat with Geoff beside me.

'Ah—are you sure you're *ready*, Billie?' Nikos says.

'You nervous?' I say, and he laughs. Nervously.

Geoff talks me through the takeoff and it all goes well.

'What a nice little beast,' I say.

'Into a twenty mile an hour headwind, takeoff's only six-fifty feet,' says Geoff.

'Wow, six-fifty! Hear that, Nikos?'

'Mmm,' he says.

Soon we're almost back at Sydney Harbour. Geoff contacts the radio room at the base, we get a heading and circle lower and start coming in as the sun is setting.

The control launches have already laid out the bobbing flare path. It glows in the dusk—four golden lamps at the corners of the mile-long landing channel and the row of eight green lights marking the left-hand side.

'Fantastic!' I say. 'Nikos, this is what it's like for the flying boats! Oh, look at those flares, aren't they *gorgeous*?'

'Um,' he says. 'Concentrate, Billie.'

Closer and closer to the surface, throttle back, lovely, touch, small bump, spray flying on each side, swishing through the water, green lights flicking past the corners of my eyes and ... we glide to a stop, rolling a little.

'My God, Geoff. What a *gem*.'

He grins. 'Okay, rev a bit, approach and turn to starboard, very slowly, and—a bit further—okay, we'll just ease up to the landing—and—*excellent*.'

Geoff and I make plans to meet in a couple of days for another lesson, then after a few more I can be examined and add the qualification to my licence (which I've kept current, though I never expected to use it again).

As Nikos and I walk home in the twilight—our house is less than a mile from the base—he's surprisingly quiet.

'Are you having second thoughts?' I say.

'No ...' he says doubtfully.

'What's wrong?'

'I have a confession to make. Apart from a joy-ride in a Moth in 1932, I've never been in a plane before.'

'*Never?*' I say. 'Do you mean you've done about as much flying as I have sailing?'

'Far less.' He shakes his head. 'Jesus, Billie. I've worked with pilots for years, and I had no idea.' He turns to me. 'It's *terrifying*! You're so far off the ground and you make jokes about going to nineteen thousand feet!'

'They weren't jokes.'

'Even worse. How can you *do* that?'

'Change the flap angle, open the throttle, and off you go.'

'I'm serious. How can you put yourself in such danger without a moment's worry?'

I laugh. 'I've had plenty of worries over the years, but I'm still here. *You* could sink and get eaten by a shark, but that doesn't stop you sailing.'

'Pretty unlikely.'

'Ditto.'

'Seems a lot more likely when you're nineteen thousand *bloody* feet up in the air,' he says.

I stop and we gaze at each other, then we walk home in silence.

That was yesterday and we haven't had time to talk about the plane (or perhaps our entire future) because today Nikos is busy building a barbecue in the back yard, a brick cube topped with a metal plate.

This evening our friends are coming over to the pink palace for a joint house-warming and Sputnik-view. It's October 1957 and the papers are abuzz with the sudden launch by the Russians of a small metal sphere with four trailing antennae.

Radio hams everywhere record the eerie beep-beep-beep of Sputnik as it passes, visible at night like a moving star. Nikos, the science fiction fan, is fascinated by the satellite and what it might mean for the future.

I tease, 'For someone who hates going up in planes you're surprisingly charmed by the whole idea of flight into outer space,' but he doesn't smile as he usually would.

Still, it's a beautiful spring night and, as we're getting food ready in the kitchen, Steve and Vivy are the first to arrive, Steve with a plate of Ruby's finest salad.

She and Nikos's father aren't coming tonight. Papous is still a little miffed we're not getting married, but he was very fond of me before we mentioned it so I think he'll be all right eventually.

Vivy says hullo, looking sophisticated and bad-tempered, then goes down the outside steps to the garden and sits silhouetted beside the lit barbecue.

'What's up with Vivy, mate?' I ask Steve.

'I told her my plans,' he says. 'Guess I'd better tell you two as well.'

Nikos, chopping tomatoes, turns. 'Plans?'

'I'm going away for a while, for a year,' he says. 'I'm twenty-three, should do it while I'm young.'

'Where?' I say.

Steve grins, looking very much like his father. 'Well, um, Greece, actually. To study ancient music in Athens, the *tonoi* of Ptolemy and Aristoxenus. Fundamental to all music. We did the theory at the Conservatorium but I want to know more.'

'How will you get there?' says Nikos.

'I've been saving up and Papous says he'll help because at last I'll be learning *real* music. But I had to promise to come home speaking fluent Greek, and also visit the ancestral village and meet all the great-grand-aunties.'

I say, 'You do realise they'll call you Stavros over there, there'll be no escaping it.'

He grins again. 'That's cool.'

Nikos hugs him. 'Sounds good, son. When are you going?'

'In a month. That's why Vivy's so cross with me. I'm leaving the band and leaving her too.'

'Ah,' I say, then the bell rings.

I open the front door, and it's Lizzie and Harry and their children. We kiss and I say, 'Leo, Jenny, you've grown so much,' but as it's been three years since I last saw them it's perfectly true.

I lead them to the kitchen. 'There's lemonade for the youngsters and something stronger for the elderly. What'll you have?'

The doorbell rings again, and it's Klara, Yvonne and Claire, with Tina behind them, carrying two-year-old Róbert. A tall, slim boy is there too, and Yvonne introduces him as Tibor Adler—I knew Klara was tutoring him but we haven't met before.

Tibor is holding a plate and says shyly, 'A cheesecake from my mother. She says, welcome to Rose Bay.'

'Lovely, thanks a lot, Tibor. Come in everyone, the kitchen's along this way.'

Tina says, 'Róbert's almost asleep. Can I put him down for a rest somewhere?'

I take her to the spare room, and we tuck him into bed.

'He looks so peaceful, Teen.'

'Don't be misled by the angelic demeanour,' she says, smiling.

'How are you going?' I say.

'Very well. Run off my feet at Tempo, but in a good way.'

'And—any luck with finding László?'

Tina shakes her head. 'Moshe put out the word among his European contacts, but no response. I didn't expect anything to come of it,' she says, her chin firm.

'And you brought Moshe's son along tonight?'

'No, he came with Klara and Yvonne. He's just had a writing lesson with Klara and I think she took pity on him—he doesn't have much of a social life.'

'It's odd we're building up all these links with the Adlers. Maybe they're not as bad as they're painted,' I say as we close the door.

Tina stops and says in a low voice, 'Billie, don't be sentimental. Yes, we have connections with them, necessary connections, but never forget they're criminals, and the best we can hope for is to stay clear of the damage.'

She takes a breath. 'Come on, pour me something nice and let's join the party.'

We get drinks then I lead Tina down the steps to the yard below, where everyone is now sitting by the barbecue in our collection of second-hand chairs, beside a table with plates and cutlery.

Nikos is cooking pieces of marinated lamb, octopus, tomato, onion and eggplant on the hot plate, and the sizzling smells are glorious on the night air.

I sit beside Lizzie and say, 'How's the job at the Dockyard?'

'Wonderful, Bill,' she says. 'I can see everything going on in the harbour from my office. I've made friends too with a few old blokes who remember the four-masters. I love the place.'

'Mummy took us to see a big grey ship being launched,' says Jenny. 'It had flags and made a splash when it went in the water.'

'And a lady smashed a bottle on it and glass went *everywhere*, and nobody minded,' says Leo admiringly.

Yvie says, 'Eliza, wasn't it just a fortnight ago one of your beloved barques meet a terrible end?'

Lizzie nods. 'Yes, poor *Pamir*. Hit by a hurricane in the Caribbean and capsized. Only a handful out of eighty crewmen survived. And fifty of the dead were cadets, boys.' She sighs. 'All just boys.' Her eyes are on Leo.

'They ignored the wisdom of decades and loaded the grain *loose* instead of in the usual sacks,' says Harry. 'So it flowed like water when the ship heeled. A stupid accident waiting to happen.'

'It's twenty-eight years since we sailed on *Inverley*,' says Lizzie. 'Ever since then everyone's been predicting the end of merchant sail. But now must be the time to let it all go. Only *Passat* is left afloat, and she'll soon be laid up.'

'I am sorry, Eliza,' Klara says. 'The end of something is sad.'

'It had to happen.' Lizzie nods regretfully. 'But tonight is also the beginning of something, isn't it, Nikos? When will your futuristic satellite be overhead?'

Nikos forks cooked food onto serving platters. 'The USSR might take offence at you calling it mine, but yes—' he checks his watch, '—should be here in about ten minutes. Enough time to eat. Help yourselves, plates and cutlery are over there.'

We're quiet apart from murmurs of enjoyment, then Harry says, 'And Tibor, I hear Klara's been tutoring you. How's that going?'

Tibor says shyly, 'I've learnt a great deal. My Leaving Certificate is in a month and if I do well I'll go to university next year.'

'What do you want to study?' says Lizzie.

'Law. It's not what I want, but it should be interesting enough.'

Yvonne says, 'Actually, Tibor's been helping with Ilona's cookbook. She doesn't know the English for ingredients and procedures, and he's great at translating. He and Klara have also done some excellent introductory chapters, too.'

Tibor laughs quietly. 'I've had to learn quite a lot myself.'

'You'll be an author then, Tibor!' says Tina. 'Well done.'

He shrugs, smiling.

Claire says suddenly, pointing, 'Is *that* the Sputnik, Uncle Nikos?'

'Certainly is. Well spotted, Claire, you've got good eyes.'

'That's because they're *sharp*,' mutters Leo.

'Better than being *slippery*,' says Claire disdainfully.

'You can see the satellite more clearly now,' says Nikos. 'Near those two bright stars.'

'Alpha and Beta Centauri,' says Leo.

'Right, Leo. How did you know that?'

'I like stars,' he says. 'And I like rockets too.'

'He's moved on to this whole new world,' says Lizzie. 'We can't answer his questions, but we were hoping you could.'

'Let's have a good chat later, Leo,' Nikos says. 'I'd love to know a fellow enthusiast. To be honest, it's a lonely old business being interested in outer space around here.'

Leo sighs happily and I feel a pang of guilt.

Jenny stares at the tiny point of light. 'How far away is the Sputnik, Uncle Nikos?'

'The closest it comes to earth is one hundred and thirty miles,' says Nikos. 'Now, Jenny, if you measure that in units of nineteen thousand feet—say, let's call that a *billie*—it's nearly forty billies away. And the furthest away the orbit gets from earth is an amazing one hundred and sixty billies.'

Leo says, '*Wow.*'

Claire glances at me, puzzled. 'But why is it called a billie?'

'That's just a special way of measuring an absolutely *ridiculous* height off the ground,' says Nikos, and I laugh and nearly choke on a piece of eggplant.

Jenny says, 'But why doesn't Sputnik fall down?'

'It *is* falling down,' says Leo, 'but it's up so high and going so fast it can't reach the earth.' He looks uncertainly at Nikos, who nods and says, 'Precisely,' and Leo beams.

'Oh,' Jenny says softly. 'I didn't know that.'

Tibor, next to her, murmurs, 'I didn't either,' and Jenny smiles up at him. 'How old are you?' she says.

'I'm seventeen,' Tibor says. 'How old are you?'

'I'm six,' says Jenny.

'But I'm *eleven*,' says Leo.

'And I'm twelve,' says Claire, tucking a fair curl behind her ear. She gazes at Leo. 'Why do you always call my eyes sharp?'

He thinks for a moment. 'You look at things as if you can see right through them.'

Claire nods. 'I like that.'

'So—why do you call my eyes slippery, then?' Leo says casually.

'Because you only see what's on the surfaces of things.'

Claire goes to the table to get more food and Leo whispers to me, 'Aunty Billie, I'm going to *marry* her one day.'

I murmur, 'Well good luck with that, kid.'

The moving silver dot has now passed overhead and is approaching the horizon.

'Almost gone,' says Nikos. 'It'll be back in an hour and a half, but then on a different orbit.'

I notice Steve and Vivy standing to one side of the yard. They seem to have made up—he's holding her tightly and whispering against her hair. I remember joking to Lizzie: all that passion and heartbreak will be good for her singing. Poor old Vivy.

'Now, who's for dessert?' I say. 'I made fruit salad and Ilona's sent us a magnificent cheesecake.'

'I can recommend the cheesecake, it's the star of our book,' says Yvonne. 'Oh, I almost forgot.' She looks through her handbag and hands Tina an envelope. 'For you. Moshe just received it.'

Tina peers at it in the firelight, then glances at me in anguish.

I say, 'Okay, everyone, back upstairs for dessert. Nikos, would you put the coffee on too, please?'

Once they're all gone, Tina opens the envelope and reads the single page inside. She breathes deeply, then folds it up again.

'Is it—?'

She nods. 'He's in Paris, a pianist at a jazz club. He won't be coming back.'

'But why *not*? Jimmy's gone now.'

'He can't—he couldn't—cope with seeing Róbert in real life. With loving a child again. But he'll write and keep in touch. He says that's as much closeness as he can bear.'

She bows her head and I put my arm around her.

After a time she wipes her eyes, and says, 'It's all right. I have everything. I have my child, I have my freedom. I know László is playing his music again. That's enough.'

Later, in bed, I tell Nikos about the letter.

'Thank God he's fine,' he says. 'But poor Tina.'

'We're so lucky. Here, now, with each other.'

'After yesterday's flight I was thinking, what if I lost you—what would I *do*?' Nikos sighs. 'Probably curl up and die. But I suppose we could lose each other any day through some stupid mishap.'

We've just got to live with it. Everyone does.'

He nods. 'My fears are no reason for you to step back from what you love, Billie, and I don't want you to—not ever.'

I kiss his shoulder. 'I know. But it's me who's having second thoughts.'

'You?'

'I don't want to fly the Otter regularly. I'm getting old and my reflexes are slow. But we could hire a young pilot to do the routine work and still build up a good business to the Hawkesbury.'

Nikos strokes my face. 'Come on, you'd get your reflexes back in days. What's behind this?'

'Look, it was fun and I did all right—flying the Otter was a lot harder than it appeared.' I laugh. 'But you see, all my life I've had to fight to prove myself, and now, suddenly, I don't have to any more. I'm pretty damned good and there's an end to it.'

'Yes, you are.' Nikos wraps his arms around me and holds me against the warm length of him.

'Know what I'd really rather do? We've been so busy with all this fixing-up-the-house stuff we've neglected what we're best at.'

'Dancing?' He strokes my thigh.

'*Dancing*. Perfect substitute for flying. Even for sex, so I'm told.'

'Never for sex.'

'I want us to dress up and go out and dance till we drop, then come home and enjoy everything we have,' I say. 'Two, Three, a yacht and a pink stucco palace.'

'But you'll still get qualified for the Otter, though, and fly now and then?' Nikos says.

'Yes, I think so. Is that all right?'

'Only if you take me along with you.'

'But you *hate* being so far off the ground,' I say.

'Well, you'll just have to show me why I shouldn't hate it.'

I smile. 'You can be my First Mate if you like.'

'Me in the air, you on the yacht?' he says. 'That's a very well-balanced relationship.'

He kisses me, his mouth warm and I stretch against him.

Outside in the night the starlight glimmers, and somewhere in space a metal ball is orbiting above the earth at a distance of forty billies. Or perhaps one hundred and sixty billies.

I nudge Nikos. 'Hey, did you calculate my unit of distance from the earth on the fly?'

He laughs, content. 'Worked it out earlier. Thought you'd enjoy it.'

Thank You, Readers

Thank you for reading *Harbour of Secrets*. If you've enjoyed it, please recommend it to your friends and give it a review or rating on your favourite book site.

This is the third volume of the Tempo series, and follows *Embers at Midnight*, set in the 1940s, and *Testing the Limits*, in the 1930s.

https://seabooks.net provides links to all my books, with buying options, reviews, extracts, images and background information.

The foundation novel of the Tempo series is *Silver Highways*, set in Broome in the early twentieth century, and based upon award-winning *Redbill*.

On the website I offer a free ebook copy of *Silver Highways* to anyone who subscribes to my mailing-list (and you can unsubscribe at any time).

About the Author

I grew up at Speers Point on Lake Macquarie, NSW. My background is in science and Internet technology, but in 2000 I ran across the story of the charmed life of an old Broome pearling lugger, and discovered the joys of historical research and writing.

My first book, *Redbill: From Pearls to Peace*, won the Western Australian Premier's Book Award for Non-Fiction, and the second, *Alan Villiers: Voyager of the Winds*, won the Mountbatten Maritime Award. My novels include *Embers at Midnight, Testing the Limits, Silver Highways, Atomic Sea* and *The Turning Tide*.

I'm mother to two sons and live in the rolling hills of green South Gippsland, Victoria. I make no apologies for my passion for K-Pop and Korean TV.

You may find me on **https://seabooks.net**, where there are extracts, images and reviews of my books. (Image above by Alex Lance. Cover images from iStock.)

Acknowledgements

I'd like to thank my dear friends Alison Shields, Gillian Clarke and Ruth Carson for their insightful editing of this book; Friday-night zoomers Jane Keany, Tony Hill, Donna Karp, Kevin Karp and Michael Biber for their fine company over several lockdowns; and Joe Rowley, Alex Lance and Megan Dennis for their entertaining conversation and constant support.

Fiction by Kate Lance

EMBERS AT MIDNIGHT — Kate Lance, Seabooks Press, 2021

"The writing is beautiful and haunting. The characters are drawn with razor-sharp precision. It's compelling reading of the highest standard, full of evocative triumph and tragedy."

In the late 1930s, a group of old friends at a sunny wedding could not imagine what storms are about to engulf them.

Fierce pilot Billie is glad she's got a job at last — only trouble is it's in some little dust-up in Spain. Secretive Toby has no wish to volunteer for anything. Till he finds out for himself what *blitzkrieg* means.

Newlywed Eliza is posted to Intelligence at Singapore — safer than London, she thinks. But when fortress Singapore is reduced to embers, it is actress Izabel who is forced to play the role of her life.

TESTING THE LIMITS — Kate Lance, Seabooks Press, 2020

"I can't recommend this series highly enough: the writing is brilliant, the story wonderful, and you can't help but fall in love with the characters."

1930s England: will the sunny days of ships, flying and love ever end?

Eliza McKee sails away to a new life in London, where her glamorous aunt Izabel is a star with a secret to hide. Her brother Pete yearns to fly, but has no idea how much he needs to learn from fierce pilot Billie Quinn.

Eliza's friend Harry loves golden Charlotte, but Charlotte just loves gambling with flyboy Pete's heart. And when a great white barque encounters the coast one foggy night, not only an era of sail finds itself tested to the limits.

SILVER HIGHWAYS — Kate Lance, Seabooks Press, 2018

"A beautiful and poignant coming of age romantic tale that kept me reading from start to finish."

From pearling to war. Is there any way home?

In 1906, Lucy Fox is sailing to Melbourne with her sister Rosa, when a tragic landfall leaves her life entangled with three seamen: gentle Sam, cynical Danny and beautiful Gideon.

After Rosa's scandalous elopement, trader Min-lu draws Lucy into a new world of silks, spices and the silvery pearlshell of Broome: a place where breaking the rules is a way of life.

The Great War begins and Lucy's beloved must go to sea, where ruthless U-boats stalk the last of the old sailing ships. But with peace comes the influenza pandemic ... and Lucy discovers how cruelly she has been betrayed.

ATOMIC SEA — CM Lance, Seabooks Press, 2016

"Brilliant! Every chapter holds a twist you can't see coming. Fast moving and worth the reading ride."

Chernobyl, the nuclear power station that contaminated Europe. Fukushima, smashed into radioactive rubble by a tsunami. And now ... Broome? Worm Turning nuclear waste plant is fast-tracked on sacred ground near Broome. A certain Great Power says it'll take all responsibility. Sadly it's lying.

Life ashore becomes surprisingly threatening for scientist Lena and hacker Jessie, and their only refuge is Simon's old lugger. Sadly he's lying too. An eerie blue boat turns up with a glowing cargo, the grand opening of Worm Turning is just days away, and a cyclone called Cyril is on the move.

And Lena discovers being stuck on a committee isn't her worst nightmare after all.

THE TURNING TIDE — CM Lance, Allen & Unwin, 2014

"It took me about two pages to fall in love with this beautiful Australian book."

Mike Whalen trained as a commando in 1942 at rugged Wilsons Prom and fought in East Timor. Now a widowed academic in his sixties, and more damaged than he realises, he meets Lena, the granddaughter of his glamorous old friends Helen and Johnny.

When Johnny died in the war he left Mike with a burden of secrets, and as Lena draws him back into her family he discovers more secrets existed than he ever imagined. From the Prom to devastated Hiroshima, this is a saga of adventure and passion.

Non-Fiction by Kate Lance

ALAN VILLIERS: VOYAGER OF THE WINDS
2nd Edition, Seabooks Press, 2020. **Mountbatten Maritime Award 2009**. Fully revised and with over 100 photos.

> *"A delightful warts-and-all biography of one of the world's most notable chroniclers of seafaring life."*

"When Australian journalist Alan Villiers sailed on the last of the giant merchant windjammers in the 1920s and '30s, his writings and photographs made him famous.

Villiers crewed on beautiful *Herzogin Cecilie* and tragic *Grace Harwar*, took tiny *Joseph Conrad* around the globe, sailed on Arabian dhows, led wartime landing craft, captained *Mayflower* II across the Atlantic, and inspired sail training and ship restoration projects.

Drawn from his personal diaries, this award-winning biography of the author-adventurer reveals both his mythmaking and his achievements. It is a tribute to the greatest sailing ships ever launched —and to the extraordinary man who loved them.

REDBILL: FROM PEARLS TO PEACE
Fremantle Press, 2004.
Western Australian Premier's Award 2004 for Non-Fiction.

> *"Lance has presented the biography of Redbill with quiet passion and exquisite detail."*

Redbill is the true story of a sailing boat's voyage through a century of history. She began life as a Broome pearlshell lugger owned by the buccaneering Captain Gregory, then became naval vessel HMAS *Redbill*, bombed in Darwin during WW2.

After the war *Redbill* went pearling in Papua, then worked for Greenpeace in Tahiti, and raised funds for refugees. *Redbill* also filmed a Bass Strait voyage, *If It Doesn't Kill You* and reunited a young Aboriginal man with his long-lost family.

Finally she took on an epic voyage around the coast of Australia, to return to the North-West to face her greatest challenge yet: Rosita, the most powerful tropical cyclone to strike Broome in ninety years.